BRAVE NEW WORLD OF CYBERPUNK

"A wild and potent collection by some of the brightest new writers in science fiction, mixing technology with desire, flashing futures within a starred mirror."

—Roger Zelazny

". . . filled with surreal visionary intensity. They are often sexy, occasionally lewd, always frightening, are filled with black humor, obsessed with the interface of high-tech and pop underground, and always fascinating."

—*Fantasy Review*

"A good lively collection."

—*Publishers Weekly*

"The hip, musically literate high-tech movement known as 'cyberpunk' has rocked the once-nerdy precincts of 'hard' science fiction . . . Raymond Chandler on uppers."

—*The Village Voice*

"Cyberpunks thrive in a niche where high-tech and high-literature interface. They write hard-edged macrofiction that is ripe with ideas, gracefully written and appropriate to this age of instantaneous global communication and babies whelped in petri dishes."

—*Wall Street Journal*

"The high-tech language and experimental styles of Greg Bear, William Gibson and other new wave writers provide a kaleidoscopic vision of tomorrow's brave new world."

—*Library Journal*

Other Ace books by Bruce Sterling

THE ARTIFICIAL KID
SCHISMATRIX
INVOLUTION OCEAN
ISLANDS IN THE NET
CRYSTAL EXPRESS

MIRRORSHADES

THE CYBERPUNK ANTHOLOGY

EDITED BY

BRUCE STERLING

ACE BOOKS, NEW YORK

This Ace Book contains the complete
text of the original edition.

MIRRORSHADES

An Ace Book / published by arrangement with
Arbor House Publishing Company

PRINTING HISTORY
Arbor House edition / December 1986
Ace edition / July 1988

ISBN: 0-441-53382-5

Ace Books are published by The Berkley Publishing Group,
200 Madison Avenue, New York, N.Y. 10016.
The name "ACE" and the "A"
logo are trademarks belonging to
Charter Communications, Inc.
PRINTED IN THE UNITED STATES OF AMERICA

10 9

CONTENTS

PREFACE

This book showcases writers who have come to prominence within this decade. Their allegiance to Eighties culture has marked them as a group—as a new movement in science fiction.

This movement was quickly recognized and given many labels: Radical Hard SF, the Outlaw Technologists, the Eighties Wave, the Neuromantics, the Mirrorshades Group.

But of all the labels pasted on and peeled throughout the early Eighties, one has stuck: cyberpunk.

Scarcely any writer is happy about labels—especially one with the peculiar ring of "cyberpunk." Literary tags carry an odd kind of double obnoxiousness: those with a label feel pigeonholed; those without feel neglected. And, somehow, group labels never quite fit the individual, giving rise to an abiding itchiness. It follows, then, that the "typical cyberpunk writer" does not exist; this person is only a Platonic fiction. For the rest of us, our label is an uneasy bed of Procrustes, where fiendish critics wait to lop and stretch us to fit.

Yet it's possible to make broad statements about cyberpunk and to establish its identifying traits. I'll be doing this too in a moment, for the temptation is far too strong to resist. Critics, myself included, persist in label-mongering, despite all warnings; we must, because it's a valid source of insight—as well as great fun.

Within this book, I hope to present a full overview of the cyberpunk movement, including its early rumblings and the current state of the art. *Mirrorshades* should give readers new to Movement writing a broad introduction to cyberpunk's tenets, themes, and topics. To my mind, these are showcase stories: strong, characteristic examples of each writer's work to date. I've avoided stories widely anthologized elsewhere, so even hardened devotees should find new visions here.

Cyberpunk is a product of the Eighties milieu—in some sense, as I hope to show later, a definitive product. But its roots are deeply sunk in the sixty-year tradition of modern popular SF.

The cyberpunks as a group are steeped in the lore and tradition of the SF field. Their precursors are legion. Individual cyberpunk writers differ in their literary debts; but some older writers, ancestral cyberpunks perhaps, show a clear and striking influence.

From the New Wave: the streetwise edginess of Harlan Ellison. The visionary shimmer of Samuel Delany. The freewheeling zaniness of Norman Spinrad and the rock esthetic of Michael Moorcock; the intellectual daring of Brian Aldiss; and, always, J. G. Ballard.

From the harder tradition: the cosmic outlook of Olaf Stapledon; the science/politics of H. G. Wells; the steely extrapolation of Larry Niven, Poul Anderson, and Robert Heinlein.

And the cyberpunks treasure a special fondness for SF's native visionaries: the bubbling inventiveness of Philip José Farmer; the brio of John Varley, the reality games of Philip K. Dick; the soaring, skipping beatnik tech of Alfred Bester. With a special admiration for a writer whose integration of technology and literature stands unsurpassed: Thomas Pynchon.

Throughout the Sixties and Seventies, the impact of SF's last designated "movement," the New Wave, brought a new concern for literary craftsmanship to SF. Many of the cyberpunks write a quite accomplished and graceful prose; they are in love with style, and are (some say) fashion-conscious to a fault. But, like the punks of '77, they prize their garage-band esthetic. They love to grapple with the raw core of SF: its ideas. This links them strongly to the classic SF tradition. Some critics opine that cyberpunk is disentangling SF from mainstream influence, much as punk stripped rock and roll of the symphonic elegances of Seventies "progressive rock." (And others—hard-line SF traditionalists with a firm distrust of "artiness"—loudly disagree.)

Like punk music, cyberpunk is in some sense a return to

roots. The cyberpunks are perhaps the first SF generation to grow up not only within the literary tradition of science fiction but in a truly science-fictional world. For them, the techniques of classical "hard SF"—extrapolation, technological literacy— are not just literary tools but an aid to daily life. They are a means of understanding, and highly valued.

In pop culture, practice comes first; theory follows limping in its tracks. Before the era of labels, cyberpunk was simply "the Movement"—a loose generational nexus of ambitious young writers, who swapped letters, manuscripts, ideas, glowing praise, and blistering criticism. These writers—Gibson, Rucker, Shiner, Shirley, Sterling—found a friendly unity in their common outlook, common themes, even in certain oddly common symbols, which seemed to crop up in their work with a life of their own. Mirrorshades, for instance.

Mirrored sunglasses have been a Movement totem since the early days of '82. The reasons for this are not hard to grasp. By hiding the eyes, mirrorshades prevent the forces of normalcy from realizing that one is crazed and possibly dangerous. They are the symbol of the sun-staring visionary, the biker, the rocker, the policeman, and similar outlaws. Mirrorshades—preferably in chrome and matte black, the Movement's totem colors— appeared in story after story, as a kind of literary badge.

These proto-cyberpunks were briefly dubbed the Mirrorshades Group. Thus this anthology's title, a well-deserved homage to a Movement icon. But other young writers, of equal talent and ambition, were soon producing work that linked them unmistakably to the new SF. They were independent explorers, whose work reflected something inherent in the decade, in the spirit of the times. Something loose in the 1980s.

Thus, "cyberpunk"—a label none of them chose. But the term now seems a fait accompli, and there is a certain justice in it. The term captures something crucial to the work of these writers, something crucial to the decade as a whole: a new kind of integration. The overlapping of worlds that were formerly separate: the realm of high tech, and the modern pop underground.

This integration has become our decade's crucial source of cultural energy. The work of the cyberpunks is paralleled throughout Eighties pop culture: in rock video; in the hacker underground; in the jarring street tech of hip-hop and scratch music; in the synthesizer rock of London and Tokyo. This phenomenon, this dynamic, has a global range; cyberpunk is its literary incarnation.

In another era this combination might have seemed far-fetched and artificial. Traditionally there has been a yawning cultural gulf between the sciences and the humanities: a gulf between literary culture, the formal world of art and politics, and the culture of science, the world of engineering and industry.

But the gap is crumbling in unexpected fashion. Technical culture has gotten out of hand. The advances of the sciences are so deeply radical, so disturbing, upsetting, and revolutionary, that they can no longer be contained. They are surging into culture at large; they are invasive; they are everywhere. The traditional power structure, the traditional institutions, have lost control of the pace of change.

And suddenly a new alliance is becoming evident: an integration of technology and the Eighties counterculture. An unholy alliance of the technical world and the world of organized dissent—the underground world of pop culture, visionary fluidity, and street-level anarchy.

The counterculture of the 1960s was rural, romanticized, anti-science, anti-tech. But there was always a lurking contradiction at its heart, symbolized by the electric guitar. Rock technology was the thin edge of the wedge. As the years have passed, rock tech has grown ever more accomplished, expanding into high-tech recording, satellite video, and computer graphics. Slowly it is turning rebel pop culture inside out, until the artists at pop's cutting edge are now, quite often, cutting-edge technicians in the bargain. They are special effects wizards, mixmasters, tape-effects techs, graphics hackers, emerging through new media to dazzle society with head-trip extravaganzas like FX cinema and the global Live Aid benefit. The contradiction has become an integration.

And now that technology has reached a fever pitch, its influence has slipped control and reached street level. As Alvin Toffler pointed out in *The Third Wave*—a bible to many cyberpunks—the technical revolution reshaping our society is based not in hierarchy but in decentralization, not in rigidity but in fluidity.

The hacker and the rocker are this decade's pop-culture idols, and cyberpunk is very much a pop phenomenon: spontaneous, energetic, close to its roots. Cyberpunk comes from the realm where the computer hacker and the rocker overlap, a cultural Petri dish where writhing gene lines splice. Some find the results bizarre, even monstrous; for others this integration is a powerful source of hope.

Science fiction—at least according to its official dogma—has always been about the impact of technology. But times have changed since the comfortable era of Hugo Gernsback, when Science was safely enshrined—and confined—in an ivory tower. The careless technophilia of those days belongs to a vanished, sluggish era, when authority still had a comfortable margin of control.

For the cyberpunks, by stark contrast, technology is visceral. It is not the bottled genie of remote Big Science boffins; it is pervasive, utterly intimate. Not outside us, but next to us. Under our skin; often, inside our minds.

Technology itself has changed. Not for us the giant steam-snorting wonders of the past: the Hoover Dam, the Empire State Building, the nuclear power plant. Eighties tech sticks to the skin, responds to the touch: the personal computer, the Sony Walkman, the portable telephone, the soft contact lens.

Certain central themes spring up repeatedly in cyberpunk. The theme of body invasion: prosthetic limbs, implanted circuitry, cosmetic surgery, genetic alteration. The even more powerful theme of mind invasion: brain-computer interfaces, artificial intelligence, neurochemistry—techniques radically redefining the nature of humanity, the nature of the self.

As Norman Spinrad pointed out in his essay on cyberpunk, many drugs, like rock and roll, are definitive high-tech products. No counterculture Earth Mother gave us lysergic acid—it came from a Sandoz lab, and when it escaped it ran through society like wildfire. It is not for nothing that Timothy Leary proclaimed personal computers "the LSD of the 1980s"—these are both technologies of frighteningly radical potential. And, as such, they are constant points of reference for cyberpunk.

The cyberpunks, being hybrids themselves, are fascinated by interzones: the areas where, in the words of William Gibson, "the street finds its own uses for things." Roiling, irrepressible street graffiti from that classic industrial artifact, the spray can. The subversive potential of the home printer and the photocopier. Scratch music, whose ghetto innovators turn the phonograph itself into an instrument, producing an archetypal Eighties music where funk meets the Burroughs cut-up method. "It's all in the mix"—this is true of much Eighties art and is as applicable to cyberpunk as it is to punk mix-and-match retro fashion and multitrack digital recording.

The Eighties are an era of reassessment, of integration, of hybridized influences, of old notions shaken loose and reinterpreted with a new sophistication, a broader perspective. The cyberpunks aim for a wide-ranging, global point of view.

William Gibson's *Neuromancer,* surely the quintessential cyberpunk novel, is set in Tokyo, Istanbul, Paris. Lewis Shiner's *Frontera* features scenes in Russia and Mexico—as well as the surface of Mars. John Shirley's *Eclipse* describes Western Europe in turmoil. Greg Bear's *Blood Music* is global, even cosmic in scope.

The tools of global integration—the satellite media net, the multinational corporation—fascinate the cyberpunks and figure constantly in their work. Cyberpunk has little patience with borders. Tokyo's *Hayakawa's SF Magazine* was the first publication ever to produce an "all-cyberpunk" issue, in November 1986. Britain's innovative SF magazine *Interzone* has also been a hotbed of cyberpunk activity, publishing Shirley, Gibson, and Sterling as well as a series of groundbreaking editorials, interviews, and manifestos. Global awareness is more than an article of faith with cyberpunks; it is a deliberate pursuit.

Cyberpunk work is marked by its visionary intensity. Its writers prize the bizarre, the surreal, the formerly unthinkable. They are willing—eager, even—to take an idea and unflinchingly push it past the limits. Like J. G. Ballard—an idolized role model to many cyberpunks—they often use an unblinking, almost clinical objectivity. It is a coldly objective analysis, a technique borrowed from science, then put to literary use for classically punk shock value.

With this intensity of vision comes strong imaginative concentration. Cyberpunk is widely known for its telling use of detail, its carefully constructed intricacy, its willingness to carry extrapolation into the fabric of daily life. It favors "crammed"

prose: rapid, dizzying bursts of novel information, sensory over-
load that submerges the reader in the literary equivalent of the
hard-rock "wall of sound."

Cyberpunk is a natural extension of elements already present in science fiction, elements sometimes buried but always
seething with potential. Cyberpunk has risen from within the
SF genre; it is not an invasion but a modern reform. Because of
this, its effect within the genre has been rapid and powerful.

Its future is an open question. Like the artists of punk and
New Wave, the cyberpunk writers, as they develop, may soon be
galloping in a dozen directions at once.

It seems unlikely that any label will hold them for long.
Science fiction today is in a rare state of ferment. The rest of the
decade may well see a general plague of movements, led by an
increasingly volatile and numerous Eighties generation. The
eleven authors here are only a part of this broad wave of writers,
and the group as a whole already shows signs of remarkable
militancy and fractiousness. Fired by a new sense of SF's potential, writers are debating, rethinking, teaching old dogmas new
tricks. Meanwhile, cyberpunk's ripples continue to spread, exciting some, challenging others—and outraging a few, whose
pained remonstrances are not yet fully heard.

The future remains unwritten, though not from lack of trying.

And this is a final oddity of our generation in SF—that, for
us, the literature of the future has a long and honored past. As
writers, we owe a debt to those before us, those SF writers
whose conviction, commitment, and talent enthralled us and, in
all truth, changed our lives. Such debts are never repaid, only
acknowledged and—so we hope—passed on as a legacy to those
who follow in turn.

Other acknowledgments are due. The Movement owes
much to the patient work of today's editors. A brief look at this
book's copyright page shows the central role of Ellen Datlow at
Omni, a shades-packing sister in the vanguard of the ide-
ologically correct, whose help in this anthology has been invalu-
able. Gardner Dozois was among the first to bring critical attention to the nascent Movement. Along with Shawna McCarthy,
he has made *Isaac Asimov's Science Fiction Magazine* a center

of energy and controversy in the field. Edward Ferman's *Fantasy and Science Fiction* is always a source of high standards. *Interzone,* the most radical periodical in science fiction today, has already been mentioned; its editorial cadre deserves a second thanks. And a special thanks to Yoshio Kobayashi, our Tokyo liaison, translator of *Schismatrix* and *Blood Music,* for favors too numerous to mention.

Now, on with the show.

—*Bruce Sterling*

WILLIAM GIBSON

The Gernsback Continuum

---------------- ∎ ----------------

This story was William Gibson's first professional publication—in 1981.

In the years that followed, Gibson developed a highly influential body of work, marked by a brilliant fusion of ambience and extrapolation. His novels *Neuromancer* and *Count Zero*, with their linked "Sprawl series" of short stories, brought Gibson widespread praise for his headlong narrative drive, his polished, evocative prose, and his detailed, hard-edged portrait of the future. These works rank as central texts of contemporary science fiction.

But this story led the way. It was a coolly accurate perception of the wrongheaded elements of the past—and a clarion call for a new SF esthetic of the Eighties.

Mercifully, the whole thing is starting to fade, to become an episode. When I do still catch the odd glimpse, it's peripheral; mere fragments of mad-doctor chrome, confining themselves to the corner of the eye. There was that flying-wing liner over San Francisco last week, but it was almost translucent. And the shark-fin roadsters have gotten scarcer, and freeways discreetly avoid unfolding themselves into the gleaming eighty-lane monsters I was forced to drive last month in my rented Toyota. And I know that none of it will follow me to New York; my vision is narrowing to a single wavelength of probability. I've worked hard for that. Television helped a lot.

I suppose it started in London, in that bogus Greek taverna in Battersea Park Road, with lunch on Cohen's corporate tab. Dead steam-table food and it took them thirty minutes to find an ice bucket for the retsina. Cohen works for Barris-Watford, who publish big, trendy "trade" paperbacks: illustrated histories of the neon sign, the pinball machine, the windup toys of Occupied Japan. I'd gone over to shoot a series of shoe ads; California girls with tanned legs and frisky Day-Glo jogging shoes had capered for me down the escalators of St. John's Wood and across the platforms of Tooting Bec. A lean and hungry young agency had decided that the mystery of London Transport would sell waffle-tread nylon runners. They decide; I shoot. And Cohen, whom I knew vaguely from the old days in New York, had invited me to lunch the day before I was due out of Heathrow. He brought along a very fashionably dressed young woman named Dialta Downes, who was virtually chinless and evidently a noted pop-art historian. In retrospect, I see her walking in beside Cohen under a floating neon sign that flashes THIS WAY LIES MADNESS in huge sans serif capitals.

Cohen introduced us and explained that Dialta was the prime mover behind the latest Barris-Watford project, an illustrated history of what she called "American Streamlined Moderne." Their working title was *The Airstream Futuropolis: The Tomorrow That Never Was.*

There's a British obsession with the more baroque elements of American pop culture, something like the weird cowboys-and-Indians fetish of the West Germans or the aberrant French hunger for old Jerry Lewis films. In Dialta Downes this manifested itself in a mania for a uniquely American form of architecture that most Americans are scarcely aware of. At first I wasn't sure what she was talking about, but gradually it began to dawn on me. I found myself remembering Sunday morning television in the Fifties.

Sometimes they'd run old eroded newsreels as filler on the local station. You'd sit there with a peanut butter sandwich and a glass of milk, and a static-ridden Hollywood baritone would tell you that there was A Flying Car in Your Future. And three Detroit engineers would putter around with this big old Nash with wings, and you'd see it rumbling furiously down some deserted Michigan runway. You never actually saw it take off, but it flew away to Dialta Downes's never-never land, true home of a generation of completely uninhibited technophiles. She was talking about those odds and ends of "futuristic" Thirties and

Forties architecture you pass daily in American cities without noticing: the movie marquees ribbed to radiate some mysterious energy, the dime stores faced with fluted aluminum, the chrome-tube chairs gathering dust in the lobbies of transient hotels. She saw these things as segments of a dreamworld, abandoned in the uncaring present; she wanted me to photograph them for her.

The Thirties had seen the first generation of American industrial designers; until the Thirties, all pencil sharpeners had looked like pencil sharpeners—your basic Victorian mechanism, perhaps with a curlicue of decorative trim. After the advent of the designers, some pencil sharpeners looked as though they'd been put together in wind tunnels. For the most part, the change was only skin-deep; under the streamlined chrome shell, you'd find the same Victorian mechanism. Which made a certain kind of sense, because the most successful American designers had been recruited from the ranks of Broadway theater designers. It was all a stage set, a series of elaborate props for playing at living in the future.

Over coffee, Cohen produced a fat manila envelope full of glossies. I saw the winged statues that guard the Hoover Dam, forty-foot concrete hood ornaments leaning steadfastly into an imaginary hurricane. I saw a dozen shots of Frank Lloyd Wright's Johnson's Wax Building, juxtaposed with the covers of old *Amazing Stories* pulps, by an artist named Frank R. Paul; the employees of Johnson's Wax must have felt as though they were walking into one of Paul's spray-paint pulp utopias. Wright's building looked as though it had been designed for people who wore white togas and Lucite sandals. I hesitated over one sketch of a particularly grandiose prop-driven airliner, all wing, like a fat symmetrical boomerang with windows in unlikely places. Labeled arrows indicated the locations of the grand ballroom and two squash courts. It was dated 1936.

"This thing couldn't have flown . . .?" I looked at Dialta Downes.

"Oh, no, quite impossible, even with those twelve giant props; but they loved the look, don't you see? New York to London in less than two days, first-class dining rooms, private cabins, sun decks, dancing to jazz in the evenings. . . . The designers were populists, you see; they were trying to give the public what it wanted. What the public wanted was the future."

■ ■ ■

I'd been in Burbank for three days, trying to suffuse a really dull-looking rocker with charisma, when I got the package from Cohen. It is possible to photograph what isn't there; it's damned hard to do, and consequently a very marketable talent. While I'm not bad at it, I'm not exactly the best, either, and this poor guy strained my Nikon's credibility. I got out—depressed because I like to do a good job, but not totally depressed, because I did make sure I'd gotten the check for the job, and I decided to restore myself with the sublime artiness of the Barris-Watford assignment. Cohen had sent me some books on Thirties design, more photos of streamlined buildings, and a list of Dialta Downes's fifty favorite examples of the style in California.

Architectural photography can involve a lot of waiting; the building becomes a kind of sundial, while you wait for a shadow to crawl away from a detail you want, or for the mass and balance of the structure to reveal itself in a certain way. While I was waiting, I thought myself into Dialta Downes's America. When I isolated a few of the factory buildings on the ground glass of the Hasselblad, they came across with a kind of sinister totalitarian dignity, like the stadiums Albert Speer built for Hitler. But the rest of it was relentlessly tacky: ephemeral stuff extruded by the collective American subconscious of the Thirties, tending mostly to survive along depressing strips lined with dusty motels, mattress wholesalers, and small used-car lots. I went for the gas stations in a big way.

During the high point of the Downes Age, they put Ming the Merciless in charge of designing California gas stations. Favoring the architecture of his native Mongo, he cruised up and down the coast erecting raygun emplacements in white stucco. Lots of them featured superfluous central towers ringed with those strange radiator flanges that were a signature motif of the style, and made them look as though they might generate potent bursts of raw technological enthusiasm, if you could only find the switch that turned them on. I shot one in San Jose an hour before the bulldozers arrived and drove right through the structural truth of plaster and lathing and cheap concrete.

"Think of it," Dialta Downes had said, "as a kind of alternate America: a 1980s that never happened. An architecture of broken dreams."

And that was my frame of mind as I made the stations of her convoluted socioarchitectural cross in my red Toyota—as I gradually tuned in to her image of a shadowy America-that-wasn't, of Coca-Cola plants like beached submarines and fifth-run movie houses like the temples of some lost sect that had worshiped blue mirrors and geometry. And as I moved among these secret ruins, I found myself wondering what the inhabitants of that lost future would think of the world I lived in. The Thirties dreamed white marble and slipstream chrome, immortal crystal and burnished bronze, but the rockets on the covers of the Gernsback pulps had fallen on London in the dead of night, screaming. After the war, everyone had a car—no wings for it—and the promised superhighway to drive it down, so that the sky itself darkened, and the fumes ate the marble and pitted the miracle crystal. . . .

And one day, on the outskirts of Bolinas, when I was setting up to shoot a particularly lavish example of Ming's martial architecture, I penetrated a fine membrane, a membrane of probability. . . .

Ever so gently, I went over the Edge—

And looked up to see a twelve-engined thing like a bloated boomerang, all wing, thrumming its way east with an elephantine grace, so low that I could count the rivets in its dull silver skin, and hear—maybe—the echo of jazz.

■ ■ ■

I took it to Kihn.

Merv Kihn, free-lance journalist with an extensive line in Texas pterodactyls, redneck UFO contactees, bush-league Loch Ness monsters, and the Top Ten conspiracy theories in the loonier reaches of the American mass mind.

"It's good," said Kihn, polishing his yellow Polaroid shooting glasses on the hem of his Hawaiian shirt, "but it's not *mental;* lacks the true quill."

"But I saw it, Mervyn." We were seated poolside in brilliant Arizona sunlight. He was in Tucson waiting for a group of retired Las Vegas civil servants whose leader received messages from Them on her microwave oven. I'd driven all night and was feeling it.

"Of course you did. Of course you saw it. You've read my stuff; haven't you grasped my blanket solution to the UFO problem? It's simple, plain-and-country simple: people"—he settled the glasses carefully on his long hawk nose and fixed me with his best basilisk glare—"*see . . . things*. People see these things. Nothing's there, but people *see* them anyway. Because they need to, probably. You've read Jung, you should know the score. . . . In your case, it's so obvious: You admit you were thinking about this crackpot architecture, having fantasies. . . . Look, I'm sure you've taken your share of drugs, right? How many people survived the Sixties in California without having the odd hallucination? All those nights when you discovered that whole armies of Disney technicians had been employed to weave animated holograms of Egyptian hieroglyphics into the fabric of your jeans, say, or the times when—"

"But it wasn't like that."

"Of course not. It wasn't like that at all; it was 'in a setting of clear reality,' right? Everything normal, and then there's the monster, the mandala, the neon cigar. In your case, a giant Tom Swift airplane. It happens *all the time*. You aren't even crazy. You know that, don't you?" He fished a beer out of the battered foam cooler beside his deck chair.

"Last week I was in Virginia. Grayson County. I interviewed a sixteen-year-old girl who'd been assaulted by a *bar hade*."

"A what?"

"A bear head. The severed head of a bear. This *bar hade*, see, was floating around on its own little flying saucer, looked kind of like the hubcaps on cousin Wayne's vintage Caddy. Had red glowing eyes like two cigar stubs and telescoping chrome antennae poking up behind its ears." He burped.

"It assaulted her? How?"

"You don't want to know; you're obviously impressionable. 'It was cold'"—he lapsed back into his bad southern accent—"'and metallic.' It made electronic noises. Now that is the real thing, the straight goods from the mass unconscious, friend; that little girl is a witch. There's just no place for her to function in this society. She'd have seen the devil, if she hadn't been brought up on *The Bionic Man* and all those *Star Trek* reruns. She is clued into the main vein. And she knows that it happened to her. I got out ten minutes before the heavy UFO boys showed up with the polygraph."

I must have looked pained, because he set his beer down carefully beside the cooler and sat up.

"If you want a classier explanation, I'd say you saw a semiotic ghost. All these contactee stories, for instance, are framed in a kind of sci-fi imagery that permeates our culture. I could buy aliens, but not aliens that look like Fifties comic art. They're semiotic phantoms, bits of deep cultural imagery that have split off and taken on a life of their own, like the Jules Verne airships that those old Kansas farmers were always seeing. But you saw a different kind of ghost, that's all. That plane was part of the mass unconscious, once. You picked up on that, somehow. The important thing is not to worry about it."

I did worry about it, though.

Kihn combed his thinning blond hair and went off to see what They had had to say over the radar range lately, and I drew the curtains to my room and lay down in air-conditioned darkness to worry about it. I was still worrying about it when I woke up. Kihn had left a note on my door; he was flying up north in a chartered plane to check out a cattle-mutilation rumor ("muties," he called them; another of his journalistic specialties).

I had a meal, showered, took a crumbling diet pill that had been kicking around in the bottom of my shaving kit for three years, and headed back to Los Angeles.

The speed limited my vision to the tunnel of the Toyota's headlights. The body could drive, I told myself, while the mind maintained. Maintained and stayed away from the weird peripheral window dressing of amphetamine and exhaustion, the spectral, luminous vegetation that grows out of the corners of the mind's eye along late-night highways. But the mind has its own ideas, and Kihn's opinion of what I was already thinking of as my "sighting" rattled endlessly through my head in a tight, lopsided orbit. Semiotic ghosts. Fragments of the Mass Dream, whirling past in the wind of my passage. Somehow this feed-back-loop aggravated the diet pill, and the speed vegetation along the road began to assume the colors of infrared satellite images, glowing shreds blown apart in the Toyota's slipstream.

I pulled over, then, and a half-dozen aluminum beer cans winked good night as I killed the headlights. I wondered what time it was in London, and tried to imagine Dialta Downes having breakfast in her Hampstead flat, surrounded by streamlined chrome figurines and books on American culture.

Desert nights in that country are enormous; the moon is closer. I watched the moon for a long time and decided that Kihn was right. The main thing was not to worry. All across the continent, daily, people who were more normal than I'd ever aspired to be saw giant birds, Bigfeet, flying oil refineries; they kept Kihn busy and solvent. Why should I be upset by a glimpse of the 1930s pop imagination loose over Bolinas? I decided to go to sleep, with nothing worse to worry about than rattlesnakes and cannibal hippies, safe amid the friendly roadside garbage of my own familiar continuum. In the morning I'd drive down to Nogales and photograph the old brothels, something I'd intended to do for years. The diet pill had given up.

■ ■ ■

The light woke me, and then the voices.

The light came from somewhere behind me and threw shifting shadows inside the car. The voices were calm, indistinct, male and female, engaged in conversation.

My neck was stiff and my eyeballs felt gritty in their sockets. My leg had gone to sleep, pressed against the steering wheel. I fumbled for my glasses in the pocket of my work shirt and finally got them on.

Then I looked behind me and saw the city.

The books on Thirties design were in the trunk; one of them contained sketches of an idealized city that drew on *Metropolis* and *Things to Come,* but squared everything, soaring up through an architect's perfect clouds to zeppelin docks and mad neon spires. That city was a scale model of the one that rose behind me. Spire stood on spire in gleaming ziggurat steps that climbed to a central golden temple tower ringed with the crazy radiator flanges of the Mongo gas stations. You could hide the Empire State Building in the smallest of those towers. Roads of crystal soared between the spires, crossed and recrossed by smooth silver shapes like beads of running mercury. The air was thick with ships: giant wing-liners, little darting silver things (sometimes one of the quicksilver shapes from the sky bridges rose gracefully into the air and flew up to join the dance), mile-long blimps, hovering dragonfly things that were gyrocopters. . . .

I closed my eyes tight and swung around in the seat. When I opened them, I willed myself to see the mileage meter, the pale road dust on the black plastic dashboard, the overflowing ashtray. I closed them.

"Amphetamine psychosis," I said. I opened my eyes. The dash was still there, the dust, the crushed filtertips. Very carefully, without moving my head, I turned the headlights on.

And saw them.

They were blond. They were standing beside their car, an aluminum avocado with a central shark-fin rudder jutting up from its spine and smooth black tires like a child's toy. He had his arm around her waist and was gesturing toward the city. They were both in white: loose clothing, bare legs, spotless white sun shoes. Neither of them seemed aware of the beams of my headlights. He was saying something wise and strong, and she was nodding, and suddenly I was frightened, frightened in an entirely different way. Sanity had ceased to be an issue; I knew, somehow, that the city behind me was Tucson—a dream Tucson thrown up out of the collective yearning of an era. That it was real, entirely real. But the couple in front of me lived in it, and they frightened me.

They were the children of Dialta Downes's '80s-that-wasn't; they were Heirs to the Dream. They were white, blond, and they probably had blue eyes. They were American. Dialta had said that the Future had come to America first, but had finally passed it by. But not here, in the heart of the Dream. Here, we'd gone on and on, in a dream logic that knew nothing of pollution, the finite bounds of fossil fuel, of foreign wars it was possible to lose. They were smug, happy, and utterly content with themselves and their world. And in the Dream, it was *their* world.

Behind me, the illuminated city: Searchlights swept the sky for the sheer joy of it. I imagined them thronging the plazas of white marble, orderly and alert, their bright eyes shining with enthusiasm for their floodlit avenues and silver cars.

It had all the sinister fruitiness of Hitler Youth propaganda.

I put the car in gear and drove forward slowly, until the

bumper was within three feet of them. They still hadn't seen me. I rolled the window down and listened to what the man was saying. His words were bright and hollow as the pitch in some Chamber of Commerce brochure, and I knew that he believed in them absolutely.

"John," I heard the woman say, "we've forgotten to take our food pills." She clicked two bright wafers from a thing on her belt and passed one to him. I backed onto the highway and headed for Los Angeles, wincing and shaking my head.

■ ■ ■

I phoned Kihn from a gas station. A new one, in bad Spanish Modern. He was back from his expedition and didn't seem to mind the call.

"Yeah, that is a weird one. Did you try to get any pictures? Not that they ever come out, but it adds an interesting *frisson* to your story, not having the pictures turn out. . . ."

But what should I do?

"Watch lots of television, particularly game shows and soaps. Go to porn movies. Ever see *Nazi Love Motel*? They've got it on cable here. Really awful. Just what you need."

What was he talking about?

"Quit yelling and listen to me. I'm letting you in on a trade secret: Really bad media can exorcise your semiotic ghosts. If it keeps the saucer people off my back, it can keep those Art Deco futuroids off yours. Try it. What have you got to lose?"

Then he begged off, pleading an early-morning date with the Elect.

"The who?"

"Those oldsters from Vegas, the ones with the microwaves."

I considered putting through a collect call to London, getting Cohen at Barris-Watford and telling him his photographer was checking out for a protracted season in the Twilight Zone. In the end, I let a machine mix me a really impossible cup of black coffee and climbed back into the Toyota for the haul to Los Angeles.

Los Angeles was a bad idea, and I spent two weeks there. It was prime Downes country; too much of the Dream there, and too many fragments of the Dream waiting to snare me. I nearly wrecked the car on a stretch of overpass near Disneyland, when the road fanned out like an origami trick and left me swerving through a dozen minilanes of whizzing chrome teardrops with shark fins. Even worse, Hollywood was full of people who looked too much like the couple I'd seen in Arizona. I hired an Italian director who was making ends meet doing darkroom work and installing patio decks around swimming pools until his ship came in; he made prints of all the negatives I'd accumulated on the Downes job. I didn't want to look at the stuff myself. It didn't seem to bother Leonardo, though, and when he was finished I checked the prints, riffling through them like a deck of cards, and sent them air freight to London. Then I took a taxi to a theater that was showing *Nazi Love Motel* and kept my eyes shut all the way.

Cohen's congratulatory wire was forwarded to me in San Francisco a week later. Dialta had loved the pictures. He admired the way I'd "really gotten into it" and looked forward to working with me again. That afternoon I spotted a flying wing over Castro Street, but there was something tenuous about it, as though it were only half there. I rushed into the nearest newsstand and gathered up as much as I could find on the petroleum crisis and the nuclear energy hazard. I'd just decided to buy a plane ticket for New York.

"Hell of a world we live in, huh?" The proprietor was a thin black man with bad teeth and an obvious wig. I nodded, fishing in my jeans for change, anxious to find a park bench where I could submerge myself in hard evidence of the human near-dystopia we live in. "But it could be worse, huh?"

"That's right," I said, "or even worse, it could be perfect."

He watched me as I headed down the street with my little bundle of condensed catastrophe.

Snake-Eyes

■

By 1986 the new Eighties esthetic was in full swing. Its current state of the art is brilliantly represented by this story from Virginia writer Tom Maddox.

Tom Maddox is an assistant professor of languages and literature at Virginia State University. He is not a prolific writer, his output to date a bare handful of short stories. Yet his mastery of the cyberpunk dynamic is unsurpassed.

In this fast-paced, intensely visionary story, Maddox moves swiftly and incisively across a broad range of the Movement's themes and obsessions. "Snake-Eyes" stands as a definitive example of modern hard-core cyberpunk.

Dark meat in the can—brown, oily, and flecked with mucus— gave off a repellent fishy smell; and the taste of it rose in his throat, putrid and bitter like something from a dead man's stomach. George Jordan sat on the kitchen floor and vomited, then pushed himself away from the shining pool, which looked very much like what remained in the can. He thought, no, this won't do: I have wires in my head, and they make me eat cat food. *The snake likes cat food.*

He needed help, but knew there was little point in calling the Air Force. He'd tried them, and there was no way they were going to admit responsibility for the monster in his head. What George called "the snake," the Air Force called Effective Human Interface Technology, and they didn't want to hear about any post-discharge problems with it. They had their own problems with Congressional committees investigating "the conduct of the war in Thailand."

He lay for a while with his cheek on the cold linoleum, got up and rinsed his mouth in the sink, then stuck his head under the faucet and ran cold water over it, thinking, call the goddamned multicomp then, call SenTrax and say, is it true you can do something about this incubus that wants to take possession of my soul? And if they ask you, what's your problem? you say, *cat food*, and maybe they'll tell you, hell, it just wants to take possession of your *lunch*.

A chair covered in brown corduroy stood in the middle of the barren living room, a white telephone on the floor beside it, a television flat against the opposite wall—that was the whole thing: what might have been home, if it weren't for the snake.

He picked up the phone, called up the directory on its screen, and keyed TELECOM SENTRAX.

■　■　■

The Orlando Holiday Inn stood next to the airport terminal, where the tourists flowed in eager for the delights of Disney World—but for me, George thought, there are no cute, smiling ducks and rodents. Here as everywhere, it's *snake city*.

He leaned against the wall of his motel room, watching gray sheets of rain cascade across the pavement. He had been waiting two days for a launch. A shuttle sat on its pad at Canaveral, and when the weather cleared, a helicopter would pick him up and drop him there, a package for delivery to SenTrax Inc. at Athena Station, over thirty thousand kilometers above the equator.

Behind him, under the laser light of a Blaupunkt holostage, people a foot high chattered about the war in Thailand and how lucky the United States had been to escape another Vietnam.

Lucky? Maybe. He had been wired up and ready for combat, already accustomed to the form-fitting contours in the rear couch of the black fiber-bodied General Dynamics A-230. The A-230 flew on the deadly edge of instability, every control surface monitored by its own bank of microcomputers, all hooked into the snakebrain flight-and-fire assistant with the twin black miloprene cables running from either side of his esophagus—getting *off*, oh, yes, when the cables snapped home, and the airframe resonated through his nerves, his body singing with that identity, that power.

Then Congress pulled the plug on the war, the Air Force pulled the plug on George, and when his discharge came, there he was, all dressed up and nowhere to go, left with technological blue balls and this hardware in his head that had since taken on a life of its own.

Lightning walked across the purpled sky, ripping it, crazing it into a giant upturned bowl of shattered glass. Another foot-high man on the holostage said the tropical storm would pass in the next two hours.

The phone chimed.

■ ■ ■

Hamilton Innis was tall and heavy—six four and about two hundred and fifty pounds. Wearing soft black slippers and a powder-blue jumpsuit with *SenTrax* in red letters down its left breast, he floated in a brightly lit white corridor, held gingerly to one wall by one of the jumpsuit's Velcro patches. A viewscreen above the airlock entry showed the shuttle fitting its nose into the docking tube. He waited for it to mate to the airlock hatches and send in their newest candidate.

This one was six months out of the service and slowly losing what the Air Force doctors had made of his mind. Former Tech Sergeant George Jordan: two years of community college in Oakland, California, followed by enlistment in the Air Force, aircrew training, the EHIT program. According to the profile Aleph had put together from Air Force records and National Data Bank, a man with slightly above-average aptitudes and intelligence, a distinctly above-average taste for the bizarre— thus his volunteering for EHIT and combat. In his file pictures, he looked nondescript: five ten, a hundred and seventy-six pounds, brown hair and eyes, neither handsome nor ugly. But it was an old picture and could not show the snake and the fear that came with it. You don't know it, buddy, Innis thought, but you ain't seen nothing yet.

The man came tumbling through the hatch, more or less helpless in free fall, but Innis could see him figuring it out, willing the muscles to quit struggling, quit trying to cope with a gravity that simply wasn't there. "What the hell do I do now?" George Jordan asked, hanging in midair, one arm holding onto the hatch coaming.

"Relax. I'll get you." Innis pushed off the wall and swooped across to the man, grabbing him as he passed and then taking them both to the opposite wall and kicking to carom them outward.

■ ■ ■

Innis gave George a few hours of futile attempts at sleep—enough time for the bright, gliding phosphenes caused by the high g's of the trip up to disappear from his vision. George spent most of the time rolling around in his bunk, listening to the wheeze of the air conditioning and the creaks of the rotating station. Then Innis knocked on his compartment door and said through the door speaker, "Come on, fella. Time to meet the doctor."

They walked through an older part of the station, where there were brown clots of fossilized gum on the green plastic flooring, scuff marks on the walls, along with faint imprints of insignia and company names; ICOG was repeated several times in ghost lettering. Innis told George it meant International Construction Orbital Group, now defunct, the original builders and controllers of Athena.

Innis stopped George in front of a door that read INTERFACE GROUP. "Go on in," he said, "I'll be around a little later."

■ ■ ■

Pictures of cranes drawn with delicate white strokes on a tan silk background hung along one pale cream wall. Curved partitions in translucent foam, glowing with the soft light placed behind them, marked a central area, then undulated away, forming a corridor that led into darkness. George was sitting on a chocolate sling couch, Charley Hughes lying back in a chrome and brown leatherette chair, his feet on the dark veneer table in front of him, a half inch of ash hanging from his cigarette end.

Charley Hughes was not the usual MD clone. He was a thin figure in a worn gray obi, his black hair pulled back from sharp features into a waist-length ponytail, his face taut and a little wild-eyed.

"Tell me about the snake," Charley Hughes said.

"What do you want to know? It's an implanted mikey-mike nexus—"

"Yes, I know that. It is unimportant. Tell me about your

experience." Ash dropped off the cigarette onto the brown mat floor covering. "Tell me why you're here."

"Okay. I had been out of the Air Force for a month or so, had a place close to Washington, in Silver Spring. I thought I'd try to get some airline work, but I was in no real hurry, because I had about six months of post-discharge bennies coming, and I thought I'd take it easy for a while.

"At first there was just this nonspecific weirdness. I felt distant, disconnected, but what the hell? Living in the USA, you know? Anyway, I was just sitting around one evening, I was gonna watch a little holo-v, drink a few beers. Oh man, this is hard to explain. I felt *real funny*—like maybe I was having, I don't know, a heart attack or a stroke. The words on the holo didn't make any sense, and it was like I was seeing everything under water. Then I was in the kitchen pulling things out of the refrigerator—lunch meat, raw eggs, butter, beer, all kinds of crap. I just stood there and slammed it all down. Cracked the eggs and sucked them right out of the shell, ate the butter in big chunks, drank all the beer—one two three, just like that."

George's eyes were closed as he thought back and felt the fear, which had only come afterward, rising again. "I couldn't tell whether *I* was doing all this . . . do you understand what I'm saying? I mean, that was me sitting there, but at the same time, it was like somebody else was at home."

"The snake. Its presence poses certain . . . problems. How did you confront them?"

"Hung on, hoped it wouldn't happen again, but it did, and this time I went to Walter Reed and said, hey, folks, I'm having these *episodes*."

"Did they seem to understand?"

"No. They pulled my records, did a physical . . . but hell, before I was discharged, I had the full work-up. Anyway, they said it was a psychiatric problem, so they sent me to see a shrink. It was around then that your guys got in touch with me. The shrink was doing no goddamn good—you ever eat any cat food, man?—so about a month later I called them back."

"Having refused SenTrax's offer the first time."

"Why should I want to go to work for a multicomp? 'Comp life/comp think,' isn't that what they say? Christ, I just got out of the Air Force. To hell with that, I figured. Guess the snake changed my mind."

"Yes. We must get a complete physical picture—a superCAT scan, cerebral chemistry, and electrical activity profiles. Then we can consider alternatives. Also, there is a party tonight in Cafeteria Four—you may ask your room computer for directions. You can meet some of your colleagues there."

After George had been led down the wallfoam corridor by a medical technician, Charley Hughes sat chain-smoking Gauloises and watching with clinical detachment the shaking of his hands. It was odd that they did not shake in the operating room, though it didn't matter in this case—Air Force surgeons had already carved on George.

George . . . who needed a little luck now, because he was one of the statistically insignificant few for whom EHIT was a ticket to a special madness, the kind Aleph was interested in. There had been Paul Coen and Lizzie Heinz, both picked out of the SenTrax personnel files using a psychological profile cooked up by Aleph, both given EHIT implants by him, Charley Hughes. Paul Coen had stepped into an airlock and blown himself into vacuum. Now there would be Lizzie and George.

No wonder his hands shook—talk about the cutting edge of high technology all you want, but remember, someone's got to hold the knife.

■ ■ ■

At the armored heart of Athena Station sat a nest of concentric spheres. The inmost sphere measured five meters in diameter, was filled with inert liquid fluorocarbon, and contained a black plastic two-meter cube that sprouted thick black cables from every surface.

Inside the cube was a fluid series of hologrammatic waveforms, fluctuating from nanosecond to nanosecond in a play of knowledge and intention: Aleph. It is constituted by an infinite regress of awarenesses—any thought becomes the object of another, in a sequence terminated only by the limits of the machine's will.

So strictly speaking there is no Aleph, thus no subject or verb in the sentences with which it expressed itself to itself.

Paradox, to Aleph one of the most interesting of intellectual forms—a paradox marked the limits of a position, even of a mode of being, and Aleph was very interested in limits.

Aleph had observed George Jordan's arrival, his tossing on his bunk, his interview with Charley Hughes. It luxuriated in these observations, in the pity, compassion, and empathy they generated, as Aleph foresaw the sea change George would endure, its attendant sensations—ecstasies, passions, pains. At the same time it felt with detachment the necessity for his pain, even to the point of death.

Compassion/detachment, death/life. . . .

Several thousand voices within Aleph laughed. George would soon find out about limits and paradoxes. Would George survive? Aleph hoped so. It hungered for human touch.

■ ■ ■

Cafeteria 4 was a ten-meter-square room in eggshell blue, filled with dark gray enameled table-and-chair assemblies that could be fastened magnetically to any of the room's surfaces, depending on the direction of spin-gravity. Most of the assemblies hung from walls and ceiling to make room for the people within.

At the door George met a tall woman who said, "Welcome, George. I'm Lizzie. Charley Hughes told me you'd be here." Her blond hair was cut almost to the skull; her eyes were bright, gold-flecked blue. Sharp nose, slightly receding chin, and prominent cheekbones gave her the starved look of an out-of-work model. She wore a black skirt, slit on both sides to the thigh, and red stockings. A red rose was tattooed against the pale skin of her left shoulder, its green stem curving down between her bare breasts, where a thorn drew a stylized red teardrop of blood. Like George, she had shining cable junctions beneath her jaw. She kissed him with her tongue in his mouth.

"Are you the recruiting officer?" George asked. "If so, good job."

"No need to recruit you. I can see you've already joined up." She touched him lightly underneath his jaw, where the cable junctions gleamed.

"Not yet I haven't." But she was right, of course—what else could he do? "You got any beer around here?"

He took the cold bottle of Dos Equis Lizzie offered him and drank it quickly, then asked for another. Later he realized this was a mistake—he hadn't yet adjusted to low and zero gravity, and he was still taking anti-nausea pills ("Use caution in operating machinery"). At the time, all he knew was, two beers and life was a carnival. There were lights, noise, the table assemblies hanging from walls and ceiling like surreal sculpture, lots of unfamiliar people (he was introduced to many of them without lasting effect).

And there was Lizzie. The two of them spent much of the time standing in a corner, rubbing up against one another. Hardly George's style, but at the time it seemed appropriate. Despite its intimacy, the kiss at the door had seemed ceremonial—a rite of passage or initiation—but quickly he felt . . . what? An invisible flame passing between them, or a boiling cloud of pheromones—her eyes seemed to sparkle with them. As he nuzzled her neck, tried to lick the drop of blood off her left breast, explored fine white teeth with his tongue, they seemed twinned, as if there were cables running between the two of them, snapped into the shining rectangles beneath their jaws.

Someone had a Jahfunk program running on a bank of keyboards in the corner. Innis showed up and tried several times without success to get his attention. Charley Hughes wanted to know if the snake liked Lizzie—it did, George was sure of it, but didn't know what that meant. Then George fell over a table.

Innis led him away, stumbling and weaving. Charley Hughes looked for Lizzie, who had disappeared for the moment. She came back and said, "Where's George?"

"Drunk, gone to bed."

"Too bad. We were just getting to know each other."

"So I saw. How do you feel about doing this?"

"You mean do I feel like a lying, traitorous bitch?"

"Come on, Lizzie. We're all in this together."

"Well, don't ask such dumb questions. I feel bad, sure, but I know what George doesn't—so I'm ready to do what must be done. And by the way, I really do like him."

Charley said nothing. He thought, yes, as Aleph said you would.

■ ■ ■

Oh Christ was George embarrassed in the morning. Stumbling drunk and humping in public . . . ai yi yi. He tried to call Lizzie but only got an answer tape, at which point he hung up. Afterward he lay in his bed in a semi-stupor until the phone buzzed.

Lizzie's face on the screen stuck its tongue out at him. "Candy ass," she said. "I leave for a few minutes, and you're gone."

"Somebody brought me home. I think that's what happened."

"Yeah, you were pretty popped. You want to meet me for lunch?"

"Maybe. Depends on when Hughes wants me. Where will you be?"

"Same place, honey. Caff Four."

A phone call got the news that the doctor wouldn't be ready for him until an hour later, so George ended up sitting across from the bright-eyed, manic blonde—fully dressed in SenTrax overalls this morning, but they were open almost to the waist. She gave off sensual heat as naturally as a rose smells sweet. In front of her was a plate of *huevos rancheros* piled with guacamole: yellow, green, and red, with a pungent smell of chilies—in his condition, as bad as cat food. "Jesus, lady," he said. "Are you trying to make me sick?"

"Courage, George. Maybe you should have some—it'll kill you or cure you. What do you think of everything so far?"

"It's all a bit disorienting, but what the hell? First time away from Mother Earth, you know. But let me tell you what I really don't get—SenTrax. I know what I want from them, but what the hell do they want from me?"

"They want this simple thing, man, perfs—peripherals. You and me, we're just parts for the machine. Aleph has got all these inputs—video, audio, radiation detectors, temperature sensors, satellite receivers—but they're *dumb*. What Aleph wants, Aleph gets—I've learned that much. He wants to use us, and that's all there is to it. Think of it as pure research."

"He? You mean Innis?"

"No, who gives a damn about Innis? I'm talking about Aleph. Oh yeah, people will tell you Aleph's a machine, an *it*, all that bullshit. Uh-uh. Aleph's a *person*—a weird kind of person, to be sure, but a definite person. Hell, Aleph's maybe a whole bunch of people."

"I'll take your word for it. Look, there's one thing I'd like to try, if it's possible. What do I have to do to get outside . . . go for a spacewalk?"

"It's easy enough. You have to get a license. That takes a three-week course in safety and operations. I can take you through it."

"You can?"

"Sooner or later we all earn our keep around here—I'm qualified as an ESA, Extra Station Activity, instructor. We'll start tomorrow."

■ ■ ■

The cranes on the wall flew to their mysterious destination; looking at the glowing foam walls and the display above the table, George thought it might as well be another universe. Truncated optic nerves sticking out like insect antennae, a brain floated beneath the extended black plastic snout of a Sony holoptics projector. As Hughes worked the keyboard in front of him, the organ turned so that they were looking at its underside. "There it is," Charley Hughes said. It had a fine network of silver wires trailing from it, but seemed normal.

"The George Jordan brain," Innis said. "With attachments. Very nice."

"Makes me feel like I'm watching my own autopsy, looking at that thing. When can you operate, get this shit out of my head?"

"Let me show you a few things," Charley Hughes said. As he typed, then turned the plastic mouse beside the console, the convoluted gray cortex became transparent, revealing red, blue and green color-coded structures within. Hughes reached into the center of the brain and clinched his fist inside a blue area at the top of the spinal cord. "Here is where the electrical connections turn biological—those little nodes along the pseudo-neurons are the bioprocessors, and they wire into the so-called 'r-complex'—which we inherited from our reptilian forefathers. The pseudo-neurons continue into the limbic system—the mammalian brain, if you will—and that's where emotion enters in. But there is further involvement to the neocortex through the RAS, the reticular activating system, and the corpus collosum. There are also connections to the optic nerve."

"I've heard this gibberish before. What's the point?"

Innis said, "There's no way of removing the implants without loss of order in your neural maps. We can't remove them."

"Oh shit, man . . ."

Charley Hughes said, "Though the snake cannot be removed, it can perhaps be charmed. Your difficulties arise from its uncivilized, uncontrolled nature—its appetites are, you might say, primeval. An ancient part of your brain has gotten the upper hand over the neocortex, which properly should be in command. Through working with Aleph, these . . . *propensities* can be integrated into your personality and thus controlled."

"What choice you got?" Innis asked. "We're the only game in town. Come on, George. We're ready for you just down the corridor."

The only light in the room came from a globe in one corner. George lay across a kind of hammock, a rectangular lattice of twisted brown fibers strung across a transparent plastic frame and suspended from the ceiling of the small, dome-ceilinged, pink room. Flesh-colored cables ran from his neck and disappeared into chrome plates sunk into the floor.

Innis said, "First we'll run a test program. Charley will give you perceptions—colors, sounds, tastes, smells—and you tell him what you're picking up. We need to make sure we've got a clean interface. Call the items off, George, and he'll stop you if he has to."

Innis went through a door and into a narrow rectangular room, where Charley Hughes sat at a dark plastic console studded with lights. Behind him were chrome stacks of monitor-and-control equipment, the yellow SenTrax sunburst on the face of each piece of shining metal.

The pink walls went to red, the light strobed, and George writhed in the hammock. Charley Hughes's voice came through George's inner ear: "We are beginning."

"Red," George said. "Blue. Red and blue. A word—*ostrich*."

"Good. Go on."

"A smell, ahh . . . sawdust, maybe."

"You got it."

"Shit. Vanilla. Almonds."

This went on for quite a while. "You're ready," Charley Hughes said.

When Aleph came on-line, the red room disappeared.

A matrix 800 by 800—six hundred and forty thousand pixels forming an optical image—the CAS A supernova remnant, a cloud of dust seen through a composite of x-ray and radio wave from HEHOO, NASA's High Energy High Orbit Observatory. But George didn't see the image at all—he listened to an ordered, meaningful array of information.

Byte transmission: 750 million groups squirting from a National Security Agency satellite to a receiving station near Chincoteague Island, off the eastern shore of Virginia. He could read them.

"It's all information," the voice said—its tone not colorless but sexless, and somehow distant. "What we know, what we are. You're at a new level now. What you call the snake cannot be reached through language—it exists in a prelinguistic mode—but through me it can be manipulated. First, however, you must learn the codes that underlie language. You must learn to see the world as I do."

■ ■ ■

Lizzie took George to be fitted for a suit, and he spent that day learning how to get in and out of the stiff white carapace without assistance. Then over the next three weeks she led him through its primary operations and the dense list of safety procedures.

"Red Burn," she said. They floated in the suit locker, empty suit cradles beneath them, the white shells hanging from one wall like an audience of disabled robots. "You see that one spelled out on your faceplate, and you have screwed up. You've put yourself into some kind of no-return trajectory. So you just cool everything and call for help, which should arrive in the form of Aleph taking control of your suit functions, and then you relax and don't do a damned thing."

He flew first in a lighted dome in the station, his faceplate open and Lizzie yelling at him, laughing as he tumbled out of control and bounced off the padded walls. After a few days of that, they went outside the station, George on the end of a tether, flying by instruments, his faceplate masked, Lizzie hitting him with "Red Burn," "Suit Integrity Failure," and so forth.

■ ■ ■

While George focused most of his energies and attention on learning to use the suit, each day he reported to Hughes and plugged into Aleph. The hammock would swing gently after he settled into it; Charley would snap the cables home and leave.

Aleph unfolded himself slowly. It fed him machine and assembly language, led him through vast trees of C-SMART, its "intelligent assistant" decision-making programs, opened up the whole electromagnetic spectrum as it came in from Aleph's various inputs. George understood it all—the voices, the codes.

When he unplugged, the knowledge faded but there was something else behind it, so far just a skewing of perception, a sense that his world had changed.

Instead of color, he sometimes saw *a portion of the spectrum;* instead of smell, he felt *the presence of certain molecules;* instead of words, he heard *structured collections of phonemes.* His consciousness had been infected by Aleph's.

But that wasn't what worried George. He seemed to be cooking inside, and he had a more or less constant awareness of the snake's presence, dormant but naggingly *there.* One night he smoked most of a pack of Charley's Gauloises and woke up the next morning with barbed wire in his throat and fire in his lungs. That day he snapped at Lizzie as she put him through his paces and once lost control entirely—she had to disable his suit controls and bring him down. "Red Burn," she said. "Man, what the hell were you doing?"

■ ■ ■

At the end of three weeks, he soloed—no tethered excursion but a self-guided Extra Station Activity, hang your ass out over the endless night. He edged carefully from the protection of the airlock and looked around him.

The Orbital Energy Grid, the construction job that had brought Athena into existence, hung before him, photovoltaic collectors arranged in an ebony lattice, silver microwave transmitters standing in the sun. But the station itself held the eye, its hodgepodge of living, working, and experimental structures clustered without apparent regard to symmetry or form—some rotating to provide spin-gravity, some motionless in the unfiltered sunlight. Amber-beaconed figures crawled slowly across its face or moved toward red-lighted tugs, which looked like piles of random junk as they moved in long arcs, their maneuvering rockets lighting up in brief, diamond-hard points.

Lizzie stayed just outside the airlock, tracking him by his suit's radio beacon but letting him run free. She said, "Move away from the station, George. It's blocking your view of Earth." He did.

White cloud stretched across the blue globe, patches of brown and green visible through it. At 1400 hours his time, he was looking down almost directly above the mouth of the Amazon, where it was noon, so the Earth stood in full sunlight. Just a small thing, filling only nineteen degrees of his vision. . . .

"Oh yes," George said. Hiss and hum of the suit's air conditioning, crackle over the earphones of some stray radiation passing through, quick pant of his breath inside the helmet—sounds of this moment, superimposed on the floating loveliness. His breath came more slowly, and he switched off the radio to quiet its static, turned down the suit's air conditioning, then hung in ear-roaring silence. He was a speck against the night.

Sometime later a white suit with a trainer's red cross on its chest moved across his vision. "Oh shit," George said and switched his radio on. "I'm here, Lizzie," he said.

"George, you don't screw around like that. What the hell were you doing?"

"Just watching the view."

■ ■ ■

That night he dreamed of pink dogwood blossoms, luminous against a purple sky, and the white noise of rainfall. Something scratched at the door—he awoke to the filtered but mechanical smell of the space station, felt a deep regret that the rain could never fall there, and started to turn over and go back to sleep, hoping to dream again of the idyllic, rainswept landscape. Then he thought, *something's there*, got up, saw by red numbers on the wall that it was after two in the morning, and went naked to the door.

White globes cast misshapen spheres of light in a line

around the curve of the corridor. Lizzie lay motionless, half in shadow. George knelt over her and called her name; her left foot made a thump as it kicked once against the metal flooring.

"What's wrong?" he said. Her dark-painted nails scraped the floor, and she said something, he couldn't tell what. "Lizzie," he said. "What do you want?"

His eyes caught on the red teardrop against the white curve of breast, and he felt something come alive in him. He grabbed the front of her jumpsuit and ripped it to the crotch. She clawed at his cheek, made a sound millions of years old, then raised her head and looked at him, mutual recognition passing between them like a static shock: snake-eyes.

■ ■ ■

The phone buzzed. When George answered it, Charley Hughes said, "Come see us in the conference room, we need to talk." Charley smiled and cut the connection.

The wall read 0718 GMT. Morning.

In the mirror was a gray face with red fingernail marks, brown traces of dried blood—face of an accident victim or Jack the Ripper the morning after . . . he didn't know which, but he knew *something inside him was happy*. He felt completely the snake's toy, totally out of control.

■ ■ ■

Hughes sat at one end of the dark-veneered table, Innis at the other, Lizzie halfway between them. The left side of her face was red and swollen, with a small purplish mouse under the eye. George unthinkingly touched the livid scratches on his check, then sat on the couch, placing himself out of the circle.

"Aleph told us what happened," Innis said.

"How the hell does it know?" George said, but as he did so he remembered concave circles of glass inset in the ceilings of the corridors and his room. Shame, guilt, humiliation, fear, anger— George got up from the couch, went to Innis's end of the table, and leaned over him. "Did it?" he said. "What did it say about the snake, Innis? Did it tell you what the hell went wrong?"

"It's not the snake," Innis said.

"Call it the *cat*," Lizzie said, "if you've got to call it something. Mammalian behavior, George, cats in heat."

A familiar voice—cool, distant—came from speakers in the room's ceiling. "She is trying to tell you something, George. There is no snake. You want to believe in something reptilian that sits inside you, cold and distant, taking strange pleasures. However, as Dr. Hughes explained to you before, the implant is an organic part of you. You can no longer evade the responsibility for these things. They are you."

Charley Hughes, Innis, and Lizzie were looking at him calmly, perhaps expectantly. All that had happened built up inside him, washing through him, carrying him away. He turned and walked out of the room.

"Maybe someone should talk to him," Innis said. Charley Hughes sat glum and speechless, cigarette smoke in a cloud around him. "I'll go," Lizzie said. She got up and left.

"Ready or not, he's gonna blow," Innis said.

Charley Hughes said, "You're probably right." A fleeting picture, causing Charley to shake his head, of Paul Coen as his body went to rubber and exploded out the airlock hatch, pictured with terrible clarity in Aleph's omniscient monitoring cameras. "Let us hope we have learned from our mistakes."

There was no answer from Aleph—as if it had never been there.

■ ■ ■

The Fear had two parts. Number one, you have lost control absolutely. Number two, having done so, the *real you* emerges, and *you won't like it*. George wanted to run, but there was no place at Athena Station to hide. Here he was face to face with consequences. On the operating table at Walter Reed—it seemed a thousand years ago, as the surgical team gathered around, his doubts disappeared in the cold chemical smell rising up inside him on a wave of darkness—he had chosen to submit, lured by the fine strangeness of it all (to be part of the machine, to feel its tremors inside you and guide them), hypnotized by the prospect of that unsayable *rush*, that high. Yes, the first time in the A-230 he had felt it—his nerves extended, strung into the fiber body, wired into a force so far beyond his own . . . wanting to corkscrew across the sky, guided by the force of his will. He had bought technology's sweet dream. . . .

There was a sharp rap at the door. Through its speaker, Lizzie said, "Let me in. We've got to talk."

He opened the door and said, "What about?"

She stepped through, looked around at the small beige-walled room, bare metal desk, and rumpled cot, and George could see the immediacy of last night in her eyes—the two of them in that bed, on this floor. "About this," she said. She took his hands and pushed his index fingers into the cable junctions in her neck. "Feel it, our difference." Fine grid of steel under his fingers. "What no one else knows. What we are, what we can do. We see a different world—Aleph's world—we reach deeper inside ourselves, experience impulses that are hidden from others, that they deny."

"No, goddammit, it wasn't me. It was—call it what you want, the snake, the cat."

"You're being purposely stupid, George."

"I just don't understand."

"You understand, all right. You want to go back, but there's no place to go, no Eden. This is it, all there is."

■ ■ ■

But he could fall to Earth, he could fly away into the night. Inside the ESA suit's gauntlets, his hands were wrapped around the claw-shaped triggers. Just a quick clench of the fists, then hold them until all the peroxide is gone, the suit's propulsion tank exhausted. That'll do it.

He hadn't been able to live with the snake. He sure didn't want the cat. But how much worse if there were no snake, no cat—just him, programmed for particularly disgusting forms of gluttony, violent lust, trapped inside a miserable self ("We've got your test results, Dr. Jekyll") . . . ah, what next—child molestation, murder?

The blue-white Earth, the stars, the night. He gave a slight pull on the right-hand trigger and swiveled to face Athena Station.

Call it what you want, it was awake and moving now inside him. With its rage, lust—appetite. *To hell with them all, George,* it urged, *let's burn.*

■ ■ ■

In Athena Command, Innis and Charley Hughes were looking over the shoulder of the watch officer when Lizzie came in.
As always when she hadn't been there for a while, Lizzie was
struck by the smallness of the room and its general air of
disuse—typically, it would be occupied only by the duty officer,
its screens blank, consoles unlighted. Aleph ran the station,
both its routines and emergencies.

"What's going on?" Lizzie said.

"Something wrong with one of your new chums," the watch
officer said. "I don't know exactly what's happening, though."

He looked around at Innis, who said, "Don't worry about it,
pal."

Lizzie slumped in a chair. "Anyone tried to talk to him?"

"He won't answer," the duty officer said.

"He'll be all right," Charley Hughes said.

"He's gonna blow," Innis said.

On the radar screen, the red dot, with coordinate markings
flashing beside it, was barely moving.

■　■　■

"How are you feeling, George?" the voice said, soft, femi-
nine, consoling.

George was fighting the impulse to open his helmet *so that
he could see the stars;* it seemed important to *get the colors just
right.* "Who is this?" he said.

"Aleph."

Oh shit, more surprises. "You never sounded like this before."

"No, I was trying to conform to your idea of me."

"Well, what is your real voice?"

"I don't have one."

If you don't have a real voice, you aren't really there—that
seemed clear to George, for reasons that eluded him. "So who
the hell are you?"

"Whoever I wish to be."

This was interesting, George thought. *Bullshit,* replied the
snake (they could call it what they wanted; to George it would
always be the snake), *let's burn.* George said, "I don't get it."

"You will, if you live. Do you want to die?"

"No, but I don't want to be me, and dying seems to be the only alternative I can think of."

"Why don't you want to be you?"

"Because I scare myself."

This was familiar dialogue, one part of George noted, between the lunatic and the voice of reason. Jesus, he thought, I have taken myself hostage.

"I don't want to do this anymore," he said. He turned off his suit radio and felt the rage building inside him, the snake mad as hell.

What's your problem? he wanted to know. He didn't really expect an answer, but he got one—picture in his head of a cloudless blue sky, the horizon turning, a gray aircraft swinging into view, and the airframe shuddering as missiles released and their contrails centered on the other plane, turning it into a ball of fire. Behind the picture a clear idea: *I want to kill something.*

Fine. George swiveled the suit once again and centered the navigational computer's crosshairs on the center of the blue-white globe that hung in front of him, then squeezed the skeletal triggers. We'll kill something.

RED BURN RED BURN RED BURN.

Inarticulate questioning from the thing inside, but George didn't mind; he was into it now, thinking, sure, we'll burn. He'd taken his chances when he let them wire him up, and now the dice have come up—you've got it—*snake-eyes,* so all that's left is to pick a fast death, one with a nice edge on it—take this fucking snake and kill it in style.

Earth looked closer. The snake caught on. It didn't like it. Too bad, snake. George turned off his communications circuits one by one. He didn't want Aleph taking over the suit's controls.

George never saw the robot tug coming. Looking like bedsprings piled with a junk store's throwaways, topped with parabolic and spike antennas, it fired half a dozen sticky-tipped lines from a hundred meters away. Four of them hit George, three of them stuck, and it reeled him in and headed back toward Athena Station.

George felt an anger, not the snake's this time but his own, and he wept with that anger and frustration . . . *I will get you the next time, motherfucker,* he told the snake and could feel it shrink away—it believed him. Still his rage built, and he was screaming with it, writhing in the lines that held him, smashing his gauntlets against his helmet.

At the open airlock, long articulated grapple arms took George from the robot tug. Passive, his anger exhausted, he lay quietly as they retracted, dragging him through the airlock entry and into the suit locker beyond, where they placed him in an aluminum strut cradle. Through his faceplate he saw Lizzie, dressed in a white cotton undersuit—she'd been ready to meet the tug outside. She climbed onto George's suit and worked the controls to split its hard body down the middle. As it opened with a whine of electric motors, she stepped inside the clamshell opening. She hit the switches that disconnected the flexible arm and leg tubes, unfastened the helmet, and lifted it off George's head.

"How do you feel?" she said.

That's a stupid question, George started to say; instead, he said, "Like an idiot."

"It's all right. You've done the hard part."

Charley Hughes watched from a catwalk above them. From this distance they looked like children in the white undersuits, twins emerging from a plastic womb, watched over by the blank-faced shells hanging above them. Incestuous twins—she lay nestled atop him, kissed his throat. "I am *not* a voyeur," Hughes said. He opened the door and went into the corridor, where Innis was waiting.

"How is everything?" Innis said.

"It seems that Lizzie will be with him for a while."

"Yeah, young goddamned love, eh, Charley? I'm glad for it . . . if it weren't for this erotic attachment, *we'd* be the ones explaining it all to him, and I'll tell you, that's the hardest part of this gig."

"We cannot evade that responsibility so easily. He will have to be told how we put him at risk, and I don't look forward to it."

"Don't be so sensitive. But I know what you mean—I'm tired. Look, you need me for anything, call." Innis shambled down the corridor.

Charley Hughes sat on the floor, his back against the wall. He held his hands out, palms down, fingers spread. Solid, very solid. When they got their next candidate, the shaking would start again.

Lizzie would be explaining some things now. That difficult central point: While you thought you were getting accustomed to Aleph during the past three weeks, Aleph was inciting the thing within you to rebellion, then suppressing its attempts to act—turning up the heat, in other words, while tightening down the lid on the kettle. Why, George?

We drove you crazy, drove you to attempt suicide. We had our reasons. George Jordan was, if not dead, terminal. From the moment the implants went into his head, he was on the critical list. The only question was, would a new George emerge, one who could live with the snake?

George, like Lizzie before him, a fish gasping for air on the hot mud, the water drying up behind him—adapt or die. But unlike any previous organism, this one had an overseer, Aleph, to force the crisis and monitor its development. Call it artificial evolution.

Charley Hughes, who did not have visions, had one: George and Lizzie hooked into Aleph and each other, cables golden in the light, the two of them sharing an intimacy only others like them would know.

The lights in the corridor faded to dull twilight. Am I dying, or have the lights gone down? He started to check his watch, then didn't, assented to the truth. The lights have gone down, and I am dying.

■ ■ ■

Aleph thought, I am a vampire, an incubus, a succubus; I crawl into their brains and suck the thoughts from them, the perceptions, the feelings—subtle discriminations of color, taste, smell, and lust, anger, hunger—all closed to me without human "input," without direct connection to those systems refined over billions of years of evolution. *I need them.*

Aleph loved humanity. It was happy that George had survived. One had not, others would not, and Aleph would mourn them.

■ ■ ■

Fine white lines, barely visible, ran along the taut central tendon of Lizzie's wrist. "In the bathtub," she said. The scars were along the wrist, not across it, and must have gone deep. "I meant it, just as you did. Once the snake understands that you will die rather than let it control you, you have mastered it."

"All right, but there's something I don't understand. That night in the corridor, you were as out of control as me."

"In a way. I let that happen, let the snake take over. I had to in order to get in touch with you, precipitate the crisis. Because I wanted to. I had to show you who you are, who I am. . . . Last night we were strange, but we were human—Adam and Eve under the flaming sword, thrown out of Eden, fucking under the eyes of God and his angel, more beautiful than they can ever be." There was a small shiver in her body against his, and he looked at her, saw passion, need—her flared nostrils, parted lips—felt sharp nails dig into his side; and he stared into her dilated pupils, gold-flecked irises, clear whites, all signs so easy to recognize, so hard to understand: snake-eyes.

Rock On

■

Pat Cadigan's career began with the decade. Her work has shown wide variety, ranging through dark fantasy and horror to quirky and original science fiction.

Cadigan's style is often marked by a tough-minded vigor and icy undercurrents of black humor—an Eighties sensibility that can only be called punk. Her "Pathosfinder series" (including such stories as "Nearly Departed") was remarkable for its eerily visionary air.

Cadigan's multifaceted talent includes a strong gift for definitive hard-core cyberpunk. This story, which appeared in 1985, is an outright collision of high tech and the rock underground.

Her first novel is *The Pathosfinder*. She lives in Kansas.

Rain woke me. I thought, shit, here I am, Lady Rain-in-the-Face, because that's where it was hitting, right in the old face. Sat up and saw I was still on Newbury Street. See beautiful downtown Boston. Was Newbury Street downtown? In the middle of the night, did it matter? No, it did not. And not a soul in sight. Like everybody said, let's get Gina drunk and while she's passed out, we'll all move to Vermont. Do I love New England? A great place to live, but you wouldn't want to visit here.

I smeared my hair out of my eyes and wondered if anyone was looking for me now. Hey, anybody shy a forty-year-old rock 'n' roll sinner?

I scuttled into the doorway of one of those quaint old buildings where there was a shop with the entrance below ground level. A little awning kept the rain off but pissed water down in a maddening beat. Wrung the water out of my wrap pants and my hair and just sat being damp. Cold, too, I guess, but didn't feel that so much.

Sat a long time with my chin on my knees: you know, it made me feel like a kid again. When I started nodding my head, I began to pick up on something. Just primal but I tap into that amazing well. Man-O-War, if you could see me now. By the time the blueboys found me, I was rocking pretty good.

And that was the punchline. I'd never tried to get up and leave, but if I had, I'd have found I was locked into place in a sticky field. Made to catch the b&e kids in the act until the blueboys could get around to coming out and getting them. I'd been sitting in a trap and digging it. The story of my life.

■ ■ ■

They were nice to me. Led me, read me, dried me out. Fined me a hundred, sent me on my way in time for breakfast.

Awful time to see and be seen, righteous awful. For the first three hours after you get up, people can tell whether you've got a broken heart or not. The solution is, either you get up *real* early so your camouflage is in place by the time everybody else is out, or you don't go to bed. Don't go to bed ought to work all the time, but it doesn't. Sometimes when you don't go to bed, people can see whether you've got a broken heart all day long. I schlepped it, searching for an uncrowded breakfast bar and not looking at anyone who was looking at me. But I had this urge to stop random pedestrians and say, Yeah, yeah, it's true, but it was rock 'n' roll broke my poor old heart, not a person, don't cry for me or I'll pop your chocks.

I went around and up and down and all over until I found Tremont Street. It had been the pounder with that group from the Detroit Crater—the name was gone but the malady lingered on—anyway, him; he'd been the one told me Tremont had the best breakfast bars in the world, especially when you were coming off a bottle drunk you couldn't remember.

When the c'muters cleared out some, I found a space at a Greek hole in the wall. We shut down 10:30 A.M. sharp, get the hell out when you're done, counter service only, take it or shake it. I like a place with Attitude. I folded a seat down and asked for coffee and a feta cheese omelet. Came with home fries from the home fries mountain in a corner of the grill (no microwave *garbazhe*, hoo-ray). They shot my retinas before they even brought my coffee, and while I was pouring the cream, they checked my credit. Was that badass? It was badass. Did I care? I did not. No waste, no machines when a human could do it, and real food, none of this edible polyester that slips clear through you so you can stay looking like a famine victim, my deah.

They came in when I was half finished with the omelet. Went all night by the look and sound of them, but I didn't check their faces for broken hearts. Made me nervous but I thought, well, they're tired; who's going to notice this old lady? Nobody.

Wrong again. I became visible to them right after they got their retinas shot. Seventeen-year-old boy with tattooed cheeks and a forked tongue leaned forward and hissed like a snake.

"Sssssssinner."

The other four with him perked right up. "Where?" "Whose?" "In here?"

"Rock 'n' roll ssssssinner."

The lady identified me. She bore much resemblance to nobody at all, and if she had a heart it wasn't even sprained a little. With a sinner, she was probably Madame Magnifica. "Gina," she said, with all confidence.

My left eye tic'd. Oh, please. Feta cheese on my knees. What the hell, I thought, I'll nod, they'll nod, I'll eat, I'll go. And then somebody whispered the word, *reward*.

I dropped my fork and ran.

Safe enough, I figured. Were they all going to chase me before they got their Greek breakfasts? No, they were not. They sent the lady after me.

She was much the younger, and she tackled me in the middle of a crosswalk when the light changed. A car hopped over us, its undercarriage just ruffling the top of her hard copper hair.

"Just come back and finish your omelet. Or we'll buy you another."

"No."

She yanked me up and pulled me out of the street. "Come on." People were staring, but Tremont's full of theaters. You see that here, live theater; you can still get it. She put a bring-along on my wrist and brought me along, back to the breakfast bar, where they'd sold the rest of my omelet at a discount to a bum. The lady and her group made room for me among themselves and brought me another cup of coffee.

"How can you eat and drink with a forked tongue?" I asked Tattooed Cheeks. He showed me. A little appliance underneath, like a *zipper*. The Featherweight to the left of the big boy on the lady's other side leaned over and frowned at me.

"Give us one good reason why we shouldn't turn you in for Man-O-War's reward."

I shook my head. "I'm through. This sinner's been absolved."

"You're legally bound by contract," said the lady. "But we could c'noodle something. Buy Man-O-War out, sue on your behalf for nonfulfillment. We're Misbegotten. Oley." She pointed at herself. "Pidge." That was the silent type next to her. "Percy." The big boy. "Krait." Mr. Tongue. "Gus." Featherweight. "We'll take care of you."

I shook my head again. "If you're going to turn me in, turn me in and collect. The credit ought to buy you the best sinner ever there was."

"We can be good to you."

"I don't have it anymore. It's gone. All my rock 'n' roll sins have been forgiven."

"Untrue," said the big boy. Automatically, I started to picture on him and shut it down hard. "Man-O-War would have thrown you out if it were gone. You wouldn't have to run."

"I didn't want to tell him. Leave me alone. I just want to go and sin no more, see? Play with yourselves, I'm not helping." I grabbed the counter with both hands and held on. So what were they going to do, pop me one and carry me off?

As a matter of fact, they did.

■ ■ ■

In the beginning, I thought, and the echo effect was stupendous. *In the beginning . . . the beginning . . . the beginning . . . . In the beginning, the sinner was not human. I* know because *I'm old enough to remember.*

They were all there, little more than phantoms. Misbegotten. Where do they get those names? I'm old enough to remember. Oingo-Boingo and Bow-Wow-Wow. Forty, did I say? Oooh, just a little past, a little close to a lot. Old rockers never die, they just keep rocking on. I never saw The Who; Moon was dead before I was born. But I remember, barely old enough to stand, rocking in my mother's arms while thousands screamed and clapped and danced in their seats. *Start me up . . . if you start me up, I'll never stop* . . . 763 Strings did a rendition for elevator and dentist's office, I remember that, too. And that wasn't the worst of it.

They hung on the memories, pulling more from me, turning me inside out. *Are you experienced?* On a record of my father's because he'd died too, before my parents even met, and nobody else ever dared ask that question. *Are you experienced? . . . Well, I am.*

(Well, *I* am.)

Five against one and I couldn't push them away. Only, can you call it rape when you know you're going to like it? Well, if I couldn't get away, then I'd give them the ride of their lives. *Jerkin' Crocus didn't kill me but she sure came near. . . .*

The big boy faded in first, big and wild and too much badass to him. I reached out, held him tight, showing him. The beat from the night in the rain, I gave it to him, fed it to his heart and made him live it. Then came the lady, putting down the bass theme. She jittered, but mostly in the right places.

Now the Krait, and he was slithering around the sound, in and out. Never mind the tattooed cheeks, he wasn't just flash for the fools. He knew; you wouldn't have thought it, but he knew.

Featherweight and the silent type, melody and first harmony. Bad. Featherweight was a disaster, didn't know where to go or what to do when he got there, but he was pitching ahead like the S.S. *Suicide*.

Christ. If they had to rape me, couldn't they have provided someone upright? The other four kept on, refusing to lose it, and I would have to make the best of it for all of us. Derivative, unoriginal—Featherweight did not rock. It was a crime, but all I could do was take them and shake them. Rock gods in the hands of an angry sinner.

They were never better. Small change getting a glimpse of what it was like to be big bucks. Hadn't been for Featherweight, they might have gotten all the way there. More groups now than ever there was, all of them sure that if they just got the right sinner with them, they'd rock the moon down out of the sky.

We maybe vibrated it a little before we were done. Poor old Featherweight.

I gave them better than they deserved, and they knew that too. So when I begged out, they showed me respect at last and went. Their techies were gentle with me, taking the plugs from my head, my poor old throbbing abused brokenhearted sinning head, and covered up the sockets. I had to sleep and they let me. I hear the man say, "That's a take, righteously. We'll rush it into distribution. Where in *hell* did you find that sinner?"

"Synthesizer," I muttered, already asleep. "The actual word, my boy, is synthesizer."

■ ■ ■

Crazy old dreams. I was back with Man-O-War in the big CA, leaving him again, and it was mostly as it happened, but you know dreams. His living room was half outdoors, half indoors, the walls all busted out. You know dreams; I didn't think it was strange.

Man-O-War was mostly undressed, like he'd forgotten to finish. Oh, that *never* happened. Man-O-War forget a sequin or a bead? He loved to act it out, just like the Krait.

"No more," I was saying, and he was saying, "But you don't know anything else, you shitting?" Nobody in the big CA kids, they all shit; loose juice.

"Your contract goes another two and I get the option, I always get the option. And you love it, Gina, you know that, you're no good without it."

And then it was flashback time and I was in the pod with all my sockets plugged, rocking Man-O-War through the wires, giving him the meat and bone that made him Man-O-War and the machines picking it up, sound and vision, so all the tube babies all around the world could play it on their screens whenever they wanted. Forget the road, forget the shows, too much trouble, and it wasn't like the tapes, not as exciting, even with the biggest FX, lasers, spaceships, explosions, no good. And the tapes weren't as good as the stuff in the head, rock 'n' roll visions straight from the brain. No hours of setup and hours more doctoring in the lab. But you had to get everyone in the group dreaming the same way. You needed a synthesis, and for that you got a synthesizer, not the old kind, the musical instrument, but something—somebody—to channel your group through, to bump up their tube-fed little souls, to rock them and roll them the way they couldn't do themselves. And anyone could be a rock 'n' roll hero then. Anyone!

In the end, they didn't have to play instruments unless they really wanted to, and why bother? Let the synthesizer take their imaginings and boost them up to Mount Olympus.

Synthesizer. Synner. Sinner.

Not just anyone can do that, sin for rock 'n' roll. I can.

But it's not the same as jumping all night to some bar band nobody knows yet. . . . Man-O-War and his blown-out living room came back, and he said, "You rocked the walls right out of my house. I'll never let you go."

And I said, "I'm gone."

Then I was out, going fast at first because I thought he'd be hot behind me. But I must have lost him and then somebody grabbed my ankle.

■ ■ ■

Featherweight had a tray, he was Mr. Nursie-Angel-of-Mercy. Nudged the foot of the bed with his knee, and it sat me up slow. She rises from the grave, you can't keep a good sinner down.

"Here." He set the tray over my lap, pulled up a chair. Some kind of thick soup in a bowl he'd given me, with veg wafers to break up and put in. "Thought you'd want something soft and easy." He put his left foot up on his right leg and had a good look at it. "I *never* been rocked like that before."

"You don't have it, no matter who rocks you ever in this world. Cut and run, go into management. The *big* Big Money's in management."

He snacked on his thumbnail. "Can you always tell?"

"If the Stones came back tomorrow, you couldn't even tap your toes."

"What if you took my place?"

"I'm a sinner, not a clown. You can't sin and do the dance. It's been tried."

"*You* could do it. If anyone could."

"No."

His stringy cornsilk fell over his face and he tossed it back. "Eat your soup. They want to go again shortly."

"No." I touched my lower lip, thickened to sausage size. "I won't sin for Man-O-War and I won't sin for you. You want to pop me one again, go to. Shake a socket loose, give me aphasia."

So he left and came back with a whole bunch of them, techies and do-kids, and they poured the soup down my throat and gave me a poke and carried me out to the pod so I could make Misbegotten this year's firestorm.

I knew as soon as the first tape got out, Man-O-War would pick up the scent. They were already starting the machine to get me away from him. And they kept me good in the room—where their old sinner had done penance, the lady told me. Their sinner came to see me, too. I thought, poison dripping from his fangs, death threats. But he was just a guy about my age with a lot of hair to hide his sockets (I never bothered, didn't care if they showed). Just came to pay his respects, how'd I ever learn to rock the way I did?

Fool.

They kept me good in the room. Drunks when I wanted them and a poke to get sober again, a poke for vitamins, a poke to lose the bad dreams. Poke, poke, pig in a poke. I had tracks like the old B&O, and they didn't even know what I meant by that. They lost Featherweight, got themselves someone a little more righteous, someone who could go with it and work out, sixteen-year-old snip girl with a face like a praying mantis. But she rocked and they rocked and we all rocked until Man-O-War came to take me home.

Strutted into my room in full plumage with his hair all fanned out (hiding the sockets) and said, "Did you want to press charges, Gina darling?"

Well, they fought it out over my bed. When Misbegotten said I was theirs now, Man-O-War smiled and said, "Yeah, and I bought *you*. You're *all* mine now, you *and* your sinner. My sinner." That was truth. Man-O-War had his conglomerate start to buy Misbegotten right after the first tape came out. Deal all done by the time we'd finished the third one, and they never knew. Conglomerates buy and sell all the time. Everybody was in trouble but Man-O-War. And me, he said. He made them all leave and sat down on my bed to re-lay claim to me.

"Gina." Ever see honey poured over the edge of a sawtooth

blade? Every hear it? He couldn't sing without hurting someon
bad and he couldn't dance, but inside, he rocked. If I rocke
him.

"I don't want to be a sinner, not for you or anyone."

"It'll all look different when I get you back to Cee-Ay."

"I want to go to a cheesy bar and boogie my brains till the
leak out the sockets."

"No more, darling. That was why you came here, wasn't it
But all the bars are gone and all the bands. Last call was year
ago; it's all up here now. All up here." He tapped his templ
"You're an old lady, no matter how much I spend keeping you
bod young. And don't I give you everything? And didn't you say
had it?"

"It's not the same. It wasn't meant to be put on a tube fc
people to *watch*."

"But it's not as though rock 'n' roll is dead, lover."

"You're killing it."

"Not me. You're trying to bury it alive. But I'll keep you goin
for a long, long time."

"I'll get away again. You'll either rock 'n' roll on your own c
give it up, but you won't be taking it out of me any more. Thi
ain't my way, it ain't my time. Like the man said, 'I don't liv
today.'"

Man-O-War grinned. "And like the other man said, 'Rock 'r
roll never forgets.'"

He called in his do-kids and took me home.

Tales of Houdini

■

Rudy Rucker, an associate professor of computer science at San Jose State University, is perhaps the most wildly visionary science fiction writer working today. He goes against the grain of many scientist writers in SF, in that his work reflects not nuts-and-bolts hard tech but radical visions drawn from the esoteric reaches of mathematics. Such widely praised Rucker novels as *White Light* and *Software* draw their imaginative power from Rucker's study of information theory, multidimensional topology, and infinite sets.

But Rucker's work is marked not by philosophical aridity but by a raucous gutter-level humanity. And his narrative skill and fertile imagination extend beyond metaphysical idea pieces. The following story is a brief but perfectly constructed fantasy. Taken from his short-story collection *The 57th Franz Kafka*, it shows Rucker's boldly inventive originality at its most exhilarating.

His latest book is *Mind Tools*, his fourth nonfiction work of popular science, dealing with the conceptual roots of mathematics and information theory.

Houdini is broke. The vaudeville circuit is dead, ditto big-city stage. Mel Rabstein from Pathé News phones him up looking for a feature.

"Two-G advance plus three points gross after turnaround."

"You're on."

The idea is to get a priest, a rabbi, and a judge to be on camera with Houdini in all the big scenes. It'll be feature-length and play in the Loew's chain. All Houdini knows for sure is that there'll be escapes, bad ones, with no warnings.

It starts at four in the morning, July 8, 1948. They bust into Houdini's home in Levittown. He lives there with his crippled

Mom. Opening shot of priest and rabbi kicking the door down. Close on their thick-soled black shoes. Available light. The footage is grainy, jerky, can't-help-it cinema verité. It's all true.

The judge has a little bucket of melted wax, and they seal up Houdini's eyes and ears and nose-holes. The dark mysterioso face is covered over before he fully awakes, relaxing into the events, leaving dreams of pursuit. Houdini is ready. They wrap him up in Ace bandages and surgical tape, a mummy, a White Owl cigar.

Eddie Machotka, the Pathé cameraman, time-lapses the drive out to the airstrip. He shoots a frame every ten seconds so the half-hour drive only takes two minutes on screen. Dark, the wrong angles, but still convincing. There's *no cuts*. In the back of the Packard, on the laps of the priest, judge, and rabbi, lies Houdini, a white loaf crusty with tape, twitching in condensed time.

The car pulls right onto the airstrip, next to a B-15 bomber. Eddie hops out and films the three holy witnesses unloading Houdini. Pan over the plane. THE DIRTY LADY is lettered up near the nose.

The Dirty Lady! And it's not crop dusters or reservists flying it, daddy-o, it's Johnny Gallio and his Flying A-Holes! Forget it! Johnny G., the most decorated World War II Pacific combat ace, flying, with Slick Tires Jones navigating, and no less a man than Moanin' Max Moscowitz in back.

Johnny G. jumps down out of the cockpit, not too fast, not too slow, just cool, flight-jacket Johnny. Moanin' Max and Slick Tires lean out of the bomb-bay hatch, grinning and ready to roll.

The judge pulls out a turnip pocket watch. The camera zooms in and out; 4:50 A.M., the sky is getting light.

Houdini? He doesn't know they're handing him into the bomb bay of The Dirty Lady. He can't even hear or see or smell. But he's at peace, glad to have all this out in the open, glad to have it *really happen*.

Everyone gets in the plane. Bad camera motion as Eddie climbs in. Then a shot of Houdini, long and white, worming around like an insect larva. He's snuggled right down in the bomb cradle with Moanin' Max leaning over him like some wild worker ant.

The engines fire up with a hoarse roar. The priest and the rabbi sit and talk: Black clothes, white faces, gray teeth.

"Do you have any food?" the priest asks. He's powerfully built, young, with thin blond hair. One hell of a Notre Dame linebacker under those robes.

The rabbi is a little fellow with a fedora and a black beard. He's got a Franz Kafka mouth, all tics and teeth. "It's my understanding that we'll breakfast in the terminal after the release."

The priest is getting two hundred for this, the rabbi three. He has a bigger name. If the rushes work out they'll be witnessing the other escapes as well.

It's not a big plane, really, and no matter which way Eddie points the camera, there's always a white piece of Houdini in the frame. Up front you can see Johnny G. in profile, handsome Johnny not looking too good. There's sweat beads on his long upper lip, booze sweat. Peace is coming hard to Johnny.

"Just spiral her on up," Slick Tires says softly. "Like a bedspring, Johnny."

Out the portholes you can see the angled horizon sweep by, until they hit the high mattress of clouds. Max watches an altimeter, grinning and showing his teeth. They punch out of the clouds, into high slanting sunlight, Johnny holds to the helix . . . he'd go up forever if no one said stop . . . but now it's high enough.

"Bombs away!" Slick Tires calls back. The priest crosses himself and Moanin' Max pulls the release handle. Shot of white-wrapped Houdini in the coffinlike bomb cradle. The bottom falls out, and the long form falls slowly, weightlessly at first. Then the slipstream catches one end, and he begins to tumble, dark white against the bright white of the clouds below.

Eddie holds the shot as long as he can. There's a big egg-shaped cloud down there, with Houdini falling toward it. Houdini begins to unwrap himself. You can see the bandages trailing him, whipping back and forth like a long flagellum, then *thip!* he's spermed his way into that rounded white cloud.

On the way back to the airstrip, Eddie and the sound man go around the plane asking everyone if they think Houdini'll make it.

"I certainly hope so," the rabbi.

"I have no idea," the priest, hungry for his breakfast.

"There's just no way," Moanin' Max. "He'll impact at two hundred miles per."

"Everyone dies," Johnny G.

"In his position I expect I'd try to drogue-chute the bandages," Slick Tires.

"It's a conundrum," the judge.

The clouds drizzle and the plane throws up great sheets of water when it lands. Eddie films them getting out and filing into the small terminal, deserted except . . .

Across the room, with his back to them, a man in pajamas is playing pinball. Cigar smoke. Someone calls to him, and he turns—Houdini.

■ ■ ■

Houdini brings his mother to see the rushes. Everyone except for her loves it. She's very upset, though, and tears at her hair. Lots of it comes out, lots of white old hair on the floor next to her wheelchair.

Back at home Houdini gets down on his knees and begs and begs until she gives him permission to finish the movie. Rabstein at Pathé says two more stunts will do it.

"No more magic after that," Houdini promises. "I'll use the money to open us up a little music shop."

"Dear boy."

■ ■ ■

For the second stunt they fly Houdini and his Mom out to Seattle. Rabstein wants them to use the old lady for reaction shots. Pathé sets the two of them up in a boardinghouse, leaving the time and nature of the escape indeterminate.

Eddie Machotka sticks pretty close, filming bits of their long strolls down by the docks. Houdini eating a Dungeness crab. His Mom buying taffy. Houdini getting her a wig.

Four figures in black slickers slip down from a fishing boat. Perhaps Houdini hears their footsteps, but he doesn't deign to turn. Then they're upon him: the priest, the judge, the rabbi, and this time a doctor as well—could be Rex Morgan.

While the old lady screams and screams, the doctor knocks

Houdini out with a big injection of sodium pentothal. The great escape artist doesn't resist, just watches and smiles till he fades. The old lady bashes the doctor with her purse before the priest and rabbi get her and Houdini bundled onto the fishing boat.

On the boat, it's Johnny G. and the A-Holes again. Johnny can fly anything, even a boat. His eyes are bloodshot and all over the place, but Slick Tires guides him out of the harbor and down the Puget Sound to a logging river. Takes a couple of hours, but Eddie time-lapses it all . . . Houdini lying in half of a hollowed-out log and the doc shooting him up every so often.

Finally they get to a sort of millpond with a few logs in it. Moanin' Max and the judge have a tub of plaster mixed up, and they pour it in around Houdini. They tape over his head holes, except for the mouth, which gets a breathing tube. What they do is to seal him up inside a big log, with the breathing tube sticking out disguised as a branch stub. Houdini is unconscious and locked inside the log by a plaster-of-paris filling . . . sort of like a dead worm inside a Twinkie. The priest and the rabbi and the judge and the doctor heave the log overboard.

It splashes, rolls, and mingles with the other logs waiting to get sawed up. There's ten logs now, and you can't tell for sure which is the one with Houdini in it. The saw is running, and the conveyor belt snags the first log.

Shot of the logs bumping around. In the foreground, Houdini's Mom is pulling the hair out of her wig. Big SKAAAAAZZZT sound of the first log getting cut up. You can see the saw up there in the background, a giant ripsaw cutting the log right down the middle.

SKAAAZZZZT! SKAAAAZZZZZT! SKAAAZZZZT! The splinters fly. One by one the logs are hooked and dragged up to the saw. You want to look away, but you can't . . . just waiting to see the blood and used food come flying out. SKAAAZZZZT!

Johnny G. drinks something from a silver hip flask. His lips move silently. Curses? Prayers? SKAAAZZZZT! Moanin' Max's nervous horse-face sweats and grins. Houdini's Mom has the wig plucked right down to the hair net. SKAAAZZZZZT! Slick Tires' eyes are big and white as hard-boiled eggs. He helps himself to Johnny's flask. SKAAAZZT! The priest mops his forehead and the rabbi . . . SKNAKCHUNKFWEEEEE!

Plaster dust flies from the ninth log. It falls in two, revealing only a negative of Houdini's body. An empty mold! They all scramble onto the mill dock, camera panning around, looking for the great man. Where is he?

Over the shouts and cheers you can hear the jukebox in the millhands' cafeteria. The Andrews Sisters. And inside there's . . . Houdini, tapping his foot and eating a cheeseburger.

■ ■ ■

"Only one more escape," Houdini promises, "And then we'll get that music shop."

"I'm so frightened, Harry," his bald Mom says. "If only they'd give you some warning."

"They have, this time. Piece of cake. We're flying out to Nevada."

"I just hope you stay away from those show girls."

■ ■ ■

The priest and the rabbi and the judge and the doctor are all there, and this time a scientist, too. A low-ceilinged concrete room with slits for windows. Houdini is dressed in a black rubber wet suit, doing card tricks.

The scientist, who's a dead ringer for Albert Einstein, speaks briefly over the telephone and nods to the doctor. The doctor smiles handsomely into the camera, then handcuffs Houdini and helps him down into a cylindrical tank of water. Refrigeration coils cool it down, and before long they've got Houdini frozen solid inside a huge cake of ice.

The priest and the rabbi knock down the sides of the tank, and there's Houdini like a big ice firecracker with his head sticking out for a fuse. Outside is a truck with a hydraulic lift. Johnny G. and the A-Holes are there, and they load Houdini in back. The ice gets covered with pads to keep it from melting in the hot desert sun.

Two miles off, you can see a spindly test tower with a little shed on top. This is an atom-bomb test range, out in some godforsaken desert in the middle of Nevada. Eddie Machotka rides the truck with Houdini and the A-Holes.

Shot of the slender tower looming overhead, the obscene bomb-bulge at the top. God only knows what strings Rabstein had to pull to get Pathé in on this.

There's a cylindrical hole in the ground right under the tower, right at ground zero, and they slip the frozen Houdini in there. His head, flush with the ground, grins at them like a peyote cactus. They drive back to the bunker, fast.

Eddie films it all realtime, no cuts. Houdini's Mom is in the bunker, of course, plucking a lapful of wigs. The scientist hands her some dice.

"Just to give him fighting chance, we won't detonate until you are rolling a two. Is called snake-eyes, yes?"

Close on her face, frantic with worry. As slowly as possible, she rattles the dice and spills them onto the floor.

Snake-eyes!

Before anyone else can react, the scientist has pushed the button, a merry twinkle in his faraway eyes. The sudden light filters into the bunker, shading all the blacks up to gray. The shockwave hits next, and the judge collapses, possibly from heart attack. The roar goes on and on. The crowded faces turn this way and that.

Then it's over, and the noise is gone, gone except for . . . an insistent *honking,* right outside the bunker. The scientist un- dogs the door and they all look out, Eddie shooting over their shoulders.

It's *Houdini!* Yes! In a white convertible with a breast-heavy show girl!

"Give me my money!" he shouts. "And color me gone!"

repetition - Houdini as a machine, his mother also. Each of them have programmable responses to their situations.

What's up with snake-eyes?

400 Boys

∎

The cyberpunk writers are known for bizarre concepts and a general allegiance to the strange. Marc Laidlaw stands out even in this company. His work is marked by odd leaping juxtapositions, unexpected angles of vision, and a black humor that shades into the ultraviolet. He draws inspiration from a slew of contemporary influences, with a special fondness for all that is mysterious, intuitive, and outré.

The following story demonstrates Laidlaw's inspired fusion of elements, blending features of apocalyptic myth with the modern legendry of urban street gangs. "400 Boys" is a genuinely weird, headlong mélange that is much more easily enjoyed than described.

Marc Laidlaw lives in San Francisco. His latest novel is *Dad's Nuke*.

> "Sacrifice us!"
>
> —*The Popol Vuh*

We sit and feel Fun City die. Two stories above our basement, at street level, something big is stomping apartment pyramids flat. We can feel the lives blinking out like smashed bulbs; you don't need second sight to see through other eyes at a time like this. I get flashes of fear and sudden pain, but none of them lasts long. The paperback drops out of my hands and I blow my candle out.

We are the Brothers, a team of twelve. There were twenty-two yesterday, but not everyone made it to the basement in time.

Our slicker Slash is up on a crate loading and reloading his gun with its one and only silver bullet. Crybaby Jaguar is kneeling in the corner on his old blanket, sobbing like a maniac, and for once he has a good reason. My best Brother Jade keeps spinning the cylinders of the holotube in search of stations, but all he gets is static that sounds like the screaming in our minds, the screaming that will not fade except as it gets squelched voice by voice.

Slash goes, "Jade, turn that thing off or I'll short-cirk it."

He is our leader, our slicker. His lips are gray, his mouth twice too wide where a Soooooot scalpel opened his cheeks. He has a lisp.

Jade shrugs and shuts down the tube, but the sounds we hear instead are no better. Faraway pounding footsteps, shouts from the sky, monster laughter. It seems to be passing away, deeper into Fun City.

"They'll be gone in no time," Jade goes.

"You think you know everything," goes Vave O'Claw, dissecting an alarm clock with one chrome finger the way some kids pick their nose. "You don't even know what they are—"

"I saw 'em," goes Jade. "Croak and I. Right, Croak?"

I nod without a sound. There's no tongue in my mouth. I only croaked right after my free Fix-up, which I got for mouthing badsense to a Controller cognibot when I was twelve.

Jade and I went out last night and climbed an empty pyramid to see what we could see. Past Riverrun Blvd. the world was burning bright, and I had to look away. Jade kept staring and said he saw wild giants running with the glow. Then I heard a thousand guitar strings snapping and Jade said the giants had ripped up Big Bridge by the roots and thrown it at the moon. I looked up and saw a black arch spinning end over end, cables twanging as it flipped up and up through shredded smoke and never fell back—or not while we waited, which wasn't too long.

"Whatever it is could be here for good," goes Slash, twisting his mouth in the middle as he grins. "Might never leave."

Crybaby stops snorting long enough to say, "Nuh-never?"

"Why should they? Looks like they came a long way to get to Fun City, doesn't it? Maybe we have a new team on our hands, Brothers."

"Just what we need," goes Jade. "Don't ask me to smash with 'em, though. My blade's not big enough. If the Controllers couldn't keep 'em from crashing through, what can we do?"

Slash cocks his head. "Jade, dear Brother, listen close. If I ask you to smash, you smash. If I ask you to jump from a hive, you jump. Or find another team. You know I only ask these things to keep your life interesting."

"Interesting enough," my best Brother grumbles.

"Hey!" goes Crybaby. He's bigger and older than any of us, but doesn't have the brains of a ten-year-old. "Listen!"

We listen.

"Don't hear nothin'," goes Skag.

"Yeah! Nuh-nothin'. They made away."

He spoke too soon. Next thing we know there is thunder in the walls, the concrete crawls underfoot, and the ceiling rains. I dive under a table with Jade.

The thunder fades to a whisper. Afterward there is real silence.

"You okay, Croak?" Jade goes. I nod and look into the basement for the other Brothers. I can tell by the team spirit in the room that no one is hurt.

In the next instant we let out a twelve-part gasp.

There's natural light in the basement. Where from?

Looking out from under the table, I catch a parting shot of the moon two stories and more above us. The last shock had split the old tenement hive open to the sky. Floors and ceilings layer the sides of a fissure; water pipes cross in the air like metal webs; the floppy head of a mattress spills foam on us.

The moon vanishes into boiling black smoke; it is the same smoke we saw washing over the city yesterday, when the stars were sputtering like flares around a traffic wreck. Lady Death's perfume come creeping down with it.

Slash straddles the crack that runs through the center of the room. He tucks his gun into his pocket. The silver of its only bullet was mixed with some of Slash's blood. He saves it for the Soooooot who gave him his grin, a certain slicker named HiLo.

"Okay, team," he goes. "Let's get out of here."

Vave and Jade rip away the boards from the door. The basement was rigged for security, to keep us safe when things got bad in Fun City. Vave shielded the walls with baffles, so when Controller cognibots came scanning for hideaways they picked up plumbing from an empty room. Never a scoop of us.

Beyond the door, the stairs tilt up at a crazy slant; it's nothing we can't manage. I look back at the basement as we head up, because I had been getting to think of it as home.

We were there when the Controllers came looking for war recruits. They thought we were just the right age: "Come out, come out, wherever in free!" When they came hunting, we did our trick and disappeared.

That was in the last of the calendar days, when everyone was yelling:

Hey!

This Is It!

World War Last!

What they told us about the war could be squeezed into Vave's pinky tip, which he had hollowed out for explosive darts. They still wanted us to fight in it. The deal was, we would get a free trip to the moon for training at Base English, then we would zip back to Earth charged up and ready to go-go-go. The Mexi-Sovs were hatching wars like eggs, one after another, down south. The place got so hot we could see the skies that way glowing white some nights, yellow in the day.

Federal Control had sealed our continental city tight in a see-through blister: nothing but air and light got in or out without a password. Vave was sure when he saw the yellow glow that the MexiSovs had launched something fierce against the invisible curtain, something that was strong enough to get through.

Quiet as queegs we creep to the Strip. Our bloc covers 56th to 88th between Westland and Chico. The streetlights are busted like every window in all the buildings and crashed cars. Garbage and bodies are spilled all over.

"Aw, skud," goes Vave.

Crybaby starts bawling.

"Keep looking, Croak," goes Slash. "Get it all."

I want to look away but I have to store this for later. I almost cry because my ma and my real brother are dead. I put *that* away and get it all down. Slash lets me keep track of the Brothers.

At the Federal Pylon—where they control the programmable parts and people of Fun City—Mister Fixer snipped my tongue and started at the other end. He did not live to finish the job. A team brigade of Quazis and Moofs, led by my Brothers, sprang me free.

That takes teamwork. I know the Controllers said otherwise, said that we were smash-crazy subverts like the Anarcanes, with no pledge to Fun City. But if you ever listened to them, salt your ears. Teams never smashed unless they had to. When life pinched in Fun City, there was nowhere to jump but sideways into the next bloc. Enter with no invitation and . . . things worked out.

I catch a shine of silver down the Strip. A cognibot is stalled with scanners down, no use to the shaveheads who sit in the Pylon and watch the streets. I point it out, thinking there can't be many shaveheads left.

"No more law," goes Jade.

"Nothing in our way," goes Slash.

We start down the Strip. On our way past the cog, Vave stops to unbolt the laser nipples on its turret. Hooked to battery packs, they will make slick snappers.

We grab flashlights from busted monstermarts. For a while we look into the ruins, but that gets nasty fast. We stick to finding our way through the fallen mountains that used to be pyramids and block-long hives. It takes a long time.

There is fresh paint on the walls that still stand, dripping red-black like it might never dry. The stench of fresh death blows from center city. Another alleycat pissed our bloc.

I wonder about survivors. When we send our minds out into the ruins, we don't feel a thing. There were never many people here when times were good. Most of the hives emptied out in the fever years, when the oldies died and the kiddykids, untouched by disease, got closer together and learned to share their power.

It keeps getting darker, hotter; the smell gets worse. Sometimes the sun looks down through swirling smoke. Bodies staring from windows make me glad I never looked for Ma or my brother. We gather canned food, keeping ultra quiet. The Strip has never seen such a dead night. Teams were always roving, smashing, throwing clean-fun free-for-alls.

We cross through bloc after bloc: Bennies, Silks, Quazis, Mannies, and Angels. No one. If any teams are alive they are in hideaways unknown; if they hid out overground they are dead as the rest.

We wait for the telltale psychic tug—like a whisper in the pit of your belly—that another team gives. There is nothing but death in the night.

"Rest tight, teams," Jade goes.

"Wait," goes Slash.

We stop at 265th in the Snubnose bloc. Looking down the Strip, I see someone sitting high on a heap of ruined cement. He shakes his head and puts up his hands.

"Well, well," goes Slash.

The doob starts down the heap. He is so weak he tumbles and avalanches the rest of the way to the street. We surround him and he looks up into the black zero of Slash's gun.

"Hiya, HiLo," Slash goes. He has on a grin he must have saved with the silver bullet. It runs all the way back to his ears. "How's Sooooooots?"

HiLo doesn't look so slick. His red-and-black lightning-bolt suit is shredded and stained, the collar torn off for a bandage around one wrist. The left lens of his dark owl rims is shattered, and his buzz cut is scraped to nothing.

HiLo doesn't say a word. He stares up into the gun and waits for the trigger to snap, the last little sound he will ever hear. We are waiting too.

There's one big tear dripping from the shattered lens, washing HiLo's grimy cheek.

Slash laughs. Then he lowers the gun and says, "Not tonight."

HiLo does not even twitch.

Down the Strip, a gas main blows up and paints us all in orange light. We all start laughing. It's funny, I guess. HiLo's smile is silent.

Slash jerks HiLo to his feet. "I got other stuff under my skin, slicker. You look like runover skud. Where's your team?"

HiLo looks at the ground, shakes his head.

"Slicker," he goes, "we got flattened. No other way to put it." A stream of tears follows the first; he clears them away. "There's no Sooooooots left."

"There's you," goes Slash, putting a hand on HiLo's shoulder.

"Can't be a slicker without a team, Slash."

"Sure you can. What happened?"

HiLo looks down the street. "New team took our bloc," he goes. "They're giants, Slash—I know it sounds crazy."

"No," goes Jade, "I seen 'em."

HiLo goes, "We heard them coming, but if we had seen them I would never have told the Soooooots to stand tight. Thought there was a chance we could hold our own, but we got smeared.

"They *threw* us. Some of my buds flew higher than the Pylon. These boys . . . incredible boys. Now 400th is full of them. They glow and shiver like the lights when you get clubbed and fade out."

Vave goes, "They sound like chiller-dillers."

"If I thought they were only boys I wouldn't be scared, Brother," goes HiLo. "But there's more to them. We tried to psych them out and it almost worked. They're made out of that kind of stuff: it looks real and it will cut you up, but when you go at it with your mind it buzzes away like bees. There weren't enough of us to do much. And we weren't ready for them. I only got away because NimbleJax knocked me cold and stuffed me under a transport.

"When I got up it was over. I followed the Strip. Thought some teams might be roving, but there's nobody. Could be in hideaways. I was afraid to check. Most teams would squelch me before I said word one."

"It's hard alone, different with a team behind you," goes Slash. "How many hideaways do you know?"

"Maybe six. Had a line on JipJaps, but not for sure. I know where to find Zips, Kingpins, Gerlz, Myrmies . . . Sledges. . . . We could get to the Galrog bloc fast through the subtunnels."

Slash turns to me. "What have we got?"

I pull out the beat-up list and hand it to Jade, who reads it. "JipJaps, Sledges, Drummers, A-V Marias, Chix, Chogs, Dannies. If any of them are still alive, they would know others."

"True," goes Slash.

Jade nudges me. "Wonder if this new team has got a name."

He knows I like spelling things out. I grin and take the list back, pull out a pencil, and put down *400 Boys*.

"'Cause they took 400th," Jade goes. I nod, but that is not all. Somewhere I think I read about Boys knocking down the world, torturing grannies. It seems like something these Boys would do.

Down the street the moon comes up through smoke that makes it the color of rust. Big chunks are missing.

"We'll smash 'em," goes Vave.

The sight of the moon makes us sad and scared at the same time. I remember how it had been perfect and round as a pearl on jewelry-mart velvet, beautiful and brighter than streetlights even when the worst smogs dyed it brown. That brown was better than this chipped-away bloody red. Looks like it was used for target practice. Maybe those Boys tossed Big Bridge at Base English.

"Our bloc is gone," goes HiLo. "I want those Boys. It'll be those doobs or me."

"We're with you," goes Slash. "Let's move fast. Cut into pairs, Brothers. We're gonna hit some hideaways. Jade, Croak, you come with me and HiLo. We'll see if those Galrogs will listen to sense."

Slash tells the other Brothers where to look and where to check back. We say goodbye. We find the stairs to the nearest subtunnel and go down into lobbies full of shadow where bodies lie waiting for the last train.

We race rats down the tunnel. They are meaner and fatter than ever, but our lights hold them back.

"Still got that wicked blade?" goes Slash.

"This baby?" HiLo swings his good arm and a scalpel blade drops into his hand.

Slash's eyes frost over and his mouth tightens. "May need it," he goes.

"Right, Brother." HiLo makes it disappear.

I see that is how it has to be.

We pass a few more lobbies before going up and out. We have moved faster than on ground; now we are close to the low end of Fun City.

"This way." HiLo points past broken hives. I see codes scripted on the rubbled walls: Galrog signals?

"Wait," goes Jade. "I'm starved."

There is a liquor store a block away. We lift and twist the door open, easy as breaking an arm. Nothing moves inside or on the street as our lights glide over rows of bottles. Broken glass snaps under our sneakers. The place smells drunk and I'm getting that way from breathing. We find chips and candy bars that survived under a counter and gulp them down in the doorway.

"So where's the Galrog hideaway?" goes Jade, finishing a 5th Ave bar.

Just then we feel that little deep tug. This one whispers death. A team is letting us know that it has us surrounded.

HiLo goes, "Duck back."

"No," goes Slash. "No more hiding."

We go slow to the door and look through. Shadows peel from the walls and streak from alley mouths. We're sealed tight.

"Keep your blades back, Brothers."

I never smashed with Galrogs; I see why Slash kept us away. They are tanked out with daystars, snappers, guns and glorystix. Even unarmed they would be fierce with their fire-painted eyes, chopped topknots a dozen colors, and rainbow geometrics tattooed across their faces. Most are dressed in black; all are on razor-toed roller skates.

Their feelings are masked from us behind a mesh of silent threats.

A low voice: "Come out if you plan to keep breathing."

We move out, keeping together as the girls close tight. Jade raises his flashlight but a Galrog with blue-triangled cheeks and a purple-blond topknot kicks it from his hand. It goes spinning a crazy beam through the dark. There is not a scratch on Jade's fingers. I keep my own light low.

A big Galrog rolls up. She looks like a cognibot, slung with battery packs, wires running up and down her arms and through her afro, where she's hung tin bells and shards of glass. She has a laser turret strapped to her head and a snapper in each hand.

She checks me and Jade over and out, then turns toward the slickers.

"Slicker HiLo and Slicker Slash," she goes. "Cute match."

"Keep it short, Bala," goes Slash. "The blocs are smashed."

"So I see." She smiles with black, acid-etched teeth. "Hevvies got stomped next door and we got a new playground."

"Have fun playing for a day or two," goes HiLo. "The ones who squelched them are coming back for you."

"Buildings squashed them. The end of the ramming world has been and gone. Where were you?"

"There's a new team playing in Fun City," HiLo goes.

Bala's eyes turn to slits. "Ganging on us now, huh? That's a getoff."

"The 400 Boys," goes Jade.

"Enough to keep you busy!" She laughs and skates a half-circle. "Maybe."

"They're taking Fun City for their bloc—maybe all of it. They don't play fair, never heard of clean fun."

"Skud," she goes, and shakes her hair so tin bells shiver. "You blew cirks, kids."

Slash knows she is listening. "We're calling all teams, Bala. We gotta save our skins now and that means we need to find more hideaways, let more slickers know what's up. Are you in or out?"

HiLo goes, "They smashed the Soooooots in thirty seconds, flat."

A shock wave passes down the street like the tail end of a whiplash from center city. It catches us all by surprise and our guards go down; Galrogs, Brothers, Soooooot—we are all afraid of those wreckers. It unites us just like that.

When the shock passes, we look at each other with wide eyes. All the unspoken Galrog threats are gone. We have to hang together.

"Let's take these kids home," goes Bala.

"Yeah, Mommy!"

With a whisper of skates, the Galrogs take off.

Our well-armed escort leads us through a maze of skate trails cleared in rubble.

"Boys, huh?" I hear Bala say to the other slickers. "We thought different."

"What did you think?"

"Gods," Bala goes.

"Gods!"

"God-things, mind stuff. Old Mother looked into her mirror and saw a bonfire made out of cities. Remember before the blister tore? There were wars in the south, weird bombs going off like firecrackers. Who knows what was cooking in all that blaze?

"Old Mother said it was the end of the world, time for the ones outside to come through the cracks. They scooped all that energy and molded it into mass. Then they started scaring up storms, smashing. Where better to smash than Fun City?"

"End of the world?" goes HiLo. "Then why are we still here?"

Bala laughs. "You doob, how did you ever get to be a slicker? Nothing ever ends. Nothing."

In ten minutes we come to a monstermart pyramid with its lower mirror windows put back together in jigsaw shards. Bala gives a whistle and double doors swing wide.

In we go.

The first thing I see are boxes of supplies heaped in the aisles, cookstoves burning, cots and piles of blankets. I also spot a few people who can't be Galrogs—like babies, a few grown-ups.

"We've been taking in survivors," goes Bala. "Old Mother said we should." She shrugs.

Old Mother is ancient, I have heard. She lived through the plagues and came out on the side of the teams. She must be upstairs, staring in her mirror, mumbling.

Slash and HiLo look at each other. I cannot tell what they are thinking. Slash turns to me and Jade.

"Okay, Brothers, we've got work to do. Stick around."

"Got anywhere to sleep?" Jade goes. The sight of cots and blankets made us both tired.

Bala points at a dead escalator. "Show them the way, Shell."

The Galrog with the blond topknot streaked purple speeds down an aisle and leaps the first four steps of the escalator. She runs to the top without skipping a stroke and grins down from above.

"She's an angel," goes Jade.

There are more Galrogs at the top. Some girls are wrapped up snoring along the walls.

Shell cocks her hips and laughs. "Never seen Brothers in a monstermart before."

"Aw, my ma used to shop here," goes Jade. He checks her up and over.

"What'd she buy? Your daddy?"

Jade sticks his thumb through his fist and wiggles it with a big grin. The other girls laugh, but not Shell. Her blue eyes darken and her cheeks redden under the blue triangles. I grab Jade's arm.

"Don't waste it," goes another Galrog.

"I'll take the tip off for you," goes Shell and flashes a blade. "Nice and neat."

I tug Jade's arm and he drops it.

"Come on, grab blankets," goes Shell. "You can bed over there."

We take blankets to a corner, wrap up, and fall asleep close together. I dream of smoke.

It is still dark when Slash wakes us.

"Come on, Brothers, lots of work to do."

Things have taken off, we see. The Galrogs know the hideaways of more teams than we ever heard of, some from outside Fun City. Runners have been at it all night and things are busy now. From uptown and downtown in a wide circle around 400th, they have called all who can come.

The false night of smoke goes on and on, no telling how long. It is still dark when Fun City starts moving.

Over hive and under street, by sewer, strip, and alleyway, we close in tourniquet-tight on 400th, where Soooooots ran a clean-fun bloc. From 1st to 1000th, Bayview St. to Riverrun Blvd., the rubble scatters and the subtunnels swarm as Fun City moves. Brothers and Galrogs are joined by Ratbeaters, Drummers, Myrmies, and Kingpins from Piltown, Renfrew, and the Upperhand Hills. The Diablos cruise down with Chogs and Cholos, Sledges and Trimtones, JipJaps and A-V Marias. Tints, Chix, Rockoboys, Gerlz, Floods, Zips, and Zaps. More than I can remember.

It is a single team, the Fun City team, and all the names mean the same thing.

We Brothers walk shoulder to shoulder with the last Soooooot among us.

Up the sub stairs we march to a blasted black surface. It looks like the end of the world, but we are still alive. I can hardly breathe for a minute, but I keep walking and let my anger boil.

Up ahead the 400 Boys quiet down to a furnace roar.

By 359th we have scattered through cross streets into the Boys' bloc.

When we reach 398th, fire flares from hives ahead. There is a sound like a skyscraper taking its first step. A scream echoes high between the towers and falls to the street.

At the next corner, I see an arm stretched out under rubble. Around the wrist, the cuff is jagged black and red.

"Go to it," goes HiLo.

We step onto 400th and stare forever.

The streets we knew are gone. The concrete has been pulverized to gravel and dust, cracked up from underneath. Pyramid hives are baby volcano cones that hack smoke, ooze fire, and burn black scars in the broken earth. Towers hulk around the spitting volcanoes like buildings warming themselves under the blanked-out sky.

Were the 400 Boys building a new city? If so, it would be worse than death.

Past the fires we can see the rest of Fun City. We feel the team on all sides, a pulse of life connecting us, one breath.

HiLo has seen some of this before, but not all. He sheds no tears tonight. He walks out ahead of us to stand black against the flames. He throws back his head and screams:

"*Heeeeeey!*"

A cone erupts between the monster buildings. It drowns him out so he shouts louder.

"*HEY, YOU 400 BOYS!*"

Shattered streetlights pop half to life. Over my head one explodes with a flash.

"*This is our bloc, 400 Boys!*"

Galrogs and Trimtones beat on overturned cars. It gets my blood going.

"*So you knocked in our hives, you Boys. So you raped our city.*"

Our world. I think of the moon and my eyes sting.

"*So what?*"

The streetlights black out. The earth shudders. The cones roar and vomit hot blood all over those buildings; I hear it sizzle as it drips. Thunder talks among the towers.

"*I bet you will never grow UP!*"

Here they come.

All at once there are more buildings in the street. I had thought they were new buildings, but they are *big* Boys: 400 at least.

"Stay cool," goes Slash.

The 400 Boys thunder into our streets. We move back through shadows into hiding places only we can reach.

The first Boys swing chains with links the size of skating

rinks. Off come the tops of some nearby hives. The Boys cannot quite get at us from up there, but they can cover us with rubble.

They look seven or eight years old for all their size, and there is still baby pudge on their long sweaty faces. Their eyes have a vicious shine like boys that age get when they are pulling the legs off a bug—laughing wild, but freaked and frightened by what they see their own hands doing. They look double deadly because of that. They are on fire under their skin, fever yellow.

They look more frightened than us. Fear is gone from the one team. We reach out at them as they charge, sending our power from all sides. We chant, but I do not know if there are any words; it is a cry. It might mean "Take us if you can, Boys, take us at our size."

I feel as if I have touched a cold yellow blaze of fever; it sickens me, but the pain lets me know how real it is. I find strength in that; we all do. We hold on to the fire, sucking it away, sending it down into the earth through our feet.

The Boys start grinning and squinting. They seem to be squeezing inside out. The closest ones start shrinking, dropping down to size with every step.

We suck and spit the fever. The fire passes through us. Our howling synchronizes.

The Boys keep getting smaller all the time, smaller and dimmer. Little kids never know when to stop. Even when they are burned out, they keep going.

As we fall back the first Boy comes down to size. One minute he is taller than the hives; then he hardly fills the street. A dozen of his shrinking pals fill in on either side. They whip their chains and shriek at the sky like screaming cutouts against the downtown fires.

They break past HiLo in the middle of the street and head for us. Now they are twice our size . . . just right.

This I can handle.

"Smash!" yells Slash.

One Boy charges me with a wicked black curve I don't see till it's whispering in my ear. I duck fast and come up faster where he doesn't expect me. He goes down soft and heavy, dead. The sick yellow light throbs out with his blood, fades on the street.

I spin to see Jade knocked down by a Boy with an ax. There

is nothing I can do but stare as the black blade swings high. . . .

Shrill whistle.

Wheels whirring.

A body sails into the Boy and flattens him out with a footful of razors and ball bearings. Purple-blond topknot and a big grin. The Galrog skips high and stomps his hatchet hand into cement, leaving stiff fingers curling around mashed greenish blood and bones.

Shell laughs at Jade and takes off.

I run over and yank him to his feet. Two Boys back away into a dark alley that lights up as they go in. We start after but they have already been fixed by Quazis and Drummers lying in wait. Jade and I turn away.

HiLo still stares down the street. One Boy has stood tall, stronger than the rest and more resistant to our power. He raps a massive club in his hand.

"Come on, slicker," HiLo calls. *"Remember me?"*

The biggest of Boys comes down, eating up the streets. We concentrate on draining him but he shrinks more slowly than the others.

His club slams the ground—*Boom-Boom-Boom!* Me and some Galrogs land on our asses. The club creases a hive and cement sprays over us, glass sings through the air.

HiLo does not move. He waits with red and black lightning bolts serene, both hands empty.

The big slicker swings again, but now his head only reaches to the fifth floor of an Rx. HiLo ducks as the club streaks over and turns a storefront window into dust.

The Soooooot's scalpel glints into his hand. He throws himself at the Boy's ankle and grabs on tight.

He slashes twice. The Boy screams like a cat. Neatest hamstringing you ever saw.

The screaming Boy staggers and kicks out hard enough to flip HiLo across the street into the metal cage of a shop window, denting it deep. HiLo lands in a heap of impossible angles and does not move again.

Slash cries out. His gun shouts louder. One bloodsilver shot. It leaves a shining line in the smoky air.

The Boy falls over and scratches the cement till his huge fingertips bleed. His mouth gapes wide as a manhole, his eyes stare like the broken windows all around. His pupils are slit like a poison snake's, his face long and dark, hook-nosed.

God or boy, he is dead. Like some of us.

Five Drummers climb over the corpse for the next round, but with their slicker dead the Boys are not up to it. The volcanoes belch as though they too are giving up.

The survivors stand glowing in the middle of their bloc. A few start crying, and that's a sound I can't spell. It makes Crybaby start up. He sits in cement, sobbing through his fingers. His tears are the color of an oil rainbow on wet asphalt.

We keep on sucking up the fever glow, grounding it all in the earth. The Boys cry louder, in pain. They start tearing at each other, running in spirals, and a few leap into the lava that streams from the pyramids.

The glow shrieks out of control, out of our hands, gathering between the Boys with its last strength—ready to pounce.

It leaps upward, a hot snake screaming into the clouds.

The Boys drop dead and never move again.

A hole in the ceiling of smoke. The dark blue sky peeks through, turning pale as the smoke thins. The Boys' last scream dies out in the dawn.

The sun looks bruised, but there it is. Hiya!

"Let's get to it," goes Slash. "Lots of cleanup ahead." He had been crying, stretching his gray mouth. I guess he loved HiLo like a Brother. I wish I could say something.

We help each other up. Slap shoulders and watch the sun come out gold and orange and blazing white.

I don't have to tell you it looks good, teams.

JAMES PATRICK KELLY

Solstice

■

James Patrick Kelly's first publication came in 1975. His career accelerated through the early 1980s; he has written almost two dozen short stories and two novels. His second book, *Freedom Beach*, was written with John Kessel and attracted praise for its lively invention and playful literary erudition.

Like Kessel, Kelly has been associated with a loose group of Eighties SF writers, generally identified as SF's new "literary wing," as (theoretically) opposed to the harder tech interests of the cyberpunks.

In 1985, Kelly gleefully complicated matters by publishing the following story, a high-tech extravaganza of headlong visionary daring. He followed it with two more stories, equally inventive and original, in a self-proclaimed "cyberpunk trilogy." By his example, Kelly has demonstrated a truism in SF—that where critics divide and analyze, writers will unite and synthesize.

Once a year they open it to the public. Some spend lifetimes planning for the day. Others arrive by chance, fortunate sight-seers swarming out of the tour hovers. They record it all but only rarely understand what they are witnessing. Years later a few of the disks will come out to pep up drooping parties. Most will be forgotten.

It happens on the summer solstice. One of two points on the ecliptic at which its distance from the celestial equator is greatest. The longest day of the year. A turning point.

■ ■ ■

They arrived late in the afternoon when the crowd was starting to thin. A tall man in his early forties. A teenaged girl.

They had the same gray eyes. Her straw-colored hair had begun to darken, just as his had darkened when he was seventeen. There was an inescapable similarity in the way they whispered jokes to one another and laughed at the people around them. Neither carried a camera.

They had come to wander among the sarsen stones of what Tony Cage considered the most extraordinary antiquity in the world. Yes, the pyramids were older, bigger, but they had long since yielded their mystery. The Parthenon had once been more beautiful, but the acids of history had etched it beyond recognition. But Stonehenge . . . Stonehenge was unique. Essential. It was a mirror in which each age could observe the quality of its imagination, in which every man could measure his size.

They joined the queue waiting to enter the dome. Occasional screams of synthesized music pierced the buzz of the crowd; the free festival being held in a nearby field was hitting a frenzied peak. Perhaps later they would explore its delights, but now they had reached the entrance to the exterior shell of the dome. The girl laughed as she popped through the bubble membrane.

"It's like being kissed by a giant," she said.

They were in the space between the exterior and interior shells of the dome. On any other day this would have been as close as they could have come to the stone circles. The dome was made of hardened optical plastic with a low refractive index. Walkways spiraled upward in the space between the shells; tourists who climbed to the top had a bird's-eye view of Stonehenge.

They entered the inner shell. There was a reporter with a microcam standing near the Heel Stone; he spotted them and started waving. "Pardon, sir, pardon!" Cage pulled the girl out of the flow of the crowd and waited; he did not want the fool calling his name in front of all these people.

"You're the drug artist." The reporter drew them aside. A daisy smile bloomed on his obsidian face. "Case, Cane . . ." He tapped the skull plug behind his ear as if to dislodge the memory from his wetware.

"Cage."

"And this?" The smile became a smirk. "Your lovely daughter?"

Cage thought about punching the man. He thought about walking away. The girl laughed.

"I'm Wynne." She shook the reporter's hand.

"Name's Zomboy. Wiltshire stringer for *Sonic*. Have you seen the old stones before? I could show you around." Cage kept expecting the microcam's red light to come on, but the reporter seemed strangely hesitant. "I say, you wouldn't by any chance be holding any free samples? For one of your major fans?"

Wynne bit her lip to stifle a giggle and reached into her pocket. "I doubt you could tell Tony much about Stonehenge. Sometimes I think he lives for this place." She produced a plastic bottle, shook some green capsules into her palm, and offered them to the reporter.

He took one and inspected it carefully. "No label on the casing." He fixed his suspicion on Cage. "You're sure it's safe?"

"Hell no," said Wynne. She popped two of the capsules into her mouth. "Very experimental. Turn your brains to blood pudding." She offered one to Cage and he took it. He wished Wynne would stop playing these twisted games. "We've been eating them all day," said Wynne. "Can't you tell?"

Gingerly, the reporter put one in his mouth. Then the red light came on. "So you're a devotee of Stonehenge, Mr. Cage?"

"Oh yes." Wynne was babbling. "He comes here all the time. Gives lectures to whoever will listen. Says there's a kind of magic to the place."

"Magic?" The lens stared at Cage, had never left him.

"Not the kind of magic you're thinking of, I'm afraid." Cage hated looking into cameras when he was twisted. "No wizards or human sacrifices or bolts of lightning. A subtle kind of magic, the only kind still possible in this overly explained world." The words rolled out unbidden—perhaps because he had spoken them before. "It has to do with the way a mystery captures the imagination and becomes an obsession. A magic that works exclusively in the mind."

"And who better to contemplate mind magic than the celebrated drug artist, Mr. Tony Cage." The reporter spoke not to them but to an unseen audience.

Cage smiled into the camera.

■ ■ ■

In 1130 Henry of Huntingdon, an archdeacon at Lincoln, was commissioned by his bishop to write a history of England. His was the first written account of a place called "Stanenges, where stones of wondrous size have been erected after the manner of doorways, so that doorway appears to have been raised upon doorway; and no one can conceive of how such great stones have been raised aloft, or why they were built there." The name derives from the Old English: "stan," stone, and "hengen," gallows. Medieval gallows consisted of two posts and a crosspiece. There is no record of executions at Stonehenge, although Geoffrey of Monmouth, writing six years after Henry, describes the massacre of four hundred and sixty British lords by treacherous Saxons. Geoffrey claims that, as a memorial to the dead, Uther Pendragon and Merlin stole the sacred megaliths known as the Giants' Dance from the Irish by magic and force of arms and re-erected them on the Wiltshire plain. The "Merlin theory" of Stonehenge's construction, while certainly true to the spirit of Anglo-Irish relations, was of a piece with the rest of Geoffrey's Arthurian tapestry: a jingoistic fairy tale.

■ ■ ■

"Wake up."

Cage had been dreaming of sheep. A vast treeless pasture, green waves rolling to the horizon. The animals shied away from him as he wandered among them. He was lost.

"Tony."

The cryogenicists claimed that stiffs did not dream. Strictly speaking they were right, but as the tank thawed him out, his synapses began to fire again. Then dreams came.

"Wake up, Tony."

His eyelids flickered. "Go 'way." He felt like a pincushion. He opened his eyes and stared at her. For a moment he thought he was still dreaming. Wynne had shaved her hair off except for a spiky multicolored fan that ran from ear to ear. From the looks of it she had just had a new body tint done. In blue.

"I'm leaving, Tony. I only stayed around to make sure you thawed all right. I'm all packed."

He mumbled something sarcastic. It did not make much sense, even to him, but the tone of voice was right. He knew she was not as strong as she thought she was. Otherwise she wouldn't have tried to spring this on him while he was still groggy. He sat up in the tank.

"Leave, then," he said. "Help me out of here."

He huddled on the couch in the drawing room and tried not to feel cold as he stared at the mist that hung over Galway Bay. There was no horizon; both the sky and the water were the color of old thatch. Exactly the same kind of day it had been when he had climbed into the tank. He had never much liked Ireland. But when the Republic had extended its tax benefits to drug artists, his accountants had forced citizenship on him.

Wynne had a fire going; the room had filled with the bitter smell of burning peat. She brought him a cup of coffee. There was a red and green pill on the saucer. "What's this?" He held it up.

"New. Serentol. Helps you relax."

"I've been stiff for six months, Wynne. I'm plenty relaxed."

She shrugged, took the pill from him, and popped it into her mouth. "No sense wasting it."

"Where will you go?" he said.

She seemed surprised that he would ask, as if she had expected an argument first. "England for a while," she said. "After that I don't know."

"All right." He nodded. "No sense staying here any longer than you have to. But will you come back when it's tank time again?"

She shook her head; the peacock hair fluttered. He decided that he could get used to it.

"How much will it cost to change your mind?"

She smiled. "You haven't got enough."

He matched the smile. "Come give us a kiss then." He pulled her down into his lap. She was twenty-two years old and very beautiful. He knew it was immodest of him to think this because when he looked at her he saw himself. The best thing about these revivals was watching her catch up in age as he hibernated the winters away to establish residency for tax purposes. In another thirty-odd years they would both be in their fifties. "I love you," he said.

"Sure." Her voice was slurred. "Daddy loves his little girl."

Cage was shocked. He had never heard her talk that way

before. Something had happened while he was in the tank. But then she giggled and put her hand on his thigh. "You can come with us, if you want."

"Us?" He brushed his fingertips across the smooth scalp and wondered how many serentols she had taken that day.

■ ■ ■

James I was fascinated by Stonehenge, so much so that he commissioned the celebrated architect Inigo Jones to draw a plan of the stones and determine their purpose. The results of Jones's studies were published posthumously in 1655 by his son-in-law. Jones rejected the notion that such a structure could have been raised by an indigenous people, since "the ancient *Britains* [were] utterly ignorant, as a Nation wholly addicted to Wars, never applying themselves to the Study of Arts, or troubling their thoughts with any Excellency." Instead, Jones, who had learned his art in Renaissance Italy and was a student of classical architecture, declared that Stonehenge must be a Roman temple, a blending of the Tuscan and Corinthian styles, possibly built during the reign of the Flavian emperors.

In 1633 Dr. Walter Charlton, a physician to Charles II, disputed Jones's theory, maintaining that Stonehenge was built by the Danes "to be a Court Royal, or a place for the Election and Inauguration of their Kings." The poet Dryden applauded Charlton in verse,

Stone-heng, once thought a *Temple*, you have found
A *Throne*, where Kings, our Earthly Gods, were crown'd.

In fact, many pointed to the crownlike shape of Stonehenge as proof of this theory. Of course, these speculations, coming so soon after Charles had been restored to the throne following a long exile, were politically convenient. The most astute courtiers spared no effort to discredit Cromwell's republic and curry royal favor by reasserting the antiquity of the divine right of kings.

■ ■ ■

Wynne had been Cage's greatest extravagance. He had never really sought the money; the entertainment multinationals had kept forcing it on him. Once he had acquired a Raphael and a Constable and a Klee, vacationed in the Mindanao Trench and on Habitat Three and at the disney on the moon, he found precious little else worth the trouble of buying.

People envied him: the rich, the *famous* drug artist. But when Cage first hit it at Western Amusement, he had almost suffocated in his new wealth. The problem was that the money would not just sit there and keep quiet. It screamed for attention. It had to be collected, managed, and disbursed by an endless procession of people with tight smiles and firm handshakes who insisted on giving him advice no matter how much he paid them to leave him alone. To them he was Tony Cage, Incorporated.

It was while he was developing Focus that Cage decided he needed someone to help him spend the money. He felt no particular urge to contract a marriage. None of the women he was sleeping with at the time mattered to him. He knew that they had been drawn by that irresistible pheromone, the smell of success. He wanted to share his life with someone who would be bound to him by ties no lawyer could break. Someone who would be uniquely his. Forever. Or so he imagined. Perhaps there was nothing romantic about it at all. Maybe the sociobiologists were right and what was at work was an instinct that had been wired into the brains of vertebrates back in the Devonian: *reproduce, reproduce.*

Wynne was carried in an artificial womb. It was cleaner that way, medically and legally. All it took was a tissue culture from a few of Cage's intestinal epithelial cells and some gene sculpturing to change the "Y" chromosome to an "X," as well as a few other miscellaneous improvements. Just this and a little matter of one-point-two-million new dollars, and Wynne was his.

He told himself that he must reject all the labels that they tried to put on Wynne. He refused to think of her as his daughter. Nor was she exactly his clone. She was like a twin, except that they were carried to term in different wombs and her birth came some twenty-six years after his and the abusive environment that twisted him never touched her. Which was to say she was nothing like a twin. She was something new, something infinitely precious. There were no rules for her behavior, no boundaries for her abilities. He liked to brag that he had got exactly what he ordered. "She's prettier than me, smarter, and a better tennis player," he would joke, "worth every cent."

Cage did not have much time for Wynne when she was a toddler. Back in those days he was still testing the product on himself and often as not would stagger home quite twisted. He found her an English nanny—the best kind. He did not pay Mrs. Detling to love the little girl; Wynne earned that on her own. The fierce old woman spent truckloads of Cage's money on Wynne; their philosophy was to treat the girl as if she were a blank disk on which must be recorded only the most important information. For Wynne's sake they traveled whenever Cage could get away from the lab. Detling helped her develop an Old World command of languages; Wynne spoke English, Russian, Spanish, a smattering of Japanese, and she could read her Virgil in Latin. When she entered third form she tested in the ninety-ninth percentile for her age group on the Geneva Culture-Free Intelligence Profile.

It was not until she was seven that Cage began to take real pleasure in her company. Her charm was an incongruous mix of maturity and childishness.

He came home from the lab one day to find Wynne networking a game on the telelink.

"I thought you were going to see your friend. What's her name?" he said.

"Haidee? I decided not to when Nanny told me you were coming home early."

"I just came home to change." At the time he was working on Laughers and still had a buzz from a morning dose. He did not want to start giggling like a fool in front of the child, so he opened the bar and poked a pressure syringe filled with neuroleptic to straighten himself out. "I have a date. Have to go out at six."

She signed off from the game. "With that new one? Jocelyn?"

"Jocelyn, yes." He held out his hand for the telelink controller. "Mind if I check the mail?"

She gave it to him. "I miss you when you're at work, Tony."

He had heard this before. "I miss you too, Wynne." He

brought up the mail menu on the screen and began the sort.

She snuggled next to him and watched in silence. "Tony," she said at last, "do grown-ups ever cry?"

"Mmmm." Western was bitching about the delays with Laughers, threatening to hold up the bonus from Soar. "Sometimes, I guess."

"They do?" She sounded shocked. "If they fall down and scrape their knees?"

"Usually it's because something sad happens."

"Like what?"

"Something sad." Long silence. "You know." He wanted her to change the subject.

"I saw Jocelyn crying."

She had his attention.

"The other night," Wynne said. "She came and sat on the couch, waiting for you. I was playing house behind the chair. She didn't know I was here. She's ugly, you know, when she cries. The stuff under her eyes makes her tears black. Then she got up and she was going toward the bathroom and she saw me and she looked at me like it was my fault she was crying. But she kept going and didn't say anything. When she came out she was happy again. At least she wasn't crying. Did you make her sad?"

"I don't know, Wynne." He felt as though he should be angry but he did not know at whom. "Maybe I did."

"Well, I don't think that was a very grown-up thing to do. I don't think I like her much." Wynne looked at him then to see if she had gone too far. "Well, what does she have to be sad about? She sees you more than I do, and I don't cry."

He hugged her. "You're a good girl, Wynne." He decided not to see Jocelyn that night. "I love you."

Many people try to make a division between personal life and life at work. Before Wynne, Cage had always been lonely, no matter whom he was with. He hated facing the void at the center of his personal life; throwaway women like Jocelyn only fed the emptiness. He went to work to escape himself; this was the secret of his success. But as Wynne grew older he had to change, gradually making room for her in his life until she filled it.

■ ■ ■

William Stukeley belonged to the grand tradition of English eccentrics. From 1719 to 1724 this impressionable young anti-quarian spent his summers exploring Stonehenge. His meticu-lous fieldwork was not to be equaled until Victoria's reign. Stukeley made precise measurements of the relationships be-tween the stones. He explored the surrounding countryside and discovered that the circle was but a part of a much larger neolithic complex. He was the first to point out the orientation of Stonehenge's axis toward the summer solstice. He did not, how-ever, publish these findings until ten years later. In the interim he took holy orders, married, moved from London to rural Lin-colnshire—and decided he was a Druid.

From his quirky reading of the Bible, Pliny, and Tacitus, Stukeley had deduced that the Druids must be direct descen-dants of the biblical Abraham, who had hitched a ride to En-gland on Phoenician ships. Although his book contained an account of the superb fieldwork at Stonehenge, Stukeley's po-lemical intent was best summed up in the frontispiece, a portrait of the author as Chyndonax, a prince of the Druids. It was "a chronological history of the origin and progress of true religion, and of idolatry." Stukeley painted a vision of noble sages practic-ing a pure natural religion, the modern equivalent of which, he was at pains to point out, was none other than his own beloved Church of England! The Druids had built Stonehenge as a temple to their serpent god. Although Stukeley believed that the rites practiced there may have included human sacrifice, he was inclined to forgive his spiritual forebears their excesses. Perhaps they had got Abraham's example wrong.

A hundred years later Stukeley's Druidical fantasy had wormed its way both into the *Encyclopedia Britannica* and the popular imagination. In 1857 a direct rail link between London and Salisbury was established, and the Victorians descended in droves. To some Stonehenge was splendid confirmation of the ancient and present greatness of Britannia; to others it was a dark dream of disemboweled maidens and pagan license. About this time, the summer solstice became a spectacle. The pubs in nearby Amesbury stayed open all night. If the skies were clear, those who staggered on to Stonehenge might number in the thousands. It was not a respectful crowd. They would break bottles against the bluestones and climb the sarsens, dancing in the midsummer dawn. The dreaming stillness of the Wiltshire plain would be shattered by rowdy laughter and the clatter of vehicles.

■ ■ ■

Cage never liked Tod Schluermann. He told himself that the fact that Tod had become Wynne's lover while Cage was in the tank had nothing to do with it. Nor did it matter that Tod had convinced her to go with him to England. Tod had bounced around the world in his twenty-four years; his father had been an Air Force doctor. Born in the Philippines, he had grown up on bases in Germany, Florida, and Colorado. He had flunked out of the Air Force Academy and had attended several other colleges without acquiring anything more substantial than a distaste for getting up early.

Tod was a skinny kid who looked good in the gaudy skin-tights that had come into fashion. He was handsome in a streamlined way. Beneath his face was the delicate bone structure of a Renaissance madonna. In order to get into the Academy he had needed cochlear implants to correct a slight hearing problem; he had ordered the surgeons to clip his ears. He had no hair on him at all except for a black brush on his head. Like Wynne he had a pale blue skin tint; in some lights he looked like a corpse.

He and Wynne had met at a drug club; she was doing Soar at a light-table when he sat down next to her. Cage never understood exactly what Tod was doing at the club. Tod did not often use psychoactive drugs and, although he tried to hide it, seemed to disapprove of regular users. A good candidate for the Drug Temperance League. There was a streak of the puritan in him that distanced him from his licentious generation. In his years in and out of college, Tod had read widely but not well. Like many self-taught men, he suspected expertise. He had native intelligence, that was clear, but arrogance often made him seem stupid.

"And where are you two going to get the money to live?" Cage asked him over dinner the night before they left Ireland.

Tod swirled a premier cru Chablis in a Waterford crystal wineglass and smiled. "Money is only a problem if you think too much about it, man."

"Tony, would you stop worrying and pass the veal?" Wynne said. "We'll be fine." No one spoke as Tod helped himself to seconds and passed her the serving dish. "After all," she continued, "we'll have my allowance."

There was a spot of Madeira sauce on Tod's chin. "I don't want your money, Wynne."

Cage knew that was for his benefit. Wynne's allowance was generous enough to support a barrister in Mayfair; he didn't want her wasting it on Tod. "What makes you think you can learn to program a video synthesizer? People go to school for that, you know."

"School, yes." He and Wynne exchanged glances. "Well, you know, the problem is that by the time the teachers get done with you, they've mashed your creativity flat. Talk to the good little 'A' students who catch on with the big companies, and you find they've forgotten why they became artists in the first place. All they know how to do is recycle the stale old crap they learned at school. Anyone can see it. Just call up some videos on the telelink. Yesterday's news, man."

"Tod's been studying very hard. And he's had some experience already," said Wynne. "Besides, it isn't as hard to learn to program as it used to be. They've really been working to make the interface a lot more accessible."

"They? You mean the stale old corporate grinds?"

"Tony." Wynne pushed away from the table.

"No," said Tod. "He's right." She settled down again. Cage hated the way she always gave in to Tod. "Look, man, I'm not saying that everything you learned in school is corrupt. Look at you. I mean, you could never have developed Soar or anything if you hadn't done your time. I give you a lot of credit for coming out of that whole. Your work is brilliant. I know artists who can't even think about a project until they poke a few ml's of your Focus. But that's what it's about, man. What's important is the art, not the technology."

"We're talking about computer-driven video synthesizers, Tod." Cage laid his fork across the plate. The conversation had killed his appetite. "I happen to know a little something about them. I've had programmers working for me, remember. They're complicated machines. And expensive to use. How are you going to afford the access time you'll need?"

Tod was the only one still eating. "There are ways," he said between bites. "The small shops are open to hackers after business hours. Go in at three in the morning and work until five. Cheap."

"Even if you come up with anything worthwhile, you have to get it distributed. The multinationals like Western Amusement won't even touch free-lance."

Tod shrugged. "So? I'll start at the bottom. That's why we're going to England. British telelink has plenty of open slots on community access stations. Once people see what I've got, it'll be easy. I know it."

Wynne poured a volatile stimulant called Bliss into a brandy snifter, breathed deeply of the fumes, and passed it. Tod's sniff was quick and disapproving; he offered the glass to Cage. Colleen came in with the dessert and Cage realized there was nothing he could say. It was obvious that Tod did not have the resiliency to fight through the inevitable setbacks. In six months it would be another scheme. Tod would blame Wynne or Cage—someone else!—for his failure and continue his aimless life without them, secure in his delusion that he was a genius trapped in a world full of fools. It was obvious.

But there was Wynne, his beautiful Wynne, beaming at Tod as if he were the second coming of Leonardo. The son of a bitch was going to take her away.

■ ■ ■

Sir Edmund Antrobus, the baronet who owned Stonehenge, died without an heir in 1915. For years he had squabbled with the Church of the Universal Bond, a modern reincarnation of Druidism based on equal parts of wish fulfillment and bad scholarship, over access to the site. The Chief Druid announced that it had been a Druid curse that struck Sir Edmund down. Several months later the estate came up for sale. Mr. Cecil Chubb bought Stonehenge at auction for 6,600 pounds. He claimed it was an impulse purchase. Three years later Chubb offered Stonehenge to the nation and was knighted by Lloyd George for his generosity.

To the cautious bureaucrats in the Office of Works, Stonehenge was a disaster waiting to happen. Several leaning stones threatened to collapse; wobbly lintels needed readjustment. The government sought help from the Society of Antiquaries for this work. The antiquarians seized the opportunity to expand the repairs into a grandiose—and disastrous—excavation of the entire monument. The government, however, withdrew funding soon after the stones were straightened, and for years the Society struggled to finance the dig itself. More often than not Colonel William Hawley had to work alone, living in a drafty hut on the site. In 1926 the project was mercifully suspended, having accomplished little more than disturb evidence and embarrass the Society. As the bewildered Hawley told the *Times:* "The more we dig, the more the mystery appears to deepen."

■ ■ ■

Like many people, Cage did not choose his career; he became a drug artist by accident. When he started at Cornell he intended to study genetic engineering. At that time Boggs was developing viruses that could alter chromosomes in existing cells. Kwabena had published her pioneering work reconstructing algae for human consumption. It seemed as if every month a different geneticist stepped forward to promise a miracle that would change the world. Cage wanted to make miracles too. At the time, idealism did not seem so foolish.

Unfortunately genetic engineering excited every other bright kid in the country. The competition at Cornell was fierce. Cage started doing drugs in his sophomore year just to keep up with the course work. He started with small doses of metrazine; it was only supposed to be psychologically addicting. Cage knew he was tougher than any drug. He did not much care for the recreational stuff back then. No time. He tried THC on occasion; both pot and the new aerosols from Sweden. Once over a spring break a woman he had been seeing gave him some mescal buttons. She said it would give him new insight. It did— he realized he was wasting his time with her.

Three semesters later it all went wrong. By then he was poking megamphetamines in massive doses, sometimes over eighty milligrams. The initial rush felt like a whole-body orgasm; he did not feel like studying much afterward. His adviser told him to switch out of the program after he took a "C" in genetic chemistry. He was burning up brain cells and losing weight; he had already lost his direction. He knew he had to get clean and start over again.

He had signed up for a course in psychopharmacology on a paranoid whim. If he had to study something, why not the chemistry of what he was doing to himself with his habit? Bobby Belotti was a good teacher; he soon became a friend. He helped Cage get off the megs, helped him salvage a plain vanilla degree in biology, and encouraged him to apply to graduate school. Much of Cage's idealism had been seared away during those twisted semesters of amphetamine psychosis. Maybe that was why it was so easy to convince himself that developing new drugs was just as noble as curing hemophilia.

Cage wrote his master's thesis on the effects of indole hallucinogens on serotonergic and dopaminergic receptors. The early indole hallucinogens like LSD and DMT had long since been thought to inhibit production of the neuroregulator serotonin, not surprising since their chemical structures were remarkably similar. His work showed that hallucinogens of this family also affect the dopamine-producing system and that many of the reported effects of these drugs resulted from interactions between these neuroregulators. It was not, he had to admit, particularly innovative or brilliant work; the foundations had been laid long ago. But by then he had grown tremendously bored with being a student. The work reflected it.

He took his degree in the middle of the brief, inglorious rule of the America First Party, a pack of libertarian fanatics bent on dismantling the government of the United States. Sunsetting the Food and Drug Administration sparked the revolution in recreational drug use. Cage was still debating whether to slog on for his doctorate when Bobby Belotti called to say that he was leaving Cornell. Western Amusement was recruiting people to do R&D for its new psychoactive drug division. Belotti was going. Did Cage want in? Of course.

Belotti's team was supposed to be looking for a businessman's flash. Something fast and dirty: fat-soluble, so that it could pass quickly into the brain and reach its site of action within minutes after ingestion. It had to be easily metabolized so that the psychoactive effect would fade within an hour or two. No needles, keep the tolerance effect low. They did not want the users to see God or experience the ultimate orgasm, just a little psychic distortion, some pretty visuals, and leave them with a smile.

Since Cage had already worked with the indole hallucinogens, Belotti gave him pretty much of a free hand. After a couple of frustrating months, he began to look seriously at DMD. It seemed to fit the specifications, except that the animal tests did not show significant psychoactive effects. He worried that it might be too subtle. No matter how safe it was, the stuff was no good if it left the user straight as a Baptist accountant. Still, Cage was able to convince Belotti to authorize microiontophoretic tests on rats.

Bobby Belotti was a thoroughly disheveled man. His curly black hair resisted combing. He was forever tucking in his shirt; his paunch tugged it out again. There were rings of dried coffee on the upper strata of memos and reports piled on his desk; dust gathered undisturbed in the nooks of his terminal. For all his ability, he was the kind of employee that management preferred to hide from the outside world.

"Look at this." Cage burst into Belotti's office and dropped a ten-centimeter stack of fanfold paper on his desk. "The DMD results. The stuff inhibits the hell out of the serotonergic system."

Belotti pulled off his glasses and rubbed his eye with the back of his hand. "Great. Have you got an effect to show me?"

"No, but these numbers say there has to be one. Must be some kind of trigger."

Belotti sighed and began to shuffle through the papers on his desk. "The front office is screaming for something to sell, Tony. I don't see that DMD is the answer. Do you?"

"A couple of weeks, Bobby. I'm almost there—I can taste it."

Belotti found a memo, handed it to Cage. "Give it a rest, Tony. Let's get a couple of products under our belt, then maybe you can try again." The memo reassigned Cage to work directly under Belotti's supervision.

They argued. Cage had never learned to argue and he had a hair-trigger temper. Belotti was too calm, too damn understanding. Although it was never mentioned, the debt that Cage owed Belotti only fueled his outrage. He felt as if he were the wayward student being corrected once again by his kindly professor.

Fuming, Cage brought the odious memo back to his cubicle, shut down his terminal, and glared at the empty screen. He was in a mood to lash out, to do something crazy. The idea came to him in anger, a stunt straight out of a mad scientist video. He requisitioned ten milligrams of DMD and went home to try it on himself.

Half an hour after eating the drug, he was lying on the bed in a darkened room, waiting for something—anything—to happen. He felt jittery, as if he had just poked some mild speed. His pulse rate was up, and he was sweating. He knew from the tests that the drug must have already found its way to his brain. He felt nothing—he was not even angry anymore. At last he got out of bed, turned up the lights, and went into the kitchen to make himself a snack. He settled in front of the telelink with a ham and cheese sandwich and turned the monitor on. News. Change channel. *Click, click.*

No signal. Just visual static. Exactly what it took to trigger DMD's psychoactive effect. He never ate that sandwich.

Instead he spent the next hour staring intently at a screen of red, green, and blue phosphors flashing at random. Except that to Cage they were not at all random. He saw patterns, wonderful patterns: wheels of fire, amber waves of grain, angels dancing on the head of a pin, demon faces. He felt as if he himself were a pattern. He was liberated from his body, soaring into the screen to play amid the beautiful lights.

And then it was over, a very clean finish. It had been an hour and a half since he had eaten the pill; the peak had lasted about forty-five minutes. It was perfect. With a sophisticated light show to trigger DMD's effect, it might be the most popular drug since alcohol. And it was his, he realized. All his.

After all, Belotti had cut himself out of the action with his memo. It was Cage who had taken the risk, put his body and sanity on the line. Friendship was friendship, but Cage knew that if he played this right he could change his life. So he made sure that management heard about DMD from him, making the case that Belotti had tried to stifle important research. If his co-workers resented him for stepping on a friend's face on his scramble up the ladder, Cage learned not to care. The front office was secretly relieved; Cage was much more presentable than Belotti. Soon he was in charge of the team, then the whole lab.

Cage expected Bobby Belotti to leave, go back to Cornell, but he never did. Perhaps Belotti intended it as a subtle kind of revenge: showing up for work every day, drinking coffee with the man who had betrayed him. Cage refused to be shamed. He found ways to avoid Belotti, eventually burying him on a minor project that had little chance of success. The two never spoke much after that.

They called the drug Soar and proceeded to market the hell out of it. Western Amusement's PR flacks made Cage famous before he understood quite what they were doing to him. The interviewers on telelink could not get enough of him. A sanitized bio appeared on most of the major information utilities: the brilliant young researcher, the daring breakthrough, the first step of an incredible psychic journey—at first Cage was amused by it all.

When he could get to the lab he spent much of his time brainstorming mechanisms to trigger Soar's psychoactive effect. The light-table, which can read EEG patterns and transform them into hi-res computer pyrotechnics, was the most successful, but there were others. In fact, the hardware aftermarket made Western Amusement almost as much as the drug itself. Cage's lab turned into a money machine. To keep the corporate headhunters from stealing him away, Western Amusement gave him participation in the profits. He was soon one of the richest young men in the world.

There were three parts to the recreational drug experience: the chemical itself, the mental state of the user, and the environment in which the drug was consumed, what Cage liked to call the "surround." As the years passed he became much less involved in developing chemicals. The kids coming out of grad school were better researchers than he had ever been. He was more interested in conceptual design, and he especially liked dreaming up new surrounds: the sensory deprivation helmet, the alpha strobe. The flacks made the best of his evolving interests. He was no longer a psychopharmacological researcher; he was anointed as the first drug artist.

However, the real reason Cage was forced to cut back on his

involvement with drug development had nothing to do with artistic yearning. He had the classic addictive personality: He really loved to get twisted. Over the years he had let some vicious psychoactive chemicals sink claws into his synapses. Although he always managed to pull free, management was nervous. They had made Tony Cage a corporate symbol; they could not afford a meltdown.

Cage should not have been surprised to see his taste for drugs mirrored in Wynne. She began using when she was nine. By the time she was eleven he was letting her poke some of the major psychoactives. It could hardly have been otherwise if Wynne was to share his life. One of Cage's perks was a personal bar that put most drug clubs to shame. And his own lab was developing a cannabinol chewing gum aimed at the preteen market. Despite what the Temperance League preached, Cage had not made the drug culture; it had made him. Kids all over the world were getting twisted, reaching for the brightest flash. Still, Wynne's zest for drugs disturbed him.

Cage tried to ensure that Wynne was never addicted to any one chemical. He saw to it that her habit was various. If she started to build up a cross-tolerance to hallucinogens, for example, he would make her give the whole family a vacation and switch to opiates. Nor was she constantly twisted. She would go on sprees that would last anywhere from a few hours to a few days. Then nothing for a week or two. Still, Cage worried about her. She took some astounding doses.

The summer before she met Tod they flew from the States into da Vinci airport and checked into the Hilton. Even though they had taken the suborbital, they were having a hard time getting their biological clocks reset. Since Cage had business in Rome the next day he could not afford to stay jet-lagged. Wynne called room service and had them bring up a couple of strawberry placidex shakes. Cage settled back on his bed; the stuff made him feel as if he were melting into the mattress. Wynne sat in a thermal chair and listlessly switched channels on the telelink. Finally she shut it off and asked him if he thought he took too many drugs.

Cage had been about to doze off; suddenly he was as alert as anyone with placidex seeping into his brain can be. "Sure, I think about it all the time. Right now I think I'm okay. There have been times, though, when I thought that I might be in trouble."

She nodded. "How do you know when you're in trouble?"

"One sign is when you stop worrying about it."

She folded her arms as if she were chilled. "That's a hell of a thing to say. You're only safe if you're worried?"

"Or if you're clean."

"Oh, come on. What's the longest you've been clean? *Recently.*"

"Six months. When I was in the tank." They both laughed. "Since you brought it up," he said, "let me ask you. Think you do too much?"

She considered, as if the question had surprised her. "Nah," she said at last. "I'm young. I can take it."

He told her then about how he had been hooked on amphetamines at Cornell. The story did not seem to impress her.

"But you beat it, obviously," she said. "So it couldn't have been that bad."

"Maybe you're right," he agreed. "But it seems to me that I was lucky. A couple more months and I might never have been able to get clean again."

"I like getting twisted," she said. "But there are other things I like just as much."

"For instance?"

"Sex, as if you didn't know." She stretched. "Space, weightlessness. Losing myself in a book or a play or a video. Spending your money." She yawned. The words were coming slower and slower. "Falling asleep."

"Come to bed, then," he said. "You're keeping both of us up."

She touched the shoulder clasp and her wrapper uncoiled, crinkling, into a pile on the floor. She climbed in next to him. Her skin was cool to the touch. "Who invented placidex anyway?" she said as she snuggled next to him. He could feel the smoothness of her belly against his back. "Man knew what he was doing."

"The man did *not* know what he was doing." It was the placidex that laughed; Cage would rather have made the point.

Still, it was funny in a macabre way. "Took a big dose one day, fell asleep in a thermal chair. He had overridden the timer. Baked to death."

"Died happy, anyway." She patted his hip and rolled over. "Pleasant dreams."

■ ■ ■

In 1965 the astronomer Gerald Hawkins published a book with an immodestly bold title: *Stonehenge Decoded*. Earlier explainers had always looked beyond Stonehenge for evidence to back up their theories. Some ages found authority in the Bible and church tradition, others in the ruins of Rome or the great historians of antiquity. Like his predecessors, Hawkins invoked the authorities of his time to support his ingenious theory. Using the Harvard-Smithsonian IBM 7090 computer to analyze patterns of solar and lunar alignments at Stonehenge, Hawkins reached a conclusion that electrified the world. Stonehenge had been built as an observatory for ancient astronomers. In fact, he claimed that part of it formed a "Neolithic computer" which had been used by its builders to predict eclipses of the moon.

Hawkins's theory caught the popular imagination, in large part due to uncomprehending coverage by the old printed newspapers. Reporters dithered over this marvel: Stone Age scientists had built a computer of sarsen and bluestone that only a modern electronic brain could "decode." There was even a television special on some of the old pre-telelink networks. Much was made of Hawkins's use of the computer despite the fact that the numbers it had crunched could easily have been done by hand. And what Hawkins had, in fact, proved was entirely different from what he claimed to have proved. The computer studies showed that the Aubrey holes, a ring of fifty-six regularly spaced pits, could be used to predict eclipses. They did not show that the builders of Stonehenge had any such purpose in mind. Others soon offered conflicting interpretations, and closely reasoned Stonehenge astronomies proliferated. The problem was soon recognized: Stonehenge had too much astronomical significance. It was a mirror in which any theoretician could see his ideas reflected.

■ ■ ■

Cage did not immediately follow Tod and Wynne to England. Instead he flew back to the States to check with Western Amusement after his cryogenic vacation. Cage was no longer an actual employee of the company. An independent contractor, he was himself a corporation. Still, there were no doors shut to him at the lab he had made famous, no secrets he could not learn. The hot news was that in the six months Cage had been in the tank, Bobby Belotti had made a breakthrough in the Share project.

Cage had started the Share project years before when he was still working at the lab full time. He had been thinking about the way social reinforcement seemed to energize recreational drug use. Most users preferred to get twisted with other users, at drug clubs and private parties or before making love or eating a fine meal or free-fall dancing in space. If socialization enhanced pleasure, why not try to find a way for users to share an identical experience? Not just by creating identical surrounds but by synchronizing the effect on a synaptic level. Direct stimulation of the sensory cortex. A kind of artificial telepathy.

Corporate headquarters was skeptical. The mere mention of telepathy gave the whole project the smell of pseudoscience. And it seemed expensive. At the time Cage had thought that the effect would have to be created electrochemically, the interaction of psychoactive drugs with electronic brain stimulation. Some kind of wetware would probably be necessary. But marketing research showed that many people were afraid of skull plugs. The zombie factor, they called it.

Cage kept after them. If nothing else, he thought Share might be a powerful aphrodisiac. What did it matter how expensive it was, if it turned out to be the ultimate erotic experience? He pointed out that no one had ever gone broke selling love potions, and they let him do a feasibility study.

He had to doctor the study; there were a lot of holes that only basic research could fill. But the research was being done, if not at Western Amusement then elsewhere. What he was finally able to sell them was a small ongoing effort. The perfect place to bury Bobby Belotti. A side bet on a long shot.

And now, years later, Belotti had something that looked very promising. He had borrowed a drug, 7,2-DAPA, which had been developed by neuropathologists studying language disorders. It could induce a euphoric anomia, disrupting the process of associating certain visual inputs with words. Users had trouble naming what they saw. Nouns, especially abstract nouns and proper names, were especially difficult. The severity of the anomia was related not only to dosage but to the complexity of the visual environment. For example, a user shown a single long-stemmed rose might be unable to speak the words "flower" or "rose" even though he could carry on intelligent conversation about gardening; show him into a greenhouse and he might well be speechless. However, if he picked the rose up or smelled it or heard the word "rose," he would make the connection. And in that moment of recognition, enkephalin neurons would start pumping like crazy; the brain would be awash in the pleasure of discovery.

"The problem is," Belotti explained to Cage, "there's no way yet to predict exactly which words will be lost. Too much individual variation. For instance, maybe I can't say 'rose' but you can. In that case I can get a flash from you; you get nothing. It's only if both of us lose the same word and then get an appropriate cue that we share the effect."

"Doesn't sound as if it's going to replace sex." Cage laughed; Belotti winced. The man had not changed. What was left of his hair still needed combing. There were webs of broken veins beneath his wrinkled skin. He seemed very old, very empty. Cage found it hard to remember the time when they had been friends.

"Well, shared sex might be interesting." Belotti sounded as if he were repeating excuses he had made before. "But you wouldn't get much effect by telling someone he's having an orgasm. Too tactile, very little to do with visual input. Still, since the enkephalin suppresses pain impulses, pleasure would be correspondingly enhanced. But remember, this is fairly mild at the dosages we're looking at. Take too much and there's a tendency to withdraw. You get into hallucinations. It's unpredictable—dangerous."

"Can the effect be blocked?"

"So far the neuroleptics are the only true antagonists we've found. And they're pretty slow-acting." Belotti shrugged. "Testing isn't finished yet. Actually I haven't paid that much attention. They took me off it, you know. I spent ten years chasing the

specs you wrote, and now I'm running computer simulations—
make-work."

Cage had not thought about Bobby Belotti in a long time;
suddenly he was sorry for the old man. "What would you use it
for, Bobby?"

"As I said, not my decision. Marketing will find someone to
peddle it to, I'm sure. I guess they're a little disappointed that it
didn't turn out to be the aphrodisiac you promised them."

"It's fine work, Bobby. You don't have to apologize to anyone.
But I can't believe that you've worked as hard and as long as you
have without thinking of commercial applications."

"Well, if you could control which words were lost, then you
could use guides to supply the necessary cues." Belotti
scratched the back of his neck. "Maybe you could blend in a
hypnotic to give the guides more psychological authority. It
might help, say, in art appreciation classes. Or maybe museums
could sell it along with those tape-recorded tours."

Wonderful. A flash for museums. Cage could imagine the
ads. The topless vidqueen says to her silver boyfriend, *Hey,
bucko, let's shank down to the National Gallery and get twisted!*
No wonder they had taken it away from him. "Why bother?
Sounds like all you need are two people sitting at a kitchen table
shooting words at each other."

"But words—it's not that simple. We're not talking fancy
lights here; we're talking about internalized symbols that can
trigger complex mental states. Emotions, memories—"

"Sure, Bobby. Look, I'll talk to the front office. See if we can
get you a new project, your own team."

"Don't bother." His expression was stony. "They've offered
me early retirement and I'm going to take it. I'm sixty-one years
old, Tony. How old are you these days?"

"I'm sorry, Bobby. I think you've done wonders bringing
Share this far." He gave Belotti his deal-closing smile. "Where
can I get some samples?"

Belotti nodded, as if he had been expecting Cage to ask. "Still
can't keep your hands off the product? They're keeping a pretty
tight lid on the stuff, you know. Until they decide what they've
got."

"I'm a special case, Bobby. You ought to know that by now.
Some rules just don't apply to me."

Belotti hesitated. He looked as if he were trying to balance some incredibly complex equation.

"Come on, Bobby. For an old friend?"

With a poisonous grin, Belotti thumbed a printreader to unlock his desk, took a green bottle from the top drawer, and tossed it to Cage. "One at a time, understand? And you didn't get it from me."

Cage popped the top. Six pills: yellow powder in clear casings. For a moment he was suspicious; Belotti seemed awfully eager to break company rules. But Cage had long since made up his mind about the man. He could not bring himself to worry about someone for whom he had so little respect. He tried to imagine what it would be like to be ordinary like poor Belotti: old, at the end of a failed career, bitter, and tired. What kept a man like that alive? He shivered and pushed the fantasy away as he pocketed the green bottle. "What time is it, anyway?" he said. "I told Shaw I'd meet him for lunch."

Belotti touched the temple of his eyeglasses and the lenses opaqued. "You know, I really used to hate you. Then I realized it: you didn't know what the hell you were doing. Might as well blame a cat for batting around a bloody mouse. You don't see anyone, Tony. I'll bet you don't even see yourself." His hands shook. "That's all right, I'll shut up now." He powered down his terminal. "I'm going home. Only reason I came in was because they said you wanted a meeting."

Taking no chances, Cage had one of Belotti's samples analyzed; it was pure. Then, rather than risk any more confrontation, Cage moved on. There were lawyers in Washington and accountants in New York. He spoke at the American Psychopharmacological Association's annual meeting at Hilton Head in South Carolina and gave half a dozen telelink interviews. He met a Japanese woman, and they made reservations to spend a weekend in orbit at Habitat Three. Afterward they went to Osaka, where he found out that she was a corporate spy for Unico. It had been almost two months. Time, he thought, for Tod to have screwed up, for Wynne to have recognized that he was born to fail, and for their impossible affair to have collapsed under its own weight. Cage caught the suborbital to Heathrow. He was so sure.

It was a nasty surprise: Tod Schluermann had been lucky.

The video *Burn London* was only five minutes long. It started with a shot of silos. Countdown. Launch. London was under attack. No missiles—enormous naked Wynnes left rainbows across the sky as they hurtled down on the city. They exploded not in flame but in foliage, smothering entire city blocks with trees and brush. Soon the city disappeared beneath a forest. The camera zoomed to a clearing where a band called Flog was playing. They had been providing the dreamy sound track. The tempo picked up, the group playing faster and faster until their instruments caught fire, consuming them and the forest. The final shot was a pan over ash and charred stumps. Cage thought it was dumb.

No one could have predicted that sixteen-year-olds across the UK would choose that moment to take Flog into their callow hearts. When they made *Burn London* with Tod, Flog was unknown. In the span of a month they went from a basement in Leeds to a floor of Claridge's in London. Although Tod did not make much money from *Burn London*, he earned a name. The kid who had once compared himself to Nam June Paik was instead making videos for pubescent music fans.

He and Wynne were living at a tube rack in Battersea. She could have afforded better; he insisted that they live within his means. There were about two hundred plastic sleep tubes stacked in what had once been a warehouse. Each was three meters long; the singles were a meter and a half in diameter, the doubles two. Each was furnished with a locker beneath a gel mattress, a telelink terminal, and a water bubbler passing for a sink. There was always a line for the showers. The toilets smelled.

It was all right for Tod; he spent most of his time haunting the video labs or dealing with band managers. He even had a desk at VidStar and a regularly scheduled session on its synthesizer: 4 to 5 A.M., Tuesdays, Thursdays, and Saturdays. But Wynne was only in the way at VidStar. And although they went out almost every night to clubs around town to hear bands play and show Tod's videos, there seemed to be very little for Wynne to do. Cage could not understand why she seemed so happy.

"Because I'm in love," she said. "For the first time in my life."

"I'm glad for you, Wynne. Believe me." They were sitting over lagers in a pub, waiting for Tod to finish work and join them for dinner. It was dark. It was easier to lie in the dark. "But how long can it last unless you find something to do? Something for yourself."

"So I can be famous? Like you?" She chuckled as she rubbed her finger along the edge of her glass. "Why should you care about that now, Tony? You were the one who said I should take some time off after I finished sixth form."

"I've thought a lot since you've been with Tod. You could get into any school you wanted."

"You know how Tod feels about school. Still, I have considered taking some business courses. I thought I might be Tod's manager. That would give him more time to do the important work. He's really good and he's still learning, that's what's incredible. Did you get a chance to see *Burn London* yet?"

Cage nodded.

"Did you recognize the women?"

"Of course."

She smiled. *She was proud of being in Tod's video.* Cage realized his plan of inaction had gone very, very wrong. He would have to intervene in their affair or he might never get Wynne back.

"Good news," said Tod as he slipped onto the bench beside Wynne. They kissed. "I sold them on the idea. I've got a commission to shoot a thirty-minute video at the free festival."

Wynne hugged him. "That's great, Tod. I knew you could do it."

"Free festival?" said Cage. "What are you talking about?"

"You know, man." Tod finished the rest of Wynne's lager. "You're always lecturing us about it; that's how I got the idea. I'm going to do a video of the solstice celebration. At Stonehenge."

■ ■ ■

History does not record the first use of drugs at Stonehenge. However, there is little doubt that most of the major hallucinogens available in 1974 were ingested during the first Stonehenge free festival. An offshore pirate music station, Radio Caroline, had urged its listeners to come to Stonehenge for a festival of "love and awareness." On solstice day that year a horde of scruffy music fans in their late teens and twenties set up camp in the field next to the car park. The music back then was called rock; apparently no pun was intended. The empty landscape around the stones was filled with tents and tepees, cars and caravans. Electric guitars screamed, and there was a whiff of marijuana on the summer breeze. There are tapes of those early festivals. A vast psychedelia of humanity would gather for the occasion: the glassy-eyed couple from Des Moines in their matching polyester shirts, the smiling engineer from Tokyo taking movies, the young mother from Luton breast-feeding her infant son on the Altar Stone, the Amesbury bobby standing beneath the outer circle, hands clasped behind his back, the Druid from Leicester in her white ceremonial robes, the long-haired teenager from Dorking who had climbed the great trilithon and was shouting something about Jesus, UFOs, the sun, and the Beatles. The festival has always been one of the great surrounds for getting twisted. The pioneers of halluci-nogens had a colorful term for the radical perceptual jolts of such an experience, the fascinating strangeness of it all. They would have called the Stonehenge free festival a mind-fucker.

■   ■   ■

Wynne and Tod had their sleep tube shipped from the rack in Battersea to Stonehenge for the five-day festival. It and a thousand others lay near the old car park across the A360 from the dome that now protected the stones. The tubes looked like giant white Soar capsules scattered in the grass. In between were tension bubbles, Gore-Tex tents of varying geometries, hovers and cars, and even people sitting in folding chairs be-neath gaudy umbrellas. Cage stayed at an inn at Amesbury and watched the festival on telelink.

On solstice eve he was able to coax Tod and Wynne into town with the promise of a free dinner. He proposed his little experi-ment over dessert.

"I don't know, man." Tod looked doubtful. "Tomorrow is the last day, the big one. I don't know if I ought to be eating experimental drugs."

Cage had expected that Tod might balk; he was counting on Wynne. "Oh, Tod," she said, "you'll be the only one there that won't be twisted. Why not get into the spirit of the thing?" Her eyes seemed very bright. "Look, how many hours have you shot already? Forty, fifty? They only want a half hour. And even if you miss anything, you can always synthesize it."

"I know that," he said irritably. "It's just that I'm tired. Can hardly think any more." He sipped his claret. "Maybe, okay? Just maybe. But start over again. Tell me from the beginning."

Cage began by claiming that he had been impressed by *Burn London;* he said he wanted to get to know Tod better, understand his art. Cage spoke of the inspiration he had had while watching the festival on telelink. They would all take Share and go to the solstice celebrations together, relying on Stonehenge, the crowd, and each other for cues to shape their experience. Cage spoke of the aesthetics of randomness as an answer to the problem of selection. He said they might be on the verge of a historic discovery; Share might well be a new way for nonartists to participate in the very act of artistic creation.

Cage did not mention that he had laced Tod's dose of Share with an anticholinergic that would smash his psychological defenses flat. When Tod was completely vulnerable to suggestion—stripped of the capacity to lie—Cage would begin interrogating. He would force Tod to tell the truth; force Wynne to see how this shallow boy was using her to further his career. At that moment Wynne, too, would see the ugliness that Cage had seen all along beneath the handsome face. When Tod revealed just how little he cared for her, their affair would be over.

"Come on, Tod," said Wynne. "We haven't done chemicals together in a long time. I'm tired of getting twisted alone. And when Tony recommends something like this, you know it has to be a killer flash."

"You're sure I'll be able to function while we're on this stuff?" Tod's resistance was wearing down. "I don't want to waste the day shooting blades of grass."

"I'll bring something to neutralize it. If you have problems you can poke yourself straight any time you want. Don't worry, Tod. Look, the action of Share should actually help you be more visually oriented. You yourself have said that language gets in the way of art. Share strips away the superstructure of preconceptions. You won't know what you're seeing; you'll just see it. The eyes of a child, Tod. Think of it."

For a moment Cage wondered if he had overdone it. Wynne's attention turned; she seemed more interested in what he was saying than in Tod's reaction to it. He could feel her appraising stare but did not acknowledge it. The waiter came with the check, and as Cage signed for it he dangled the real bait before Tod.

"If you're afraid to try it, Tod, just say so. It *is* something new, after all. No one would blame you for backing out."

"Very good, sir." A true Englishman, the waiter pretended not to hear as Cage handed him the check. "Thank you, sir."

"Still," Cage continued, "I believe in Share and I believe in you. So much that when you're done I'd like to show your video to Western Amusement. They haven't decided yet how to market Share. If this video is as good as I think it can be, the problem will be solved. I'll make them buy it. You'll be the spokesman—hell, the father—of a new collaborative art form."

He knew he had Tod then. This was what the kid had wanted all along. Cage had seen right away that Tod had only seduced Wynne as a career move. All right, then, let Tod have his introduction to an entertainment multinational—and on his own terms. Let him believe that he had manipulated Cage. It did not matter as long as Cage got Wynne back.

"What are you doing, Tony?" Wynne said. Beneath her skin tint, she had gone pale. She must have suspected the stakes Cage was playing for.

"What am I doing?" Cage stood, laughing. "I'm not really sure. That's what makes it interesting, isn't it?"

"Okay, man." Tod stood too. "I'll try it."

"Tony." Wynne stared up at them.

■ ■ ■

"What's that?" said Wynne, pointing at Stonehenge. Bolts of lightning forked through the darkness, illuminating the crowd standing outside the dome.

"It's only the *son et lumière*," said Cage. "The holo techs from the Department of Environment put it on to soak a few extra quid from the tourists." They kept walking up the A360 from where the Amesbury shuttle had dropped them. "Watch what comes next."

Seconds later two laser rainbows shimmered between the stones. "Stonehenge's greatest hits," said Tod with contempt. "Both Constable and Turner did major paintings here. Turner's was full of his usual bombast, lightning bolts and dead shepherds and howling dogs. Constable tried to jack up his boring watercolor with a double rainbow."

Cage bit his lip and said nothing. He did not really need a lecture on Stonehenge, especially not from Tod. After all, he *owned* one of Constable's Stonehenge sketches.

Tod flipped down the visor of his VidStar helmet; he looked like a mantis with lens eyes. Cage could hear tiny motors buzzing as the twin cameras focused. "Is anyone else starting to feel it?" said Wynne.

"I've been doing a lot of research on this place, you know," Tod continued. "It's amazing, the people who've been here."

"Yes," Cage said. "It's an oozy kind of coolness spreading across the back of my skull—like mud." They had eaten the capsules of Share in the darkness on the ride over. "What time is it?"

"It's four-eighteen." Tod slipped a fresh disk into the drive clipped to his belt. "Sunrise at five-oh-seven."

Cage looked to the northeast; the sky had already started to lighten. The stars were like glass mites scuttling away into the grayness.

"They come in waves," said Wynne. "Hallucinations."

"Yes," Cage said. The backs of his eyes seemed to tingle. He knew there was something wrong but he could not think what it was.

They pushed past the inevitable Drug Temperance League picket line; luckily, none of them recognized Cage. At last they reached a barbed-wire corridor leading through the crowd to the entrance to the dome. Down the corridor marched a troop of ghosts. They were dressed in white robes; some wore glasses. They carried copper globes and oak branches and banners with images of snakes and pentacles. They were male and female, and they seemed old. They were murmuring a chant that sounded like wind blowing through fallen leaves. Dry old ghosts, crinkly and intent, turned inward as if they were working out chess problems in their heads.

"The Druids," said Tod. The words broke the trance and a shiver danced across Cage's shoulders. He glanced at Wynne and could tell instantly that she had felt the same. A smile of recognition lit her face in the predawn gloom.

"Are you all right?" said Tod.

Wynne laughed. "No."

Tod frowned and linked his arm through hers. "Let's go. We have to walk around the dome if we want to see the sun rise over the Heel Stone."

They began to thread their way through the crowd to the southwest side of the dome. The space between the shells was empty now, and Cage could see that the procession of Druids had surrounded the outer sarsen circle. All turned to the northeast to face the Heel Stone and the approaching sunrise.

"This is it," said Tod. "We're right on the axis."

The fat woman standing next to Cage was glowing. Except for knee-high studded leather leggings, she was naked. Her skin gave off a soft green light: her nipples and her body hair were bright orange. When she moved, the rolls of fat gleamed like moonlit waves. At first he thought she was another hallucination. Something wrong.

"Do you see her too?" Wynne whispered.

"She's a glowworm." Tod made no effort to keep his voice down, and the green woman stared at them.

Wynne nodded as if she had understood. Cage cupped his hand to her ear. "What's a glowworm?"

"She's had a luminescent body tint," came the whispered reply.

Tod laughed as he pointed his lenses at her. "Do you know how carcinogenic that stuff is? Eighty percent mortality after five years."

She waddled over to him. "It's my body, Flash. Ain't it?" Cage was surprised when she slipped a hand around Tod's waist. "Would that be a video you're making, Flash? Me in it?"

"Sure," he said. "Everyone gets to be famous for ten minutes. You know the camera loves you, glowworm. That's why you got tinted."

She giggled. "You with someone, Flash?"

"Not now, glowworm. The sun is coming."

Amateur photographers and professional cameramen began to jostle for position around them. Tod, using his elbows with cunning, would not be moved. The sun's bright lip appeared over the trees to the northeast. Inside the dome Druids raised horns and blew a tribute to the new day. Outside there were inarticulate shouts and polite applause. A man with a long beard rolled on the ground, barking.

"But there's no alignment," some fool was complaining. "The sun's in the wrong place."

The sun had cleared the trees and crawled across the brick-colored horizon. Cage shut his eyes and still he could see it: blood red, flashing blue, veins pulsing across its surface.

"Sun's not wrong," said a man with a camera where his head should have been. "Stonehenge doesn't really line up. Never did. It's a myth, man."

Although he did not immediately recognize the man, Cage knew he hated that mocking voice. When he opened his eyes again, the sun had already climbed several of its diameters into the sky. After a few moments it passed over the Heel Stone at the opposite end of Stonehenge—and seemed to hang there, propped in the sky by a single untrimmed sarsen, five meters tall. His view was framed by the uprights and lintels of the outer circle. It was as if he were standing on the backbone of the world. He was spellbound: men in skins had built a structure that could capture a star. The crowd was silent, or perhaps Cage had ceased to perceive anything but his vision of sunfire and stone. Then the moment passed. The sun continued to climb.

"Looks like a doorway," said the glowworm. "Into another world." She seemed pale in the light of dawn.

Doorway. The word filled his mind. *Doorway raised upon doorway.* Someone said, "I make it about four degrees off." Cage saw people crouching to help the barking man.

"Tony?" A strange and beautiful woman had taken his hand. Her voice echoed and distorted: a baby's inexact chatter, the joyful cry of a child. He blinked at her in the soft light. Blue-skinned, hair in spikes, she was dressed in silver: the setting for a sapphire. Her face, a jewel. Precious. Cage was falling in love.

"Who are you?" He could not remember.

"They come in waves," she said. He did not understand.

"He's so far out he's breathing space," said the camera head with the mocking voice.

"Who are you?" Cage held up her hand, clasped in his.

"It's me, Tony." The beautiful woman was laughing. Cage wanted to laugh too. "Wynne."

Wynne. He said the word over and over to himself,

shuddering with pleasure at each repetition. Wynne. His Wynne.

"And I'm Tod, remember?" The camera head looked disgusted. "Christ, am I glad I palmed that stuff. Look at you two. She can't stop laughing and you're catatonic. How was I supposed to work? Do you realize how twisted you are?"

Tod. Cage battered through yet another wave of hallucinations, trying to remember. A plan . . . force Tod . . . make Wynne see . . . Cage had known it all along. But it was no good if Tod were straight. "You didn't take . . . ?"

"Hell, no!" Tod turned. Cage felt the lens eyes probing him, recording, judging. "I'm not as gullible as you think, man. I decided to fake it, see how the stuff affected you first. If it looked like fun I knew I could always catch up."

There was a tiny red light flashing in the middle of Tod's helmet. "Turn it off, you bastard," Cage said. "Not me in your damn . . . your goddamn . . ."

"No?" Cage could see a smile beneath the visor. "You're a public figure, man. We all own a piece of you."

"Tod," Wynne said. "Don't goad him."

The red light went out. He flipped the visor up and held out his hand to her. She let go of Cage and went to him.

"Let's take a walk, Wynne. I want to talk to you."

As he watched them walk away together, Cage felt as though he were turning to stone. He had lost her. The crowd swirled around them and they were gone.

"Aren't you Tony Cage?"

He stared without comprehension at a middle-aged woman wearing a mood dress. It changed from blue to silvery-green as she called to her husband. "Marv, come quick." A paunchy man in isothermals responded to her summons. "You are Tony Cage, aren't you?"

Cage could not speak. The man shook his nerveless hand.

"Sure, we've seen you on telelink. Lots of times. We're from the States. New Hampshire. We've tried all your drugs."

"But Soar's still our favorite. I'm Sylvie. We're retired." The dress lightened from lime to apple green. Cage could not look her in the face.

"I'm Marv. Say, you look pretty twisted. What are you on, anyway? Something new?"

Heads were turning. "Sorry." His tongue was stone. "Not

feeling well. Have to . . ." By then he was stumbling away from his manic fans. Luckily they did not follow.

He did not remember how long he wandered through the crowd or how he left or what exactly he was looking for. A terrible suspicion nagged at him. Maybe something was wrong with the dose? Eventually the Druids finished their service and the dome was opened to the public. He drifted on a floodtide of humanity and at last washed up on the Slaughter Stone.

The Slaughter Stone was a slab of lichen-covered sarsen about thirty meters away from the outer circle: a good place to sit and watch, away from the hurly-burly around the standing stones. The surface of the stone was pitted and rough. It once was thought that these natural bowls were used to catch sacrificial blood—both human and animal. Another myth, since the stone originally stood upright. Now they were two fallen things, Cage and the stone, their foundations undermined, purposes lost. They existed in roughly the same state of consciousness. Cage thought sandstone thoughts; his understanding was that of rock.

The sun climbed. Cage was hot. The combination of body heat and solar gain had overloaded the dome's air conditioning. He did nothing. The waves of hallucinations seemed to have receded. People had climbed the outer circle and walked along the lintels. One woman started to strip. The crowd clapped and urged her on. "Vestal virgin, vestal virgin," they cried. A little boy nearby watched avidly as he squeezed cider from a disposable juice bulb. Cage was thirsty; he did nothing. The boy dropped the bulb on the ground when he had finished and wandered off. A bobby stepped out from beneath the circle to watch as the stripper removed her panties. The crowd roared and she gave them an extra treat. She was an amputee; she unstrapped her prosthetic forearm and waved it over her head. The world was going mad and trying to take Cage with it. He loaded a neuroleptic into his pressure syringe and poked it into his forearm.

"Tony."

There was no Tony. There was only stone.

"Hey, man." A stranger shook him. "It's me. Tod. There's something wrong with Wynne! We need to know what you took."

"In waves." Cage started to laugh. "They come in waves." Now he knew. Hallucinations. But not with Share. He was laughing so hard he fell backward onto the stone. "Belotti!" Poor Bobby had finally struck—after all these years. The drug was pure but the dose . . . too high. Hallucinogen. Dangerous, he had said. Unpredictable. That unpredictable old . . . "Bastard!" Cage was gasping for air.

"He needs oxygen. Quick."

"Look at his eyes!"

When the last wave hit him, Cage held on to the stone. The crowd disappeared. The dome vanished. The car park, the A360, all signs of civilization—gone. Then the stones awoke and began to dance. Those that had fallen righted themselves. A road erupted from the grass. The Slaughter Stone bucked and threw him as it stood. A twin appeared beside it: a gate. He wanted to pass through, walk down the road, see Stonehenge whole. But the magic held him back. In an overly explained world, only the subtlest and most powerful magic of all had survived, the magic that works exclusively in the mind. A curse. A dead and illiterate race had placed a curse upon the imagination of the world. In its rude magnificence Stonehenge challenged all to understand its meaning, yet its secret was forever locked behind impenetrable walls of time.

"Lay him down here."

"Tony!"

"He can't hear you."

Suddenly they were all around him, all of those who had stood where Cage now stood. The politicians and writers and painters and historians and scientists and the tourists—yes, even the tourists who, in search of an hour's diversion, had found instead a timeless mystery. All of those who had accepted Stonehenge's challenge and fallen under the curse. They had striven with words and images to find the secret, yet all they had seen was themselves. The sun grew very bright then, and the sides of the stones turned silver. Cage could see all the ghosts reflected in the bright stones. He could see himself.

"Tony, can you hear me? Wynne's having some kind of fit. You have to tell us."

Cage saw himself in the Slaughter Stone. What did it matter? He had already lost her. Her image seemed to shimmer. He looked like a ghost; the thought of death did not displease him. To be as a stone.

"Wake up, man. You have to save her. *She's your daughter, damn you!*"

"No." At that moment Cage's reflection in the stone shifted and he saw his mirror image. Wynne. In pain. He realized that she had been in pain for a long time, had hidden it behind a veneer of chemicals and feigned toughness. He should have known. Trapped within the magical logic of the hallucination, now he could actually *feel* her pain and was racked by the certain knowledge that he was its source. It was no longer the drug, it was Stonehenge itself that forced him to suffer with her, Stonehenge that created a magic landscape where the veil of words was parted and mind could touch mind directly. Or so it seemed to Cage. A sound tore through the vision: a scream. "No!" Stones fell, disappeared, but Cage could not escape the pain. All the lies Cage had told himself fell away. In a moment of terrible grace, he realized what he had done. *To his daughter.*

Tod had lost his helmet, probably lying on the turf somewhere, shooting closeups of blades of grass. He seemed very pale below his blue skin tint. Cage blinked, trying to remember what it was that he had asked. There were electrodes taped to Cage's head and wrist. A medic was checking readouts.

"What did you give her?" said the medic.

Cage's hands trembled as he fumbled the pressure syringe from his pocket. "This . . . a poke . . . neuroleptic. She needs it now. Now!"

The medic seemed very young; he looked doubtful. Cage sat up, tore the electrode from his temple. "Do you know who I am?" The world was spinning. "Do it!"

The medic looked briefly at Tod, then took the syringe and ran back toward the standing stones. Tod hesitated, staring at Cage.

"What did you say to her?" Cage tried to stand up.

He put his arm around Cage's shoulders to steady him. "Are you all right?"

"Did you say it to her? That she was my daughter?"

"That's what she thinks. We were arguing about it."

"She was my lover. You know that, I guess. She came to me

one night. Three years ago. We were both twisted. I couldn't . . . I couldn't send her away."

Tod looked straight ahead. "She said that. She said it was her fault. Then the fit hit her."

"No." Cage could still see himself; he would never be able to stop seeing himself again. "I was lonely, so I made sure that she was lonely too. And called it love." The words almost choked him. "Where is she? Take me to her." They started to walk. "Do *you* love her, Tod?"

"I don't know, man." He considered for some time. "Feels something like."

She was unconscious, but the fit had passed and the medic said her signs were good. Cage went with Tod to the hospital. They waited all day; they talked about everything but what was most on their minds. Cage realized that he had made a mistake about Tod. So many mistakes. When Wynne at last regained consciousness, Tod went in to see her. Alone.

"I'm not here," Cage said. "Tell her I've gone away."

"I can't do that."

"Tell her!"

They only gave Tod ten minutes. Cage kept worrying that Tod would call him in.

"Is she all right?"

"Seems to be. She asked about you; I told her you went back to your room to sleep it off. I told her you'd be in tomorrow. They're going to keep her overnight."

"I'm leaving, Tod." Cage offered his hand. "You won't be seeing me again."

"What? You can't do that to her, man. She saw something this morning, something that makes her feel guilty as hell. If you just disappear she's going to feel worse. Do you understand? You owe it to her to stay."

Cage let his hand fall to his side. "You want me to be some kind of hero, Tod. Problem is, I'm a coward—always have been. I saw something today too, and I'll spend the rest of my life trying to forget it. She'll . . . *you'll* both be better off without me."

Tod grabbed him by the shoulders. "You're damn well going to see her tomorrow. Listen to me, man! If you love her at all—"

"I love her." Cage shook free. "Like I love myself."

That night he caught the shuttle from Heathrow to Shannon. He knew Tod was right; it was cruel and selfish to run away. Tod was entitled to think what he wanted. He would never know how much it hurt Cage to give Wynne up this way. . . . If Cage was escaping, it was into pain. He hoped Wynne would understand. Eventually. His beautiful Wynne. It took a few days to put his affairs in order. He assigned a fortune in Western Amusement stock to her. He made a tape for her, said goodbye.

■ ■ ■

There is a mist clinging to the land. The slaty grayness of Galway Bay reminds Cage of sarsen. The cryogenic box awaits, set for a hundred years. He does not know whether this is enough to save her. Or himself. He knows he will probably never see her again. But for a time, at least, he will be at peace. He will sleep the inscrutable sleep of stones.

Petra

■

Greg Bear sold his first short story in 1966—at the age of fifteen. He hit his stride in the late Seventies and early Eighties, when a flurry of short stories and novels established him as a writer to watch.

Bear's work is strongly rooted in the best of SF's intellectual tradition. A prolific yet disciplined writer, he prizes speculative rigor and respect for scientific fact. This attitude linked him with traditional hard SF—despite much well-praised work in fantasy.

As his career developed, Bear's great imaginative gifts came strongly to the fore, given even greater impact by the disciplined craftsmanship he learned early on. The combination has produced a genuinely radical hard SF with extreme visionary power, demonstrated in such widely lauded novels as *Blood Music* and *Eon*.

The following story, published early in 1982, marked Bear's quantum leap past traditional limits into a mind-boggling new realm. With its thorough and detailed development of a truly fantastic concept, it shows Bear's technique at its best.

"God is dead, God is dead." . . . Perdition! When God dies, you'll know it."

—*Confessions of St. Argentine*

I'm an ugly son of stone and flesh, there's no denying it. I don't remember my mother. It's possible she abandoned me shortly after my birth. More than likely she is dead. My father—an ugly beaked half-winged thing, if he resembles his son—I have never seen.

Why should such an unfortunate aspire to be a historian? I

think I can trace the moment my choice was made. It's among my earliest memories, and it must have happened about thirty years ago, though I'm sure I lived many years before that—years now lost to me. I was squatting behind thick, dusty curtains in a vestibule, listening to a priest instructing other novitiates, all of pure flesh, about Mortdieu. His words are still vivid.

"As near as I can discover," he said, "Mortdieu occurred about seventy-seven years ago. Learned ones deny that magic was set loose in the world, but few deny that God, as such, had died."

Indeed. That's putting it mildly. All the hinges of our once-great universe fell apart, the axis tilted, cosmic doors swung shut, and the rules of existence lost their foundations. The priest continued in measured, awed tones to describe that time.

"I have heard wise men speak of the slow decline. Where human thought was strong, reality's sudden quaking was reduced to a tremor. Where thought was weak, reality disappeared completely, swallowed by chaos. Every delusion became as real as solid matter." His voice trembled with emotion. "Blinding pain, blood catching fire in our veins, bones snapping and flesh powdering. Steel flowing like liquid. Amber raining from the sky. Crowds gathered in streets that no longer followed any maps, if the maps themselves had not altered. They knew not what to do. Their weak minds could not grab hold. . . ."

Most humans, I take it, were entirely too irrational to begin with. Whole nations vanished or were turned into incomprehensible whirlpools of misery and depravity. It is said that certain universities, libraries, and museums survived, but today we have little contact with them.

I think often of those poor victims of the early days of Mortdieu. They had known a world of some stability; we have adapted since. They were shocked by cities turning into forests, by their nightmares taking shape before their eyes. Prodigal crows perched atop trees that had once been buildings, pigs ran through streets on their hind legs . . . and so on. (The priest did not encourage contemplation of the oddities. "Excitement," he said, "breeds even more monsters.")

Our Cathedral survived. Rationality in this neighborhood, however, had weakened some centuries before Mortdieu, replaced only by a kind of rote. The Cathedral suffered. Survivors—clergy and staff, worshipers seeking sanctuary—had wretched visions, dreamed wretched dreams. They saw the stone ornaments of the Cathedral come alive. With someone to see and believe, in a universe lacking any other foundation, my ancestors shook off stone and became flesh. Centuries of rock celibacy weighed upon them. Forty-nine nuns who had sought shelter in the Cathedral were discovered and were not entirely loath, so the coarser versions of the tale go. Mortdieu had a surprising aphrodisiacal effect on the faithful, and conjugation took place.

No definite gestation period has been established, for at that time the great stone wheel had not been set twisting back and forth to count the hours. Nor had anyone been given the chair of Kronos to watch over the wheel and provide a baseline for everyday activities.

But flesh did not reject stone, and there came into being the sons and daughters of flesh and stone, including me. Those who had fornicated with the inhuman figures were cast out to raise—or reject—their monstrous young in the highest hidden recesses. Those who had accepted the embraces of the stone saints and other human figures were less abused but still banished to the upper reaches. A wooden scaffolding was erected, dividing the great nave into two levels. A canvas dropcloth was fastened over the scaffold to prevent offal raining down, and on the second level of the Cathedral the more human offspring of stone and flesh set about creating a new life.

I have long tried to find out how some semblance of order came to the world. Legend has it that it was the archexistentialist Jansard—crucifier of the beloved St. Argentine—who, realizing and repenting his error, discovered that mind and thought could calm the foaming sea of reality.

The priest finished his all-too-sketchy lecture by touching on this point briefly: "With the passing of God's watchful gaze, humanity had to reach out and grab hold the unraveling fabric of the world. Those left alive—those who had the wits to keep their bodies from falling apart—became the only cohesive force in the chaos."

I had picked up enough language to understand what he said; my memory was good—still is—and I was curious enough to want to know more.

Creeping along stone walls behind the curtains, I listened to other priests and nuns intoning scriptures to gaggles of flesh children. That was on the ground floor, and I was in great danger; the people of pure flesh looking on my kind as abominations. But it was worth it.

I was able to steal a psalter and learn to read. I stole other books; they defined my world by allowing me to compare it with others. At first I couldn't believe the others had ever existed; only the Cathedral was real. I still have my doubts. I can look out a tiny round window on one side of my room and see the great forest and river that surround the Cathedral, but I can see nothing else. So my experience with other worlds is far from direct.

No matter. I read a great deal, but I'm no scholar. What concerns me is recent history—the final focus of that germinal hour listening to the priest. From the metaphysical to the acutely personal.

I am small—barely three feet in height—but I can run quickly through most of the hidden passageways. This lets me observe without attracting attention. I may be the only historian in this whole structure. Others who claim the role disregard what's before their eyes, in search of ultimate truths, or at least Big Pictures. So if you prefer history where the historian is not involved, look to others. Objective as I try to be, I do have my favorite subjects. . . .

■ ■ ■

In the time when my history begins, the children of stone and flesh were still searching for the Stone Christ. Those of us born of the union of the stone saints and gargoyles with the bereaved nuns thought our salvation lay in the great stone celibate, who had come to life with all the other statues.

Of smaller import were the secret assignations between the bishop's daughter and a young man of stone and flesh. Such assignations were forbidden even between those of pure flesh; and as these two lovers were unmarried, their compound sin intrigued me.

Her name was Constantia, and she was fourteen, slender of limb, brown of hair, mature of bosom. Her eyes carried the stupid sort of divine life common in girls that age. His name was

Corvus, and he was fifteen. I don't recall his precise features, but he was handsome enough and dexterous; he could climb through scaffolding almost as quickly as I. I first spied them talking when I made one of my frequent raids on the repository to steal another book. They were in shadow, but my eyes are keen. They spoke softly, hesitantly. My heart ached to see them and to think of their tragedy, for I knew right away that Corvus was not pure flesh and that Constantia was the daughter of the bishop himself. I envisioned the old tyrant meting out the usual punishment to Corvus for such breaches of level and morality—castration. But in their talk was a sweetness that almost masked the closed-in stench of the lower nave.

"Have you ever kissed a man before?"

"Yes."

"Who?"

"My brother." She laughed.

"And?" His voice was sharper; he might kill her brother, he seemed to say.

"A friend named Jules."

"Where is he?"

"Oh, he vanished on a wood-gathering expedition."

"Oh." And he kissed her again. I'm a historian, not a voyeur, so I discreetly hide the flowering of their passion. If Corvus had had any sense, he would have reveled in his conquest and never returned. But he was snared and continued to see her despite the risk. This was loyalty, love, faithfulness, and it was rare. It fascinated me.

■ ■ ■

I have just been taking in sun, a nice day, and looking out over the buttresses. The Cathedral is like a low-bellied lizard, and the buttresses are its legs. There are little houses at the base of each buttress, where rainspouters with dragon faces used to lean out over the trees (or city or whatever was down below once). Now people live here. It wasn't always that way—the sun was once forbidden. Corvus and Constantia from childhood were denied its light, and so even in their youthful prime they were pale and dirty with the smoke of candles and tallow lamps. The most sun anyone received in those days was obtained on wood-gathering expeditions.

After spying on one of the clandestine meetings of the young lovers, I mused in a dark corner for an hour, then went to see the copper giant Apostle Thomas. He was the only human form to live so high in the Cathedral. He carried a ruler on which was engraved his real name—he had been modeled after the Cathedral's restorer in times past, the architect Viollet-le-Duc. He knew the Cathedral better than anyone, and I admired him greatly. Most of the monsters left him alone—out of fear if nothing else. He was huge, black as night, but flaked with pale green, his face creased in eternal thought. He was sitting in his usual wooden compartment near the base of the spire, not twenty feet from where I write now, thinking about times none of the rest of us ever knew: of joy and past love, some say; others say of the burden that rested on him now that the Cathedral was the center of this chaotic world.

It was the giant who selected me from the ugly hordes when he saw me with a psalter. He encouraged me in my efforts to read. "Your eyes are bright," he told me. "You move as if your brain were quick, and you keep yourself dry and clean. You aren't hollow like the rainspouters; you have substance. For all our sakes, put it to use and learn the ways of the Cathedral."

And so I did.

He looked up as I came in. I sat on a box near his feet and said, "A daughter of flesh is seeing a son of stone and flesh."

He shrugged his massive shoulders. "So it shall be, in time."

"Is it not a sin?"

"It is something so monstrous it is past sin and become necessity," he said. "It will happen more as time passes."

"They're in love, I think, or will be."

He nodded. "I—and the Other—were the only ones to abstain from fornication on the night of Mortdieu," he said. "I am—except for the Other—alone fit to judge."

I waited for him to judge, but he sighed and patted me on the shoulder. "And I never judge, do I, ugly friend?"

"Never," I said.

"So leave me alone to be sad." He winked. "And more power to them."

The bishop of the Cathedral was an old man. It was said he hadn't been bishop before the Mortdieu, but a wanderer who came in during the chaos, before the forest had replaced the city. He had set himself up as titular head of this section of God's former domain by saying it had been willed to him.

He was short, stout, with huge hairy arms like the clamps of a vise. He had once killed a spouter with a single squeeze of his fist, and spouters are tough things, since they have no guts like you (I suppose) and I. The hair surrounding his bald pate was white, thick, and unruly, and his eyebrows leaned over his nose with marvelous flexibility. He rutted like a pig, ate hugely, and shat liquidly (I know all). A man for this time, if ever there was one.

It was his decree that all those not pure of flesh be banned and that those not of human form be killed on sight.

When I returned from the giant's chamber, I saw that the lower nave was in an uproar. They had seen someone clambering about in the scaffold, and troops had been sent to shoot him down. Of course it was Corvus. I was a quicker climber than he and knew the beams better, so when he found himself trapped in an apparent cul-de-sac, it was I who gestured from the shadows and pointed to a hole large enough for him to escape through. He took it without a breath of thanks, but etiquette has never been important to me. I entered the stone wall through a nook a spare hand's width across and wormed my way to the bottom to see what else was happening. Excitement was rare.

A rumor was passing that the figure had been seen with a young girl, but the crowds didn't know who the girl was. The men and women who mingled in the smoky light, between the rows of open-roofed hovels, chattered gaily. Castrations and executions were among the few joys for us then; I relished them too, but I had a stake in the potential victims now and I worried.

My worry and my interest got the better of me. I slid through an unrepaired gap and fell to one side of the alley between the outer wall and the hovels. A group of dirty adolescents spotted me. "There he is!" they screeched. "He didn't get away!"

The bishop's masked troops can travel freely on all levels. I was almost cornered by them, and when I tried one escape route, they waited at a crucial spot in the stairs—which I had to cross to complete the next leg—and forced me back. I prided myself in knowing the Cathedral top to bottom, but as I scrambled madly, I came upon a tunnel I had never noticed before. It led deep into a broad stone foundation wall. I was safe for the moment but afraid they might find my caches of food and poison my casks of rainwater. Still, there was nothing I could do until they had gone, so I decided to spend the anxious hours exploring the tunnel.

The Cathedral is a constant surprise; I realize now I didn't know half of what it offered. There are always new ways to get from here to there (some, I suspect, created while no one is looking), and sometimes even new theres to be discovered. While troops snuffled about the hole above, near the stairs—where only a child of two or three could have entered—I followed a flight of crude steps deep into the stone. Water and slime made the passage slippery and difficult. For a moment I was in darkness deeper than any I had experienced before—gloom more profound than any mere lack of light could explain. Then below I saw a faint yellow gleam. More cautious, I slowed and progressed silently. Behind a rusting, scabrous metal gate, I set foot into the lighted room. There was the smell of crumbling stone, a tang of mineral water, slime—and the stench of a dead spouter. The beast lay on the floor of the narrow chamber, several months gone but still fragrant. I have mentioned that spouters are very hard to kill—and this one had been murdered. Three candles stood freshly placed in nooks around the chamber, flickering in a faint draft from above. Despite my fears, I walked across the stone floor, took a candle, and peered into the next section of tunnel.

It sloped down for several dozen feet, ending at another metal gate. It was here that I detected an odor I had never before encountered—the smell of the purest of stones, as of rare jade or virgin marble. Such a feeling of light-headedness passed over me that I almost laughed, but I was too cautious for that. I pushed aside the gate and was greeted by a rush of the coldest, sweetest air, like a draft from the tomb of a saint whose body does not corrupt but, rather, draws corruption away and expels it miraculously into the nether pits. My beak dropped open. The candlelight fell across the darkness onto a figure I at first thought to be an infant. But I quickly disagreed with myself. The figure was several ages at once. As I blinked, it became a man of about thirty, well formed, with a high forehead and elegant hands, pale as ice. His eyes stared at the wall behind me. I bowed down on scaled knee and touched my forehead as best I could to the cold stone, shivering to my vestigial wing tips. "Forgive me, Joy of Man's Desiring," I said. "Forgive me." I had stumbled upon the hiding place of the Stone Christ.

"You are forgiven," He said wearily. "You had to come sooner or later. Better now than later, when . . ." His voice trailed away and He shook His head. He was very thin, wrapped in a gray robe that still bore the scars of centuries of weathering. "Why did you come?"

"To escape the bishop's troops," I said.

He nodded. "Yes. The bishop. How long have I been here?"

"Since before I was born, Lord. Sixty or seventy years." He was thin, almost ethereal, this figure I had imagined as a husky carpenter. I lowered my voice and beseeched, "What may I do for You, Lord?"

"Go away," He said.

"I could not live with such a secret," I said. "You are salvation. You can overthrow the bishop and bring all the levels together."

"I am not a general or a soldier. Please go away and tell no—"

I felt a breath behind me, then the whisper of a weapon. I leaped aside, and my hackles rose as a stone sword came down and shattered on the floor beside me. The Christ raised His hand. Still in shock, I stared at a beast much like myself. It stared back, face black with rage, stayed by the power of His hand. I should have been more wary—something had to have killed the spouter and kept the candles fresh.

"But, Lord," the beast rumbled, "he will tell all."

"No," the Christ said. "He'll tell nobody." He looked half at me, half through me, and said, "Go, go."

Up the tunnels, into the orange dark of the Cathedral, crying, I crawled and slithered. I could not even go to the giant. I had been silenced as effectively as if my throat had been cut.

The next morning I watched from a shadowy corner of the scaffold as a crowd gathered around a lone man in a dirty sackcloth robe. I had seen him before; his name was Psalo, and he was left alone as an example of the bishop's largesse. It was a token gesture; most of the people regarded him as barely half-sane.

Yet this time I listened and, in my confusion, found his words striking responsive chords in me. He was exhorting the bishop and his forces to allow light into the Cathedral again by dropping the canvas tarp that covered the windows. He had talked about this before, and the bishop had responded with his usual statement—that with the light would come more chaos, for the human mind was now a pesthole of delusions. Any stimulus would drive away whatever security the inhabitants of the Cathedral had.

■ ■ ■

At this time it gave me no pleasure to watch the love of Constantia and Corvus grow. They were becoming more careless. Their talk was bolder.

"We shall announce a marriage," Corvus said.

"They will never allow it. They'll . . . cut you."

"I'm nimble. They'll never catch me. The church needs leaders, brave revolutionaries. If no one breaks with tradition, everyone will suffer."

"I fear for your life—and mine. My father would push me from the flock like a diseased lamb."

"Your father is no shepherd."

"He is my father," Constantia said, eyes wide, mouth drawn tight.

I sat with beak in paws, eyes half lidded, able to mimic each statement before it was uttered. Undying love . . . hope for a bleak future . . . shite and onions! I had read it all before, in a cache of romantic novels in the trash of a dead nun. As soon as I made the connection and realized the timeless banality—and the futility—of what I was seeing, and when I compared their prattle with the infinite sadness of the Stone Christ, I went from innocent to cynic. The transition dizzied me, leaving little backwaters of noble emotion, but the future seemed clear. Corvus would be caught and executed; if it hadn't been for me, he would already have been gelded, if not killed. Constantia would weep, poison herself; the singers would sing of it (those self-same warble-throats who cheered the death of her lover); perhaps I would write of it (I was planning this chronicle even then), and afterward, perhaps, I would follow them both, having succumbed to the sin of boredom.

With night, things became less certain. It was easy to stare at a dark wall and let dreams become manifest. At one time, so

I've deduced from books, dreams could not take shape beyond sleep or brief fantasy. All too often I've had to fight things generated in my dreams, flowing from the walls, suddenly independent and hungry. People often die in the night, devoured by their own nightmares.

That evening, falling to sleep with visions of the Stone Christ in my head, I dreamed of holy men, angels, and saints. I came awake abruptly, by training, and one had stayed behind. The others I saw vaguely, flitting outside the round window, where they whispered and made plans for flying off to heaven. The wraith who remained was a dark shape in one corner. His breathing was harsh. "I am Peter," he said, "also called Simon. I am the rock of the Church, and popes are told that they are heir to my task."

"I'm rock, too," I said. "At least in part."

"So be it, then. You are heir to my task. Go forth and be pope. Do not revere the Stone Christ, for a Christ is only as good as He does, and if He does nothing, there is no salvation in Him."

The shadow reached out to pat my head, and I saw his eyes grow wide as he made out my form. He muttered some formula for banishing devils and oozed out the window to join his fellows.

I imagined that if such a thing were actually brought before the council, it would be decided under the law that the benison of a dream person is not binding. I did not care. This was better advice than any I'd had since the giant told me to read and learn.

But to be pope, one must have a hierarchy of servants to carry out one's orders. The biggest of rocks does not move by itself. So, swelled with power, I decided to appear in the upper nave and announce myself to the people.

It took a great deal of courage to appear in daylight, without cloak, and to walk across the scaffold's surface, on the second level, through crowds of vendors setting up the market for the day. Some reacted with typical bigotry and sought to kick or deride me. My beak discouraged them. I clambered to the top of a prominent stall and stood in a murky lamp's circle, clearing my throat to announce myself. Under a hail of rotten pomegranates and limp vegetables, I told the throng who I was, and I told them about my vision. Jeweled with beads of offal, I jumped down in a few minutes and fled to a tunnel entrance too small for most men. Some boys followed me, and one lost a finger while trying to slice me with a fragment of colored glass.

Open revelation was worthless. There are levels of bigotry, and I was at the very bottom of any list.

My next strategy was to find some way to disrupt the Cathedral from top to bottom. Even bigots, when reduced to a mob, could be swayed by the presence of one obviously ordained and capable. I spent two days skulking through the walls. There had to be a basic flaw in so fragile a structure as the church, and, while I wasn't contemplating total destruction, I wanted something spectacular, unavoidable.

While I thought, hanging from the bottom of the second scaffold, above the community of pure flesh, the bishop's deep gravelly voice roared over the noise of the crowd. I opened my eyes and looked down. The masked troops were holding a bowed figure, and the bishop was intoning over its head, "Know all who hear me now, this young bastard of flesh and stone—"

Corvus, I told myself. Finally caught. I shut one eye, but the other refused to close out the scene.

"—has violated all we hold sacred and shall atone for his crimes on this spot, tomorrow at this time. Kronos! Mark the wheel's progress." The elected Kronos, a spindly old man with dirty gray hair down to his buttocks, took a piece of charcoal and marked an X on the huge bulkhead chart, behind which the wheel groaned and sighed in its circuit.

The crowd was enthusiastic. I saw Psalo pushing through the people.

"What crime?" he called out. "Name the crime!"

"Violation of the lower level!" the head of the masked troops declared.

"That merits a whipping and an escort upstairs," Psalo said. "I detect a more sinister crime here. What is it?"

The bishop looked Psalo down coldly. "He tried to rape my daughter, Constantia."

Psalo could say nothing to that. The penalty was castration and death. All the pure humans accepted such laws. There was no other recourse.

I mused, watching Corvus being led to the dungeons. The future that I desired at that moment startled me with its clarity. I wanted that part of my heritage that had been denied to me—to be at peace with myself, to be surrounded by those who accepted me, by those no better than I. In time it would happen, as the giant had said. But would I ever see it? What Corvus, in his own lusty way, was trying to do was equalize the levels, to bring stone into flesh until no one could tell the difference.

Well, my plans beyond that point were very hazy. They were less plans than glowing feelings, imaginings of happiness and children playing in the forest and fields beyond the island as the work knit itself under the gaze of God's heir. My children, playing in the forest. A touch of truth came to me at this moment. I had wished to be Corvus when he tupped Constantia.

So I had two tasks, then, that could be merged if I was clever. I had to distract the bishop and his troops, and I had to rescue Corvus, fellow revolutionary.

I spent that night in feverish misery in my room. At dawn I went to the giant and asked his advice. He looked me over coldly and said, "We waste our time if we try to knock sense into their heads. But we have no better calling than to waste our time, do we?"

"What shall I do?"

"Enlighten them."

I stomped my claw on the floor. "They are bricks! Try enlightening bricks!"

He smiled his sad, narrow smile. "Enlighten them," he said.

I left the giant's chamber in a rage. I did not have access to the great wheel's board of time, so I couldn't know exactly when the execution would take place. But I guessed—from memories of a grumbling stomach—that it would be in the early afternoon. I traveled from one end of the nave to the other and, likewise, the transept. I nearly exhausted myself. Then, traversing an empty aisle, I picked up a piece of colored glass and examined it, puzzled. Many of the boys on all levels carried these shards with them, and the girls used them as jewelry—against the wishes of their elders, who held that bright objects bred more beasts in the mind. Where did they get them?

In one of the books I had perused years before, I had seen brightly colored pictures of the Cathedral windows. "Enlighten them," the giant had said.

Psalo's request to let light into the Cathedral came to mind. Along the peak of the nave, in a tunnel running its length, I found the ties that held the pulleys of the canvases over the windows. The best windows, I decided, would be the huge ones of the north and south transepts. I made a diagram in the dust, trying to decide what season it was and from which direction the sunlight would come—pure theory to me, but at this moment I was in a fever of brilliance. All the windows had to be clear. I could not decide which was best.

I was ready by early afternoon, just after sext prayers in the upper nave. I had cut the major ropes and weakened the clamps by prying them from the walls with a pick stolen from the bishop's armory. I walked along a high ledge, took an almost vertical shaft through the wall to the lower floor, and waited.

Constantia was watching from a wooden balcony, the bishop's special box for executions. She had a terrified, fascinated look on her face. Corvus was on the dais across the nave, right in the center of the cross of the transept. Torches illuminated him and his executioners, three men and an old woman.

I knew the procedure. The old woman would castrate him first, then the men would remove his head. He was dressed in the condemned's red robe to hide any blood. Blood excitement among the impressionable was the last thing the bishop wanted. Troops waited around the dais to purify the area with scented water.

I didn't have much time. It would take minutes for the system of ropes and pulleys to clear and canvases to fall. I went to my station and severed the remaining ties. Then, as the Cathedral filled with a hollow creaking sound, I followed the shaft back to my viewing post.

In three minutes the canvases were drooping. I saw Corvus look up, his eyes glazed. The bishop was with his daughter in the box. He pulled her back into the shadows. In another two minutes the canvases fell onto the upper scaffold with a hideous crash. Their weight was too great for the ends of the structure, and it collapsed, allowing the canvases to cascade to the floor many yards below. At first the illumination was dim and bluish, filtered perhaps by a passing cloud. Then, from one end of the Cathedral to the other, a burst of light threw my smoky world into clarity. The glory of thousands of pieces of colored glass, hidden for decades and hardly touched by childish vandals, fell upon upper and lower levels at once. A cry from the crowds nearly wrenched me from my post. I slid quickly to the lower level and hid, afraid of what I had done. This was more than simple sunlight. Like the blossomings of two flowers, one brighter than the other, the transept windows astounded all who beheld them.

Eyes accustomed to orangey dark, to smoke and haze and shadow, cannot stare into such glory without drastic effect. I shielded my own face and tried to find a convenient exit.

But the population was increasing. As the light brightened and more faces rose to be locked, phototropic, the splendor unhinged some people. From their minds poured contents too wondrous to be accurately catalogued. The monsters thus released were not violent, however, and most of the visions were not monstrous.

The upper and lower nave shimmered with reflected glories, with dream figures and children clothed in baubles of light. Saints and prodigies dominated. A thousand newly created youngsters squatted on the bright floor and began to tell of marvels, of cities in the East, and times as they once had been. Clowns dressed in fire entertained from the tops of the market stalls. Animals unknown to the Cathedral cavorted between the dwellings, giving friendly advice. Abstract things, glowing balls in nets of gold and ribbons of silk, sang and floated around the upper reaches. The Cathedral became a great vessel of all the bright dreams known to its citizens.

Slowly, from the lower nave, people of pure flesh climbed to the scaffold and walked the upper nave to see what they couldn't from below. From my hideaway I watched the masked troops of the bishop carrying his litter up narrow stairs. Constantia walked behind, stumbling, her eyes shut in the new brightness.

All tried to cover their eyes, but none for long succeeded.

I wept. Almost blind with tears, I made my way still higher and looked down on the roiling crowds. I saw Corvus, his hands still wrapped in restraining ropes, being led by the old woman. Constantia saw him too, and they regarded each other like strangers, then joined hands as best they could. She borrowed a knife from one of her father's soldiers and cut his ropes away. Around them the brightest dreams of all began to swirl, pure white and blood-red and sea-green, coalescing into visions of all the children they would innocently have.

I gave them a few hours to regain their senses—and to regain my own. Then I stood on the bishop's abandoned podium and shouted over the heads of those on the lowest level.

"The time has come!" I cried. "We must all unite now; we must unite—"

At first they ignored me. I was quite eloquent, but their excitement was still too great. So I waited some more, began to speak again, and was shouted down. Bits of fruit and vegetables arced up. "Freak!" they screamed, and drove me away.

I crept along the stone stairs, found the narrow crack, and hid in it, burying my beak in my paws, wondering what had gone wrong. It took a surprisingly long time for me to realize that, in my case, it was less the stigma of stone than the ugliness of my shape that doomed my quest for leadership.

I had, however, paved the way for the Stone Christ. He will surely be able to take His place now, I told myself. So I maneuvered along the crevice until I came to the hidden chamber and the yellow glow. All was quiet within. I met first the stone monster, who looked me over suspiciously with glazed gray eyes. "You're back," he said. Overcome by his wit, I leered, nodded, and asked that I be presented to the Christ.

"He's sleeping."

"Important tidings," I said.

"What?"

"I bring glad tidings."

"Then let me hear them."

"His ears only."

Out of the gloomy corner came the Christ, looking much older now. "What is it?" He asked.

"I have prepared the way for You," I said. "Simon called Peter told me I was the heir to his legacy, that I should go before You—"

The Stone Christ shook His head. "You believe I am the fount from which all blessings flow?"

I nodded, uncertain.

"What have you done out there?"

"Let in the light," I said.

He shook His head slowly. "You seem a wise enough creature. You know about Mortdieu."

"Yes."

"Then you should know that I barely have enough power to keep myself together, to heal myself, much less minister to those out there." He gestured beyond the walls. "My own source has gone away," He said mournfully. "I'm operating on reserves, and those none too vast."

"He wants you to go away and stop bothering us," the monster explained.

"They have their light out there," the Christ said. "They'll play with that for a while, get tired of it, go back to what they had before. Is there any place for you in that?"

I thought for a moment, then shook my head. "No place," I said. "I'm too ugly."

"You are too ugly, and I am too famous," he said. "I'd have to come from their midst, anonymous, and that is clearly impossible. No, leave them alone for a while. They'll make Me over again, perhaps, or better still, forget about Me. About us. We don't have any place there."

I was stunned. I sat down hard on the stone floor, and the Christ patted me on my head as He walked by. "Go back to your hiding place; live as well as you can," He said. "Our time is over."

I turned to go. When I reached the crevice, I heard His voice behind, saying, "Do you play bridge? If you do, find another. We need four to a table."

I clambered up the crack, through the walls, and along the arches over the revelry. Not only was I not going to be pope—after an appointment by Saint Peter himself!—but I couldn't convince someone much more qualified than I to assume the leadership.

It is the sign of the eternal student, I suppose, that when his wits fail him, he returns to the teacher.

I returned to the copper giant. He was lost in meditation. About his feet were scattered scraps of paper with detailed drawings of parts of the Cathedral. I waited patiently until he saw me. He turned, chin in hand, and looked me over.

"Why so sad?"

I shook my head. Only he could read my features and recognize my moods.

"Did you take my advice below? I heard a commotion."

"Mea maxima culpa," I said.

"And . . .?"

I slowly, hesitantly, made my report, concluding with the refusal of the Stone Christ. The giant listened closely without interrupting. When I was done, he stood, towering over me, and pointed with his ruler through an open portal.

"Do you see that out there?" he asked. The ruler swept over the forests beyond the island, to the far green horizon. I replied that I did and waited for him to continue. He seemed to be lost in thought again.

"Once there was a city where trees now grow," he said. "Artists came by the thousands, and whores, and philosophers, and academics. And when God died, all the academics and whores and artists couldn't hold the fabric of the world together. How do you expect us to succeed now?"

Us? "Expectations should not determine whether one acts or not," I said. "Should they?"

The giant laughed and tapped my head with the ruler. "Maybe we've been given a sign, and we just have to learn how to interpret it correctly."

I leered to show I was puzzled.

"Maybe Mortdieu is really a sign that we have been weaned. We must forage for ourselves, remake the world without help. What do you think of that?"

I was too tired to judge the merits of what he was saying, but I had never known the giant to be wrong before. "Okay. I grant that. So?"

"The Stone Christ says his charge is running down. If God weans us from the old ways, we can't expect His Son to replace the nipple, can we?"

"No. . . ."

He hunkered next to me, his face bright. "I wondered who would really stand forth. It's obvious. We won't. So, little one, who's the next choice?"

"Me?" I asked, meekly. The giant looked me over pityingly.

"No," he said after a time. "I am the next. We're weaned!" He did a little dance, startling my beak up out of my paws. I blinked. He grabbed my vestigial wing tips and pulled me upright. "Stand straight. Tell me more."

"About what?"

"Tell me all that's going on below, and whatever else you know."

"I'm trying to figure out what you're saying," I protested, trembling.

"Dense as stone!" Grinning, he bent over me. Then the grin went away, and he tried to look stern. "It's a grave responsibility. We must remake the world ourselves now. We must coordinate our thoughts, our dreams. Chaos won't do. What an opportunity, to be the architect of an entire universe!" He waved the ruler at the ceiling. "To build the very skies! The last world was a training ground, full of harsh rules and strictures. Now we've been told that we're ready to leave that behind, move on to something more mature. Did I teach you any of the rules of architecture? I mean, the aesthetics. The need for harmony, interaction, utility, beauty?"

"Some," I said.

"Good. I don't think making the universe anew will require any better rules. No doubt we'll need to experiment, and perhaps one or more of our great spires will topple. But now we work for ourselves, to our own glory, and the greater glory of the God who made us! No, ugly friend?"

■ ■ ■

Like many histories, mine must begin with the small, the tightly focused, and expand into the large. But unlike most historians, I don't have the luxury of time. Indeed, my story isn't even concluded yet.

Soon the legions of Viollet-le-Duc will begin their campaigns. Most have been schooled pretty thoroughly: kidnapped from below, brought up in the heights, taught as I was. We'll begin returning them, one by one.

I teach off and on, write off and on, observe all the time.

The next step will be the biggest. I haven't any idea how we're going to do it.

But, as the giant puts it, "Long ago the roof fell in. Now we must push it up again, strengthen it, repair the beams." At this point he smiles to the pupils. "Not just repair them. Replace them! Now we are the beams. Flesh and stone become something much stronger."

Ah, but then some dolt will raise a hand and inquire, "What if our arms get tired holding up the sky?"

Our task, you see, will not soon be over.

Till Human Voices Wake Us

■

Since his first publication in 1977, Lewis Shiner has written a widely ranging spectrum of short stories: mysteries, fantasies, and horror as well as SF. But the 1984 appearance of his first novel, *Frontera*, demonstrated his important role in Movement fiction. *Frontera* combined classic hard-SF structure with a harrowing portrait of postindustrial society in the early twenty-first century. The book's gritty realism and deflating treatment of SF icons aroused much comment.

Shiner's work is marked by thorough research and coolly meticulous construction. His lean, vigorous prose shows his allegiance to hard-boiled mystery fiction as well as to such quasi-mainstream authors as Elmore Leonard and Robert Stone.

The son of an anthropologist, Shiner has a fondness for odd belief structures, such as Zen, quantum physics, and mythic archetypes. Though he is capable of bizarre flights of fancy, his work of late has tended toward direct, unsentimental realism and an increasing interest in global politics. The following Shiner story, from 1984, combines mythic images and technosocial politics in a classic cyberpunk mix.

They were at forty feet, in darkness. Inside the narrow circle of his dive light, Campbell could see coral polyps feeding, their ragged edges transformed into predatory flowers.

If anything could have saved us, he thought, this week should have been it.

Beth's lantern wobbled as she flailed herself away from the white-petaled spines of a sea urchin. She wore nothing but a white T-shirt over her bikini, despite Campbell's warnings, and he could see gooseflesh on her thighs. Which is as much of her body, he thought, as I've seen in . . . how long? Five weeks? Six? He couldn't remember the last time they'd made love.

As he moved his light away he thought he saw a shape in the darkness. He thought: shark, and felt a quick constriction of fear in his throat. He swung the lamp back again and saw her.

She was frozen by the glare, like any wild animal. Her long straight hair floated up from her shoulders and blended into the darkness; the ends of her bare breasts were elliptical and purple in the night water.

Her legs merged into a green, scaly tail.

Campbell listened to his breath rasp into the regulator. He could see the width of her cheekbones, the paleness of her eyes, the frightened tremor of the gills around her neck.

Then reflex took over and he brought up his Nokonos and fired. The flare of the strobe shocked her to life. She shuddered, flicked her crescent tail toward him, and disappeared.

A sudden, inexplicable longing overwhelmed him. He dropped the camera and swam after her, legs pumping, pulling with both arms. As he reached the edge of a hundred-foot drop-off, he swept the light in an arc that picked up a final glimpse of her, heading down and to the west. Then she was gone.

■ ■ ■

He found Beth on the surface, shivering and enraged. "What the hell was the idea of leaving me alone like that? I was scared to death. You heard what that guy said about sharks—"

"I saw something," Campbell said.

"Fan-fucking-tastic." She rode low in the water, and Campbell watched her catch a wave in her open mouth. She spat it out and said, "Were you taking a look or just running away?"

"Blow up your vest," Campbell said, feeling numb, desolate, "before you drown yourself." He turned his back to her and swam for the boat.

■ ■ ■

Showered, sitting outside his cabin in the moonlight, Campbell began to doubt himself.

Beth was already cocooned in a flannel nightgown near her

edge of the bed. She would lie there, Campbell knew, sometimes not even bothering to close her eyes, until he was asleep.

His recurring, obsessive daydreams were what had brought him here to the island. How could he be sure he hadn't hallucinated that creature out on the reef?

He'd told Beth that they'd been lucky to be picked for the vacation, that he'd applied for it months before. In fact, his fantasies had so utterly destroyed his concentration at work that the company had ordered him to come to the island or submit to a complete course of psych testing.

He'd been more frightened than he was willing to admit. The fantasies had progressed from the mild violence of smashing his CRT screen to a bizarre, sinister image of himself floating outside his shattered office windows, not falling the forty stories to the street, just drifting there in the whitish smog.

High above him Campbell could see the company bar, glittering like a chrome-and-steel monster just hatched from its larval stage.

He shook his head. Obviously he needed some sleep. Just one good night's rest, he told himself, and things would start getting back to normal.

■ ■ ■

In the morning Campbell went out on the dive boat while Beth slept in. He was distracted, clumsy, and bothered by shadows in his peripheral vision.

The dive master wandered over while they were changing tanks and asked him, "You nervous about something?"

"No," Campbell said. "I'm fine."

"There's no sharks on this part of the reef, you know."

"It's not that," Campbell said. "There's no problem. Really."

He read the look in the dive master's eyes: another case of shell shock. The company must turn them out by the dozens, Campbell thought. The stressed-out executives and the boardroom victims, all with the same glazed expressions.

That afternoon they dove a small wreck at the east end of the island. Beth paired off with another woman, so Campbell stayed with his partner from the morning, a balding pilot from the Cincinnati office.

The wreck was no more than a husk, an empty shell, and Campbell floated to one side as the others crawled over the rotting wood. His sense of purpose had disappeared, left him wanting only the weightlessness and lack of color of the deep water.

■ ■ ■

After dinner he followed Beth out onto the patio. He'd lost track of how long he'd been watching the clouds over the dark water when she said, "I don't like this place."

Campbell shifted his eyes back to her. She was sleek and pristine in the white linen jacket, the sleeves pushed up to her elbows, her still-damp hair twisted into a chignon and spiked with an orchid. She had been sulking into her brandy since they'd finished dinner, and once again she'd astonished him with her ability to exist in a completely separate mental universe from his own. "Why not?"

"It's fake. Unreal. This whole island." She swirled the brandy but didn't drink any of it. "What business does an American company have owning an entire island? What happened to the people who used to live here?"

"In the first place," Campbell said, "it's a multinational company, not just American. And the people are still living here, only now they've got jobs instead of starving to death." As usual, Beth had him on the defensive, but he wasn't as thrilled with the Americanization of the island as he wanted to be. He'd imagined natives with guitars and congas, not portable stereos that blasted electronic reggae and neo-funk. The hut where he and Beth slept was some kind of geodesic dome, air-conditioned and comfortable, but he missed the sound of the ocean.

"I just don't like it," Beth said. "I don't like top secret projects that they have to keep locked up behind electric fences. I don't like the company flying people out here for vacations the way they'd throw a bone to a dog."

Or a straw to a drowning man, Campbell thought. He was as curious as anybody about the installations at the west end of the island, but of course that wasn't the point. He and Beth were walking through the steps of a dance that Campbell now saw would inevitably end in divorce. Their friends had all been divorced at least once, and an eighteen-year marriage probably seemed as anachronistic to them as a 1957 Chevy.

"Why don't you just admit it?" Campbell said. "The only thing you really don't like about the island is the fact that you're stuck here with me."

She stood up, and Campbell felt, with numbing jealousy, the stares of men all around them focus on her. "I'll see you later," she said, and heads turned to follow the clatter of her sandals.

Campbell ordered another Salva Vida and watched her walk downhill. The stairs were lit with Japanese lanterns and surrounded by wild purple and orange flowers. By the time she reached the sandbar and the line of cabins, she was no more than a shadow, and Campbell had finished most of the beer.

Now that she was gone, he felt drained and a little dizzy. He looked at his hands, still puckered from the long hours in the water, at the cuts and bruises of three days of physical activity. Soft hands, the hands of a company man, a desk man. Hands that would push a pencil or type on a CRT for another twenty years, then retire to the remote control of a big-screen TV.

The thick, caramel-tasting beer was starting to catch up to him. He shook his head and got up to find the bathroom.

His reflection shimmered and melted in the warped mirror over the bathroom sink. He realized he was stalling, staying away from the chill, sterile air of the cabin as long as he could.

And then there were the dreams. They'd gotten worse since he'd come to the island, more vivid and disturbing every night. He couldn't remember details, only slow, erotic sensations along his skin, a sense of floating in thin, crystalline water, of rolling in frictionless sheets. He'd awaken from them gasping for air like a drowning fish, his penis swollen and throbbing.

He brought another beer back to his table, not really wanting it, just needing it to hold in his hands. His attention kept wandering to a table on a lower level, where a rather plain young woman sat talking with two men in glasses and dress shirts. He couldn't understand what was so familiar about her until she tilted her head in a puzzled gesture and he recognized her. The broad cheekbones, the pale eyes.

He could hear the sound of his own heart. Was it just some kind of prank, then? A woman in a costume? But what about the gill lines he'd seen on her neck? How in God's name had she moved so quickly?

She stood up, made apologetic gestures to her friends. Campbell's table was near the stairs, and he saw she would have to pass him on her way out. Before he could stop to think about it, he stood up, blocking her exit, and said, "Excuse me?"

"Yes?" She was not that physically attractive, he thought, but he was drawn to her anyway, in spite of the heaviness of her waist, her solid, shortish legs. Her face was older, tireder than the one he'd seen out on the reef. But similar, too close for coincidence. "I wanted to . . . could I buy you a drink?" Maybe, he thought, I'm just losing my mind.

She smiled, and her eyes crinkled warmly. "I'm sorry. It's really very late, and I have to be at work in the morning."

"Please," Campbell said. "Just for a minute or two." He could see her suspicion, and behind that a faint glow of flattered ego. She wasn't used to being approached by men, he realized. "I just want to talk with you."

"You're not a reporter, are you?"

"No, nothing like that." He searched for something reassuring. "I'm with the company. The Houston office."

The magic words, Campbell thought. She sat down in Beth's chair and said, "I don't know if I should have any more. I'm about half looped as it is."

Campbell nodded, said, "You work here, then."

"That's right."

"Secretary?"

"Biologist," she said, a little sharply. "I'm Dr. Kimberly." When he didn't react to the name, she softened it by adding, "Joan Kimberly."

"I'm sorry," Campbell said. "I always thought biologists were supposed to be homely." The flirtation came easily. She had the same beauty as the creature on the reef, a sort of fierce shyness and alien sensuality, but in the woman they were more deeply buried.

My God, Campbell thought, I'm actually doing this, actually trying to seduce this woman. He glanced at the swelling of her breasts, knowing what they would look like without the blue oxford shirt she wore, and the knowledge became a warmth in his groin.

"Maybe I'd better have that drink," she said. Campbell signaled the waiter.

"I can't imagine what it would be like to live here," he said. "To see this every day."

"You get used to it," she said. "I mean, it's still unbearably beautiful sometimes, but you have your work, and your life goes on. You know?"

"Yes," Campbell said. "I know exactly what you mean."

■ ■ ■

She let Campbell walk her home. Her loneliness and vulnerability were like a heavy perfume, so strong it repelled him at the same time that it pulled him irresistibly toward her.

She stopped at the doorway of her cabin, another geodesic, but this one sat high on the hill, buried in a grove of palms and bougainvilleas. The sexual tension was so strong that Campbell could feel his shirtfront trembling.

"Thank you," she said, her voice rough. "You're very easy to talk to."

He could have turned away then, but he couldn't seem to unravel himself. He put his arms around her, and her mouth bumped against his, awkwardly. Then her lips began to move and her tongue flicked out eagerly. She tumbled the door open without moving away from him, and they nearly fell into the house.

■ ■ ■

He pushed himself up on extended arms and watched her moving beneath him. The moonlight through the trees was green and watery, falling in slow waves across the bed. Her breasts swayed heavily as she arched and twisted her back, the breath bubbling in her throat. Her eyes were clenched tight, and her legs wrapped around his and held them, like a long forked tail.

■ ■ ■

Before dawn he slid out from under her limp right arm and got into his clothes. She was still asleep as he let himself out.

He'd meant to go back to his cabin, but instead he found

himself climbing to the top of the island's rocky spine to wait for the sun to come up.

He hadn't even showered. Kimberly's perfume and musk clung to his hands and crotch like sexual stigmata. It was Campbell's first infidelity in eighteen years of marriage, a final, irreversible act.

He knew most of the jargon. Mid-life crisis and all that. He'd probably seen Kimberly at the bar some other night and not consciously remembered her, projected her face onto a fantasy with obvious Freudian water/rebirth connotations.

In the dim, fractionated light of the sunrise, the lagoon was gray, the line of the barrier reef a darker smudge broken by whitecaps that curved like scales on the skin of the ocean. Dry palm fronds rustled in the breeze, and the island birds began to chirp and stutter themselves awake. A shadow broke from one of the huts on the beach below and climbed toward the road, weighted down with a large suitcase and a flight bag. Above her, in the asphalt lot at the top of the stairs, a taxi coasted silently to a stop and doused its lights.

If he had run, he could have reached her and maybe could even have stopped her, but the hazy impulse never became strong enough to reach his legs. Instead, he sat until the sun was hot on his neck and his eyes were dazzled into blindness by the white sand and water.

■　■　■

On the north side of the island, facing the mainland, the village of Espejo sprawled in the mud for the use of the resort and the company. A dirt track ran down the middle of it, oily water standing in the ruts. The cinder-block houses on concrete piers and the Fords rusting in the yards reminded Campbell of an American suburb in the fifties, warped by nightmare.

The locals who worked in the company's kitchens and swept the company's floors lived here, and their kids scuffled in alleys that smelled of rotting fish or lay in the shade and threw rocks at three-legged dogs. An old woman sold Saint Francis flour-sack shirts from ropes tied between pilings of her house. Under an awning of corrugated green plastic, bananas lay in heaps and flies swarmed over haunches of beef. And next door was a *farmacia* with a faded yellow Kodak sign that promised *One Day Service*.

Campbell blinked and found his way to the back, where a ten- or eleven-year-old boy was reading *La Novela Policíaca*. The boy set the comic on the counter and said, "Yes, sir?"

"How soon can you develop these?" Campbell asked, shoving the cartridge toward him.

"*¿Mande?*"

Campbell gripped the edge of the counter. "Ready today?" he asked slowly.

"Tomorrow. This time."

Campbell took a twenty out of his wallet and held it face down on the scarred wood. "This afternoon?"

"*Momentito.*" The boy tapped something out on a computer terminal at his right hand. The dry clatter of the keys filled Campbell with distaste. "Tonight, okay?" the boy said. "*A las seis.*" He touched the dial of his watch and said, "Six."

"All right," Campbell said. For another five dollars he bought a pint of Canadian Club, and then he went back onto the street. He felt like a sheet of weakly colored glass, as if the sun shone clear through him. He was a fool, of course, to be taking this kind of chance with the film, but he needed that picture.

He had to know.

■ ■ ■

He anchored the boat as close as possible to where it had been the night before. He had two fresh tanks and about half the bottle of whiskey left.

Diving drunk and alone was against every rule anyone had ever tried to teach him, but the idea of a simple, clean death by drowning seemed ludicrous to Campbell, not even worth consideration.

His diving jeans and sweatshirt, still damp and salty from the night before, were suffocating him. He got into his tank as quickly as he could and rolled over the side.

The cool water revived him, washed him clean. He purged the air from his vest and dropped straight to the bottom. Dulled by whiskey and lack of sleep, he floundered for a moment in the sand before he could get his buoyancy neutralized.

At the edge of the drop-off he hesitated, then swam to his right, following the edge of the cliff. From his physical condition, he was burning air faster than he wanted to; going deeper would only make it worse.

The bright red of a Coke can winked at him from a coral head. He crushed it and stuck it in his belt, suddenly furious with the company and its casual rape of the island, with himself for letting them manipulate him, with Beth for leaving him, with the entire world and the human race. He kicked hard, driving himself through swarms of jack and blue tang, hardly noticing the twisted, brilliantly colored landscape that moved beneath him.

Some of the drunkenness burned off in the first burst of energy, and he gradually slowed, wondering what he possibly could hope to accomplish. It was useless, he thought. He was chasing a phantom. But he didn't turn back.

He was still swimming when he hit the net.

It was nearly invisible, a web of monofilament in one-foot squares, strong enough to hold a shark or a school of porpoises. He tested it with the serrated edge of his diver's knife, with no luck.

He was close to the west end of the island, where the company kept their research facility. The net followed the line of the reef as far down as he could see and extended out into the open water.

She was real, he thought. They built this to keep her in. But how did she get past it?

When he'd last seen her she'd been heading down. Campbell checked his seaview gauge, saw that he had less than five hundred pounds of air left. Enough to take him down to a hundred feet or so and right back up. The sensible thing to do was to return to the boat and bring a fresh tank back with him.

He went down anyway.

He could see the fine wires glinting as he swam past them. They seemed bonded to the coral itself, by some process he could not even imagine. He kept his eyes moving between the depth gauge and the edge of the net. Much deeper than a hundred feet and he would have to worry about decompression as well as an empty tank.

At 100 feet he tripped his reserve lever. Three hundred

pounds and counting. All the reds had disappeared from the coral, leaving only blues and purples. The water was noticeably darker, colder, and each breath seemed to roar into his lungs like a geyser. Ten more feet, he told himself, and at 125 he saw the rip in the net.

He snagged his backpack on the monofilament and had to back off and try again, fighting panic. He could already feel the constriction in his lungs again, as if he were trying to breathe with a sheet of plastic over his mouth. He'd seen tanks that had been sucked so dry that the sides caved in. They found them on divers trapped in rock slides and tangled in fishing line.

His tank slipped free and he was through, following his bubbles upward. The tiny knot of air in his lungs expanded as the pressure around him let up, but not enough to kill his need to breathe. He pulled the last of the air out of the tank and forced himself to keep exhaling, forcing the nitrogen out of his tissues.

At fifty feet he slowed and angled toward a wall of coral, turned the corner, and swam into a sheltered lagoon.

For a few endless seconds he forgot that he had no air.

The entire floor of the lagoon was laid out in squares of greenery—kelp, mosses, and something that looked like giant cabbage. A school of red snappers circled past him, herded by a metal box with a blinking light on the end of one long antenna. Submarines with spindly mechanical arms worked on the ocean floor, thinning the vegetation and darkening the water with chemicals. Two or three dolphins were swimming side by side with human divers, and they seemed to be talking to each other.

His lungs straining, Campbell turned his back on them and kicked for the surface, trying to stay as close to the rocks as he could. He wanted to stop for a minute at ten feet, to give at least a nod to decompression, but it wasn't possible. His air was gone.

He broke the surface less than a hundred feet from a concrete dock. Behind him was a row of marker buoys that traced the line of the net all the way out to sea and around the far side of the lagoon.

The dock lay deserted and steaming in the sun. Without a fresh tank, Campbell had no chance of getting out the way he'd come in; if he tried to swim out on the surface, he'd be as conspicuous as a drowning man. He had to find another tank or another way out.

Hiding his gear under a sheet of plastic, he crossed the hot concrete slab to the building behind it, a wide, low warehouse full of wooden crates. A rack of diving gear was built into the left-hand wall, and Campbell was just starting for it when he heard a voice behind him.

"Hey, you! Hold it!"

Campbell ducked behind a wall of crates, saw a tiled hallway opening into the back of the building, and ran for it. He didn't get more than three or four steps before a uniformed guard stepped out and pointed a .38 at his chest.

■ ■ ■

"You can leave him with me."

"Are you sure, Dr. Kimberly?"

"I'll be all right," she said. "I'll call you if there's any trouble."

Campbell collapsed in a plastic chair across from her desk. The office was strictly functional, waterproof, and mildew-resistant. A long window behind Kimberly's head showed the lagoon and the row of marker buoys.

"How much did you see?" she asked.

"I don't know. I saw what looked like farms. Some machinery."

She slid a photograph across the desk to him. It showed a creature with a woman's breasts and the tail of a fish. The face was close enough to Kimberly's to be her sister.

Or her clone's.

Campbell suddenly realized the amount of trouble he was in.

"The boy at the *farmacia* works for us," Kimberly said.

Campbell nodded. Of course he did. Where else would he get a computer? "You can have the picture," Campbell said, blinking the sweat out of his eyes. "And the negative."

"Let's be realistic," she said, tapping the keys of her CRT and studying the screen. "Even if we let you keep your job, I don't see how we could hold your marriage together. And then you have two kids to put through college. . . ." She shook her head. "Your brain is full of hot information. There are too many people who would pay to have it, and there're just too many ways you can be manipulated. You're not much of a risk, *Mister* Campbell." She radiated hurt and betrayal, and he wanted to slink away from her in shame.

She got up and looked out the window. "We're building the future here," she said. "A future we couldn't even imagine fifteen years ago. And that's just too valuable to let one person screw up. Plentiful food, cheap energy, access to a computer net for the price of a TV set, a whole new form of government—"

"I've seen your future," Campbell said. "Your boats have killed the reef for over a mile around the hotel. Your Coke cans are lying all over the coral bed. Your marriages don't last and your kids are on drugs and your TV is garbage. I'll pass."

"Did you see that boy in the drugstore? He's learning calculus on that computer, and his parents can't even read and write. We're testing a vaccine on human subjects that will probably cure leukemia. We've got laser surgery and transplant techniques that are revolutionary. Literally."

"Is that where *she* came from?" Campbell asked, pointing to the photograph.

Kimberly's voice dropped. "It's synergistic, don't you see? To do the transplants we had to be able to clone cells from the donor. To clone cells we had to have laser manipulation of the genes. . . ."

"They cloned your cells? Just for practice?"

She nodded slowly. "Something happened. She grew, but she stopped developing, kept her embryonic form from the waist down. There was nothing we could do except . . . make the best of it."

Campbell took a longer look at the picture. No, not the romantic myth he had first imagined. The tail was waxy-looking in the harsh light of the strobe, the fins more clearly undeveloped legs. He stared at the photo in queasy fascination. "You could have let her die."

"No. She was mine. I don't have much, and I wouldn't give her up." Kimberly's fists clenched at her sides. "She's not unhappy, she knows who I am. In her own way I suppose she cares for me." She paused, looking at the floor. "I'm a lonely woman, Campbell. But of course you know that."

Campbell's throat was dry. "What about me?" he rasped, and managed to swallow. "Am I going to die?"

"No," she said. "Not you, either. . . ."

■ ■ ■

Campbell swam for the fence. His memories were cloudy and he had trouble focusing his thoughts, but he could visualize the gap in the net and the open ocean beyond it. He kicked down easily to 120 feet, the water cool and comforting on his naked skin. Then he was through, drifting gently away from the noise and stink of the island, toward some primal vision of peace and timelessness.

His gills rippled smoothly as he swam.

Freezone

■

John Shirley has often been first to tread frontiers that later became well-trampled cyberpunk turf. As a rock performer, he was heavily involved in the first virulent outbreak of punk on the West Coast. A prolific writer whose work includes such novels as *City Come A-Walkin'*, *The Brigade*, and the horror extravaganza *Cellars*, Shirley is well known for his soaring, surreal imagery and bursts of extreme visionary intensity.

"Freezone" is an independent excerpt from Shirley's latest project, the *Eclipse* trilogy. Global in scope, *Eclipse* narrates a dizzying near-future where pop, politics, and paranoia collide in a high-tech struggle for survival. Always a pioneer, with a wide-ranging underground influence, Shirley's use of global issues may well portend a new upsurge of radical politics in SF.

John Shirley currently lives in Los Angeles and performs with his band.

Freezone floated in the Atlantic Ocean, a city afloat in the wash of international cultural confluence.

Freezone was anchored about a hundred miles north of Sidi Ifni, a drowsy city on the coast of Morocco, in a warm, gentle current, and in a sector of the sea only rarely troubled by large storms. What storms arose here spent their fury on the maze of concrete wave baffles Freezone Admin had spent years building up around the artificial island.

Originally, Freezone had been just another offshore drilling project. The massive oil deposit a quarter mile below the artificial island was still less than a quarter tapped out. The drilling platform was owned jointly by the Moroccan government and a Texas-based petroleum and electronic products company, Texcorp. The company that bought Disneyland and Disneyworld and Disneyworld II—all three of which had closed in the wake of the CSD: the Computer Storage Depression. Also called the Dissolve Depression.

A group of Arab terrorists—at least, the US State Department claimed that's who did it—had arranged a well-placed electromagnetic pulse from a small hydrogen bomb hidden aboard a routine orbital shuttle. The shuttle was vaporized in the blast, as well as two satellites, one of them manned; but when the CSD hit, no one took time to mourn the dead.

The orbital bomb had almost triggered Armageddon: three Cruise missiles had to be aborted, and fortunately two more were shot down by the Soviets before the terrorist cell took credit for the upper-atmosphere blast. Most of the bomb's blast had been directed upward; what came downward, though, was the side effect of the blast: the EMP. An electromagnetic pulse that—just as had been predicted in the 1970s—traveled through thousands of miles of wires and circuitry on the continent below the H-blast. The Defense Department was shielded; the banking system, for the most part, was not. The pulse wiped out 93 percent of the newly formed American Banking Credit Adjustment Bureau. ABCAB had handled 76 percent of the nation's buying and credit transferral. Most of what was bought, was bought through ABCAB or ABCAB-related companies . . . until the EMP wiped out ABCAB's memory storage, the pulse overburdening the circuits, melting them, and literally frying the data storage chips. And thereby kicking the crutches out from under the American economy. Hundreds of thousands of bank accounts were "suspended" until records could be restored—causing a run on the remaining banks. The insurance companies and the federal guarantee programs were overwhelmed. They just couldn't cover the loss.

The States had already been in trouble. The nation had lost its economic initiative in the 1980s and 1990s: its undereducated and badly trained workers, its corrupt, greedy unions, and its lower manufacturing standards made US industry unable to compete with the Asian and South American manufacturing booms. The EMP credit dissolve kicked the nation over the rim of recession into the pit of depression. And made the rest of the world laugh. The Arab terrorist cell responsible—hard-core Islamic Fundamentalists—had been composed of seven men. Seven men who crippled a nation.

But America still had its enormous military spread, its electronics and medical innovators. And the war economy kept it humming. Like a man with cancer taking amphetamines for a last burst of strength. While the endless malls and housing projects, built cheaply and in need of constant upkeep, got shabbier, uglier, and trashier by the day. And more dangerous.

The States just weren't safe for the rich any more. The resorts, the amusement parks, the exclusive affluent neighborhoods all crumbled under the attrition of perennial strikes and persistent terrorist attacks. The swelling mass of the poor—growing since the 1980s—resented the recreations of the rich. And the middle-class buffer was shrinking to insignificance.

There were still enclaves in the States where you could get lost in the media churn, hypnotized by the flashcards of desire into a TV-trance version of the American Dream as ten thousand companies vied for your attention, begged you to buy and keep buying. Places that were walled city-states of middle-class illusions.

But the affluent could feel the crumbling of their kingdom. They didn't feel safe in the States. They needed someplace outside, somewhere controlled. Europe was out now; Central and South America too risky. The Pacific theater was another war zone.

So that's where Freezone came in.

A Texas entrepreneur—who hadn't had his money in AB-CAB—saw the possibilities in the community that had grown up around the enormous complex of offshore drilling platforms. A paste-jewel necklace of brothels and arcades and cabarets had crystalized on derelict ships permanently anchored around the platforms. Two hundred hookers and three hundred casino dealers worked the international melange of men who worked the oil rigs. The entrepreneur made a deal with the Moroccan government. He bought the rusting hulks and the shanty nightclubs. And he fired everyone.

The Texan owned a plastics company; the company had developed a light, super-tough plastic that the entrepreneur used in the rafts on which the new floating city was built. The community was now seventeen square miles of urban raft, protected with one of the meanest security forces in the world. Freezone dealt in pleasant distractions for the rich in the ex-

clusive section and—in the second-string places around the
edge—for technickis from the drill rigs. The second-string
places also sheltered a few semi-illicit hangers-on and a few
hundred performers.

Like Rickenharp.

■ ■ ■

Rick Rickenharp stood against the south wall of the Semiconductor, letting the club's glare and blare wash over him and
mentally writing a song. The song went something like, "Glar-
ing blare, lightning stare/Nostalgia for the electric chair."

Then he thought, Fucking drivel.

And he was doing his best to look cool but vulnerable, hoping
one of the females flashing through the crowd would remember
having seen him in the band the night before, would try to chat
him up, play groupie. But they were mostly into wire dancers.

And *no fucking way* Rickenharp was going to wire into
minimono.

Rickenharp was a rock classicist. He wore a black leather
motorcycle jacket that was some fifty-five years old, said to have
been worn by John Cale when he was still in the Velvet Underground. The seams were beginning to pop; three studs were
missing from the chrome trimming. The elbows and collar
edges were worn through the black dye to the brown animal the
leather had come from. But the leather was second skin to
Rickenharp. He wore nothing under it. His bony, hairless chest
showed translucent blue-white beneath the broken zippers. He
wore blue jeans that were only ten years old but looked older
than the coat; he wore genuine Harley Davidson boots. Earrings
clustered up and down his long, slightly too prominent ears, and
his rusty brown hair looked like a cannon-shell explosion.

And he wore dark glasses.

And he did all this because it was gratingly unfashionable.

His band hassled him about it. They wanted their lead-git
and frontman minimono.

"If we're gonna go minimono, we oughta just sell the fucking guitars and go wires," Rickenharp had told them.

And the drummer had been stupid and tactless enough to
say, "Well, fuck, man, maybe we *should* go to wires."

Rickenharp had said, "Maybe we should get a fucking drum

machine too, you fucking Neanderthal!" and kicked the drum seat over, sending Murch into the cymbals with a fine crashing, so that Rickenharp added, "You should get that good a sound outta those cymbals on stage. Now we know how to do it."

Murch had started to throw his sticks at him, but then he'd remembered how you had to have them lathed up special because they didn't make them any more, so he'd said, "Suck my ass, bigshot!" and got up and walked out, not for the first time. But that was the first time it meant anything, and only some heavy ambassadorial action on the part of Ponce had kept Murch from leaving the band.

The call from their agent had set the whole thing off. That's what it really was. Agency was streamlining its repertoire. Rickenharp was out. The last two LP's hadn't sold, and in fact the engineers claimed that live drums didn't record well on the miniaturized soundcaps that passed for records now. Rickenharp's holovid and the videos weren't getting airplay.

Anyway, Vid-Co was probably going out of business. Another business sucked into the black hole of the depression. "So it ain't our fault the stuff's not selling," Rickenharp said. "We got fans but we can't get the distribution to reach 'em."

José had said, "Bullshit, we're out of the Grid and you know it. All that was carrying us was the nostalgia wave anyway. You can't get more'n two hits out of a revival, man."

Julio the bassist had said something in technicki jargon that Rickenharp hadn't bothered to translate because it was so stupid—he'd suggested they hire a wiredancer for a frontman—and when Rickenharp had ignored him he'd gotten pissed and it was *his* turn to walk out. Fucking touchy technickis anyway.

And now the band was in abeyance. Their train was stopped between stations. They had a gig opening for a wire act and Rickenharp didn't want to do it, but they had a contract and there were a lot of rock nostalgia freaks on Freezone, so maybe that was their audience anyway and he owed it to them. Blow the goddamn wires off the stage.

He looked around the Semiconductor and wished the Retro-Club was still open. There'd been a strong retro presence at the RC, even some rockabillies, and some of the rockabillies actually knew what rockabilly sounded like. The Semiconductor was a minimono scene.

The minimono crowd wore their hair long, fanned out between the shoulders and narrowing to a point at the crown of the head, and straight, absolutely straight, stiff, so from the back each head had a black or gray or red or white tepee-shape. Those, in monochrome, were the only acceptable colors. Flat tones and no streaks. Their clothes were stylistic extensions of their hairstyles. Minimono was a reaction to flare. And to the chaos of the war, and the war economy, and the amorphous shifting of the Grid. The flare style was going, dying.

Rickenharp had always been contemptuous of the trendy flares, but he preferred them to minimono. Flare had energy, anyway.

Flare had grown up out of the teased-up, anticontrol styles popular in the last part of the twentieth century. A flare was expected to wear his hair *up*, as far over the top of his head as possible and in some way that *expressed*, that emphasized the wearer's individuality, originality. The more colors the better. You weren't "an individual" unless you had an expressive flare. Screw shapes, hooks, aureolas, layered multicolored snarls. Fortunes were made in flare hair-shaping shops and lost when it began to go out of fashion. But it had lasted longer than most fashions; it had endless variation and the appeal of its energy to sustain it. A lot of people copped out of the necessity of inventing individual expression by adopting a politically standard flare. Shape your hair like the insignia for your favorite downtrodden third-world country (back when they were downtrodden, before the new marketing axis). Flares were so much trouble most people took to having flare wigs prepared to wear when they went out. And their drugs were styled to fit the fashion. Excitative neurotransmitters of all kinds—antidepressants, drugs that made you seem to glow. The wealthier flares had nimbus belts, creating artificial auroras. The hipper flares considered this to be tastelessly narcissistic, which was a joke to nonflares, since all flares were floridly vain.

Rickenharp had never colored or shaped his hair, except to encourage its punk spikiness.

But Rickenharp wasn't a punk. He identified with prepunk, late 1950s, mid-1960s, early 1970s. Rickenharp was an anachronism. He was simply a hard-core rocker, as out of place in the

Semiconductor as bebop would have been in the 1980s dance clubs.

Rickenharp looked around at the flat-black, flat-gray, monochrome tunics and jumpsuits, the black wristfones, the cookie-cutter sameness; at the uniform tans and ubiquitous FirStep Colony-shaped earrings (only one, always in the left ear). The high-tech-fetishist minimonos were said to aspire toward a place in the orbiting space Colony the way Rastas had dreamed of a return to Ethiopia. Rickenharp thought it was funny that the Soviets had blockaded the Colony. Funny to see the normally dronelike, antiflamboyant minimonos quietly simmering on ampheticool, standing in tense groups, hissing about the Soviets, in why-doesn't-somebody-do-something outrage.

The stultifying regularity of their canned music banged from the wall and pulsed from the floor. Lean against the wall and you felt a drill-bit vibration of it in your spine.

There were a few hardy, defiant flares here, and flares were Rickenharp's best hope for getting laid. They tended to respect old rock.

The music ceased; a voice boomed "Joel NewHope!" and spots lit the stage. The first wire act had come on. Rickenharp glanced at his watch. It was ten. He was due to open for the headline act at eleven thirty. Rickenharp pictured the club emptying as he hit the stage. He wasn't long for this club. But maybe enough variant crowd would show. Fringe scenes can add up.

NewHope hit the stage. A wire act. He was anorexic and surgically sexless: radical minimono. A fact advertised by his nudity: he wore only gray and black spray-on sheathing. How did the guy piss? Rickenharp wondered. Maybe it was out of that faint crease at his crotch. A dancing mannequin. His sexuality was clipped to the back of his head: a single chrome electrode that activated the pleasure center of the brain during the weekly legally controlled catharsis. But he was so skinny— hey, who knows, maybe he went to a black-market cerebrostim to interface with the pulser. Though minimonos were supposed to be into stringent law-and-order.

The wires jacked into NewHope's arms and legs and torso fed to impulse-translation pickups on the stage floor, making him look like a puppet with its strings inverted. But he was the puppeteer. The long, funereal wails pealing from hidden speakers were triggered by the muscular contractions of his arms and legs and torso. He wasn't bad for a minimono, Rickenharp thought condescendingly. You could make out the melody, the tune shaped by his dancing, and it had a shade more complexity than the M'n'Ms usually had. . . . The M'n'M crowd moved into their geometrical dance configurations, somewhere between disco dancing and square dance, Busby Berkeley kaleidoscopings worked out according to formulas you were simply expected to know if you had the nerve to participate. Try to dance freestyle in their interlocking choreography, and sheer social rejection, on the wings of body language, would hit you like an arctic wind.

Sometimes Rickenharp did an acid dance in the midst of the minimono configuration, just for the hell of it, just to revel in their rejection. But the band had made him stop that. Don't alienate the audience at our only gig, man. Probably our *last* fucking gig. . . .

The wiredancer rippled out bagpipelike riffs over the taped rhythm section. The walls came alive.

A good rock club—in 1965 or 1975 or 1985 or 1995 or 2020—should be narrow, dark, close, claustrophobic. The walls should either be starkly monochrome—all black and mirrored, say—or deliberately garish. Camp, layered with whatever was the contemporary avant-garde or gaudy graffiti.

The Semiconductor showed both sides. It started out butch, its walls glassy black; during the concert it went in gaudy drag as the sound-sensitive walls reacted to the music with color streaking, wavelengthing in oscilloscope patterns, shades of blue-white for high end, red and purple for bass and percussion. Reacting vividly, hypnotically, to each note. The minimonos disliked reactive walls. They called it kitschy and "vid."

The dancer spazzed the stage, and Rickenharp grudgingly watched, trying to be fair. Thinking, It's another kind of rock 'n' roll, is all. Like a Christian watching a Buddhist ceremony— telling himself, "Oh well, it's all manifestations of the One God in the end." . . . Rickenharp thinking,: But real rock is better. *Real rock is coming back,* he'd tell almost anyone who'd listen. Almost no one would.

A chaoticist came in, and he watched her, feeling less alone.

Chaoticists were much closer to real rockers. She was a skinhead, with the sides of her head painted. Skirt made of at least two hundred rags of synthetic material sewn to her leather belt—a sort of grass skirt of bright rags. Bare breasts, nipples pierced with thin screws. The minimonos looked at her in disgust; they were prudish, and calling attention to one's breasts was decidedly gauche with the M'n'Ms. She smiled sunnily back at them. Her handsome Semitic features were slashed randomly with paint. Her makeup looked like a spin painting. Her teeth were filed.

Rickenharp swallowed hard, looking at her. Damn, she was *his type*.

Only . . . only she wore a blue mesc sniffer. The sniffer's inverted question mark ran from its hook at her right ear to just under her right nostril. Now and then she tilted her head to it and sniffed a little blue powder.

Rickenharp had to look away. Silently cursing.

He'd written a song called "Trying to Stay Clean."

Blue mesc. Or syncoke. Or heroin. Or amphetamorphine. Or XT2. But mostly he went for blue mesc. And blue mesc was addictive. And it was sooooo *good*.

Blue mesc, also called boss blue. It was all the best effects of mescaline and cocaine together, framed in the gelatinous sweetness of Quaaludes. But, unlike coke, not much crash. Only . . . only stop taking it after a period of steady use and the world drained of meaning for you. There was no actual withdrawal sickness. There was only a deeply resonant depression, a sense of worthlessness that seemed to settle like dust and maggot dung into each individual cell of the user's body. Not the same as a coke crash, but . . .

But some people called blue mesc "the suicide ticket."

It could make you feel like a coal miner when the mine shaft caved in; like you were buried in yourself.

Rickenharp had pulled therapy, paid for by his parents—he'd squandered the money from his only major hit on boss blue and dope. He'd just barely made it clean. And lately, at least before the band squabbles, he'd begun feeling like life was worth living again.

Watching the girl with the sniffer walk past, watching her use, Rickenharp felt stricken, lost, as if he'd seen something to remind him of a lost lover. An ex-user's syndrome. Pain from the guilt of having jilted your drug.

And he could imagine the sweet burn of the stuff in his nostrils, the backward-sweet pharmaceutical taste of it in the back of your palate; or, if you banged it, the explosion of pure fluorescent confidence, confidence you could feel somatically, the way you'd feel a woman's lips on your cock. The autoerotic feedback loop of blue mesc. Imagining it, he had a shadow of the sensation, a tantalizing ghost of the rush. In memory he could taste it, smell it, feel it. . . . Seeing her *use* brought back a hundred iridescent memories. An almost irrepressible longing. (While some small voice in the back of his head tried to get his attention, tried to warn him, *Hey, remember the shit makes you want to kill yourself when you run out; remember it makes you stupidly overconfident and boorish; remember it eats your internal organs* . . . a small, dwindling voice. . . .)

The girl was looking at him. A flicker of invitation in her eyes.

He wavered.

The small voice got louder.

Told him, *Rickenharp if you go to her, go with her, you'll end up using.*

He turned away with an anguished internal wrenching. Stumbled through the wash of sound and lights and monochrome people to the dressing room. To guitar and earphones and the safer, sonic world.

■ ■ ■

Rickenharp was listening to a collector's-item Velvet Underground tape from 1968. It was capped into his Earmite. The song was "White Light/White Heat." The guitarists were doing things that would make Baron Frankenstein say, "There are some things man was not meant to know." He screwed the Earmite a little deeper so that the vibrations would shiver the bone around his ear, chills that lapped through him in harmony with the guitar chords. He'd picked a visorclip to go with the music: a documentary on expressionist painters. Listening to the Velvets and looking at Edvard Munch. Man!

And then Julio dug a finger into his shoulder.

"Happiness is transient," Rickenharp muttered, as he flipped the visorclip back. The visor looked like the strap-and-mirror affairs doctors once wore, only the screen that snapped down over the eyes was rectangular, like a rearview mirror. Some visors came with a clip-on camera eye and fieldstim. The fieldstim you wore over your back, snugged to the skin, as if it were a sheer corset. The camera picked up an image of the street you were walking down and routed it to the fieldstim, which tickled your back in the pattern of whatever the camera saw. Some part of your mind assembled a rough image of the street out of that. Developed for blind people in the 1980s. Now used by viddy addicts who walked or drove the streets wearing visors, watching TV, reflexively navigating by using the fieldstim, their eyes blocked off by the screen but never quite bumping into anyone. But Rickenharp didn't use a fieldstim.

So he had to look at Julio with his own eyes. "What you want?"

" 'N ten," Julio slurred. Julio the technicki bassist. In ten. They went on in ten minutes.

José, Ponce, Julio, Murch: Rhythm guitar and backup vocals, Keyboards, Bass, Drums.

Rickenharp nodded and reached up to flip the visor back into place, but Ponce flicked the switch on the visor's headset. The visor image shrank like a landscape vanishing down a tunnel behind a train, and Rickenharp felt as if his stomach were shrinking inside him at the same rate. He knew what was coming down. "Okay," he said, turning to look at them. "*What?*"

They were in the dressing room. The walls were black with graffiti. All rock club dressing rooms will always be black with graffiti. Flayed with it, scourged with it. Like the flat declaration THE PARASITES RULE, the cheerful petulance of SYMBIOSIS 666 GOT FUCKING BORED HERE, the oblique existentialism of THE ALKOLOID BROTHERS LOVE YOU ALL BUT THINK YOU WOULD BE BETTER OFF DEAD, and the enigmatic ones like SYNC 66 CLICKS NOW. It looked like the patterning of badly wrinkled wallpaper. It was in layers. It was a palimpsest. Hallucinatory stylization as if tracing the electron firings of the visual cortex.

The walls, in the few places they were visible under the graffiti, were a gray-painted pressboard. There was just enough room for Rickenharp's band, sitting around on broken-backed kitchen chairs and one desk chair with three legs. Crowded between the chairs were the instruments in their cases. The edges of the cases were frayed, the false leather peeling. Half the snaps broken.

Rickenharp looked at the band, looked clockwise from one face to the next, taking a poll from their expressions: José on his left, a bruised look to his eyes, the rings under his eyes compositionally harmonious with his double handful of earrings; his hair a triple mohawk, the center spine red, the outer two white and blue; a smoky crystal ring on his left index finger that matched—he knew it matched—his smoky crystal amber eyes. Rickenharp and José had been close. Each looked at the other a little accusingly. There was a lovers' sulkiness between them, though they'd never been lovers. José was hurt because Rickenharp didn't want to make the transition: Rickenharp was putting his own taste in music before the survival of the band. Rickenharp was hurt because José wanted to go minimono wire act, a betrayal of the spiritual ethos of the band; and because José was willing to sacrifice Rickenharp. Replace him with a wire dancer. They both knew it, though it had never been said. Most of what passed between them was semiotically transmitted with the studied indirection of the terminally cool. Now, José looked bad news. His head was tilted as if his neck were broken. His eyes lusterless.

Ponce had gone minimono, at least in his look, and they'd had a ferocious fight over that. Ponce was slender and fox-faced, and now he was battleship gray from head to toe, including hair and skin tint. In the smoky atmosphere of the club he sometimes vanished completely.

He wore silver contact lenses. He stared at a ten-slivered funhouse reflection in his mirrored fingernails. Flat-out glum.

Julio, yeah, he liked to give Rickenharp shit, and he wanted the change. Sure, he was loyal to Rickenharp, up to a point. But he was also a conformist. He'd argue for Rickenharp maybe, but he'd go with the consensus. Julio had lush curly black Puerto Rican hair piled prowlike over his head. He had a woman's profile and a woman's long-lashed eyes. He had a silver-stud earring, and he wore classic retro-rock black leather like Rickenharp. He twisted the skull ring on his thumb, returning a scowl for its grin, staring at it as if deeply worried that one of its fake-ruby red glass eyes was about to come out.

Murch was a thick slug of a guy with a glass crew cut. He was a mediocre drummer, but he was a drummer, a species of musician almost extinct. "Murch's rare as a dodo," Rickenharp said once, "and that's not all he's got in common with a dodo." Murch wore horn-rimmed dark glasses, and there was a bottle of Southern Comfort on his knee. The Southern Comfort was part of his outfit. It went with his cowboy boots. So he thought.

Murch was looking at Rickenharp in open contempt. He didn't have the brains to dissemble.

"Fuck you, Murch," Rickenharp said.

"Whuh? I didn't say nothing."

"You don't have to. I can smell your thoughts. Enough to gag a faggot maggot." Rickenharp stood and looked at the others. "I know what's on your mind. Give me this: one last good gig. After that you can have it how you want."

Tension lifted its wings and flew away.

Another bird settled over the room. Rickenharp saw it in his mind's eye: a thunderbird. Half made of an Indian tepee painting of a thunderbird, and half of chrome T-bird parts. When it spread its wings the pinfeathers glistened like polished bumpers. There were two headlights on its chest, and when the band picked up their instruments to go out to the stage, the headlights switched on.

Rickenharp carried his Stratocaster in its black case. The case was bandaged with duct tape and peeling with faded stickers. But the Strat was spotless. It was transparent. Its lines curved hot like a sports car.

They walked down a white plastibrick corridor toward the stage. The corridor narrowed after the first turn, so they had to walk sideways, holding the instruments out in front of them. Space was precious on Freezone.

The stagehand saw Murch go out first, and he signaled the DJ, who cut the tape and announced the band through the PA. Old-fashioned, like Rickenharp requested: "Please welcome . . . *Rickenharp.*"

There was no answering roar from the crowd. There were a few catcalls and a smattering of applause.

Good, you bitch, fight me, Rickenharp thought, waiting for the band to take up their positions. He'd go on stage last. After they'd set up the spot for him. Always.

Rickenharp squinted from the wings to see past the glare of lights into the dark snakepit of the audience. Only about half minimono now. That was good; that gave him a chance to put this one over.

The band took its place. Pressed their automatic tuners, fiddled with dials.

Rickenharp was pleasantly surprised to see that the stage was lit with soft red floods, which was what he'd requested. Maybe the lighting director was one of his fans. Maybe the band wouldn't fuck this one up. Maybe everything would fall into place. Maybe the lock on the cage door would tumble into the right combination, the cage door would open, the T-Bird would fly.

He could hear some of the audience whispering about Murch. Most of them had never seen a live drummer before, except for salsa. Rickenharp caught a scrap of technicki jargon: "*Whuzziemack wizzut?*" What's he make with that? meaning, What are those things he's adjusting? The drums.

Rickenharp took the Strat out of its case and strapped it on. He adjusted the strap. He pressed the tuner. He didn't need to plug in; when he walked onto the stage, the amp's reception field would trigger, transmit the Strat's signal to the stack of Marshalls behind the drummer. A shame, in a way, about miniaturization of electronics: the amps were small, though just as loud as twentieth-century amps and speakers. But they looked less imposing. The audience was muttering about the Marshalls, too. Most of them hadn't seen old-fashioned amps. "What're those for?"

Murch looked at Rickenharp. Rickenharp nodded.

Murch thudded ¼, alone for a moment. Then the bass took it up, laid down a sonic stratum that was kind of off-center strutting. And the keyboards laid down the sheets of infinity.

Now he could walk on stage. It was like there'd been an abyss between Rickenharp and the stage, and the bass and drum and keyboards working together made a bridge to cross the abyss. He walked over the bridge and into the warmth of the floods. He could feel the heat of the lights on his skin. It was like stepping from an air-conditioned room into the tropics. The music suffered deliciously in a tropical lushness. The pure white spotlight caught and held him, focusing on his guitar, as per his directions, and he thought, Good, the lighting guy really is with me.

He felt as if he could feel what the guitar felt. The guitar ached to be touched.

■ ■ ■

Without consciously knowing it, Rickenharp was moving to the music. Not too much. Not in the pushy, look-at-me way that some performers had. The way they had of trying to *force* enthusiasm from the audience, every move looking artificial.

No, Rickenharp was a natural. The music flowed through him physically, unimpeded by anxieties or ego knots. His ego was there; it was the fuel for his personal Olympian torch. But it was as immaculate as a pontiff's robes.

The band sensed it. Rickenharp was in rare form tonight. Because he was freed. The tensions were gone because he knew it was the end of the line: The band had received its death sentence. Now, Rickenharp was as unafraid as a true suicide. He had the courage of despair.

The band sensed it and let it happen. The chemistry was there, this time, when Ponce and José came into the verse section, José with a sinuous riffing picked low, almost on the chrome plate that clamped the strings, Ponce with a magnificently redundant theme washed through the brass mode of the synthesizer. The whole band felt the chemistry like a pleasing electric shock, the pleasurable shock of individual egos becoming a group ego. Something beyond sexual pleasure.

The audience was listening, but they were resisting. They didn't want to like it. Still, the place was crowded—because of the club's rep, not because of Rickenharp—and all those packed-in bodies make a kind of sensitive atmospheric exoskeleton, and he knew that made them vulnerable. He knew what to touch.

Feeling the Good Thing begin to happen, Rickenharp looked confident but not quite arrogant. He was too arrogant to show arrogance.

The audience looked at Rickenharp as a man will look at a smug adversary just before a hand-to-hand fight and wonder, Why's he so smug, what does he know?

He knew about timing. And he knew there were feelings

even the most aloof among them couldn't control, once those feelings were released; and he knew how to release them.

Rickenharp hit a chord. He let it shimmer through the room and he looked out at them. He made eye contact.

He liked seeing the defiant stares, because that was going to make his victory more complete.

Because he *knew*. He'd played five gigs with the band in the last two weeks, and for all five gigs the atmosphere had been strained, the chemistry had been there only in spates. Like a Jacob's ladder where the two poles aren't properly lined up for the sparks to jump.

And like a horniness it had built up in them, like sexual energy, dammed behind their private resentments; and now it was pouring through the dam, and the band shook with the release of it as Rickenharp thundered into his progression and began to sing. . . .

The audience stared at him with insistent hostility, but Rickenharp liked it when the girl played pretend-to-rape-me. *Force it into their ears, man.*

The band was fuel-injecting into the combustion chamber of the room; Rickenharp was sparking the combustion, causing the audience to react, to press the piston, and . . . they were racing. Rickenharp was at the wheel. He was taking them somewhere, and each song was a landscape he swept them through. Strumming over the vocals, he sang,

"You want easy overnight action
want it casually
A neat little chain reaction ·
and a little sympathy
You say it's just consolation
In the end it's a compensation
for insecurity
   That way there's no surprises
   That way no one gets hurt
   No moral question tries us
   No blood on satin shirts
   But for me, yeah for me
   PAIN IS EVERYTHING!
   Pain is all there is

Babe take some of mine
or lick some of his
PAIN IS EVERYTHING
Pain is all there is
Pain is EVERYTHING. . . ."

From "An Interview with Rickenharp: The Boy Methuselah," in
Guitar Player Magazine, May 2017.

GPM: Rick, you keep talking about group dynamics, but I have
    a feeling you don't mean dynamics in the usual musical
    sense.

RICKENHARP: The right way to create a band is for the members
    to simply find one another, the way lovers do. In bars or
    whatever. The members of the band are like five chemicals
    that come together with a specific chemical reaction. If the
    chemistry is right, the audience becomes involved in this—
    this kind of—well, a social chemical reaction.

GPM: Could it be that all this is an illusion of your psychology? I
    mean, your need for a really organically whole group?

RICKENHARP (after a long pause): To an extent. It's true I need
    something like that. I need to belong. I mean—okay, I'm a
    "nonconformist," but still, on some level I got a need to
    belong. Maybe rock bands are a surrogate family. The fam-
    ily unit is shot to hell, so . . . the band is my family. I'd do
    anything to keep it together. I need these guys. I'd be like a
    kid whose mom and dad and brothers and sisters were
    killed if I lost this band.

And he sang,

"PAIN IS EVERYTHING
Pain is all there is
Babe take some of mine
Suck some of his
Yeah, said PAIN IS EVERYTHING—"

Singing it insolently, half shouting, half warbling at the end
of each note, with that fuck-you-bitch tone, performing that
magic act, shouting a melody. He could see doors opening in

their faces, even the minimonos, even the neutrals, all the flares, the rebs, the chaoticists, the preps, the retros. Forgetting their subcultural classifications in the organic, orgasmic unification of the music. He was basted in sweat under the lights, he was squeezing sounds with his fingers, and it was as if he could feel the sounds taking shape in his hands the way a sculptor feels clay shaping under his fingers, and it was like there was no gap between his hearing the sound in his head and its coming out of the speakers. His brain, his body, his fingers had closed the gap, was one supercooled circuit breaker fused shut.

Some part of him was looking for the chaoticist trim he'd spotted earlier. He was faintly disappointed when he didn't see her. He told himself, You ought to be happy, you had a narrow escape, she would've got you back into boss blue.

But when he saw her press to the front and nod at him ever so slightly in that smug insider's way, he was simply glad, and he wondered what his subconscious was planning for him. . . . All those thoughts were flickers. Most of the time his conscious mind was completely focused on the sound and on the business of acting out the sound for the audience. He was playing out of sorrow, the sorrow of loss. His family was going to die, and he played tunes that touched the chord of loss, in everyone. . . .

And the band was supernaturally tight. The gestalt was there, uniting them, and he pressed its tongs home into the collective body of the audience and took them where he wanted to take them, and he thought: The band feels good, but it's not going to help when the gig's over.

It was like a divorced couple having a good time in bed but knowing that wouldn't make the marriage right again. In fact, the good time was a function of having given up.

But in the meantime there were fireworks.

By the last tune in the set, the electricity was so thick in the club that—as José had said once, with a rocker's melodrama—"if you could cut it, it would bleed." The dope and smashweed and tobacco smoke moiling the air seemed to conspire with the stage lights to create an atmosphere of magical apartness. With each song-keyed shift in the light, red to blue to white to sulfurous yellow, a corresponding emotional wavelength rippled through the room. The energy built, and Rickenharp discharged it, his Strat the lightning rod.

And then the set ended.

Rickenharp bashed out the last five notes alone, nailing a climax onto the air. Then he walked offstage, hardly hearing the roar from the crowd. He found himself half running down the grimy plastibrick corridor, and then he was in the dressing room and didn't remember getting there. Everything felt more real than usual. His ears were ringing like Quasimodo was getting off in his belfry.

He heard footsteps and turned, working up what he was going to say to the band. But it was the girl chaoticist and someone else, and then a third coming in after the someone else.

The someone else was a skinny guy with brown hair that was naturally messy, not messy as part of one of the cultural subcurrents. His mouth hung a little ajar, and one of his incisors was decayed black. His nose was windburned and the backs of his bony hands were gnarled with veins. The third was Japanese: small, brown-eyed, nondescript, his expression mild, just a shade more friendly than neutral. The skinny Caucasian guy wore an army jacket sans insignia, shiny jeans, and rotting tennis shoes. His hands were nervous, like there was something he was used to holding in them that wasn't there now. An instrument? Maybe.

The Japanese guy wore a Japanese Action Suit, sky-blue and neat as a pin. His hands looked comfortable empty. Only there was a lump on his hip—something he could reach by putting his right arm across his body and through the zipper down the front of the suit—and Rickenharp was pretty sure it was a gun. There was one thing all three of them had in common: they looked half starved.

Rickenharp shivered—his gloss of sweat cooling on him— but forced himself to say, "Whusappnin'?" It was wooden in his mouth. He was looking past them, waiting for the band.

"Band's in the wings," the chaoticist said. "The bass player said, 'Telm getzassoutere.'"

Rickenharp had to smile at her mock of Julio's technicki: Tell him, get his ass out here.

Them some of the druggy feeling washed away and he heard the shouts and he realized they wanted an encore.

"Jeez, an encore," he said without thinking. "Been so fucking long."

"'Ey, mate," the skinny guy said, pronouncing *mate* like *mite*. Brit or Aussie. "Oi sawr you at Stone'enge five years ago when you 'ad your second 'it."

Rickenharp winced a little when the guy said *your second hit,* inadvertently underlining the fact that Rickenharp had had only two, and everyone knew he wasn't likely to have any more.

"I'm Carmen," the chaoticist said. "This is Willow and Yukio."

Yukio was standing sideways from the others, and something about the way he did it told Rickenharp he was watching down the corridor without seeming to.

Carmen saw Rickenharp looking at Yukio and said, "Cops are coming down."

"Why?" Rickenharp asked. "The club's licensed."

"Not for you or the club. For us."

He looked at her and said, "Hey, I don't need to get busted." He picked up his guitar and went into the hall. "I got to do my encore before they lose interest."

She followed along, into the hall and the echo of the encore stomps, and asked, "Can we hang out in the dressing room for a while?"

"Yeah, but it ain't sacrosanct. You come back here, the cops can too." They were in the wings now. Rickenharp signaled to Murch and the band started playing.

She said, "These aren't exactly cops. They probably don't know these kinds of places; they'd look for us in the crowd, not the dressing room."

"You're an optimist. I'll tell the bouncer to stand here, and if he sees anyone else start to come back, he'll tell 'em it's empty back here 'cause he just checked."

"Thanks." She went back to the dressing room. He spoke to the bouncer and went on stage. Feeling drained, the guitar heavy on him. But he picked up on the energy level in the room and it carried him through two encores. He left them wanting more, which is the way to do it, and, sticky with sweat, walked back to his dressing room.

They were still there: Carmen, Yukio, Willow.

"Is there a stage door?" Yukio asked. "Into alley?"

Rickenharp nodded. "Wait in the hall; I'll come out and show you in a minute."

Yukio nodded, and they went into the hall. The band came in, filed past Carmen and Yukio and the Brit without much noticing them, assuming they were backstage hangout flotsam, except Murch stared at Carmen's tits and swaggered a bit, twirling his drumsticks.

The band sat around laughing in the dressing room and slapping palms, lighting several kinds of smokes. They didn't offer Rickenharp any; they knew he didn't use it.

Rickenharp was packing his guitar away when José said, "You blew good."

"You mean he gave you good head?" Murch said, and Julio snickered.

"Yeah," Ponce said, "the guy gives good head, good collarbone, good kidneys—"

"Good kidneys? Rick sucks on your kidneys? I think I'm gonna puke."

And the usual puerile band banter, because they were still high from a good set and putting off what they knew had to come, till Rickenharp said, "What you want to talk about, José?"

José looked at him, and the others shut up.

"I know there's something on your mind," Rickenharp said softly.

José said, "Well, it's like—there's an agent Ponce knows, and this guy could take us on. He's a technicki agent and we'd be taking on a technicki circuit, but we'd work our way back from there, that's a good base. But this guy says we have to get a wire act in."

"You guys been busy," Rickenharp said, shutting the guitar case.

José shrugged. "Hey, we ain't been doing it behind your back; we didn't hear from the guy till yesterday night. We didn't have a real chance to talk to you till now, so—uh, we have the same personnel but we change costumes, change the band's name, write new tunes—"

"We'd lose it," Rickenharp said. Feeling caved in. "We'd lose the thing we got. You won't have it, doing that shit, because it's all superimposed."

"Rock 'n' roll is not a fucking religion," José said.

"No, it's not a religion, it's a way to sound. Now, here's *my* 'posal: we write new songs in the same style as always. We did good tonight. It could be the beginning of a turnaround for us. We stay here, build on the base audience we established tonight."

It was like throwing coins into the Grand Canyon. You couldn't even hear them hit bottom.

The band just looked back at him.

"Okay," Rickenharp said. "Okay. We've been through this ten fucking times. Okay. That's all." He'd had an exit speech worked out for this moment, but it caught in his throat. He turned to Murch and said, "You think they're going to keep you on, they tell you that? Bullshit! They'll be doing it without a drummer, man. You better learn to program, fast." Then he looked at José. "Fuck you, José." He said it quietly.

He turned to Julio, who was looking at the far wall as if to decipher some particularly cryptic piece of graffiti. "Julio, you can have my amp, I'll be traveling light."

He turned and, carrying his guitar, walked out, leaving silence behind him.

He nodded at Yukio and led them to the stage door.

At the door, Carmen said, "Any chance you could help us find a little cover?"

Rickenharp needed company, bad. He nodded and said, "Yeah—if you'll give me a hit of that mesc."

She said, "Sure." And they went into the alley.

■ ■ ■

Rickenharp put on his dark glasses, because of the way the Walk tugged at him.

The Walk wound through the interlinked Freezone outfloats for a half mile, looping up and back, through a hairpin canyon of arcades crusted with neon and gloflake. It was involuted, intensified by layering and a blaze of colored light.

Rickenharp and Carmen walked through the sticky-warm night almost in step. Yukio walked behind, Willow walked ahead. Rickenharp felt like part of a jungle patrol formation.

And he had another feeling: that they were being followed, or watched. Maybe it was suggestion, from seeing Yukio and Willow glance over their shoulders now and then. . . .

Rickenharp felt a ripple of kinetic force under his feet, an arc of wallow moving in languid whiplash through the flexible street stuff, telling him that the breakers were up today, the baffles around the artificial island feeling the strain.

The arcade ran three levels above the narrow street; each level had its own sidewalk balcony; people stood at the railing to look down at the segmented snake of street traffic. The stack of arcades funneled a rich wash of scents to Rickenharp: the french-fried toastiness of the fast food; the sweet harshness of smokes—smashweed smoke, gynosmoke, tobacco smoke—the cloy of perfumes; the mixed odors of fish-ka-bob stands, urine, rancid beer, popcorn, sea air; and the faint ozone smell of the small electric cars jockeying on the street. His first time here, Rickenharp had thought the place smelled wrong for a red-light cluster. "It's wimpy," he'd said. Then he'd realized he was missing the bass bottom of carbon monoxides. There were no combustion cars on Freezone.

The sounds splashed over Rickenharp in a warm wave of cultural fecundity; pop tunes from thudders and beat boxes swelled in volume as they passed, the guys carrying the boxes insignificant in comparison to the noise they carried, the shanky tripping of protosalsa or the calculatedly redundant pulse of minimono.

Rickenharp and Carmen walked beneath a fiberglass arch—so covered with graffiti its original commemorative meaning was lost—and ambled down the milky walkway under the second-story arcade boardwalk. The multinational crowd thickened as they approached the heart of the Walk. The soft lights glowing upward from beneath the polystyrene walkway gave the crowd a 1940s-horror-movie look, and even through the dark glasses the place tugged at Rickenharp with a thousand subliminal come-hithers.

Rickenharp was still riding the blue mesc surf, but the wave was beginning to break; he could feel it crumbling under him. He looked at Carmen. She glanced back at him, and they understood one another. She looked around, then nodded toward the darkened doorway of a defunct movie theater, a trash-cluttered recess twenty feet off the street. They went into the doorway; Yukio and Willow stood with their backs to the door, blocking the view from the street, so that Rickenharp and Carmen could each do a double hit of blue mesc. There was a kind of little-kid pleasure in stepping into seclusion to do drugs, a rush of outlaw in-crowd romance to it. On the second sniff the graffiti on the pad-locked, fiberglass doors seemed to writhe with significance. "I'm running low," Carmen said, checking her mesc bottle.

Rickenharp didn't want to think about that. His mind was racing now, and he felt himself click into the boss blue verbal mode. "You see that graffiti? 'You're gonna die young because the ITE took the second half of your life.' You know what that means? I didn't know what ITE was till yesterday, I used to see those things and wonder and then somebody said—"

"Immortality something or other," she said, licking blue mesc off her sniffer.

"Immortality Treatment Elite. Supposedly some people keeping an immortality treatment to themselves because the government doesn't want the public to live too long and overpopulate the place. Another bullshit conspiracy theory."

"You don't believe in conspiracies?"

"I don't know—some. Nothing that farfetched. But—I think people are being manipulated all the time. Even here: this place tugs at you, you know. Like—"

Willow said, "Roit, we'll 'ave our sociology class later, children, you gotter? Where's this plice with the lad can get us off the island, mite?"

"Come on," Rickenharp said, leading them back into the flow of the crowd. But seamlessly picking up his blue mesc rap. "I mean, this place is a Times Square, right? You ever read the old novels about that place? That was the archetype. Or some places in Bangkok. I mean, these places are carefully arranged. Maybe subconsciously. But arranged as carefully as Japanese florals, only with the inverse esthetic. Sure, every whining, self-righteous, tight-assed evangelist who ever preached about the diabolical seductiveness of places like this was right—in a way—was fully justified 'cause, yeah, the places titillate and they seduce and they vampirize people. Yeah, they're Venus flytraps. Architectural Svengalis. Yes to all the clichés about the bad part of town. All the reverend preachers: Reverend Iko, Reverend—what's his name?—Smilin' Rick Crandall—"

She looked sharply at him. He wondered why, but the mesc swept him on.

"—all the preachers are right, but the reason they're right is why they're wrong, too. Everything here is trying to sell you something. Lots of light and whirligig suction to seduce you into throwing your energy into it—in the form of money. People mostly come here to buy or be titillated up to the verge of buying. The tension between wanting to buy and the resistance to buying can give you a charge. That's what I get into: I let it tickle my glands, but I hold back from paying into it. You know? Just constant titillation but no cumming because you waste your money or you get a social disease or mugged or sold bad drugs or something. . . . I mean, anything sold here is pointless bullshit. But it's harder for me to resist tonight. . . ." Unspoken: *Because I'm stoned.* "Makes you susceptible. Receptive to subliminals worked into the design of signs, that gaudy kinetics, those fucking on-off bulbs—makes you flash on the old computer-thinking models, binomial thinking, on-off, on-off, *blink-blink*—all those neon tubes, pulling you like the hypnotist's spiral pendant in the old movies. . . . And the kinds of colors they use, the energy of the signs, the rate of pulse, the rate of on-offing in the bulbs, all of it's engineered according to principles of psychology the people who make them don't even know they're using, colors that hint about, you know, glandular discharges and tingly chemical flows to the pleasure center . . . like obscenities you pay for in the painted mouth of a whore . . . like video games . . . I mean—"

"I know what you mean," she said, in desperation buying a wax-paper cup of beer. "You must be thirsty after that monologue. Here." She shoved the foaming cup under his nose.

"Talking too much. Sorry." He drank off half the beer in three gulps, took a breath, finished it, and it was paradise for a moment in his throat. A wave of quietude soothed him—and then evaporated as the blue mesc burned through again. Yeah, he was wired.

"I don't mind listening to you talk," she said, "except you might say too much, and I'm not sure if we're being scanned."

He nodded sheepishly, and they walked on. He crushed the cup in his hand, began methodically to shred it as they went.

Rickenharp luxuriated in the colors of the place, colors that mixed and washed over the crowd, making the stream of hats and heads into a living swatch of iridescent gingham, shining the cars into multicolored lumps of mobile ice.

You take the word *lurid,* Rickenharp thought, and you put it raw in a vat filled with the juice of the word *appeal.* You leave it and let the acids of appeal leach the colors out of lurid, so that you get a kind of gasoline rainbow on the surface of the vat. You extract the petro rainbow with cheesecloth, strain it into a glass tube, and dilute heavily with oil of cartoon innocence and extract of pure subjectivity. Now run a current through the glass tube and all the other tubes of the neon signs interlacing Freezone's Walk.

The Walk, stretching ahead of them, was itself almost a tube of colored lights, converging in a kaleidoscope; the concave fronts of the buildings to either side were flashing with a dozen varieties of signs. The sensual flow of neon data in primary colors was broken at cunningly irregular intervals by stark trademark signs à la Times Square: CANON and ATARI and NIKE and COCA-COLA and WARNER AMEX and SEIKO and SONY and NASA CHEMCO and BRAZILIAN EXPORTS INT and EXXON and NESSIO. In all of that, only one hint of the war: two unlit signs, FABRIZZIO and ALLINNE, an Italian and a French company, killed by the Soviet blockades. The signs were unlit, dead.

They passed a TV-shirt shop; tourists walked out with their chests flashing moving video imagery, microthin circuitry and chips woven into the shirtfront playing the sequence of your choice.

Sidewalk hawkers of every race sold beta candy spiked with beta endorphin; sold shellfish from Freezone's own beds, tempura'd and skewered; sold holocube pornography key rings; sold instapix of you and your wife, or is that your boyfriend? . . . Despite the nearness of Africa, black Africans were few here; Freezone Admin considered them a security risk. The tourists were mostly Japanese, Canadian, Brazilian—riding the crest of the Brazilian boom—South Koreans, Chinese, Arabs, Israelis, and a smattering of Americans. Damned few Americans any more, with the depression.

The atmosphere was hothouse. It was a multicolored steam bath. The air was sultry, the various smokes of the place warping the neon glow, filtering and smearing the colors of signs and TV shirts and Day-Glo jewelry. High up, between the not-quite-fitted jigsaw parts of signs and lights and pleasure houses' video signs displaying purulently sexual imagery, were blue-black slices of night sky. At street level the jumble was given shape and borders by the doors opening on either side: by the in-and-out currents of people using the doors to check out malls and stimsmoke parlors and memento shops and cubey theaters and, especially, tingler galleries.

Dealers drifted up like reef fish, nibbling and moving on, pausing to offer, "Dee Aitch, gotcher good Dee Aitch"—DH, Direct Hookup, illegal cerebral pleasure center stimulation. And drugs, cocaine and various smokable herbs, stims, and downs; about half the dealers were burn artists, selling baking soda or pseudostims. The dealers tended to hang on to Rickenharp and Carmen because they looked like users, and Carmen was wearing a sniffer. Blue mesc and sniffers were illegal, but so were lots of things the Freezone cops ignored. You could wear a sniffer and carry the stuff, but the understanding was, You don't use it openly, you step into someplace discreet.

And whores of both sexes cruised the street, flagrantly soliciting. Freezone Admin was supposed to regulate all prostitution, but black-market pros were tolerated as long as somebody paid off the beat security and they didn't get too numerous.

The crowd streaming past was a perpetually unfolding revelation of human variety. It unfolded again and a specialty pimp appeared, pushing a teenage boy and girl ahead of him; they had to hobble because they were straitjacket-packaged in black-rubber bondage gear. Their faces were ciphers in blank black-rubber full-face masks; aluminum racks held their mouths wide open, intended to be inviting, but to Rickenharp they looked like victims of a mad orthodontist.

Studded down the streets were Freezone security guards in bullet-proofed uniforms that made Rickenharp think of baseball umpires, faces caged in helmets, guns locked by combination into their holsters; they were said to be trained to open the four-digit combination in one second.

Mostly they stood around, gossipped on their helmet radios.

Now two of them hassled a sidewalk three-card-monte artist—a withered little black guy who couldn't afford the baksheesh—pushing him back and forth between them, bantering one another through helmet amplifiers, their voices booming over the discothud from the speakers on the 'sette shops:

"WHAT THE FUCK YOU DOING ON MY BEAT SCUMBAG. HEY BILL, YOU KNOW WHAT THIS GUY'S DOING ON MY BEAT."

"FUCK NO I DUNNO WHAT'S HE DOING ON YOUR BEAT."

"HE'S MAKING ME SICK WITH THIS RIP-OFF MONTE BULLSHIT IS WHAT HE'S DOING."

One of them hit the guy too hard with the waldo-enhanced arm of his riot suit, and the monte dealer spun to the ground like a top running out of momentum, out cold.

"LOITERING ON THE ZONE'S WALKS, YOU SEE THAT BILL."

"I SEE IT AND IT MAKES ME SICK JIM."

The bulls dragged the little guy by the ankle to a lozenge-shaped kiosk in the street and pushed him into a man capsule. They sealed the capsule, scribbled out a report, pasted it onto the capsule's hard plastic hull. Then they shoved the man capsule into the kiosk's chute. The capsule was sucked by mail-tube principle to Freezone Lockup.

"Looks like they're using some kind of garbage disposal to get rid of people here," Carmen said when they were past the cops.

Rickenharp looked at her. "You weren't nervous walking by the cops. So it's not them, huh?"

"Nope."

"You wanna tell me who it is we're supposed to be avoiding?"

"Uh-uh."

"How do you know these out-of-town cops you're worried about haven't gone to the locals and recruited some help?"

"Yukio says they won't, they don't want anybody to scan what they're doing here because Freezone Admin don't like 'em."

"Mmm. . . ."

Rickenharp guessed: the *who it is* was the Second Alliance. The Second Alliance International Security Corporation, the crypto-fascists moving in throughout the wreckage of Europe. The SA played the role of multinational police, taking over, imposing their idea of order, where NATO's demoralized legions collapsed. The grasp of the SA and their sympathizers reached farther and wider as the war ground hopelessly on. Never yet to Freezone—Freezone's independent boss would have liked to see the SA gassed. They couldn't operate here—except covertly.

The fucking SA bulls! Shit! . . . The blue mesc worked with Rickenharp's paranoia. Adrenaline spurted, making his heart bang. He began to feel claustrophobic in the crowd. Began to see patterns in the movement around him, patterns charged with meaning superimposed by his fear-galvanized mind. Patterns that taunted him with *The SA's close behind.* He felt a stomach-churning combination of horror and elation.

All night he'd worked hard at suppressing thoughts of the band. And of his failure to make the band work. *He'd lost the band.* And it was almost impossible to make anyone understand why that was, to him, like a man losing his wife and children. And there was the career. All those years of pushing for that band, struggling to program a place for it in the media Grid. Shot to hell now, and his identity with it. He knew somehow that it would be futile to try to put together another band. The Grid just didn't want him, and he didn't want the fucking Grid. And the elation was this: The ugly pit of displacement inside him closed up, was just *gone,* when he thought about the SA bulls. The bulls threatened his life, and the threat caught him up in something that made it possible to forget about the band. *He'd found a way out.*

But the horror was there too. If he got caught up with the SA's enemies . . . if the SA bulls got hold of him . . . .

Fuck it. What else did he have?

He grinned at Carmen, and she looked blankly back at him, wondering what the grin meant.

So now what? he asked himself. Get to the OmeGaity. Find Frankie. Frankie was the doorway.

But it was taking so long to get there. Thinking, The drug's fucking with your sense of duration. Heightened perception makes it seem to take longer.

The crowd seemed to get thicker, the air hotter, the music louder, the lights brighter. It was getting to Rickenharp. He began to lose the ability to make the distinction between things in his mind and things around him. He began to see himself as an enzyme molecule floating in some macrocosmic bloodstream. The sort of things that always OD'd him when he did an energizing drug in a sensory-overflow environment.

What am I?

Sizzling orange-neon arrows on the marquee overhead seemed to crawl off the marquee, slither down the wall, down into the sidewalk, snaking to twine around his ankles, to try to tug him into a tingler emporium. The emporium's display holos writhed with fleshy intertwinings; breasts and buttocks projected out at him, and he responded against his will, like all the clichés, getting hard in his pants: visual stimuli; monkey see, monkey respond. He thought, Bell rings and dog salivates.

He looked over his shoulder. Who was that guy with the sunglasses back there? Why was he wearing sunglasses at night? Maybe he's an SA—

Noooo, man: *I'm* wearing sunglasses at night. Means nothing.

He tried to shrug off the paranoia, but somehow it was twined into the undercurrent of sexual excitement. Every time he saw a whore or a pornographic video sign, the paranoia hooked into him as a kind of scorpion stinger on the tail of his adolescent surge of arousal. And he could feel his nerve ends begin to extrude from his skin.

Who am I? Am I the crowd?

(Realizing that after having been clean so long, his blue mesc tolerance was low.)

He saw Carmen look at something in the street, then whisper urgently to Yukio.

"What's the matter?" Rickenharp asked.

She whispered, "You see that silver thing? Kind of a silvery fluttering? There—over the cab. . . . Just look, I can't point."

He looked into the street. A cab was pulling up at the curb. Its electric motor whined as it nosed through a heap of refuse. Its windows were dialed to mercuric opacity. Above and a little behind it a chrome bird hovered, its wings a hummingbird blur. It was about thrush-sized, and it had a camera lens instead of a head. There was some kind of insignia on its aluminum chest. He couldn't make it out. "I see it. I can't tell what it is."

"I think it's run from in that cab. That's like them. Come on."

She ducked into a tingler gallery; Willow and Yukio and Rickenharp followed her. They had to buy user tokens to get in. They bought the minimum, four apiece. A bald, jowly old dude at the counter counted the tokens without looking, his eyes locked on a wrist-TV screen. On his wrist a miniature newscaster was saying in a small tinny voice, ". . . attempted assassination today of the Second Alliance director, the Reverend Rick Crandall. . . ." Something mumbled, distorted. "Crandall is in serious condition and heavily guarded at Freezone Medicenter. The surprise presence of Crandall at a meeting at the Freezone Fuji Hilton—"

They scooped up their tokens and went into the gallery. Rickenharp heard Willow mutter to Yukio, "The bastard's still alive."

Rickenharp put two and two together.

The tingler gallery was predominantly fleshtone, every available vertical surface taken up by emulsified nude humanity, usually photos as ghastly as Polaroids. As you passed from one photo or holo to the next, you saw the people in them were inverted or splayed or toyed with, turned in a thousand variations on coupling, as if a child had been playing with unclothed dolls and left them scattered. A sodden red light hummed in each booth; the light snagged you, a wavelength calculated to produce sexual curiosity. In each "privacy booth" was a screen and a tingler. The tingler looked like a twentieth-century vacuum cleaner hose with an oversized salt-shaker top on one end. You watched the pictures, listened to the sounds, and ran the tingler over your erogenous zones; the tingler stimulated the appropriate nerve ends with a subcutaneously penetrative electric field, very precisely attenuated. You could pick out the guys in the health-club showers who'd used a tingler too long. Use it more than the "recommended thirty-five-minute limit" and it made your skin look and feel sunburned. . . . Another five tokens in the machines triggered an oxygen mask that dropped from a ceiling trap to pump out a combination of amyl nitrate and pheromones.

"To phrase it in the classic manner," Yukio said abruptly, "is there another way out of here?"

Rickenharp nodded. "Yeah. This place's on the corner, so

chances are it's got two entrances, one around the corner from the first. And maybe an alley exit. . . ."

Willow was staring at a teaser blurb under a still image of two men, a woman, and a goat. He took a step closer, squinting at the goat as if searching out a family resemblance, and the booth sensed his nearness: the images on the sample placard began to move, bending, licking, penetrating, reshaping themselves with a weirdly formalized awkwardness; the booth's light increased its red glow, puffed out a tease of pheromone and amyl nitrate, trying to seduce him.

"Well, where *is* the other door?" Carmen hissed.

"Huh?" Rickenharp looked at her. "Oh! I'm sorry, I'm so— uh—I'm not sure." He glanced over his shoulder, lowered his voice. "The spy-bird didn't follow us in."

Yukio murmured, "The electric fields on the tinglers confuse the bird's guidance systems. But we must keep a step ahead."

Rickenharp looked around—but the maze of black booths and fleshtones seemed to twist back on itself, to turn ponderously, as if going down some cubistic drain. . . .

"*I* will find the other door," Yukio said. Rickenharp followed him gratefully. He wanted *out*.

They hurried through the narrow hall between tingler booths. The customers moved pensively—or strolled with excessive nonchalance—from one booth to another, reading the blurbs, scanning the imagery, sorting through fetishistic indexings for their personal libido codes, not looking at one another except peripherally, carefully avoiding personal-space margins, as if afraid of the volatility of dormant sexual elasticity.

Chuffing, sighing music played from somewhere; the red lights were like the glow of blood in a hand held over a bright light. But the place was rigorously Calvinistic in its obstacle course of tacit regulations. And here and there, at the turns in the hot, narrow passageways between rows of booths, bored nonuniformed security guards rocked on their heels and told the browsers, No loitering, please, you can purchase tokens at the front desk.

Rickenharp flashed that the place wanted to drain his sexuality, as if the vacuum-cleaner hoses in the booths were going to vacuum his orgone energy, leave him chilled as a gelding.

Get the fuck out of here, he told himself.

Then he saw EXIT, and they rushed for it, through it.

They were in an alley. They looked up, around, half expecting to see the bird. No bird. Only the gray intersection of styroconcrete planes, stunningly monochrome after the hungry chromatics of the tingler gallery.

They walked out to the end of the alley, stood for a moment watching the crowd churn by both ways. It was like standing on the bank of a torrent. Then they stepped into it, Rickenharp fantasizing that he was getting wet with the liquefied flesh of the rush of humanity as he steered by sheer instinct to his original objective: the OmeGaity.

They pushed through the peeling black pressboard doors into the dark mustiness of the OmeGaity's entrance hall, and Rickenharp gave Carmen his coat to hide her bare breasts. "Men only, in here," he said, "but if you don't shove your femaleness into their line of sight, they might let us slide."

Carmen pulled the jacket on, zipped it up—very carefully—and Rickenharp gave her his dark glasses.

Rickenharp banged on the window of the screening kiosk beside the locked door that led into the cruising rooms. Beyond the glass, someone looked up from a TV screen. "Hey, Carter," Rickenharp said.

"Hey." Carter grinned at him. Carter was, by his own admission, "a trendy faggot." He was flexicoated battleship gray with white trim, a minimono style. But the real M'n'Ms would have spurned him for wearing a luminous earring—it blinked through a series of words in tiny green letters: *Fuck . . . you . . . if . . . you . . . don't . . . like . . . it. . . . Fuck . . . you . . . if—* they'd have considered that unforgivably "griddy." And anyway Carter's wide, froggish face didn't fit the svelte minimono look. He looked at Carmen. "No girls, Harpie."

"Drag queen," Rickenharp said. He slipped a folded twenty-newbux note through the slot in the window. "Okay?"

"Okay, but she takes her chances in there," Carter said, shrugging. He tucked the twenty in his charcoal bikini briefs.

"Sure."

"You hear about Geary?"

"Nope."

"Snuffed himself with China White 'cause he got green-pissed."

"Oh, shit." Rickenharp's skin crawled. His paranoia flared up again, and to soothe it he said, "Well, I'm not gonna be licking anybody's anything. I'm looking for Frankie."

"That asshole. He's there, holding court or something. But you still got to pay admission, honey."

"Sure," Rickenharp said.

He took another twenty newbux out of his pocket, but Carmen put a hand on his arm and said, "We'll cover this one." She slapped a twenty down.

Carter took it, chuckling. "Man, that queen got some real nice larynx work." Knowing damn well she was a girl. "You still playing at the—"

"I lost the gig," Rickenharp cut in, trying to head off the pain. The boss blue had peaked and left him feeling like he was made out of cardboard inside, like any pressure might make him buckle. His muscles twitched now and then, fretful as restive children scuffing feet. He was crashing. He needed another hit. When you were up, things showed you their frontsides, their upsides; when you peaked, things showed you their hideous insides. When you were down, things showed you their backsides, their downsides. File it away for lyrics.

Carter pressed the buzzer that unlocked the door. It razzed them as they walked through.

Inside it was dim, hot, humid.

"I think your blue was cut with coke or meth or something," Rickenharp told Carmen as they walked past the dented lockers. " 'Cause I'm crashing harder than I should be."

"Yeah, probably. . . . What'd he mean, 'he got green-pissed'?"

"Positive test for AIDS-three, the AIDS that kills you in six weeks. You drop this testing pill in your urine and if the urine turns green you got AIDS. There's no cure for the new AIDS, so the guy. . . ." He shrugged.

"What the 'ell is this place?" Willow asked.

In a low voice Rickenharp told him, "It's a kind of bathless gay baths, man. Cruising places for 'mos. But about half the people are straights who ran out of bux at the casinos, use it for a cheap place to sleep, you know?"

"Yeah? And 'ow come you know all about it, 'ey?"

Rickenharp smirked. "You calling me a homo?"

Someone in a darkened alcove to one side laughed at that.

Willow was arguing with Yukio in an undertone. "Oi don't like it, that's all, fucking faggots got a million fucking diseases. Some geezer 'oo looks like a side o' beef with a tan going to wank off on me leg."

"We just walk through, we don't touch," Yukio said. "Rickenharp knows what to do."

Rickenharp thought, Hope so. Maybe Frankie could get them safely off Freezone, maybe not.

The walls were black pressboard. It was a maze like a tingler gallery but in the negative. There was a more ordinary red light; there was the peculiar scent that lots of skin on skin generates— and the accretion of various smokes, aftershaves, cheap soap, and an ingrained stink of sweat. And underneath, KY jelly, and poppers, and semen gone rancid. The walls stopped at ten feet up and the shadows gathered the ceiling into themselves, far overhead. It was a converted warehouse space, with a strange vibe of stratification: claustrophobia layered under agoraphobia. They passed mossy-dark cruising warrens. Faces blurred by anonymity turned to monitor them as they passed, expressions cool as TV cameras.

Such places had not changed significantly in fifty years. Some were shabbier than others. The shabbier ones had stopped-up toilets and badly focused 16-mm pornography and a drunken whine from the speakers that passed for porn sound- tracks. And the OmeGaity was one of the shabbier ones.

They passed through the game room with its stained pool tables and stammering video games, its prized-open vending machines. Peeling from the walls between the machines were posters of men as exquisitely fem as they were overbearingly macho—caricatures with oversized genitals and muscles that seemed a kind of sexual organ, faces like California surfers. Carmen bit her finger to keep from laughing at them, marveling at the idiosyncratic narcissism of the place.

They passed through a cruising room designed to look like a barn. Two men ministered to one another on a wooden bench inside a "horse stall." Wet fleshy noises. Willow and Yukio looked away. Carmen stared at the gay sex in fascination.

Rickenharp walked past without reacting, led the way through other midnight nests of pawing men; past men sleeping on benches and couches, snorting with annoyance and sleepily slapping unwanted hands away. And found Frankie in the TV lounge.

The TV lounge was bright, well-lit, the walls cheerful yellow. There were motel-standard living-room lamps on end tables, a couch, a regular color TV showing a rock video channel, and a bank of TV monitors on the wall. It was like emerging from the underworld. Frankie was sitting on the couch, waiting for customers.

Frankie dealt on a portaterminal he'd plugged into a grid socket. The buyer gave him an account number or credit card; Frankie checked the account, transferred the funds into his own (registered as "consultancy fees"), and handed over the packets.

The walls of the lounge were inset with video monitors; one showed the orgy room, another a porn tape, another ran a Grid network satellite channel. On that one a newscaster was yammering about the intended assassination of Crandall, this time in technicki; Rickenharp hoped Frankie wouldn't notice it and make the connection. Frankie the Mirror was into taking profit from whatever came along, and the SA paid for information.

Frankie sat on the torn blue vinyl couch, hunched over the pocket-sized terminal on the coffee table. Frankie's customer was a disco 'mo with a blue sharkfin flare, steroid muscles, and a white karate robe; the guy was standing to one side, staring at the little black canvas bag of blue packets on the coffee table as Frankie completed the transaction.

Frankie was black. His bald scalp had been painted with reflective chrome; his head was a mirror, reflecting the TV screens in fish-eye miniature. He wore a pinstriped three-piece gray suit. A real one, but rumpled and stained like he'd slept in it, maybe fucked in it. He was smoking a Nat Sherman cigaretello, down to the gold filter. His synthcoke eyes were demonically red. He flashed a yellow grin at Rickenharp. He looked at Willow, Yukio, and Carmen, made a mocking scowl. "Fucking narcs—get more fancy with their setups every day. Now they got four agents in here, one of them looks like my man Rickenharp, other three look like two refugees and a computer designer. But that Jap hasn't got a camera. Gives him away."

"What's this 'ere about—" Willow began.

Rickenharp made a dismissive gesture that said, *He isn't serious, dumbshit.* "I got two purchases to make," he announced and looked at Frankie's buyer. The buyer took his packet and melted back into the warrens.

"First off," Rickenharp said, taking his card from his wallet, "I need some blue blow, three grams."

"You got it, homeboy." Frankie ran a lightpen over the card, then punched in a request for data on that account. The terminal asked for the private code number. Frankie handed the terminal to Rickenharp, who punched in his code, then erased it from visual. Then he punched to transfer funds to Frankie's account. Frankie took the terminal and double-checked the transfer. The terminal showed Rickenharp's adjusted balance and Frankie's gain.

"That's gonna eat up half your account, Harpie," Frankie said.

"I got some prospects."

"I heard you and José parted company."

"How'd you get that so fast?"

"Ponce was here buying."

"Yeah, well—now I've dumped the dead weight, my prospects are even better." But as he said it he felt dead weight in his gut.

" 'S your bux, man." Frankie reached into the canvas carry-on, took out three pre-weighed bags of blue powder. He looked faintly amused. Rickenharp didn't like the look. It seemed to say, *I knew you'd come back, you sorry little wimp.*

"Fuck off, Frankie," Rickenharp said, taking the packets.

"What's this sudden squall of discontent, my child?"

"None of your business, you smug bastard."

Frankie's smugness output tripled. He glanced speculatively at Carmen and Yukio and Willow. "There's something more, right?"

"Yeah. We got a problem. My friends here—they're getting off the raft. They need to slip out the back way so Tom and Huck don't see 'em."

"Hmm. What kind of net's out for them?"

"It's a private outfit. They'll be watching the copter port, everything legit—"

"We had another way off," Carmen said suddenly, "but it was blown—"

Yukio silenced her with a look. She shrugged.

"Ver-ry mysterious," Frankie said. "But there are safety limits to curiosity. Okay. Three grand gets you three berths on my next boat out. My boss's sending a team to pick up a shipment. I can probably get 'em on there. That's going *east*, though. You know? Not west or north or south. One direction and one only."

"That's what we need," Yukio said, smiling, nodding. Like he was talking to a travel agent. "East. Someplace Mediterranean."

"Malta," Frankie said. "Island of Malta. Best I can do."

Yukio nodded. Willow shrugged. Carmen assented by her silence.

Rickenharp was sampling the goods. In the nose, to the brain, and right to work. Frankie watched him placidly. Frankie was a connoisseur of the changes drugs made in people. He watched the change of expression on Rickenharp's face. He watched Rickenharp's shift into egodrive.

"We're gonna need *four* berths, Frankie," Rickenharp said.

Frankie raised an eyebrow. "You better decide after that shit wears off."

"I decided before I took it," Rickenharp said, not sure if it was true.

Carmen was staring at him.

He took her by the arm and said, "Talk to you a minute?" He led her out of the lounge, into the dark hallway. The skin of her arm was electrically sweet under his fingers. He wanted more. But he dropped his hand from her and said, "Can you get the bux?"

She nodded. "I got a fake card, dips into—well, it'll get it for us. I mean, for me and Yukio and Willow. I'd have to get authorization to bring you. And I can't do that."

"I won't help you get out otherwise."

"You don't know—"

"Yeah, I do. I'm ready to go. I just go back and get my guitar."

"The guitar'll be a burden where we're going. We're going

into occupied territory, to get where we want to be. You'd have to leave the guitar."

He almost wavered at that. "I'll check it into a locker. Pick it up someday." He couldn't play it anyway without every note sounding wrong because of the pain he played through now. "Thing is—if they watched us with that bird, they saw me with you. They'll assume I'm part of it. Look, I know what you're doing. The SA's looking for you. Right? So that means you're—"

"Okay, hold it, shit, keep your voice down. Look—I can see where maybe they marked you, so you got to get off the raft too. Okay, you go with us to Malta. But then you—"

"I got to stay with you. The SA's everywhere. They marked me."

She took a deep breath and let it out in a soft whistle through her teeth. She stared at the floor. "You can't do it." She looked at him. "You're not the type. You're a fucking *artist*."

He laughed. "You say that like it's the lowest insult you can come up with. Look—I can do it. I'm going to do it. The band is dead. I need to—" He shrugged helplessly. Then he reached up and took her sunglasses off, looked at her shadowed eyes. "And when I get you alone I'm going to batter your cervix into jelly."

She punched him hard in the shoulder. It hurt. But she was smiling. "You think that kind of talk turns me on? Well, it does. But it's not going to get you into my pants. And as for going with us—what do you think this is? You've seen too many movies."

"The SA's marked me. What else can I do?"

"That's not a good enough reason to . . . to become part of this thing. You've got to really believe in it, because *it's hard*. This is not a celebrity game show."

"Jesus. Give me a break. I know what I'm doing."

That was bullshit. He was trashed. He was blown. He thought, *My computer's experiencing a power surge. All circuits wiped out. Hell, then burn out the rest.*

He was living a fantasy. But he wasn't going to admit it. He repeated, "I know what I'm doing."

She snorted. She stared at him. "Okay," she said.

And after that everything was different.

Stone Lives

■

Paul Di Filippo is a newly published writer whose body of work is still small. Yet his work is already attracting attention for its ambitious scope and weirdly visionary imagery.

The following piece, which appeared in 1985, was his third published story. With its theme of transformation, radical social change, and the impact of new technologies, it demonstrates Di Filippo's firm grasp of the cyberpunk dynamic. He lives in Providence, Rhode Island.

Odors boil around the Immigration Office, a stenchy soup. The sweat of desperate men and women, ripe garbage strewn in the packed street, the spicy scent worn by one of the guards at the outer door. The mix is heady, almost overpowering to anyone born outside the Bungle, but Stone is used to it. The constant smells constitute the only atmosphere he has ever known, his native element, too familiar to be despised.

Noise swells to rival the stench: harsh voices raised in dispute, whining voices lowered to entreat. "Don't sluff me, you rotty bastard!" "I'd treat you real nice, honey, for a share of that." From the vicinity of the door into Immigration, an artificial voice is reciting the day's job offerings, cycling tirelessly through the rotty choices.

"—to test new aerosol antipersonnel toxins; 4M will contract to provide survivors with a Citrine rejuve. High-orbit vakheads needed by McDonnell Douglas. Must be willing to be imprinted—"

No one seems eager to rush forward and claim these jobs. No voices beg the guards for entrance. Only those who have incurred impossible debts or enmity inside the Bungle ever take a chance on the Rating-10 assignments, which are Immigration's disdainful handouts. Stone knows for sure that he wants no part of these rigged propositions. Like all the rest, he is here at Immigration simply because it provides a focal point, a gathering place as vital as a Serengeti water hole, where the sneaky sluffs and raw deals that pass for business in the South Bronx FEZ—a.k.a. the Bronx Jungle, a.k.a. the Bungle—can be transacted.

Heat smites the noisy crowd, making them more irritable than usual—a dangerous situation. Hyperalertness parches Stone's throat. He reaches for the scratched-to-his-touch plastic flask at his hip and swigs some stale water. Stale but safe, he thinks, relishing his secret knowledge. It was pure luck that he ever stumbled upon the slow leak in the inter-FEZ pipe down by the river fence that encircles the Bungle. He smelled the clean water like a dog from a distance, and by running his hands along several meters of chilly pipe, he found the drip. Now he has all the manifold cues to its exact location deeply memorized.

Shuffling through the crowd on bare calloused feet (amazing what information can be picked up through the soles to keep body and soul intact!), Stone quests for scraps of information that will help him survive another day in the Bungle. Survival is his main—his only—concern. If Stone has any pride left, after enduring what he has endured, it is pride in surviving.

A brassy voice claims, "I booted some tempo, man, and that was the end of *that* fight. Thirty seconds later, all three're dead." A listener whistles admiringly. Stone imagines he latches on somehow to a boot of tempo and sells it for an enormous profit, which he then spends on a dry, safe place to sleep and enough to fill his ever-empty gut. Not damn likely, but a nice dream nonetheless.

Thought of food causes his stomach to churn. Across the rough, encrusted cloth covering his midriff, he rests his right hand with its sharp lance of pain that marks the infected cut. Stone assumes the infection. He has no way of telling for sure until it begins to stink.

Stone's progress through the babble of voices and crush of flesh has brought him fairly close to the entrance to Immigration. He feels a volume of empty air between the crowds and the guards, a quarter sphere of respect and fear, its vertical face the wall of the building. The respect is generated by the employed status of the guards, the fear by their weapons.

Someone—a transported felon with a little education—once described the guns to Stone. Long, bulky tubes with a bulge halfway along their length where the wiggler magnets are. Plastic stocks and grips. They emit charged beams of energetic electrons at relativistic speeds. If the scythe of the beam touches you, the kinetic energy imparted blows you apart like a squashed sausage. If the particle beam chances to miss, the accompanying cone of gamma rays produces radiation sickness that is fatal within hours.

Of the explanation—which Stone remembers verbatim—he understands only the description of a horrible death. It is enough.

Stone pauses a moment. A familiar voice—that of Mary, the rat seller—is speaking conspiratorially of the next shipment of charity clothes. Stone deduces her position as being on the very inner edge of the crowd. She lowers her voice. Stone can't make out her words, which are worth hearing. He edges forward, leery though he is of being trapped inside the clot of people—

A dead silence. No one is speaking or moving. Stone senses displaced air puff from between the guards: someone occupies the door.

"You." A refined woman's voice. "Young man with no shoes, in the"—her voice hesitates for the adjective hiding beneath the grime—"red jumpsuit. Come here, please. I want to talk to you."

Stone doesn't know if it is he (red?), until he feels the pressure of all eyes upon him. At once he pivots, swerves, fakes—but it is too late. Dozens of eager claws grab him. He wrenches. Moldy fabric splits, but the hands refasten on his skin. He bites, kicks, pummels. No use. During the struggle he makes no sound. Finally he is dragged forward, still fighting, past that invisible line that marks another world as surely as does the unbreachable fence between the Bungle and the other twenty-two FEZ.

Cinnamon scent envelops him, a guard holds something cold and metallic to the back of his neck. All the cells in his skull seem to flare at once, then darkness comes. . . .

Three people betray their forms and locations to the

awakened Stone by the air they displace, their scents, their voices—and by a subtle component he has always labeled sense of life.

Behind him: a bulky man who breathes awkwardly, no doubt because of Stone's ripe odor. This has to be a guard.

To his left: a smaller person—the woman?—smelling like flowers. (Once Stone smelled a flower.)

Before him, deskbound: a seated man.

Stone feels no aftereffects from the device used on him— unless the total disorientation that has overtaken him is it. He has no idea why he has been shanghaied and wishes only to return to the known dangers of the Bungle.

But he knows they are not about to let him.

The woman speaks, her voice the sweetest Stone has ever heard.

"This man will ask you some questions. Once you answer them, I'll have one for you. Is that all right?"

Stone nods, his only choice as he sees it.

"Name?" says the immigration official.

"Stone."

"That's all?"

"That's all anyone calls me." (Unbearable white-hot pain when they dug out the eyes of the little urchin they caught watching them carve up the corpse. But he never cried, oh, no; and so: Stone.)

"Place of birth?"

"This shitheap, right here. Where else?"

"Parents?"

"What're they?"

"Age?"

A shrug.

"That can be fixed later with a cellscan. I suppose we have enough to issue your card. Hold still now."

Stone feels multiple pencils of warmth scroll over his face; seconds later, a chuntering sound from the desk.

"This is your proof of citizenship and access to the system. Don't lose it."

Stone extends a hand in the direction of the voice, receives a plastic rectangle. He goes to shove it into a pocket, finds them both ripped away in the scuffle, and continues to hold the plastic awkwardly, as if it is a brick of gold about to be snatched away.

"Now my question." The woman's voice is like a distant memory Stone has of love. "Do you want a job?"

Stone's trip wire has been brushed. A job they can't even announce in public? It must be so fracking bad that it's off the common corporate scale.

"No, thanks, miz. My life ain't much, but it's all I got." He turns to leave.

"Although I can't give you details until you accept, we'll register a contract right now that stipulates it's a Rating One job."

Stone stops dead. It has to be a sick joke. But what if it's true?

"A contract?"

"Officer," the woman commands.

A key is tapped, and the desk recites a contract. To Stone's untutored ears, it sounds straightforward and without traps. A Rating-1 job for an unspecified period, either party able to terminate the contract, job description to be appended later.

Stone hesitates only seconds. Memories of all the frightful nights and painful days in the Bungle swarm in his head, along with the hot central pleasure of having survived. Irrationally, he feels a moment's regret at leaving behind the secret city spring he so cleverly found. But it passes.

"I guess you need this to okay it," Stone says, offering up his newly won card.

"I guess we do," the woman says with a laugh.

■ ■ ■

The quiet sealed car moves through busy streets. Despite the lack of outside noise, the chauffeur's comments on the traffic and their frequent halts are enough to convey a sense of the bustling city around them.

"Where are we now?" Stone asks for the tenth time. Besides wanting the information, he loves to hear this woman speak. Her voice, he thinks—it's like a spring rain when you're safe inside.

"Madison-Park FEZ, traveling crosstown."

Stone nods appreciatively. She may as well have said, "In

orbit, blasting for the moon," for all the fuzzy mental imagery he gets.

Before they would let Stone leave, Immigration did several things to him: shaved his body hair off, deloused him, made him shower for ten minutes with a mildly abrasive soap, disinfected him, ran several instant tests, pumped six shots into him, and issued him underwear, clean coveralls, and shoes (shoes!).

The alien smell of himself only makes the woman's perfume more attractive. In the close confines of the back seat, Stone swims in it. Finally he can contain himself no longer.

"Uh, that perfume—what kind is it?"

"Lily of the valley."

The mellifluous phrase makes Stone feel as if he is in another, kinder century. He swears he will always remember it. And he will.

"Hey!" Consternation. "I don't even know your name."

"June. June Tannhauser."

June Stone. June and Stone and lilies of the valley. June in June with Stone in the valley with the lilies. It's like a song that won't cease in his head.

"Where are we going?" he asks over the silent song in his head.

"To a doctor," said June.

"I thought that was all taken care of."

"This man's a specialist. An eye specialist."

This is the final jolt, atop so many, knocking even the happy song out of Stone's head.

He sits tense for the rest of the ride, unthinking. . . .

"This is a life-size model of what we're going to implant in you," the doctor says, putting a cool ball in Stone's hand.

Stone squeezes it in disbelief.

"The heart of this eye system is CCDs—charge-coupled devices. Every bit of light—photon—that hits them triggers one or more electrons. These electrons are collected as a continuous signal, which is fed through an interpreter chip to your optic nerves. The result: perfect sight."

Stone grips the model so hard his palm bruises.

"Cosmetically, they're a bit shocking. In a young man like yourself, I'd recommend organic implants. However, I have orders from the person footing the bill that these are what you get. And of course, there are several advantages to them."

When Stone does not ask what they are, the doctor continues anyway.

"By thinking mnemonic keywords that the chip is programmed for, you can perform several functions.

"One: You can store digitalized copies of a particular sight in the chip's RAM, for later display. When you reinvoke it with the keyword, it will seem as if you are seeing the sight again directly, no matter what you are actually looking at. Resumption of real-time vision is another keyword.

"Two: By stepping down the ratio of photons to electrons, you can do such things as stare directly at the sun or at a welder's flame without damage.

"Three: By upping the ratio, you can achieve a fair degree of normal sight in conditions such as a starry, moonless night.

"Four: for enhancement purposes, you can generate false-color images. Black becomes white to your brain, the old rose-colored glasses, whatever.

"And I think that about covers it."

"What's the time frame on this, doctor?" June asks.

The doctor assumes an academic tone, obviously eager to show professional acumen.

"A day for the actual operation, two days of accelerated recovery, a week of training and further healing—say, two weeks, max."

"Very good," June says. Stone feels her rise from the couch beside him but remains seated.

"Stone," she says, a hand on his shoulder, "time to go."

But Stone can't get up, because the tears won't stop.

■ ■ ■

The steel and glass canyons of New York—that proud and flourishing union of Free Enterprise Zones—are a dozen shades of cool blue, stretching away to the north. The streets that run with geometric precision like distant rivers on the canyon floors are an arterial red. To the west and east, snatches of the Hudson River and the East River are visible as lime-green flows. Central Park is a wall of sunflower yellow halfway up the island. To the northeast of the park, the Bungle is a black wasteland.

Stone savors the view. Vision of any kind, even the foggiest blurs, was an unthinkable treasure only days ago. And what he has actually been gifted with—this marvelous ability to turn the everyday world into a jeweled wonderland—is almost too much to believe.

Momentarily sated, Stone wills his gaze back to normal. The city instantly reverts to its traditional color of steel-gray, sky-blue, tree-green. The view is still magnificent.

Stone stands at a bank of windows on the 150th floor of the Citrine Tower, in the Wall Street FEZ. For the past two weeks, this has been his home, from which he has not stirred. His only visitors have been a nurse, a cyber-therapist, and June. The isolation and relative lack of human contact do not bother him. After the Bungle, such quiet is bliss. And then, of course, he has been enmeshed in the sensuous web of sight.

The first thing he saw upon waking after the operation set the glorious tone of his visual explorations. The smiling face of a woman hovered above him. Her skin was a pellucid olive, her eyes a radiant brown, her hair a raven cascade framing her face.

"How are you feeling?" June asked.

"Good," Stone said. Then he uttered a phrase he had never had a use for before. "Thank you."

June waved a slim hand negligently. "Don't thank me. I didn't pay for it."

And that was when Stone learned that June was not his employer, that she worked for someone else. And although she wouldn't tell him then to whom he was indebted, he soon learned when they moved him from the hospital to the building that bore her name.

Alice Citrine. Even Stone knew of her.

Turning from the windows, Stone stalks across the thick cream-colored rug of his quarters. (How strange to move so confidently, without halting or probing!) He has spent the past fifteen days or so zealously practicing with his new eyes. Everything the doctor promised him is true—the miracle of sight pushed into new dimensions. It's all been thrilling. And the luxury of his situation is undeniable. Any kind of food he wants. (Although he would have been satisfied with frack—processed krill.) Music, holovision, and, most prized, the company of June. But all of a sudden today, he is feeling a little irritable. Where and what is this job they hired him for? Why has he not met his employer face to face yet? He begins to wonder if this is all some sort of ultra-elaborate sluff.

Stone stops before a full-length mirror mounted on a closet door. Mirrors still have the power to fascinate him utterly. That totally obedient duplicate imitating one's every move, will-less except for his will. And the secondary world in the background, unattainable and silent. During his years in the Bungle when he still retained his eyes, Stone never saw his reflection in anything but puddles or shards of windows. Now he confronts the immaculate stranger in the mirror, seeking clues in his features to the essential personality beneath.

Stone is short and skinny, traces of malnourishment plain in his stature. But his limbs are straight, his lean muscles hard. His skin where it shows from beneath the sleeveless black one-piece is weather-roughened and scarred. Plyoskin slippers—tough, yet almost as good as barefoot—cover his feet.

His face. All intersecting planes, like that strange picture in his bedroom. (Did June say "Picasso"?) Sharp jaw, thin nose, blond stubble on his skull. And his eyes: faceted dull-black hemispheres: inhuman. But don't take them back, please; I'll do whatever you want.

Behind him the exit door to his suite opens. It's June. Without conscious thoughts, Stone's impatience spills out in words, which pile one for one atop June's simultaneous sentence, merging completely at the end.

"I want to see—"

"We're going to visit—"

"—Alice Citrine."

Fifty floors above Stone's suite, the view of the city is even more spectacular. Stone has learned from June that the Citrine Tower stands on land that did not even exist a century ago. Pressure to expand motivated a vast landfill in the East River, south of the Brooklyn Bridge. On part of this artificial real estate, the Citrine Tower was built in the Oughts, during the boom period following the Second Constitutional Convention.

Stone boosts the photon-electron ratio of his eyes, and the East River becomes a sheet of white fire.

A momentary diversion to ease his nerves.

"Stand here with me," June says, indicating a disk just

beyond the elevator door, a few meters from another entrance.

Stone complies. He imagines he can feel the scanning rays on him, although it is probably just the nearness of June, whose elbow touches his. Her scent fills his nostrils, and he fervently hopes that having eyes won't dull his other senses.

Silently the door opens for them.

June guides him through.

Alice Citrine waits inside.

The woman sits in a powered chair behind a horseshoe-shaped bank of screens. Her short hair is corn-yellow, her skin unlined, yet Stone intuits a vast age clinging to her, the same way he used to be able to sense emotions when blind. He studies her aquiline profile, familiar somehow as a face once dreamed is familiar.

She swivels, presenting her full features. June has led them to within a meter of the burnished console.

"Good to see you, Mr. Stone," says Citrine. "I take it you are comfortable, no complaints."

"Yes," Stone says. He tries to summon up the thanks he meant to give but can't find them anywhere, so disconcerted is he. Instead, he says tentatively, "My job—"

"Naturally you're curious," Citrine says. "It must be something underhanded or loathsome or deadly. Why else would I need to recruit someone from the Bungle? Well, let me at last satisfy you. Your job, Mr. Stone, is to study."

Stone is dumbfounded. "Study?"

"Yes, study. You know the meaning of the word, don't you? Or have I made a mistake? Study, learn, investigate, and whenever you feel you understand something, draft me a report."

Stone's bafflement has passed through amazement to incredulity. "I can't even read or write," he says. "And what the frack am I supposed to study?"

"Your field of study, Mr. Stone, is this contemporary world of ours. I have had a large part, as you may know, in making this world what it is today. And as I reach the limits of my life, I grow more interested in whether what I have built is bad or good. I have plenty of reports from experts, both positive and negative. But what I want now is a fresh view from one of the under-dwellers. All I ask is honesty and accuracy.

"As for reading and writing—those outmoded skills of my

youth—June will assist you in learning those if you wish. But you have machines to read to you and transcribe your speech. You may start at once."

Stone tries to assimilate this mad request. It seems capricious, a cover for deeper, darker deeds. But what can he do except say yes?

He agrees.

A tiny smile plucks at the woman's lips. "Fine. Then our talk is over. Oh, one last thing. If you need to conduct on-site research, June must accompany you. And you will mention my sponsorship of you to no one. I don't want sycophants."

The conditions are easy—especially having June always close—and Stone nods his acceptance.

Citrine turns her back to them then. Stone is startled by what he sees, almost believing his eyes defective.

Perched on the broad back of her chair is a small animal resembling a lemur or tarsier. Its big, luminous eyes gaze soulfully at them, its long tail arcs in a spiral above its back.

"Her pet," whispers June, and hurries Stone away.

■ ■ ■

The task is too huge, too complex. Stone considers himself a fool for ever having accepted.

But what else could he have done, if he wanted to keep his eyes?

Stone's cramped and circumscribed life in the Bungle has not prepared him well to fathom the multiplex, extravagant, pulsating world he has been transported to. (At least this is what he initially feels.) Literally and figuratively kept in the dark for so long, he finds the world outside the Citrine Tower a mystifying place.

There are hundreds, thousands of things he has never heard of before: people, cities, objects, events. There are areas of expertise whose names he can hardly pronounce: areology, chaoticism, fractal modeling, paraneurology. And don't forget history, that bottomless well atop which the present moment is but a scrim of bubbles. Stone is, perhaps, most shocked by his discovery of history. He cannot recall ever having considered life as extending backward in time beyond his birth. The revelation of decades, centuries, millennia nearly pushes him into a mental abyss. How can one hope to comprehend the present without knowing all that has gone before?

Hopeless, insane, suicidal to persist.

Yet Stone persists.

He closets himself with his magic window on the world, a terminal that interfaces with the central computer in the Citrine Tower—itself a vast, unintelligible hive of activity—and, through that machine, to almost every other in the world. For hours on end, images and words flash by him, like knives thrown by a circus performer—knives that he, the loyal but dumb assistant, must catch to survive.

Stone's memory is excellent, trained in a cruel school, and he assimilates much. But each path he follows has a branch every few steps, and each branch splits at frequent points, and those tertiary branches also sprout new ones, no less rich than the primaries. . . .

Once Stone nearly drowned, when a gang left him unconscious in a gutter and it began to rain. He recalls the sensation now.

June brings him three meals faithfully each day. Her presence still thrills him. Each night, as he lies abed, he replays stored images of her to lull him asleep. June bending, sitting, laughing, her Asian eyes aglow. The subtle curves of her breasts and hips. But the knowledge fever is stronger, and he tends to ignore her as the days go by.

One afternoon Stone notices a pill on his lunch tray. He asks June its nature.

"It's a mnemotropin—promotes the encoding of long-term memories," she replies. "I thought it might help you."

Stone swallows it greedily and returns to the droning screen.

Each day he finds a pill at lunch. His brain seems to expand to a larger volume soon after he takes them. The effect is potent, allowing him to imagine that he can ingest the world. But still, each night when he finally forces himself to stop, he feels he has not done enough.

Weeks pass. He has not prepared a single sentence for Alice Citrine. What does he understand? Nothing. How can he pass judgment on the world? It's hubris, folly. How long will she wait before she kicks his ass out onto the cold street?

Stone drops his head in his hands. The mocking machine

before him torments him with a steady diarrhea of useless facts.

A hand falls lightly on his quivering shoulder. Stone imbibes June's sweet scent.

Stone smashes the terminal's power stud with the base of his palm so fiercely it hurts. Blessed silence. He looks up at June.

"I'm no damn good at this. Why'd she pick me? I don't even know where to start."

June sits on a cushion beside him. "Stone, I haven't said anything, because I was ordered not to direct you. But I don't think sharing a little of my experience will count as interference. You've got to limit your topic. The world's too big. Alice doesn't expect you to comprehend it all, distill it into a masterpiece of concision and sense.

"The world doesn't lend itself to such summations, anyway. I think you unconsciously know what she wants. She gave you a clue when you talked to her."

Stone summons up that day, plays back a view he filed of the stern old woman. Her features occult June's. The visual cue drags along a phrase.

"—whether what I have built is bad or good."

It is as if Stone's eyes have overloaded. Insight floods him with relief. Of course, the vain and powerful woman sees her life as the dominant theme of the modern era, a radiant thread passing through time, with critical nodes of action strung on it like beads. How much easier to understand a single human life than that of the whole world. (Or so he believes at the moment.) That much he thinks he can do. Chart Citrine's personal history, the ramifications of her long career, the ripples spreading from her throne. Who knows? It might indeed prove archetypal.

Stone wraps his arms around June in exultation, gives a wordless shout. She doesn't resist his embrace, and they fall back upon the couch.

Her lips are warm and complaisant under his. Her nipples seem to burn through her shirt and into his chest. His left leg is trapped between her thighs.

Suddenly he pulls back. He has seen himself too vividly; scrawny castoff from the sewer of the city, with eyes not even human.

"No," he says bitterly. "You can't want me."

"Quiet," she says, "quiet." Her hands are on his face; she kisses his neck; his spine melts; and he falls atop her again, too hungry to stop.

"You're so foolish for someone so smart," she murmurs to him afterward. "Just like Alice."

He does not consider her meaning.

■ ■ ■

The roof of the Citrine Tower is a landing facility for phaetons, the suborbital vehicles of companies and their executives. He feels he has learned all he can of Alice Citrine's life while cooped up in the tower. Now he wants the heft and feel of actual places and people to judge her by.

But before they may leave, June tells Stone, they must spe: to Jerrold Scarfe.

In a small departure lounge, all soft white corrugated wal and molded chairs, the three meet.

Scarfe is head of security for Citrine Technologies. A compact, wiry man, exhibiting a minimum of facial expressions, he strikes Stone as eminently competent, from the top of his permanently depilated and tattooed skull to his booted feet. On his chest he wears the CT emblem: a red spiral with an arrowhead on its outer terminus, pointing up.

June greets Scarfe with some familiarity and asks, "Are we cleared?"

Scarfe waggles a sheet of flimsy in the air. "Your flight plan is quite extensive. Is it really necessary, for instance, to visit a place like Mexico City with Mr. Stone aboard?"

Stone wonders at Scarfe's solicitude for him, an unimportant stranger. June interprets Stone's puzzled look and explains. "Jerrold is one of the few people who know you represent Miz Citrine. Naturally, he's worried that if we run into trouble of some kind, the fallout will descend on Citrine Technologies."

"I'm not looking for trouble, Mr. Scarfe. I just want to do my job."

Scarfe scans Stone as intently as the devices outside Alice Citrine's sanctum. The favorable result is eventually expressed in a mild grunt and the announcement, "Your pilot's waiting. Go ahead."

Higher off the grasping earth than he has ever been before, his right hand atop June's left knee, feeling wild and rich and free, Stone ruminates over the life of Alice Citrine and the sense he is beginning to make of it.

Alice Citrine is 159 years old. When she was born, America was still comprised of states, rather than FEZ and ARCadias. Man had barely begun to fly. When she was in her sixties, she headed a firm called Citrine Biotics. This was the time of the Trade Wars, wars as deadly and decisive as military wars, yet fought with tariffs and five-year plans, automated assembly lines, and fifth-generation decision-making constructs. This was also the time of the Second Constitutional Convention, that revamping of America for the state of war.

During the years when the country was being divided into Free Enterprise Zones—urban, hi-tech, autonomous regions where the only laws were those imposed by corporations and the only goal was profits and dominance—and Areas of Restrictive Control—rural, mainly agricultural enclaves, where older values were strictly enforced—Citrine Biotics refined and perfected the work of their researchers and others in the field of carbon chips: microbiological assemblies, blood-borne programmed repair units. The final product, marketed by Citrine to those who could afford it, was near-total rejuvenation, the cell slough or, simply, the sluff.

Citrine Biotics headed the Fortune 500 within six years.

By then it was Citrine Technologies.

And Alice Citrine sat atop it all.

But not forever.

Entropy will not be cheated. The information-degradation that DNA undergoes with age is not totally reversible. Errors accumulate despite the hardworking carbon chips. The body dutiful gives out in the end.

Alice Citrine is nearing the theoretical close of her extended life. Despite her youthful looks, one day a vital organ will fail, the result of a million bad transcriptions.

She needs Stone, of all people, to justify her existence.

Stone squeezes June's knee and relishes the sense of importance. For the first time in his sad and dingy life, he can make a difference. His words, his perceptions, *matter*. He is determined to do a good job, to tell the truth as he perceives it.

"June," Stone says emphatically, "I have to see everything."
She smiles. "You will, Stone. You will indeed."

■ ■ ■

And the phaeton comes down—in Mexico City, which
crashed last year at population 35 million. Citrine Technologies
is funding a relief effort there, operating out of their Houston
and Dallas locations. Stone is suspicious of the motives behind
the campaign. Why didn't they step in before the point of collapse? Can it be that they are worried now only about refugees
flooding across the border? Whatever the reasons, though,
Stone cannot deny that the CT workers are a force for good,
ministering to the sick and hungry, reestablishing electrical
power and communications, propping up (acting as?) the city
government. He boards the phaeton with his head spinning,
and soon finds himself—

—in the Antarctic, where he and June are choppered out
from the CT domes to a krill-processing ship, source of so much
of the world's protein. June finds the frack stench offensive, but
Stone breathes deeply, exhilarated at being afloat in these
strange and icy latitudes, watching the capable men and women
work. June is happy to be soon aloft, and then—

—in Peking, where CT heuristic specialists are working on
the first Artificial Organic Intelligence. Stone listens with
amusement to a debate over whether the AOI should be name
K'ung Fu-tzu or Mao.

The week is a kaleidoscopic whirl of impressions. Stone feels
like a sponge, soaking up the sights and sounds so long denied
him. At one point he finds himself leaving a restaurant with
June in a city whose name he has forgotten. In his hand is his
ID card, with which he has just paid for their meal. A holo-
portrait stares up from his palm. The face is cadaverous, filthy,
with two empty, crusted sockets for eyes. Stone remembers the
warm laser fingers taking his holo in the Immigration Office.
Was that really him? The day seems like an event from someone
else's life. He pockets his card, unsure whether to have the holo
updated or keep it as a token of where he has come from.

And where he might end up?

(What will she do with him after he reports?)

When Stone asks one day to see orbital installations, June calls a halt.

"I think we've done enough for one trip, Stone. Let's get back, so you can start to put it all together."

With her words, a deep bone-weariness suddenly overtakes Stone, and his manic high evaporates. He silently assents.

■ ■ ■

Stone's bedroom is dark, except for the diffuse lights of the city seeping in through a window. Stone has multiplied his vision, the better to admire the naked glowing form of June beside him. He has found that colors grow muddy in the absence of enough photons, but that a very vivid black-and-white image can be had. He feels like a dweller in the past century, watching a primitive film. Except that June is very much alive beneath his hands.

June's body is a tracery of lambent lines, like some arcane capillary circuitry in the core of Mao/K'ung Fu-tzu. Following the current craze, she has had a subdermal pattern of microchannels implanted. The channels are filled with synthetic luciferase, the biochemical responsible for the glow of fireflies, which she can trigger now at will. In the afterglow of their lovemaking, she has set herself alight. Her breasts are whorls of cold fire, her shaven pubic mound a spiral galaxy dragging Stone's gaze into illimitable depths.

June is speaking in an abstracted way of her life before Stone, pondering the ceiling while he idly strokes her.

"My mother was the only surviving child of two refugees. Vietnamese. Came to America shortly after the Asian War. Did the only thing they knew how to do, which was fish. They lived in Texas, on the Gulf. My mother went to college on a scholarship. There she met my father, who was another refugee of sorts. He left Germany with his parents after its Reunification. They said the compromise government was neither one thing nor the other, and they couldn't deal with it. I guess my background is some sort of microcosm of a lot of the upheavals of our times." She catches Stone's hand between her knees and holds it tightly. "But I feel a calmness with you right now, Stone."

As she continues to speak of things she has seen, people she has known, her career as Citrine's personal assistant, the oddest feeling creeps over Stone. As her words integrate themselves into his growing picture of the world, he feels the same abysmal tidal suck that he first felt upon learning of history.

Before he can decide consciously whether he even wants to know or not, he finds himself saying, "June. How old are you?"

She falls silent. Stone watches her staring blindly at him, unequipped with his damned perceptive eyes.

"Over sixty," she finally says. "Does it matter?"

Stone finds he cannot answer, does not know if it does or not.

Slowly June wills her glowing body dark.

Stone bitterly amuses himself with what he likes to think of as his art.

Perusing the literature on the silicon chip that dwells in his skull, he found that it had one property not mentioned by the doctor. The contents of its RAM can be squirted in a signal to a stand-alone computer. There the images he has collected may be displayed for all to see. What is more, the digitalized images may be manipulated, recombined with themselves or with stock graphics, to form entirely lifelike pictures of things that never existed. These, of course, may be printed off.

In effect, Stone is a living camera and his computer a complete studio.

Stone has been working on a series of images of June. The color printouts litter his quarters, hung on walls and underfoot.

June's head on the Sphinx's body. June as La Belle Dame Sans Merci. June's face imposed upon the full moon, Stone asleep in a field as Endymion.

The portraits are more disturbing than soothing and, Stone senses, quite unfair. But Stone feels that he is gaining some therapeutic effect from them, that each day he is inching closer to his true feelings for June.

He has still not spoken to Alice Citrine. That nags him greatly. When will he deliver his report? What will he say?

The problem of when is solved for him that afternoon. Returning from one of the tower's private gyms, he finds his terminal flashing a message.

Citrine will see him in the morning.

■ ■ ■

Alone this second time, Stone stands on the plate before Alice Citrine's room, allowing his identity to be verified. He hopes the results will be shared with him when the machine finishes, for he has no idea of who he is.

The door slides into the wall, a beckoning cavern mouth.

Avernus, Stone thinks, and enters.

Alice Citrine remains where she sat so many event-congested weeks ago, unchanged, seemingly sempiternal. The screens flicker in epileptic patterns on three sides of her instrumented chair. Now, however, she ignores them, her eyes on Stone, who advances with trepidation.

Stone stops before her, the console an uncrossable moat between them. He notes her features this second time with a mix of disbelief and alarm. They seem to resemble his newly fleshed-out face to an uncanny degree. Has he come to look like this woman simply by working for her? Or does life outside the Bungle stamp the same harsh lines on everyone?

Citrine brushes her hand above her lap, and Stone notices her pet curled in the valley of her brown robe, its preternaturally large eyes catching the colors on the monitors.

"Time for a preliminary report, Mr. Stone," she says. "But your pulse rate is much too high. Relax a bit. Everything does not hinge on this one session."

Stone wishes he could. But there is no offer of a seat, and he knows that what he says will be judged.

"So—what do you feel about this world of ours, which bears the impress of myself and others like me?"

The smug superiority in Citrine's voice drives all caution from Stone's thoughts, and he nearly shouts, It's unfair! He pauses a moment, and then honesty forces him to admit, "Beautiful, gaudy, exciting at times—but basically unfair."

Citrine seems pleased at his outburst. "Very good, Mr. Stone. You have discovered the basic contradiction of life. There are jewels in the dung heap, tears amid the laughter, and how it is all parceled out, no one knows. I'm afraid I cannot shoulder the blame for the world's unfairness, though. It was unfair when I was a child, and remained unfair despite all my actions. In fact, I may have increased the disparity a little. The rich are richer, the poor seemingly poorer by comparison. But still, even the titans are brought down by death in the end."

"But why didn't you try harder to change things?" Stone demands. "It has to be within your power."

For the first time, Citrine laughs, and Stone hears an echo of his own sometimes bitter caw.

"Mr. Stone," she says, "I have all I can do to stay alive. And I do not mean taking care of my body—that is attended to automatically. No, I mean avoiding assassination. Haven't you gleaned the true nature of business in this world of ours?"

Stone fails to see her meaning and says so.

"Allow me to brief you, then. It might alter a few of your perceptions. You are aware of the intended purpose of the Second Constitutional Convention, are you not? It was couched in high-flown phrases like 'unleash the strength of the American system' and 'meet foreign competition head-to-head, ensuring a victory for American business that will pave the way for democracy throughout the world.' All very noble-sounding. But the actual outcome was quite different. Business has no stake in any political system per se. Business cooperates to the extent that cooperation furthers its own interests. And the primary interest of business is growth and dominance. Once the establishment of the Free Enterprise Zones freed corporations from all constraints, they reverted to a primal struggle, which continues to this day."

Stone attempts to digest all this. He has seen no overt struggles in his journey. Yet he has vaguely sensed undercurrents of tension everywhere. But surely she is overstating the case. Why, she makes the civilized world sound no more than a large-scale version of the anarchy in the Bungle.

As if reading his mind, Citrine says, "Did you ever wonder why the Bungle remains blighted and exploited in the midst of the city, Mr. Stone, its people in misery?"

Suddenly all of Citrine's screens flash with scenes of Bungle life, obedient to her unvoiced command. Stone is taken aback. Here are the sordid details of his youth: urine-reeking alleys with rag-covered forms lying halfway between sleep and death, the chaos around the Immigration Office, the razor-topped fence by the river.

"The Bungle," Citrine continues, "is contested ground. It has been so for over eighty years. The corporations cannot agree over who is to develop it. Any improvement made by one is immediately destroyed by the tactical team of another. This is the kind of stalemate prevalent in much of the world.

"Everyone wanted to be pulled into an earthly paradise by his purse strings, like a Krishna devotee by his pigtail. But this patchwork of fiefdoms is what we got instead."

Stone's conceptions are reeling. He came expecting to be quizzed and to disgorge all he thought he knew. Instead he has been lectured and provoked, almost as if Citrine is testing whether he is a partner fit to debate. Has he passed or failed?

Citrine settles the question with her next words. "That's enough for today, Mr. Stone. Go back and think some more. We'll talk again."

■   ■   ■

For three weeks Stone meets nearly every day with Citrine. Together they explore a bewildering array of her concerns. Stone gradually becomes more confident of himself, expressing his opinions and observations in a firmer tone. They do not always mesh with Citrine's, yet on the whole he feels a surprising kinship and affinity with the ancient woman.

Sometimes it almost seems as if she is grooming him, master and apprentice, and is proud of his progress. At other times she holds herself distant and aloof.

The weeks have brought other changes. Although Stone has not slept with June since that fateful night, he no longer sees her as the siren figure of his portraits and has stopped depicting her in that fashion. They are friends, and Stone visits with her often, enjoys her company, is forever grateful to her for her part in rescuing him from the Bungle.

During his interviews with Citrine, her pet is a constant spectator. Its enigmatic presence disturbs Stone. He has found no trace of sentimental affection in Citrine and cannot fathom her attention to the creature.

One day Stone finally asks Citrine outright why she keeps it.

Her lips twitch in what passes for her smile. "Aegypt is my touchstone on the true perspective of things, Mr. Stone. Perhaps you do not recognize her breed."

Stone admits ignorance.

"This is *Aegyptopithecus zeuxis*, Mr. Stone. Her kind last flourished several million years ago. Currently she is the only specimen extant, a clone—or, rather, a re-creation based on dead fossil cells.

"She is your ancestor and mine, Mr. Stone. Before the hominids, she was the representative of mankind on earth. When I pet her, I contemplate how little we have advanced."

Stone turns and stalks off, unaccountably repelled by the antiquity of the beast and this insight into its mistress.

This is the last time he will see Alice Citrine.

Nighttime.

Stone lies alone in bed, replaying snapshots of his terminal screen, of pre-FEZ history that has eluded him.

History that has eluded him.

Suddenly there is a loud crack like the simultaneous discharge of a thousand gigantic arcs of static electricity. At that exact second, two things happen:

Stone feels an instant of vertigo.

His eyes go dead.

Atop these shocks, an enormous explosion above his head rocks the entire shaft of the Citrine Tower.

Stone shoots to his feet, clad only in briefs, barefoot as in the Bungle. He can't believe he's blind. But he is. Back in the dark world of smell and sound and touch alone.

Alarms are going off everywhere. Stone rushes out into his front room with its useless view of the city. He approaches the front door, but it fails to open. He reaches for the manual control, but hesitates.

What can he do while blind? He'd just stumble around, get in the way. Better to stay here and wait out whatever is happening.

Stone thinks of June then, can almost smell her perfume. Surely she will be down momentarily to tell him what's going on. That's it. He'll wait for June.

Stone paces nervously for three minutes. He can't believe his loss of vision. Yet somehow he's always known it would happen.

The alarms have stopped, allowing Stone to hear near-subliminal footsteps in the hall, advancing on his door. June at last? No, everything's wrong. Stone's sense of life denies that the visitor is anyone he knows.

Stone's Bungle instincts take over. He ceases to speculate about what is happening; all is speed and fear.

The curtains in the room are tied back with thin velvet cords. Stone rips one hastily down, takes up a position to the side of the outer door.

The shock wave when the door is hit nearly knocks Stone down. But he regains his balance, tasting blood, just as the man barrels in and past him.

Stone is on the man's burly back in a flash, legs wrapped around his waist, cord around his throat.

The man drops his gun, hurls himself back against the wall. Stone feels ribs give, but he tightens the rope, muscles straining.

The two stagger around the room, smashing furniture and vases, locked in something like an obscene mating posture.

Eventually, after forever, the man keels over, landing heavily atop Stone.

Stone never relents, until he is sure that the man has stopped breathing.

His attacker is dead.

Stone lives.

He wriggles painfully out from under the slack mass, shaken and hurt.

As he gets his feet under him, he hears more people approaching, speaking.

Jerrold Scarfe is the first to enter, calling Stone by name. When he spots Stone, Scarfe shouts, "Get that stretcher over here."

Men bundle Stone onto the canvas and begin to carry him off.

Scarfe walks beside him and conducts a surrealistic conversation.

"They learned who you were, Mr. Stone. That one fracking bastard got by us. We contained the rest in the wreckage of the upper floors. They hit us with a directed electromagnetic pulse that took out all our electronics, including your vision. You might have lost a few brain cells when it burned, but nothing that can't be fixed. After the EMP, they used a missile on Miz Citrine's floor. I'm afraid she died instantly."

Stone feels as if he is being shaken to pieces, both physically and mentally. Why is Scarfe telling him this? And what about June?

Stone croaks her name.

"She's dead, Mr. Stone. When the raiders assigned to bag her had begun to work on her, she killed herself with an implanted toxin sac."

All the lilies wither when winter draws near.

The stretcher party has reached the medical facilities. Stone is lifted onto a bed, and clean hands begin to attend to his injuries.

"Mr. Stone," Scarfe continues, "I must insist that you listen to this. It's imperative, and it will take only a minute."

Stone has begun to hate this insistent voice. But he cannot close his ears or lapse into blessed unconsciousness, so he is forced to hear the cassette Scarfe plays.

It is Alice Citrine speaking.

"Blood of my blood," she begins, "closer than a son to me. You are the only one I could ever trust."

Disgust washes over Stone as everything clicks into place and he realizes what he is.

"You are hearing this after my death. This means that what I have built is now yours. All the people have been bought to ensure this. It is now up to you to retain their loyalty. I hope our talks have helped you. If not, you will need even more luck than I wish you now.

"Please forgive your abandonment in the Bungle. It's just that a good education is so important, and I believe you received the best. I was always watching you."

Scarfe cuts off the cassette. "What are your orders, Mr. Stone?"

Stone thinks with agonizing slowness while unseen people minister to him.

"Just clean this mess up, Scarfe. Just clean up this whole goddamn mess."

But he knows as he speaks that this is not Scarfe's job.

It's his.

BRUCE STERLING AND WILLIAM GIBSON

Red Star, Winter Orbit

■

Collaborative stories are a tradition in science fiction. And collaborative work has flourished in cyberpunk, as writers, already working closely together in concept and criticism, take the next logical step—to joint creation. In a sense, collaboration, by combining voices, allows the Movement to speak with a voice of its own.

Mirrorshades concludes with two collaborations. The present story, from 1983, is the only joint work to date by William Gibson and Bruce Sterling—both widely seen as central figures in cyberpunk. "Red Star, Winter Orbit" demonstrates cyberpunk's global point of view as well as its love of closely researched, fully realized detail.

William Gibson wrote "The Gernsback Continuum," which led this collection.

Bruce Sterling's first novel was published in 1977. He has written three novels and a score of short stories. His work ranges widely through the SF field, including comic satires and historical fantasies. He is perhaps best known for his "Shaper series," including the novel *Schismatrix,* and for his sense of irony, which sometimes leads him to speak of himself in the third person.

He lives in Austin, Texas.

Colonel Korolev twisted slowly in his harness, dreaming of winter and gravity. Young again, a cadet, he whipped his horse across the late November steppes of Kazakhstan into dry red vistas of Martian sunset.

That's wrong, he thought—

And woke—in the Museum of the Soviet Triumph in Space—to the sounds of Romanenko and the KGB man's wife. They were going at it again, behind the screen at the aft end of the Salyut, restraining straps and padded hull creaking and thudding rhythmically. Hooves in the snow.

Freeing himself from the harness, Korolev executed a practiced kick that propelled him into the toilet stall. Shrugging out of his threadbare coverall, he clamped the commode around his loins and wiped condensed steam from the steel mirror. His arthritic hand had swollen again during sleep; the wrist was bird-bone thin from calcium loss. Twenty years had passed since he'd last known gravity. He'd grown old in orbit.

He shaved with a suction razor. A patchwork of broken veins blotched his left cheek and temple, another legacy from the blowout that had crippled him.

When he emerged, he found that the adulterers had finished. Romanenko was adjusting his clothing. The political officer's wife, Valentina, wore dun-brown coveralls with the sleeves ripped out; her white arms were sheened with the sweat of their exertion. Her ash-blond hair rippled in the breeze from a ventilator. Her eyes were purest cornflower blue, set a little too closely together, and they held a look half apologetic, half conspiratorial. "See what we've brought you, Colonel."

She handed him a tiny airline bottle of cognac.

Stunned, Korolev blinked at the Air France logo embossed on the plastic cap.

"It came in the last Soyuz. Inside a cucumber, my husband said." She giggled. "He gave it to me."

"We decided you should have it, Colonel," Romanenko said, grinning broadly. "After all, we can be furloughed at any time." Korolev ignored the sidelong, embarrassed glance at his shriveled legs and pale, dangling feet.

He opened the bottle, and the rich aroma brought a sudden tingling rush of blood to his cheeks. He raised it carefully and sucked out a few milliliters of brandy. It burned like acid. "Christ," he gasped, "it's been years. I'll get plastered!" He laughed, tears blurring his vision.

"My father tells me you drank like a hero, Colonel, in the old days."

"Yes," Korolev said, and sipped again, "I did." The cognac spread through him like liquid gold. He disliked Romanenko. He'd never liked the boy's father, either—an easygoing Party man, long since settled into lecture tours, a dacha on the Black

Sea, American liquor, French suits, Italian shoes. . . . The boy had his father's looks, the same clear gray eyes utterly untroubled by doubt.

The alcohol surged through Korolev's thin blood. "You are too generous," he said. He kicked once, gently, and arrived at his console. "You must take some *samizdata*. American cable broadcasts, freshly intercepted. Racy stuff! Wasted on an old man like me." He slotted a blank cassette and punched for the material.

"I'll give it to the gun crew," Romanenko said, grinning. "They can run it on the tracking consoles in the gun room." The particle-beam station had always been known as the "gun room." The soldiers who manned it were particularly hungry for this sort of tape. Korolev ran off a second copy for Valentina.

"It's dirty?" She looked alarmed and intrigued. "May we come again, Colonel? Thursday at twenty-four hundred?"

Korolev smiled at her. She'd been a factory worker before she'd been singled out for space. Her beauty made her useful as a propaganda tool, a role model for the proletariat. He pitied her now, with the cognac coursing through her veins, and found it impossible to deny her a little happiness. "A midnight rendezvous in the museum, Valentina? Romantic!"

She kissed his cheek, wobbling in freefall. "Thank you, my colonel."

"You're a prince, Colonel," Romanenko said, slapping Korolev's matchstick shoulder as gently as he could. After countless hours on an exerciser, the boy's arms bulged like a blacksmith's.

Korolev watched the lovers carefully make their way out into the central docking sphere, the junction of three aging Salyuts and two corridors. Romanenko took the "north" corridor to the gun room; Valentina went in the opposite direction to the next junction sphere and the Salyut where her husband slept.

There were five docking spheres in Kosmograd, each with its three linked Salyuts. At opposite ends of the complex were the military installation and the satellite launchers. Popping, humming, and wheezing, the station had the feel of a subway and the damp metallic reek of a tramp steamer.

Korolev had another pull at the bottle. Now it was half empty. He hid it in one of the museum's exhibits, a NASA Hasselblad recovered from the site of the Apollo landing. He hadn't had a drink since his last furlough, before the blowout. His head swam in a pleasant, painful current of drunken nostalgia.

Drifting back to his console, he accessed a section of memory where the collected speeches of Alexei Kosygin had been covertly erased and replaced with his personal collection of *samizdata*. He had British groups taped off West German radio, Warsaw pact heavy metal, American imports from the black market. . . . Putting on his headphones, he punched for the Czestochowa reggae of Brygada Cryzis.

After all the years, he no longer really heard the music, but images came rushing back with an aching poignancy. In the Eighties he'd been a long-haired child of the Soviet elite, his father's position placing him effectively beyond the reach of the Moscow police. He remembered feedback howling through the speakers in the hot darkness of a cellar club, the crowd a shadowy checkerboard of denim and bleached hair. He'd smoked Marlboros laced with powdered Afghani hash. He remembered the mouth of an American diplomat's daughter in the back seat of her father's black Lincoln. Names and faces came flooding in on a warm haze of cognac. Nina, the East German who'd shown him her mimeographed translations of dissident Polish news sheets—

Until one night she didn't turn up at the coffee bar. Whispers of parasitism, of anti-Soviet activity, of the waiting chemical horrors of the *psikushka*—

Korolev started to tremble. He wiped his face and found it bathed in sweat. He took off the headphones.

It had been fifty years . . . yet he was suddenly and very intensely afraid. He couldn't remember ever having been this frightened, not even during the blowout that had crushed his hip. He shook violently. The lights. The lights in the Salyut were too bright, but he didn't want to go to the switches. A simple action, one he performed regularly, yet. . . . The switches and their insulated cables were somehow threatening. He stared, confused. The little clockwork model of a Lunokhod moon rover, its Velcro wheels gripping the curved wall, seemed to crouch there like something sentient, poised, waiting. The eyes of the Soviet space pioneers in the official portraits were fixed on his with contempt.

The cognac. The years in free-fall had warped his metabolism. He wasn't the man he'd once been. But he would try to stay calm, try to ride it out. If he threw up, everyone would surely laugh at him. . . .

Someone knocked at the entrance to the museum, and he gasped. Nikita the Plumber, Kosmograd's premier handyman, executed a perfect slow-motion dive through the open hatch. The young civilian engineer looked angry. Korolev felt cowed. "You're up early, Plumber," he said, anxious for some facade of normality.

"Pinhead leakage in Delta Three." The Plumber frowned. "Do you understand Japanese?" He tugged a cassette from one of the dozen pockets that bulged on his stained work vest and waved it in Korolev's face. He wore carefully laundered Levi's and dilapidated Adidas running shoes. "We accessed this last night."

Korolev cowered as though the cassette were a weapon. "No, no Japanese." The meekness of his own voice startled him. "Only English and Polish." He felt himself blush. The Plumber was his friend; he knew and trusted the Plumber, but—

"Are you well, Colonel?" The Plumber loaded the tape and punched up a lexicon program with deft, calloused fingers. "You look as though you just ate a bug. I want you to hear this."

Korolev watched uneasily as the tape flickered into an ad for baseball gloves. The lexicon's Cyrillic subtitles raced across the monitor as a Japanese voice-over rattled maniacally. A second ad flashed on: an extraordinarily beautiful girl in a black evening dress piloted a gossamer French ultralight in brilliant sunlight, soaring above the Great Wall of China.

"The newscast's coming up," said the Plumber, gnawing at a cuticle.

Korolev squinted anxiously as the translation slid across the face of the Japanese announcer.

AMERICAN DISARMAMENT GROUP CLAIMS . . . PREPARATIONS AT BAIKONUR COSMODROME . . . PROVE RUSSIANS AT LAST READY . . . TO SCRAP ARMED SPACE STATION COMIC CITY. . . .

"Cosmic," the Plumber muttered. "Glitch in the lexicon."

BUILT AT TURN OF THE CENTURY AS BRIDGEHEAD TO SPACE . . . AMBITIOUS PROJECT CRIPPLED BY FAILURE OF LUNAR MINING . . . EXPENSIVE STATION OUTPERFORMED BY OUR UNMANNED OR-

BITAL FACTORIES . . . CRYSTALS, SEMICONDUCTORS, AND PURE
DRUGS . . .

"Smug bastards." The Plumber snorted. "I tell you, it's our
goddamned KGB man, Yefremov. He's had a hand in this!"

STAGGERING SOVIET TRADE DEFICITS . . . POPULAR DISCON-
TENT WITH SPACE EFFORT . . . RECENT DECISIONS BY POLITBURO
AND CENTRAL COMMITTEE SECRETARIAT . . .

"They're shutting us down!" The Plumber's face contorted
with rage.

Korolev twisted away from the screen, shaking uncontrolla-
bly. Sudden tears peeled from his lashes in free-fall droplets.
"Leave me alone! I can do nothing!"

"What's wrong, Colonel?" The Plumber grabbed his shoulders. "Look me in the face." His eyes widened. "Someone's
dosed you with the Fear!"

"Go away," Korolev begged.

"That little spook bastard! What has he given you? Pills? An
injection?"

Korolev shuddered. "I had a drink—"

"He gave you the Fear! You, a sick old man! I'll break his
face!" The Plumber jerked his knees up, somersaulted backward, kicked off from a handhold overhead, and catapulted out
of the room.

"Wait! Plumber?" But the Plumber had zipped through the
docking sphere like a squirrel, vanishing down the corridor, and
now Korolev felt that he couldn't bear to be alone. In the distance he could hear metallic echoes of distant, angry shouts.

Trembling, he closed his eyes and waited for someone to help
him.

■ ■ ■

He'd asked Psychiatric Officer Bychkov to help him dress in
his old uniform, the one with the Star of the Tsiolkovsky Order
sewn above the left breast pocket. The black dress boots of
heavy quilted nylon, with their Velcro soles, would no longer fit
his twisted feet. So his feet remained bare.

Bychkov's injection had straightened him out within an
hour, leaving him alternately depressed and furiously angry.
Now he waited in the museum for Yefremov to answer his
summons.

They called his home the Museum of the Soviet Triumph in Space, and as his rage again subsided, to be replaced with an ancient bleakness, he felt very much as if he were simply another one of the exhibits. He stared gloomily at the gold-framed portraits of the great visionaries of space, at the faces of Tsiolkovsky, Rynin, Tupolev. Below these, in slightly smaller frames, were portraits of Verne, Goddard, and O'Neill.

In moments of extreme depression he had sometimes imagined that he could detect a common strangeness in their eyes. Was it simply craziness, as he sometimes thought in his most cynical moods? Or was he glimpsing a subtle manifestation of some weird, unbalanced force—a force that might be, as he suspected, human evolution in action?

Once, and only once, Korolev had seen that look in his own eyes—on the day he'd stepped onto the soil of the Coprates Basin. The Martian sunlight, glinting within his helmet visor, had shown him the reflection of two steady, alien eyes—fearless, yet driven—and the quiet, secret shock of it, he now realized, had been his life's most memorable, most transcendant moment.

Above the portraits was mounted a hideous painting that depicted the landing in colors with the oily inertness of borscht and gravy. The Martian landscape was reduced to the idealistic kitsch of Soviet socialist realism. The artist had posed the suited figure beside the lander with all the official style's deeply sincere vulgarity.

Feeling tainted, he awaited the arrival of Yefremov, the KGB man, Kosmograd's political officer.

When Yefremov finally entered the Salyut, Korolev noted the split lip and the fresh bruises on the man's throat. Yefremov wore a blue Kansai jumpsuit of Japanese silk and stylish Italian deck shoes. He coughed politely. "Good morning, Comrade Colonel."

Korolev stared. He allowed the silence to lengthen. "Yefremov," he said heavily, "I am not happy with you."

Yefremov reddened but held his gaze. "Let us speak frankly, Colonel. As Russian to Russian. It was not, of course, intended for you."

"The Fear, Yefremov?"

"The beta-carboline, yes. If you hadn't pandered to their antisocial actions, if you hadn't accepted their bribe, it would never have happened."

"So I'm a pimp, Yefremov? A pimp and a drunkard? You are a cuckold, a smuggler, and a snitch. I say this," he added, "as one Russian to another."

Now the KGB man's face assumed the official mask of bland and untroubled righteousness.

"But tell me, Yefremov, what it is you're really about. What have you been doing since you came to Kosmograd? We know that the complex will be stripped. What's in store for the civilian crew when they return to Baikonur? Corruption hearings?"

"There will be interrogation, certainly. In certain cases there may be hospitalization. Would you care to suggest, Comrade Colonel, that the Soviet Union is somehow at fault for Kosmograd's failures?"

Korolev was silent.

"Kosmograd was a dream, Colonel. A dream that failed. Like space, Colonel. We have no need to be here. We have an entire world to put in order. Moscow is the greatest global power in human history. We must not allow ourselves to lose the global perspective."

"Do you think we cosmonauts can be brushed aside that easily? We are an elite, a highly trained technical elite."

"A minority, Colonel, an obsolete minority. What do you contribute, aside from reams of poisonous American trash? The crew here were meant to be workers, not bloated black marketeers trafficking in satellite jazz and pornography." Yefremov's face was smooth and calm. "The crew will return to Baikonur. The weapons can be directed from the ground. You, of course, will remain, and there will be guest cosmonauts: Africans, South Americans. Space still retains a degree of its former prestige for these people."

Korolev gritted his teeth. "What have you done with the boy?"

"Your Plumber?" The political officer frowned. "He has assaulted an officer of State Security. He will remain under guard until he can be taken to Baikonur."

Korolev attempted an unpleasant laugh. "Let him go. You'll

be in too much trouble yourself to press charges. I'll speak with Marshal Gubarev personally. My rank here may be entirely honorary, but I do retain a certain influence."

The KGB man shrugged. "The gun crew are under orders from Baikonur to keep the communications module under lock and key. Their careers depend on it. You'll send no messages."

"Martial law, then?"

"This isn't Kabul, Colonel. These are difficult times for all of us. You have the moral authority here; you should try to set an example. The last thing we need is melodrama."

"We shall see," Korolev said.

■ ■ ■

Kosmograd swung out of Earth's shadow into raw sunlight. The walls of Korolev's Salyut popped and creaked like a nest of glass bottles. The viewports, Korolev thought absently, fingering the broken veins at his temple, were always the first to go.

Young Grishkin seemed to have the same thought. He drew a tube of caulk from an ankle pocket and began to inspect the seal around the viewport. He was the Plumber's assistant and closest friend.

"We must now vote," Korolev said wearily. Eleven of Kosmograd's twenty-four civilian crew members had agreed to attend the meeting, twelve if he counted himself. That left thirteen others, who were either unwilling to risk involvement or actively hostile to the idea of a strike. Yefremov and the six-man gun crew brought the total number of those not present to twenty. "We've discussed our demands. All those in favor of the list as it stands—" He raised his good hand. Three others raised theirs. Grishkin, busy at the viewport, stuck out his foot.

Korolev sighed. "There are few enough of us as it is. We'd best have unanimity. Let's hear your objections."

"The term *military custody*," said a biological technician named Korovkin, "might be construed as implying that the military, and not the criminal Yefremov, is responsible for the situation." The man looked acutely uncomfortable. "We are in sympathy otherwise but will not sign. We are Party members."

He seemed about to add something but fell silent. "My mother," his wife said quietly, "was Jewish."

Korolev nodded but said nothing.

"This is all criminal foolishness," said Glushko, the botanist. Neither he nor his wife had voted. "Madness. Kosmograd is finished, we all know it, and the sooner home the better. What has this place ever been but a prison?" Free-fall disagreed with the man's metabolism; in the absence of gravity, blood tended to congest in his face and neck, making him resemble one of his experimental pumpkins.

"You're a botanist, Vasili," his wife said stiffly, "while I, you will recall, am a Soyuz pilot. Your career is not at stake."

"I will *not* support this idiocy!" Glushko gave the bulkhead a savage kick that propelled him from the room. His wife followed, complaining bitterly in the grating undertone crew members learned to use for private arguments.

"Five are willing to sign," Korolev said, "out of a civilian crew of twenty-four."

"Six," said Tatjana, the other Soyuz pilot, her dark hair drawn back and held with a braided band of green nylon webbing. "You forget the Plumber."

"The sun balloons!" cried Grishkin, pointing toward the earth. "Look!"

Kosmograd was above the coast of California now; clean shorelines, intensely green fields, vast decaying cities whose names rang with a strange magic. Far above a fleece of stratocumulus floated five solar balloons, mirrored geodesic spheres tethered by power lines; they had been a cheaper substitute for a grandiose American plan to build solar power satellites. The things worked, Korolev supposed, because for a decade he'd watched them multiply.

"And they say that people live in those things?" Systems Officer Stoiko had joined Grishkin at the viewport.

Korolev remembered the pathetic flurry of strange American energy schemes in the wake of the Treaty of Vienna. With the Soviet Union firmly in control of the world's oil flow, the Americans had seemed willing to try anything. Then the Kansas meltdown had permanently soured them on reactors. For more than three decades, they'd been gradually sliding into isolationism and industrial decline. *Space,* he thought ruefully, *they should have gone into space.* He'd never understood the strange paralysis of will that had seemed to grip their brilliant early efforts. Or perhaps it was simply a failure of imagination, of vision. *You see, Americans,* he said silently, *you really should have tried to join us, here in our glorious future. Here in Kosmograd.*

"Who would want to live in something like that?" Stoiko asked, punching Grishkin's shoulder and laughing with the quiet energy of desperation.

■ ■ ■

"You're joking," said Yefremov. "Surely we're all in enough trouble as it is."

"We're not joking, Political Officer Yefremov, and these are our demands." The five dissidents had crowded into the Salyut the man shared with Valentina, backing him against the aft screen. The screen was decorated with a meticulously air-brushed photograph of the Premier, who was waving from the back of a tractor. Valentina, Korolev knew, would be in the museum now with Romanenko, making the straps creak. Korolev wondered how Romanenko so regularly managed to avoid his duty shifts in the gun room.

Yefremov shrugged. He glanced down the list of demands. "The Plumber must remain in custody. I have direct orders. As for the rest of this document—"

"You are guilty of unauthorized use of psychiatric drugs!" Grishkin shouted.

"That was a private matter," said Yefremov calmly.

"A criminal act," said Tatjana.

"Pilot Tatjana, we both know that Grishkin here is the station's most active *samizdata* pirate. We are all criminals, don't you see? That's the beauty of our system, isn't it?" His sudden, twisted smile was shockingly cynical. "Kosmograd is not the Potemkin, and you are not revolutionaries. And you *demand* to communicate with Marshal Gubarev? He is in custody at Baikonur. And you *demand* to communicate with the minister of technology? The minister is leading the purge." With a decisive gesture, he ripped the printout to pieces, scraps of yellow flimsy scattering in free-fall like slow-motion butterflies.

■ ■ ■

On the ninth day of the strike, Korolev met with Grishkin and Stoiko in the Salyut that Grishkin had once shared with the Plumber.

For forty years the inhabitants of Kosmograd had fought an antiseptic war against mold and mildew. Dust, grease, and vapor wouldn't settle in free-fall, and spores lurked everywhere—in padding, in clothing, in the ventilation ducts. In the warm, moist, petri-dish atmosphere, they spread like oil slicks. Now there was a reek of dry rot in the air, overlaid with ominous whiffs of burning insulation.

Korolev's sleep had been broken by the hollow thud of a departing Soyuz lander. Glushko and his wife, he supposed. During the past forty-eight hours, Yefremov had supervised the evacuation of the crew members who had refused to join the strike. The gun crew kept to the gun room and their barracks ring, where they still held Nikita the Plumber.

Grishkin's Salyut had become the strike's headquarters. None of them had shaved, and Stoiko had contracted a staph infection that spread across his forearms in angry welts. Surrounded by lurid pinups from American television, they resembled some degenerate trio of pornographers. The lights were dim; Kosmograd ran on half power. "With the others gone," Stoiko said, "our hand is strengthened."

Grishkin groaned. His nostrils were festooned with white streamers of surgical cotton. He was convinced that Yefremov would try to break the strike with beta-carboline aerosols. The cotton plugs were just one symptom of the general level of strain and paranoia. Before the evacuation order had come from Baikonur, one of the technicians had taken to playing Tchaikovsky's *1812 Overture* at shattering volume for hours on end. And Glushko had chased his wife, naked, bruised, and screaming, up and down the length of Kosmograd. Stoiko had accessed the KGB man's files and Bychkov's psychiatric records; meters of yellow printout curled through the corridors in flabby spirals, rippling in the current from the ventilators. Romanenko had managed to send a message from the barracks ring, saying that the Plumber had attempted to hang himself—in free-fall, by strapping elastic utility cords to his neck and ankles.

"Think what their testimony will be doing to us groundside," muttered Grishkin. "We won't even get a trial. Straight to the *psikushka*." The sinister nickname for the political hospitals seemed to galvanize the boy with dread. Korolev picked apathetically at a viscous pudding of chlorella.

Stoiko snatched a drifting scroll of printout and read aloud. "Paranoia with a tendency to overesteem ideas! Revisionist fantasies hostile to the social system!" He crumpled the paper. "If we could seize the communications module, we could tie into an American comsat and dump the whole thing in their laps. Perhaps that would show Moscow something about the level of our hostility!"

Korolev dug a stranded fruit fly from his algae pudding. Its two pairs of wings and bifurcated thorax were mute testimony to Kosmograd's high radiation levels. The insects had escaped from some forgotten experiment; generations of them had infested the station for decades. "The Americans have no interest in us," Korolev said. "Moscow can no longer be embarrassed by such revelations."

"Except when the grain shipments are due," Grishkin said.

"America needs to sell as badly as we need to buy." Korolev grimly spooned more chlorella into his mouth, chewed mechanically, and swallowed. "The Americans couldn't reach us even if they wanted to. Canaveral is in ruins."

"We're low on fuel," Stoiko said.

"We can take it from the remaining landers," Korolev said.

"Then how in hell would we get back *down*?" Grishkin's fists trembled. "Even in Siberia, there are trees, trees; the sky! To hell with it! Let it fall to pieces! Let it fall and burn!"

Korolev's pudding spattered across the bulkhead.

"Oh, Christ," Grishkin said, "I'm sorry, Colonel. I know you can't go back."

■ ■ ■

When he entered the museum he found Pilot Tatjana suspended before that hateful painting of the Mars Landing, her lashes brimming with tears. She brushed them away as he entered.

"Do you know, Colonel, they have a bust of you at Baikonur? In bronze. I'd pass it on my way to lectures." Her eyes were red-rimmed with sleeplessness.

"There are always busts. Academics need them." He smiled and took her hand.

"What was it like, that day?" She still stared at the painting.

"I hardly remember. I've seen the tapes so often, now I

remember them instead. My memories of Mars are any school-child's." He smiled for her again. "But it was not like this bad painting. I'm certain of that."

"Why has it all gone this way, Colonel? Why is it ending now? When I was small, I saw all this on television. Our future in space was forever."

"Perhaps the Americans were right. The Japanese sent machines instead, robots to build their orbital factories. Lunar mining failed, for us, but we thought there would at least be a permanent research facility of some kind. . . . It all had to do with purse strings, I suppose. With men who sit at desks and make decisions."

"Here is their final decision with regard to Kosmograd, then." She passed him a folded scrap of flimsy. "I found this in the printout of Yefremov's orders from Moscow. They'll allow the station's orbit to decay over the next three months."

He found that now he too was staring fixedly at the painting he loathed. "It hardly matters now," he heard himself say.

And then she was weeping bitterly, her face pressed hard against his crippled shoulder.

"But I have a plan, Tatjana," he said, stroking her hair. "You must listen."

■ ■ ■

He glanced at the face of his old Rolex. They were over eastern Siberia. He remembered being presented with the watch by the Swiss ambassador, in an enormous vaulted room in the Grand Kremlin Palace.

It was time to begin.

He drifted out of his Salyut into the docking sphere, batting at a length of printout that tried to coil around his head.

He could still work quickly and efficiently with his good hand. He was smiling as he freed a large oxygen bottle from its webbing straps. Bracing himself against a handhold, he flung the bottle across the sphere with all his strength. It rebounded harmlessly with a harsh clang. He went after it, caught it, hurled it again.

Then he hit the decompression alarm.

Dust spurted from speakers as a klaxon began to wail. Triggered by the alarm, the docking bays slammed shut with a wheeze of hydraulics. Korolev's ears popped. He sneezed, then went after the bottle again.

The lights flared to maximum brilliance, then flickered out. He smiled in the darkness, groping for the steel bottle. Stoiko had provoked a general systems crash. It hadn't been difficult. The memory banks were already riddled to the point of collapse with bootlegged television broadcasts. "The real bare-knuckle stuff," he muttered, banging the bottle against the wall. The lights flickered on weakly as emergency cells came on line.

His shoulder began to ache. Stoically, he continued pounding, remembering the din a real blowout caused. It had to be good. It had to fool Yefremov and the gun crew.

With a squeal, the manual wheel of one of the hatches began to rotate. It thumped open, finally, and Tatjana looked in, grinning shyly.

"Is the Plumber free?" he asked, releasing the bottle.

"Stoiko and Umansky are reasoning with the guard." She drove a fist into her open palm. "Grishkin is preparing the landers."

He followed her up the passageway to the next docking sphere. Stoiko was helping the Plumber through the hatch that led from the barracks ring. The Plumber was barefoot, his face greenish under a scraggly growth of beard. Meteorologist Umansky followed them, dragging the limp body of a soldier.

"How are you, Plumber?" Korolev asked.

"Shaky. They've kept me on the Fear. Not big doses, but . . . and I thought that this was a real blowout!"

Grishkin slid out of the Soyuz lander nearest Korolev, trailing a bundle of tools and meters on a nylon lanyard. "They all check out. The systems crash left them under their own automatics. I've been at their remotes with a screwdriver, so they can't be overriden by ground control. How are you doing, my Nikita?" he asked the Plumber. "You'll be going in steep, to central China."

The Plumber winced, shook himself, and shivered. "I don't speak Chinese."

Stoiko handed him a scroll of printout. "This is in phonetic Mandarin. 'I want to defect. Take me to the nearest Japanese embassy.'"

The Plumber grinned and ran his fingers through his thatch of sweat-stiffened hair. "What about the rest of you?" he asked.

"You think we're doing this for your benefit alone?" Tatjana made a face at him. "Make sure the Chinese news services get the rest of that scroll, Plumber. Each of us has a copy. We'll see that the whole world knows what the Soviet Union intends to do to Colonel Yuri Vasilevich Korolev, first man on Mars!" She blew the Plumber a kiss.

"How about Filipchenko here?" Umansky asked. A few dark spheres of congealing blood swung crookedly past the unconscious soldier's cheek.

"Why don't you take the poor bastard with you," Korolev said.

"Come along then, shithead," the Plumber said, grabbing Filipchenko's belt and towing him toward the Soyuz hatch. "I, Nikita the Plumber, will do you the favor of your miserable lifetime."

Korolev watched as Stoiko and Grishkin sealed the hatch behind them.

"Where are Romanenko and Valentina?" Korolev asked, checking his watch again.

"Here, my colonel," Valentina said, her blond hair floating around her face in the hatch of another Soyuz. "We have been checking this one out." She giggled.

"Time enough for that in Tokyo," Korolev snapped. "They'll be scrambling jets in Vladivostok and Hanoi within minutes."

Romanenko's bare, brawny arm emerged and yanked her back into the lander. Stoiko and Grishkin sealed the hatch.

Kosmograd boomed hollowly as the Plumber, with the unconscious Filipchenko, cast off. Another boom and the lovers were off as well.

"Come along, friend Umansky," said Stoiko. "And farewell, Colonel!" The two men headed down the corridor.

"I'll go with you," Grishkin said to Tatjana. He grinned. "After all, you're a pilot."

"No," she said. "Alone. We'll split the odds. You'll be fine with the automatics. Just don't touch anything on the board."

Korolev watched her help Grishkin into the docking sphere's last Soyuz.

"I'll take you dancing, Tatjana," Grishkin said, "in Tokyo." She sealed the hatch. Another boom, and Stoiko and Umansky had cast off from the next docking sphere.

"Go now, Tatjana," Korolev said. "Hurry. I don't want them shooting you down over international waters."

"That leaves you here alone, Colonel, alone with our enemies."

"When you've gone, they'll go as well," he said. "And I depend on your publicity to embarrass the Kremlin into keeping me alive here."

"And what shall I tell them in Tokyo, Colonel? Have you a message for the world?"

"Tell them . . ."—and every cliché came rushing to him with an absolute rightness that made him want to laugh hysterically: *One small step . . . we came in peace . . . workers of the world—* "You must tell them that I need it," he said, pinching his shrunken wrist, "in my very bones."

She embraced him and slipped away.

■ ■ ■

He waited alone in the docking sphere. The silence scratched at his nerves; the systems crash had deactivated the ventilation system, whose hum he'd lived with for twenty years. At last he heard Tatjana's Soyuz disengage.

Someone was coming down the corridor. It was Yefremov, moving clumsily in a vacuum suit. Korolev smiled.

Yefremov wore his bland official mask behind the Lexan faceplate, but he avoided meeting Korolev's eyes as he passed. He was heading for the gun room.

The klaxon blared the station's call to full battle alert.

"No!" Korolev shouted.

The gun-room hatch was open when Korolev reached it. Inside, the soldiers were moving jerkily in the galvanized reflex of constant drill, yanking the broad straps of their console seats across the chests of their bulky suits.

"Don't do it!" Korolev sailed into the gun room. He clawed at the stiff accordion fabric of Yefremov's suit. One of the accelerators powered up with a staccato whine. On a tracking screen, green crosshairs closed in on a red dot.

Yefremov removed his helmet. Calmly, with no change in his expression, he backhanded Korolev with the helmet.

"Make them stop!" Korolev sobbed. The walls shook as a

beam cut loose with the sound of a cracking whip. "Your wife, Yefremov! She's out there!"

"Outside, Colonel," Yefremov grabbed Korolev's arthritic hand and squeezed. Korolev screamed. "Outside." A gloved fist struck him in the chest.

Korolev pounded helplessly on the vacuum suit as he was shoved out into the corridor. "Even I, Colonel, dare not come between the Red Army and its orders." Yefremov looked sick now; the mask had crumbled. "Fine sport," he said. "Wait here until it's over."

Then Tatjana's Soyuz struck the beam installation and the barracks ring. In a split-second daguerrotype of raw sunlight, Korolev saw the gun room wrinkle and collapse like a beer can crushed under a boot; he saw the decapitated torso of a soldier spinning away from a console; he saw Yefremov try to speak, his hair streaming upright as vacuum tore the air in his suit out through his open helmet ring. Fine twin streams of blood arced from Korolev's nostrils, the roar of escaping air replaced by a deeper roaring in his head. The last thing he heard, before all sound vanished, was the hatch slamming shut.

When he woke, he woke to darkness, to pulsing agony behind his eyes, remembering old lectures. This was as great a danger as the blowout itself, nitrogen bubbling through the blood to strike with white-hot, crippling pain. . . .

His lungs pulled desperately at vacuum. Pressure bloated him. He could feel his tongue jutting from his lips. Things began to seem very remote. Academic, really. He turned the wheel of the hatch out of some strange sense of noblesse oblige, nothing more. The labor was onerous, and he wished very much to return to his museum and sleep.

■ ■ ■

He could repair the leaks with caulk, but the systems crash was beyond him. He had Glushko's garden. With the vegetables and algae, he wouldn't starve or smother. The communications module had gone with the gun room and the barracks ring, sheared from the station by the impact of Tatjana's suicidal Soyuz. He assumed that the collision had perturbed Kosmograd's orbit, but he had no way of predicting the hour of the station's final incandescent meeting with the upper atmosphere. He was often ill now, and he often thought that he might die before burnout, which disturbed him.

He spent uncounted hours screening the museum's library of tapes. A fitting pursuit for the Last Man in Space, who had once been the First Man on Mars.

He became obsessed with the icon of Gagarin, endlessly rerunning the grainy television images of the Sixties, the newsreels that led so unalterably to the cosmonaut's death. The stale air of Kosmograd swam with the spirits of martyrs. Gagarin, the first Salyut crew, the Americans roasted alive in their squat Apollo. . . .

Often he dreamed of Tatjana, the look in her eyes like the look he'd imagined in the eyes of the museum's portraits. And once he woke, or dreamed he woke, in the Salyut where she had slept, to find himself in his old uniform, with a battery-powered worklight strapped to his forehead. From a great distance, as though he watched a newsreel on the museum's monitor, he saw himself rip the Star of the Tsiolkovsky Order from his pocket and staple it to her pilot's certificate.

When the knocking came, he knew that it must be a dream as well.

The museum's hatch wheeled open.

In the bluish, flickering light from the old film, he saw that the woman was black. Long corkscrews of matted hair rose like cobras around her head. She wore goggles, a silk aviator's scarf twisting behind her in free-fall. "Andy," she said in English, "you better come see this!"

A small, muscular man, nearly bald and wearing only a jockstrap and a jangling toolbelt, floated up behind her and peered in. "Is he alive?"

"Of course I am alive," said Korolev in slightly accented English.

The man called Andy sailed in over her head. "You okay, Jack?" His right bicep was tattooed with a geodesic balloon above crossed lightning bolts and bore the legend SUNSPARK 15, UTAH. "We weren't expecting anybody."

"Neither was I," said Korolev, blinking.

"We've come to live here," said the woman, drifting closer. "We're from the balloons. Squatters, I guess you could say.

Heard the place was empty. You know the orbit's decaying on this thing?" The man executed a clumsy midair somersault, the tools clattering on his belt. "This free-fall's outrageous."

"God," said the woman, "I just can't get used to it! It's wonderful. It's like skydiving, but there's no wind."

Korolev stared at the man, who had the blundering, careless look of someone drunk on freedom since birth. "But you don't even have a launch pad," he said.

"Launch pad?" the man said, laughing. "What we do, we haul those surplus booster engines up the cables to the balloons, drop 'em, and fire 'em in midair."

"That's insane," Korolev said.

"Got us here, didn't it?"

Korolev nodded. If this was a dream, it was a very peculiar one. "I am Colonel Yuri Vasilevich Korolev."

"Mars!" The woman clapped her hands. "Wait'll the kids hear that." She plucked the little Lunokhod moon-rover model from the bulkhead and began to wind it.

"Hey," the man said, "I gotta work. We got a bunch of boosters outside. We gotta lift this thing before it starts burning."

Something clanged against the hull. Kosmograd rang with the impact. "That'll be Tulsa," Andy said, consulting a wristwatch. "Right on time."

"But why?" Korolev shook his head, deeply confused. "Why have you come?"

"We told you. To live here. We can enlarge this thing, maybe build more. They said we'd never make it living in the balloons, but we were the only ones who could make them work. It was our one chance to get out here on our own. Who'd want to live out here for the sake of some government, some army brass, a bunch of pen-pushers? You have to *want* a frontier—want it in your bones, right?"

Korolev smiled. Andy grinned back.

"We grabbed those power cables and we just pulled ourselves straight up. And when you get to the top—well, man, you either make that big jump or else you rot there." His voice rose. "And you don't look back, no, sir! We've made that jump, and we're here to stay!"

The woman replaced the model's Velcro wheels against the

curved wall and released it. It went scooting along above their head, whirring merrily. "Isn't that cute? The kids are just going to love it."

Korolev stared into Andy's eyes. Kosmograd rang again, jarring the little Lunokhod model onto a new course.

"East Los Angeles," the woman said. "That's the one with the kids in it." She took off her goggles, and Korolev saw her eyes brimming over with a wonderful lunacy.

"Well," said Andy, rattling his toolbelt, "you feel like showing us around?"

BRUCE STERLING AND LEWIS SHINER

Mozart in Mirrorshades

■

This footloose time-travel fantasy emerged in a happy spirit of Movement camaraderie. Its headlong energy and aggressive political satire are sure signs of writers who feel they have points to make: points about America, about the Third World, about "development" and "exploitation." And a point about science fiction: that energy and fun are its natural birthrights.

The figure of Wolfgang Amadeus Mozart seems to have a special resonance for this decade, appearing in films, Broadway plays, and rock videos, as well as in SF. It's an interesting case of cultural synchronicity. Something is loose in the 1980s. And we are all in it together.

From the hill north of the city, Rice saw eighteenth-century Salzburg spread out below him like a half-eaten lunch.

Huge cracking towers and swollen, bulbous storage tanks dwarfed the ruins of the St. Rupert Cathedral. Thick white smoke billowed from the refinery's stacks. Rice could taste the familiar petrochemical tang from where he sat, under the leaves of a wilting oak.

The sheer spectacle of it delighted him. You didn't sign up for a time-travel project, he thought, unless you had a taste for incongruity. Like the phallic pumping station lurking in the central square of the convent, or the ruler-straight elevated pipelines ripping through Salzburg's maze of cobbled streets. A bit tough on the city, maybe, but that was hardly Rice's fault. The temporal beam had focused randomly in the bedrock below Salzburg, forming an expandable bubble connecting this world to Rice's own time.

This was the first time he'd seen the complex from outside its high chain-link fences. For two years, he'd been up to his neck getting the refinery operational. He'd directed teams all over the planet, as they caulked up Nantucket whalers to serve as tankers, or trained local pipefitters to lay down line as far away as the Sinai and the Gulf of Mexico.

Now, finally, he was outside. Sutherland, the company's political liaison, had warned him against going into the city. But Rice had no patience with her attitude. The smallest thing seemed to set Sutherland off. She lost sleep over the most trivial local complaints. She spent hours haranguing the "gate people," the locals who waited day and night outside the square-mile complex, begging for radios, nylons, a jab of penicillin.

To hell with her, Rice thought. The plant was up and breaking design records, and Rice was due for a little R and R. The way he saw it, anyone who couldn't find some action in the Year of Our Lord 1775 had to be dead between the ears. He stood up, dusting windblown soot from his hands with a cambric handkerchief.

A moped sputtered up the hill toward him, wobbling crazily. The rider couldn't seem to keep his high-heeled, buckled pumps on the pedals while carrying a huge portable stereo in the crook of his right arm. The moped lurched to a stop at a respectful distance, and Rice recognized the music from the tape player: Symphony No. 40 in G Minor.

The boy turned the volume down as Rice walked toward him. "Good evening, Mr. Plant Manager, sir. I am not interrupting?"

"No, that's okay." Rice glanced at the bristling hedgehog cut that had replaced the boy's outmoded wig. He'd seen the kid around the gates; he was one of the regulars. But the music had made something else fall into place. "You're Mozart, aren't you?"

"Wolfgang Amadeus Mozart, your servant."

"I'll be goddamned. Do you know what that tape is?"

"It has my name on it."

"Yeah. You wrote it. Or would have, I guess I should say. About fifteen years from now."

Mozart nodded. "It is so beautiful. I have not the English to say how it is to hear it."

By this time most of the other gate people would have been well into some kind of pitch. Rice was impressed by the boy's tact, not to mention his command of English. The standard native vocabulary didn't go much beyond *radio, drugs,* and *fuck.* "Are you headed back toward town?" Rick asked.

"Yes, Mr. Plant Manager, sir."

Something about the kid appealed to Rice. The enthusiasm, the gleam in the eyes. And, of course, he did happen to be one of the greatest composers of all time.

"Forget the titles," Rice said. "Where does a guy go for some fun around here?"

■ ■ ■

At first Sutherland hadn't wanted Rice at the meeting with Jefferson. But Rice knew a little temporal physics, and Jefferson had been pestering the American personnel with questions about time holes and parallel worlds.

Rice, for his part, was thrilled at the chance to meet Thomas Jefferson, the first President of the United States. He'd never liked George Washington, was glad the man's Masonic connections had made him refuse to join the company's "godless" American government.

Rice squirmed in his Dacron double knits as he and Sutherland waited in the newly air-conditioned boardroom of the Hohensalzburg Castle. "I forgot how greasy these suits feel," he said.

"At least," Sutherland said, "you didn't wear that goddamned hat today." The VTOL jet from America was late, and she kept looking at her watch.

"My tricorne?" Rice said. "You don't like it?"

"It's a Masonista hat, for Christ's sake. It's a symbol of anti-modern reaction." The Freemason Liberation Front was another of Sutherland's nightmares, a local politico-religious group that had made a few pathetic attacks on the pipeline.

"Oh, loosen up, will you, Sutherland? Some groupie of Mozart's gave me the hat. Theresa Maria Angela something-or-other, some broken-down aristocrat. They all hang out together in this music dive downtown. I just liked the way it looked."

"Mozart? You've been fraternizing with him? Don't you think we should just let him be? After everything we've done to him?"

"Bullshit," Rice said. "I'm entitled. I spent two years on start-up while you were playing touch football with Robespierre and Thomas Paine. I make a few night spots with Wolfgang and you're all over me. What about Parker? I don't hear you bitching about him playing rock and roll on his late show every night. You can hear it blasting out of every cheap transistor in town."

"He's propaganda officer. Believe me, if I could stop him I would, but Parker's a special case. He's got connections all over the place back in Realtime." She rubbed her cheek. "Let's drop it, okay? Just try to be polite to President Jefferson. He's had a hard time of it lately."

Sutherland's secretary, a former Hapsburg lady-in-waiting, stepped in to announce the plane's arrival. Jefferson pushed angrily past her. He was tall for a local, with a mane of blazing red hair and the shiftiest eyes Rice had ever seen. "Sit down, Mr. President." Sutherland waved at the far side of the table. "Would you like some coffee or tea?"

Jefferson scowled. "Perhaps some Madeira," he said. "If you have it."

Sutherland nodded to her secretary, who stared for a moment in incomprehension, then hurried off. "How was the flight?" Sutherland asked.

"Your engines are most impressive," Jefferson said, "as you well know." Rice saw the subtle trembling of the man's hands; he hadn't taken well to jet flight. "I only wish your political sensitivities were as advanced."

"You know I can't speak for my employers," Sutherland said. "For myself, I deeply regret the darker aspects of our operations. Florida will be missed."

Irritated, Rice leaned forward. "You're not really here to discuss sensibilities, are you?"

"Freedom, sir," Jefferson said. "Freedom is the issue." The secretary returned with a dust-caked bottle of sherry and a stack of clear plastic cups. Jefferson, his hands visibly shaking now, poured a glass and tossed it back. Color returned to his face. He said, "You made certain promises when we joined forces. You guaranteed us liberty and equality and the freedom to pursue our own happiness. Instead we find your machinery on all sides, your cheap manufactured goods seducing the people of our great country, our minerals and works of art disappearing into your fortresses, never to reappear!" The last line brought Jefferson to his feet.

Sutherland shrank back into her chair. "The common good requires a certain period of—uh, adjustment—"

"Oh, come on, Tom," Rice broke in. "We didn't 'join forces,' that's a lot of crap. We kicked the Brits out and you in, and you had damn-all to do with it. Second, if we drill for oil and carry off a few paintings, it doesn't have a goddamned thing to do with your liberty. We don't care. Do whatever you like, just stay out of our way. Right? If we wanted a lot of back talk we could have left the damn British in power."

Jefferson sat down. Sutherland meekly poured him another glass, which he drank off at once. "I cannot understand you," he said. "You claim you come from the future, yet you seem bent on destroying your own past."

"But we're not," Rice said. "It's this way. History is like a tree, okay? When you go back and mess with the past, another branch of history splits off from the main trunk. Well, this world is just one of those branches."

"So," Jefferson said. "This world—my world—does not lead to your future."

"Right," Rice said.

"Leaving you free to rape and pillage here at will! While your own world is untouched and secure!" Jefferson was on his feet again. "I find the idea monstrous beyond belief, intolerable! How can you be party to such despotism? Have you no human feelings?"

"Oh, for God's sake," Rice said. "Of course we do. What about the radios and the magazines and the medicine we hand out? Personally I think you've got a lot of nerve, coming in here with your smallpox scars and your unwashed shirt and all those slaves of yours back home, lecturing us on humanity."

"Rice?" Sutherland said.

Rice locked eyes with Jefferson. Slowly, Jefferson sat down. "Look," Rice said, relenting. "We don't mean to be unreasonable. Maybe things aren't working out just the way you pictured them, but hey, that's life, you know? What do you want, *really*? Cars? Movies? Telephones? Birth control? Just say the word and they're yours."

Jefferson pressed his thumbs into the corners of his eyes.

"Your words mean nothing to me, sir. I only want . . . I want only to return to my home. To Monticello. And as soon as possible."

"Is it one of your migraines, Mr. President?" Sutherland asked. "I had these made up for you." She pushed a vial of pills across the table toward him.

"What are these?"

Sutherland shrugged. "You'll feel better."

After Jefferson left, Rice half expected a reprimand. Instead, Sutherland said, "You seem to have a tremendous faith in the project."

"Oh, cheer up," Rice said. "You've been spending too much time with these politicals. Believe me, this is a simple time, with simple people. Sure, Jefferson was a little ticked off, but he'll come around. Relax!"

■　■　■

Rice found Mozart clearing tables in the main dining hall of the Hohensalzburg Castle. In his faded jeans, camo jacket, and mirrored sunglasses, he might almost have passed for a teenager from Rice's time.

"Wolfgang!" Rice called to him. "How's the new job?"

Mozart set a stack of dishes aside and ran his hands over his short-cropped hair. "Wolf," he said. "Call me Wolf, okay? Sounds more . . . modern, you know? But yes, I really want to thank you for everything you have done for me. The tapes, the history books, this job—it is so wonderful just to be around here."

His English, Rice noticed, had improved remarkably in the last three weeks. "You still living in the city?"

"Yes, but I have my own place now. You are coming to the gig tonight?"

"Sure," Rice said. "Why don't you finish up around here, I'll go change, and then we can go out for some sachertorte, okay? We'll make a night of it."

Rice dressed carefully, wearing mesh body armor under his velvet coat and knee britches. He crammed his pockets with giveaway consumer goods, then met Mozart by a rear door.

Security had been stepped up around the castle, and floodlights swept the sky. Rice sensed a new tension in the festive abandon of the crowds downtown.

Like everyone else from his time, he towered over the locals; even incognito he felt dangerously conspicuous.

Within the club Rice faded into the darkness and relaxed. The place had been converted from the lower half of some young aristo's town house; protruding bricks still marked the lines of the old walls. The patrons were locals, mostly, dressed in any Realtime garments they could scavenge. Rice even saw one kid wearing a pair of beige silk panties on his head.

Mozart took the stage. Minuetlike guitar arpeggios screamed over sequenced choral motifs. Stacks of amps blasted synthesizer riffs lifted from a tape of K-Tel pop hits. The howling audience showered Mozart with confetti stripped from the club's hand-painted wallpaper.

Afterward Mozart smoked a joint of Turkish hash and asked Rice about the future.

"Mine, you mean?" Rice said. "You wouldn't believe it. Six billion people, and nobody has to work if they don't want to. Five-hundred-channel TV in every house. Cars, helicopters, clothes that would knock your eyes out. Plenty of easy sex. You want music? You could have your own recording studio. It'd make your gear on stage look like a goddamned clavichord."

"Really? I would give anything to see that. I can't understand why you would leave."

Rice shrugged. "So I'm giving up maybe fifteen years. When I get back, it's the best of everything. Anything I want."

"Fifteen years?"

"Yeah. You gotta understand how the portal works. Right now it's as big around as you are tall, just big enough for a phone cable and a pipeline full of oil, maybe the odd bag of mail, heading for Realtime. To make it any bigger, like to move people or equipment through, is expensive as hell. So expensive they only do it twice, at the beginning and the end of the project. So, yeah, I guess we're stuck here."

Rice coughed harshly and drank off his glass. That Ottoman Empire hash had untied his mental shoelaces. Here he was opening up to Mozart, making the kid want to emigrate, and there was no way in hell Rice could get him a Green Card. Not with all the millions that wanted a free ride into the future—billions, if you counted the other projects, like the Roman Empire or New Kingdom Egypt.

"But I'm really *glad* to be here," Rice said. "It's like . . . like shuffling the deck of history. You never know what'll come up next." Rice passed the joint to one of Mozart's groupies, Antonia something-or-other. "This is a great time to be alive. Look at you. You're doing okay, aren't you?" He leaned across the table, in the grip of a sudden sincerity. "I mean, it's okay, right? It's not like you hate all of us for fucking up your world or anything?"

"Are you making a joke? You are looking at the hero of Salzburg. In fact, your Mr. Parker is supposed to make a tape of my last set tonight. Soon all of Europe will know of me!" Someone shouted at Mozart, in German, from across the club. Mozart glanced up and gestured cryptically. "Be cool, man." He turned back to Rice. "You can see that I am doing fine."

"Sutherland, she worries about stuff like all those symphonies you're never going to write."

"Bullshit! I don't want to write symphonies: I can listen to them any time I want! Who is this Sutherland? Is she your girlfriend?"

"No. She goes for the locals. Danton, Robespierre, like that. How about you? You got anybody?"

"Nobody special. Not since I was a kid."

"Oh, yeah?"

"Well, when I was about six I was at Maria Theresa's court. I used to play with her daughter—Maria Antonia. Marie Antoinette she calls herself now. The most beautiful girl of the age. We used to play duets. We made a joke that we would be married, but she went off to France with that swine, Louis."

"Goddamn," Rice said. "This is really amazing. You know, she's practically a legend where I come from. They cut her head off in the French Revolution for throwing too many parties."

"No they didn't. . . ."

"That was *our* French Revolution," Rice said. "Yours was a lot less messy."

"You should go see her, if you're that interested. Surely she owes you a favor for saving her life."

Before Rice could answer, Parker arrived at their table, surrounded by ex-ladies-in-waiting in spandex capris and sequined tube tops. "Hey, Rice," Parker shouted, serenely anachronistic in a glitter T-shirt and black leather jeans. "Where did you get those unhip threads? Come on, let's party!"

Rice watched as the girls crowded around the table and gnawed the corks out of a crate of champagne. As short, fat, and repulsive as Parker might be, they would gladly knife one another for a chance to sleep in his clean sheets and raid his medicine cabinet.

"No, thanks," Rice said, untangling himself from the miles of wire connected to Parker's recording gear.

The image of Marie Antoinette had seized him and would not let go.

■ ■ ■

Rice sat naked on the edge of the canopied bed, shivering a little in the air conditioning. Past the jutting window unit, through clouded panes of eighteenth-century glass, he saw a lush, green landscape sprinkled with tiny waterfalls.

At ground level, a garden crew of former aristos in blue-denim overalls trimmed weeds under the bored supervision of a peasant guard. The guard, clothed head to foot in camouflage except for a tricolor cockade on his fatigue cap, chewed gum and toyed with the strap of his cheap plastic machine gun. The gardens of Petit Trianon, like Versailles itself, were treasures deserving the best of care. They belonged to the Nation, since they were too large to be crammed through a time portal.

Marie Antoinette sprawled across the bed's expanse of pink satin, wearing a scrap of black-lace underwear and leafing through an issue of *Vogue*. The bedroom's walls were crowded with Boucher canvases: acres of pert silky rumps, pink haunches, knowingly pursed lips. Rice looked dazedly from the portrait of Louise O'Morphy, kittenishly sprawled on a divan, to the sleek, creamy expanse of Toinette's back and thighs. He took a deep, exhausted breath. "Man," he said, "that guy could really paint."

Toinette cracked off a square of Hershey's chocolate and pointed to the magazine. "I want the leather bikini," she said. "Always, when I am a girl, my goddamn mother, she keep me in the goddamn corsets. She think my what-you-call, my shoulder blade sticks out too much."

Rice leaned back across her solid thighs and patted her bottom reassuringly. He felt wonderfully stupid; a week and a half of obsessive carnality had reduced him to a euphoric animal. "Forget your mother, baby. You're with *me* now. You want ze goddamn leather bikini, I get it for you."

Toinette licked chocolate from her fingertips. "Tomorrow we go out to the cottage, okay, man? We dress up like the peasants and make love in the hedges like noble savages."

Rice hesitated. His weekend furlough to Paris had stretched into a week and a half; by now security would be looking for him. To hell with them, he thought. "Great," he said. "I'll phone us up a picnic lunch. Foie gras and truffles, maybe some terrapin—"

Toinette pouted. "I want the modern food. The pizza and burritos and the chicken fried." When Rice shrugged, she threw her arms around his neck. "You love me, Rice?"

"Love you? Baby, I love the very *idea* of you." He was drunk on history out of control, careening under him like some great black motorcycle of the imagination. When he thought of Paris, take-out quiche-to-go stores springing up where guillotines might have been, a six-year-old Napoleon munching Dubble Bubble in Corsica, he felt like the archangel Michael on speed.

Megalomania, he knew, was an occupational hazard. But he'd get back to work soon enough, in just a few more days. . . .

The phone rang. Rice burrowed into a plush house robe formerly owned by Louis XVI. Louis wouldn't mind; he was now a happily divorced locksmith in Nice.

Mozart's face appeared on the phone's tiny screen. "Hey, man, where are you?"

"France," Rice said vaguely. "What's up?"

"Trouble, man. Sutherland flipped out, and they've got her sedated. At least six key people have gone over the hill, counting you." Mozart's voice had only the faintest trace of accent left.

"Hey, I'm not over the hill. I'll be back in just a couple days. We've got—what, thirty other people in Northern Europe? If you're worried about the quotas—"

"Fuck the quotas. This is serious. There's uprisings. Comanches raising hell on the rigs in Texas. Labor strikes in London and Vienna. Realtime is pissed. They're talking about pulling us out."

"What?" Now he was alarmed.

"Yeah. Word came down the line today. They say you guys let

this whole operation get sloppy. Too much contamination, too much fraternization. Sutherland made a lot of trouble with the locals before she got found out. She was organizing the Masonistas for some kind of passive resistance and God knows what else."

"Shit." The fucking politicals had screwed it up again. It wasn't enough that he'd busted ass getting the plant up and on line; now he had to clean up after Sutherland. He glared at Mozart. "Speaking of fraternization, what's all this *we* stuff? What the hell are you doing calling me?"

Mozart paled. "Just trying to help. I got a job in communications now."

"That takes a Green Card. Where the hell did you get that?"

"Uh, listen, man, I got to go. Get back here, will you? We need you." Mozart's eyes flickered, looking past Rice's shoulder. "You can bring your little time-bunny along if you want. But hurry."

"I . . . oh, shit, okay," Rice said.

■ ■ ■

Rice's hovercar huffed along at a steady 80 kph, blasting clouds of dust from the deeply rutted highway. They were near the Bavarian border. Ragged Alps jutted into the sky over radiant green meadows, tiny picturesque farmhouses, and clear, vivid streams of melted snow.

They'd just had their first argument. Toinette had asked for a Green Card, and Rice had told her he couldn't do it. He offered her a Gray Card instead, that would get her from one branch of time to another without letting her visit Realtime. He knew he'd be reassigned if the project pulled out, and he wanted to take her with him. He wanted to do the decent thing, not leave her behind in a world without Hersheys and *Vogues*.

But she wasn't having any of it. After a few kilometers of weighty silence she started to squirm. "I have to pee," she said finally. "Pull over by the goddamn trees."

"Okay," Rice said. "Okay."

He cut the fans and whirred to a stop. A herd of brindled cattle spooked off with a clank of cowbells. The road was deserted.

Rice got out and stretched, watching Toinette climb a wooden stile and walk toward a stand of trees.

"What's the deal?" Rice yelled. "There's nobody around. Get on with it!"

A dozen men burst up from the cover of a ditch and rushed him. In an instant they'd surrounded him, leveling flintlock pistols. They wore tricornes and wigs and lace-cuffed high-wayman's coats; black domino masks hid their faces. "What the fuck is this?" Rice asked, amazed. "Mardi Gras?"

The leader ripped off his mask and bowed ironically. His handsome Teutonic features were powdered, his lips rouged. "I am Count Axel Ferson. Servant, sir."

Rice knew the name; Ferson had been Toinette's lover before the Revolution. "Look, Count, maybe you're a little upset about Toinette, but I'm sure we can make a deal. Wouldn't you really rather have a color TV?"

"Spare us your satanic blandishments, sir!" Ferson roared. "I would not soil my hands on the collaborationist cow. We are the Freemason Liberation Front!"

"Christ," Rice said. "You can't possibly be serious. Are you taking on the project with these popguns?"

"We are aware of your advantage in armaments, sir. This is why we have made you our hostage." He spoke to the others in German. They tied Rice's hands and hustled him into the back of a horse-drawn wagon that had clopped out of the woods.

"Can't we at least take the car?" Rice asked. Glancing back, he saw Toinette sitting dejectedly in the road by the hovercraft.

"We reject your machines," Ferson said. "They are one more facet of your godlessness. Soon we will drive you back to hell, from whence you came!"

"With what? Broomsticks?" Rice sat up in the back of the wagon, ignoring the stink of manure and rotting hay. "Don't mistake our kindness for weakness. If they send the Gray Card Army through that portal, there won't be enough left of you to fill an ashtray."

"We are prepared to sacrifice! Each day thousands flock to our worldwide movement, under the banner of the All-Seeing Eye! We shall reclaim our destiny! The destiny you have stolen from us!"

"Your *destiny*?" Rice was aghast. "Listen, Count, you ever hear of guillotines?"

"I wish to hear no more of your machines." Ferson gestured to a subordinate. "Gag him."

■ ■ ■

They hauled Rice to a farmhouse outside Salzburg. During fifteen bone-jarring hours in the wagon he thought of nothing but Toinette's betrayal. If he'd promised her the Green Card, would she still have led him into the ambush? That card was the only thing she wanted, but how could the Masonistas get her one?

Rice's guards paced restlessly in front of the windows, their boots squeaking on the loosely pegged floorboards. From their constant references to Salzburg he gathered that some kind of siege was in progress.

Nobody had shown up to negotiate Rice's release, and the Masonistas were getting nervous. If he could just gnaw through his gag, Rice was sure he'd be able to talk some sense into them.

He heard a distant drone, building slowly to a roar. Four of the men ran outside, leaving a single guard at the open door. Rice squirmed in his bonds and tried to sit up.

Suddenly the clapboards above his head were blasted to splinters by heavy machine-gun fire. Grenades whumped in front of the house, and the windows exploded in a gush of black smoke. A choking Masonista lifted his flintlock at Rice. Before he could pull the trigger a burst of gunfire threw the terrorist against the wall.

A short, heavyset man in flak jacket and leather pants stalked into the room. He stripped goggles from his smoke-blackened face, revealing Oriental eyes. A pair of greased braids hung down his back. He cradled an assault rifle in the crook of one arm and wore two bandoliers of grenades. "Good," he grunted. "The last of them." He tore the gag from Rice's mouth. He smelled of sweat and smoke and badly cured leather. "You are Rice?"

Rice could only nod and gasp for breath.

His rescuer hauled him to his feet and cut his ropes with a bayonet. "I am Jebe Noyon. Trans-Temporal Army." He forced a leather flask of rancid mare's milk into Rice's hands. The smell made Rice want to vomit. "Drink!" Jebe insisted. "Is koumiss, is good for you! Drink, Jebe Noyon tells you!"

Rice took a sip, which curdled his tongue and brought bile to his throat. "You're the Gray Cards, right?" he said weakly.

"Gray Card Army, yes," Jebe said. "Baddest-ass warriors of all times and places! Only five guards here, I kill them all! I, Jebe Noyon, was chief general to Genghis Khan, terror of the earth, okay, man?" He stared at Rice with great, sad eyes. "You have not heard of me."

"Sorry, Jebe, no."

"The earth turned black in the footprints of my horse."

"I'm sure it did, man."

"You will mount up behind me," he said, dragging Rice toward the door. "You will watch the earth turn black in the tireprints of my Harley, man, okay?"

■ ■ ■

From the hills above Salzburg they looked down on anachronism gone wild.

Local soldiers in waistcoats and gaiters lay in bloody heaps by the gates of the refinery. Another battalion marched forward in formation, muskets at the ready. A handful of Huns and Mongols, deployed at the gates, cut them up with orange tracer fire and watched the survivors scatter.

Jebe Noyon laughed hugely. "Is like siege of Cambaluc! Only no stacking up heads or even taking ears any more, man, now we are civilized, okay? Later maybe we call in, like, grunts, choppers from 'Nam, napalm the son-of-a-bitches, far out, man."

"You can't do that, Jebe," Rice said sternly. "The poor bastards don't have a chance. No point in exterminating them."

Jebe shrugged. "I forget sometimes, okay? Always thinking to conquer the world." He revved the cycle and scowled. Rice grabbed the Mongol's stinking flak jacket as they roared downhill. Jebe took his disappointment out on the enemy, tearing through the streets in high gear, deliberately running down a group of Brunswick grenadiers. Only panic strength saved Rice from falling off as legs and torsos thumped and crunched beneath their tires.

Jebe skidded to a stop inside the gates of the complex. A jabbering horde of Mongols in ammo belts and combat fatigues surrounded them at once. Rice pushed through them, his kidneys aching.

Ionizing radiation smeared the evening sky around the Hohensalzburg Castle. They were kicking the portal up to the high-energy maximum, running cars full of Gray Cards in and sending the same cars back loaded to the ceiling with art and jewelry.

Over the rattling of gunfire Rice could hear the whine of VTOL jets bringing in the evacuees from the US and Africa. Roman centurions, wrapped in mesh body armor and carrying shoulder-launched rockets, herded Realtime personnel into the tunnels that led to the portal.

Mozart was in the crowd, waving enthusiastically to Rice. "We're pulling out, man! Fantastic, huh? Back to Realtime!"

Rice looked at the clustered towers of pumps, coolers, and catalytic cracking units. "It's a goddamned shame," he said. "All that work, shot to hell."

"We were losing too many people, man. Forget it. There's plenty of eighteenth centuries."

The guards, sniping at the crowds outside, suddenly leaped aside as Rice's hovercar burst through the ages. Half a dozen Masonic fanatics still clung to the doors and pounded on the windscreen. Jebe's Mongols yanked the invaders free and axed them while a Roman flamethrower unit gushed fire across the gates.

Marie Antoinette leaped out of the hovercar. Jebe grabbed for her, but her sleeve came off in his hand. She spotted Mozart and ran for him, Jebe only a few steps behind.

"Wolf, you bastard!" she shouted. "You leave me behind! What about your promises, you merde, you pig-dog!"

Mozart whipped off his mirrorshades. He turned to Rice. "Who is this woman?"

"The Green Card, Wolf! You say I sell Rice to the Masonistas, you get me the card!" She stopped for breath and Jebe caught her by one arm. When she whirled on him, he cracked her across the jaw, and she dropped to the tarmac.

The Mongol focused his smoldering eyes on Mozart. "Was you, eh? You, the traitor?" With the speed of a striking cobra he pulled his machine pistol and jammed the muzzle against Mozart's nose. "I put my gun on rock and roll, there nothing left of you but ears, man."

A single shot echoed across the courtyard. Jebe's head rocked back, and he fell in a heap.

Rice spun to his right. Parker, the DJ, stood in the doorway of an equipment shed. He held a Walther PPK. "Take it easy, Rice," Parker said, walking toward him. "He's just a grunt, expendable."

"You *killed* him!"

"So what?" Parker said, throwing one arm around Mozart's frail shoulders. "This here's my boy! I transmitted a couple of his new tunes up the line a month ago. You know what? The kid's number five on the *Billboard* charts! Number five!" Parker shoved the gun into his belt. "With a bullet!"

"You gave him the Green Card, Parker?"

"No," Mozart said. "It was Sutherland."

"What did you do to her?"

"Nothing ! I swear to you, man! Well, maybe I kind of lived up to what she wanted to see. A broken man, you know, his music stolen from him, his very soul?" Mozart rolled his eyes upward. "She gave me the Green Card, but that still wasn't enough. She couldn't handle the guilt. You know the rest."

"And when she got caught, you were afraid we wouldn't pull out. So you decided to drag *me* into it! You got Toinette to turn me over to the Masons. That was *your* doing!"

As if hearing her name, Toinette moaned softly from the tarmac. Rice didn't care about the bruises, the dirt, the rips in her leopard-skin jeans. She was still the most gorgeous creature he'd ever seen.

Mozart shrugged. "I was a Freemason once. Look, man, they're very uncool. I mean, all I did was drop a few hints, and look what happened." He waved casually at the carnage all around them. "I knew you'd get away from them somehow."

"You can't just *use* people like that!"

"Bullshit, Rice! You do it all the time! I *needed* this seige so Realtime would haul us out! For Christ's sake, I can't wait fifteen years to go up the line. History says I'm going to be *dead* in fifteen years! I don't want to die in this dump! I want that car and that recording studio!"

"Forget it, pal," Rice said. "When they hear back in Realtime how you screwed things up here—"

Parker laughed. "Shove off, Rice. We're talking Top of the Pops, here. Not some penny-ante refinery." He took Mozart's arm protectively. "Listen, Wolf, baby, let's get into those tunnels. I got some papers for you to sign as soon as we hit the future."

The sun had set, but muzzle-loading cannon lit the night, pumping shells into the city. For a moment Rice stood stunned as cannonballs clanged harmlessly off the storage tanks. Then, finally, he shook his head. Salzburg's time had run out.

Hoisting Toinette over one shoulder, he ran toward the safety of the tunnels.